Buffy the Vampire Slayer™

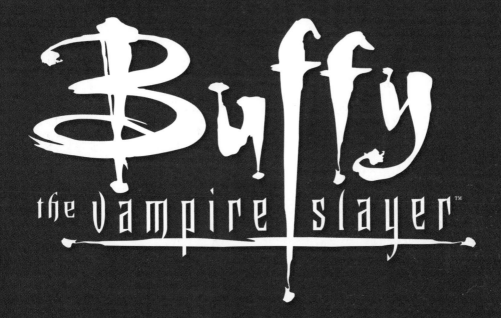

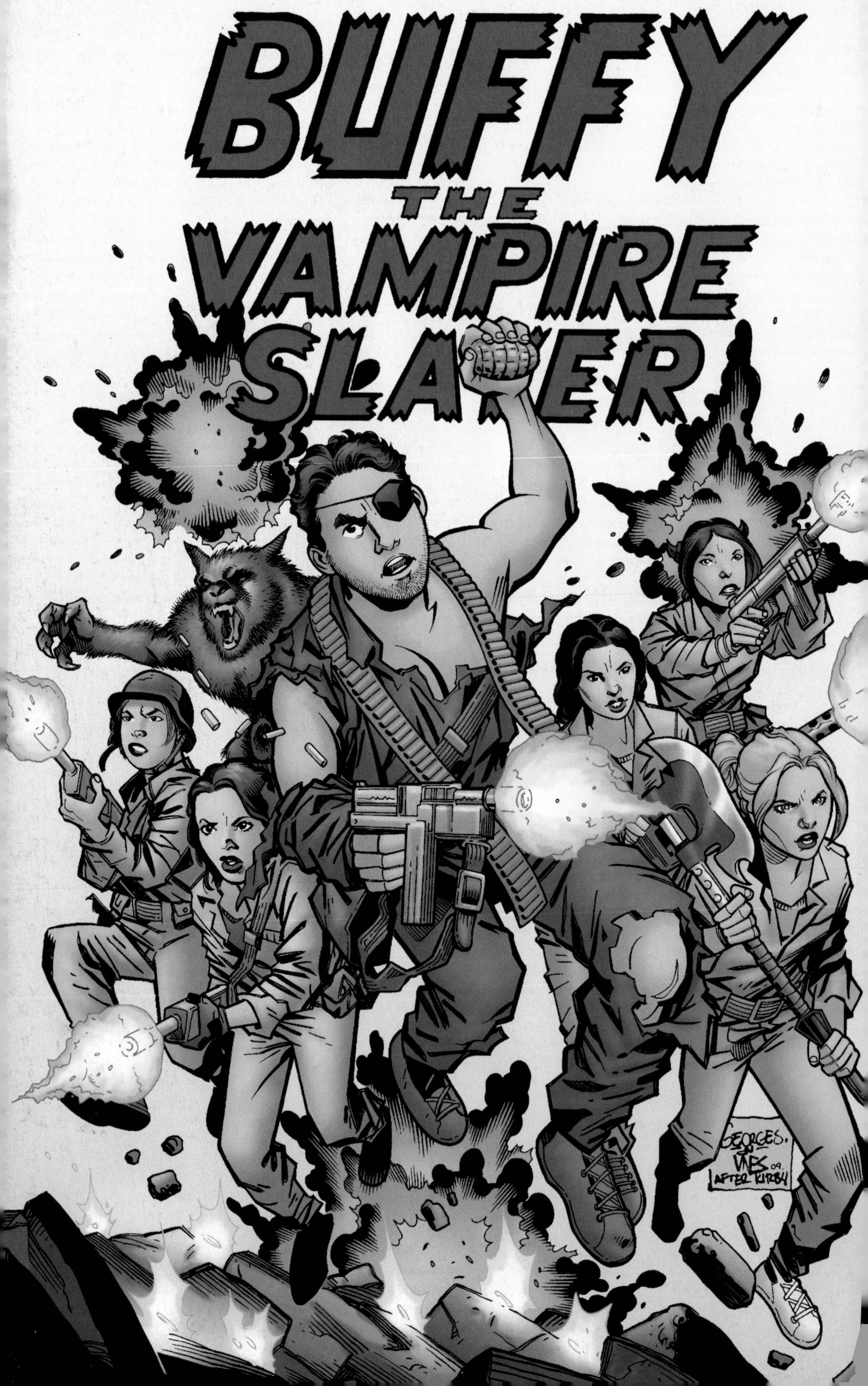
BUFFY
THE
VAMPIRE
SLAYER

Buffy the Vampire Slayer™

SEASON EIGHT VOLUME 6
RETREAT

Script **JANE ESPENSON**

Pencils **GEORGES JEANTY**

Inks **ANDY OWENS**

Colors **MICHELLE MADSEN**

Letters **RICHARD STARKINGS &
COMICRAFT'S JIMMY BETANCOURT**

Cover Artists **JO CHEN**
with **MASSIMO CARNEVALE &
ADAM HUGHES**

Executive Producer **JOSS WHEDON**

Dark Horse Books®

President & Publisher MIKE RICHARDSON

Editor SCOTT ALLIE

Associate Editor SIERRA HAHN

Assistant Editor FREDDYE LINS

Collection Designer TONY ONG

This story takes place after the end of the
television series *Buffy the Vampire Slayer*,
created by Joss Whedon.

Special thanks to Debbie Olshan at Twentieth Century Fox, Natalie Farrell, and Bob Harris.

EXECUTIVE VICE PRESIDENT Neil Hankerson · CHIEF FINANCIAL OFFICER Tom Weddle · VICE PRESIDENT OF PUBLISHING Randy Stradley · VICE PRESIDENT OF BUSINESS DEVELOPMENT Michael Martens · VICE PRESIDENT OF MARKETING, SALES, AND LICENSING Anita Nelson · VICE PRESIDENT OF PRODUCT DEVELOPMENT David Scroggy · VICE PRESIDENT OF INFORMATION TECHNOLOGY Dale LaFountain · DIRECTOR OF PURCHASING Darlene Vogel · GENERAL COUNSEL Ken Lizzi EDITORIAL DIRECTOR Davey Estrada · SENIOR MANAGING EDITOR Scott Allie · SENIOR BOOKS EDITOR Chris Warner · EXECUTIVE EDITOR Diana Schutz · DIRECTOR OF DESIGN AND PRODUCTION Cary Grazzini · ART DIRECTOR Lia Ribacchi · DIRECTOR OF SCHEDULING Cara Niece

This volume reprints the comic-book series Buffy the Vampire Slayer Season Eight #26–#30, and short stories from MySpace Dark Horse Presents #24 and #25 from Dark Horse Comics.

Published by
Dark Horse Books
A division of
Dark Horse Comics, Inc.
10956 SE Main Street
Milwaukie, OR 97222

darkhorse.com

To find a comics shop in your area,
call the Comic Shop Locator Service toll-free at (888) 266-4226.

First edition: March 2010
ISBN 978-1-59582-415-8

1 3 5 7 9 10 8 6 4 2

Printed at Interglobe Printing, Inc., Beauceville, QC, Canada

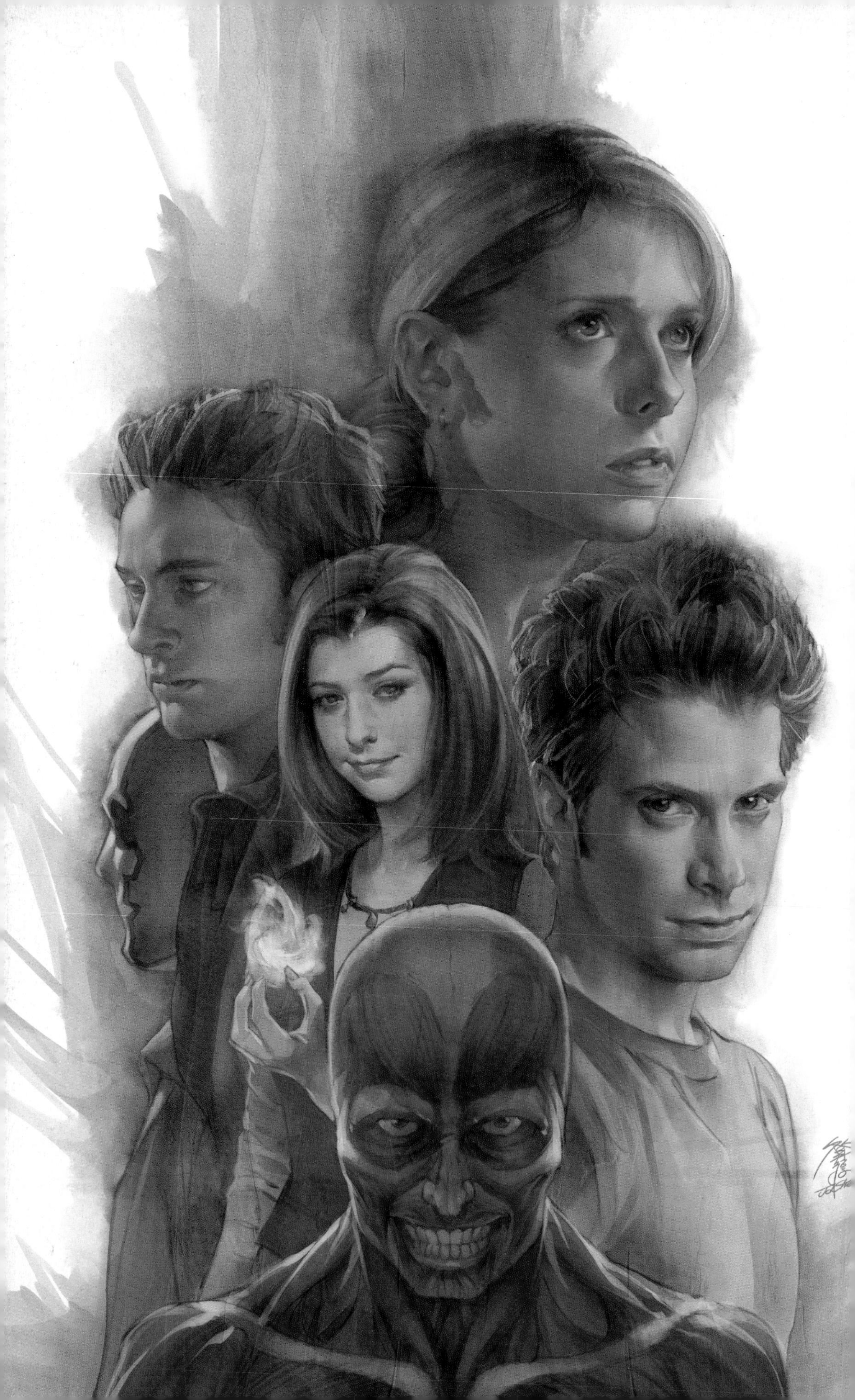

RETREAT

PART ONE

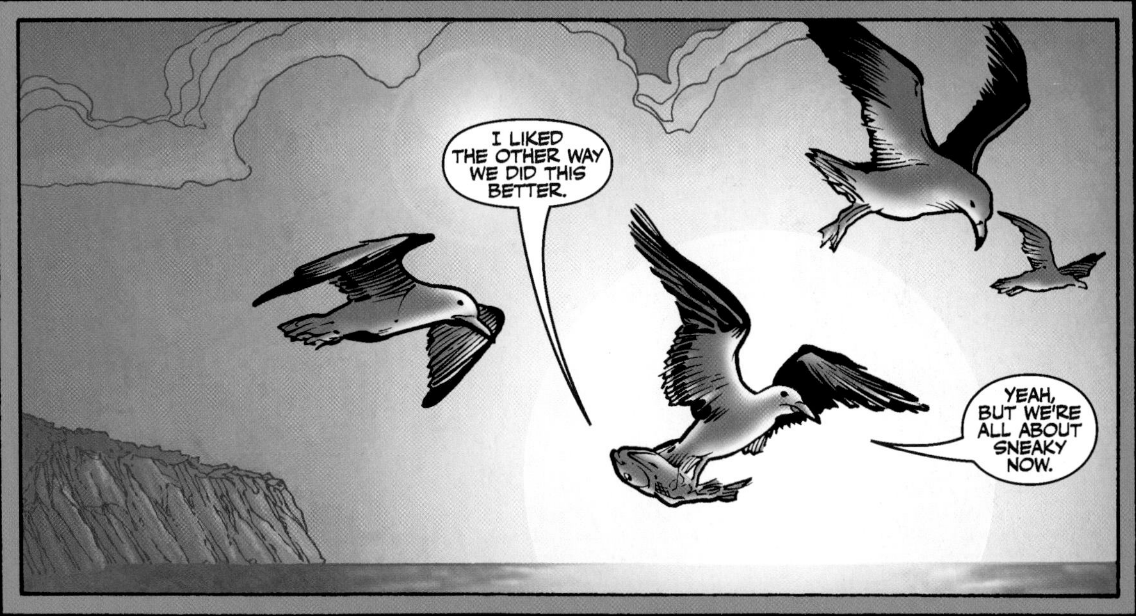
I LIKED THE OTHER WAY WE DID THIS BETTER.
YEAH, BUT WE'RE ALL ABOUT SNEAKY NOW.

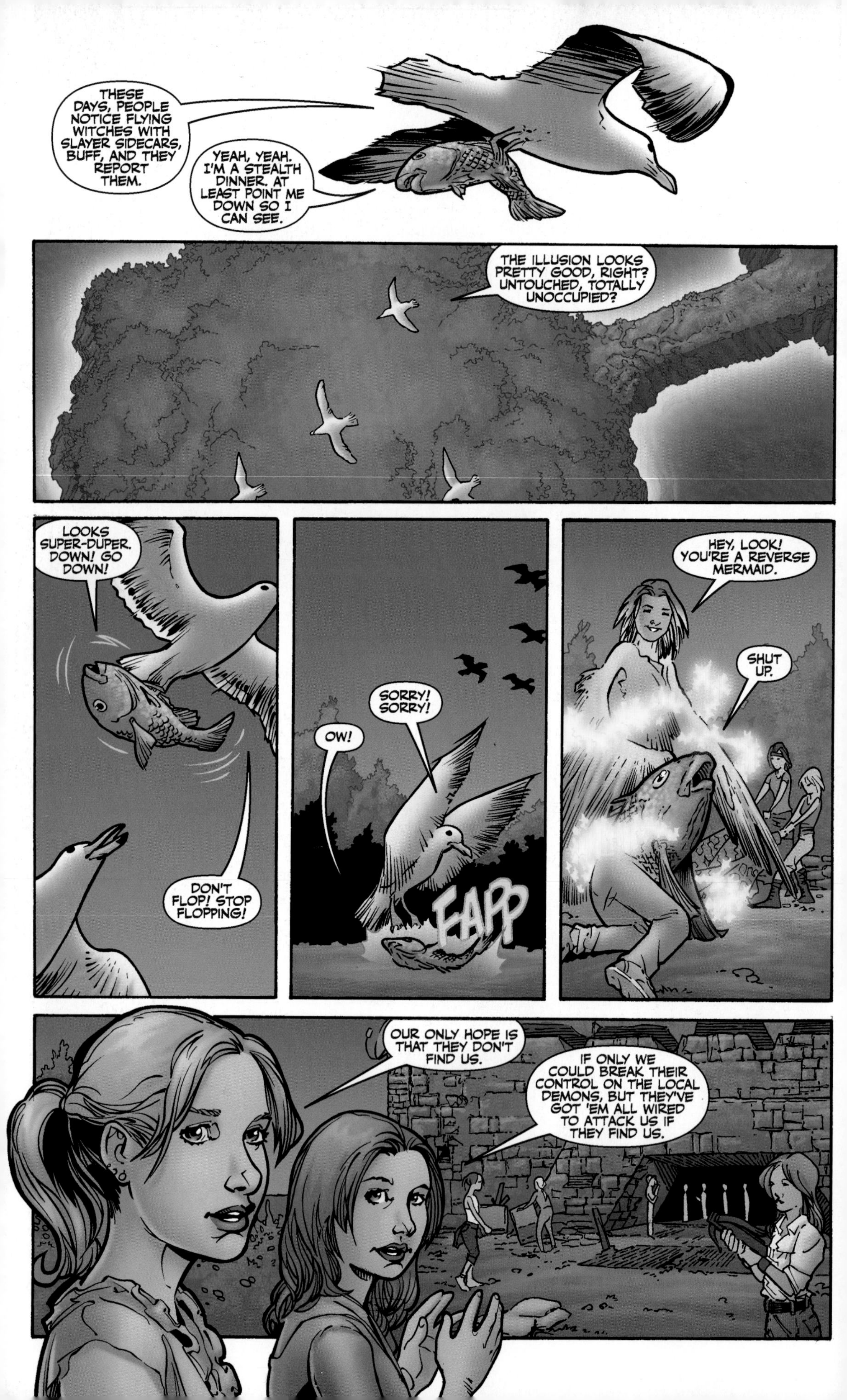
THESE DAYS, PEOPLE NOTICE FLYING WITCHES WITH SLAYER SIDECARS, BUFF, AND THEY REPORT THEM.
YEAH, YEAH. I'M A STEALTH DINNER. AT LEAST POINT ME DOWN SO I CAN SEE.
THE ILLUSION LOOKS PRETTY GOOD, RIGHT? UNTOUCHED, TOTALLY UNOCCUPIED?
LOOKS SUPER-DUPER. DOWN! GO DOWN!
DON'T FLOP! STOP FLOPPING!
SORRY! SORRY!
OW!
FAPP
HEY, LOOK! YOU'RE A REVERSE MERMAID.
SHUT UP.
OUR ONLY HOPE IS THAT THEY DON'T FIND US.
IF ONLY WE COULD BREAK THEIR CONTROL ON THE LOCAL DEMONS, BUT THEY'VE GOT 'EM ALL WIRED TO ATTACK US IF THEY FIND US.

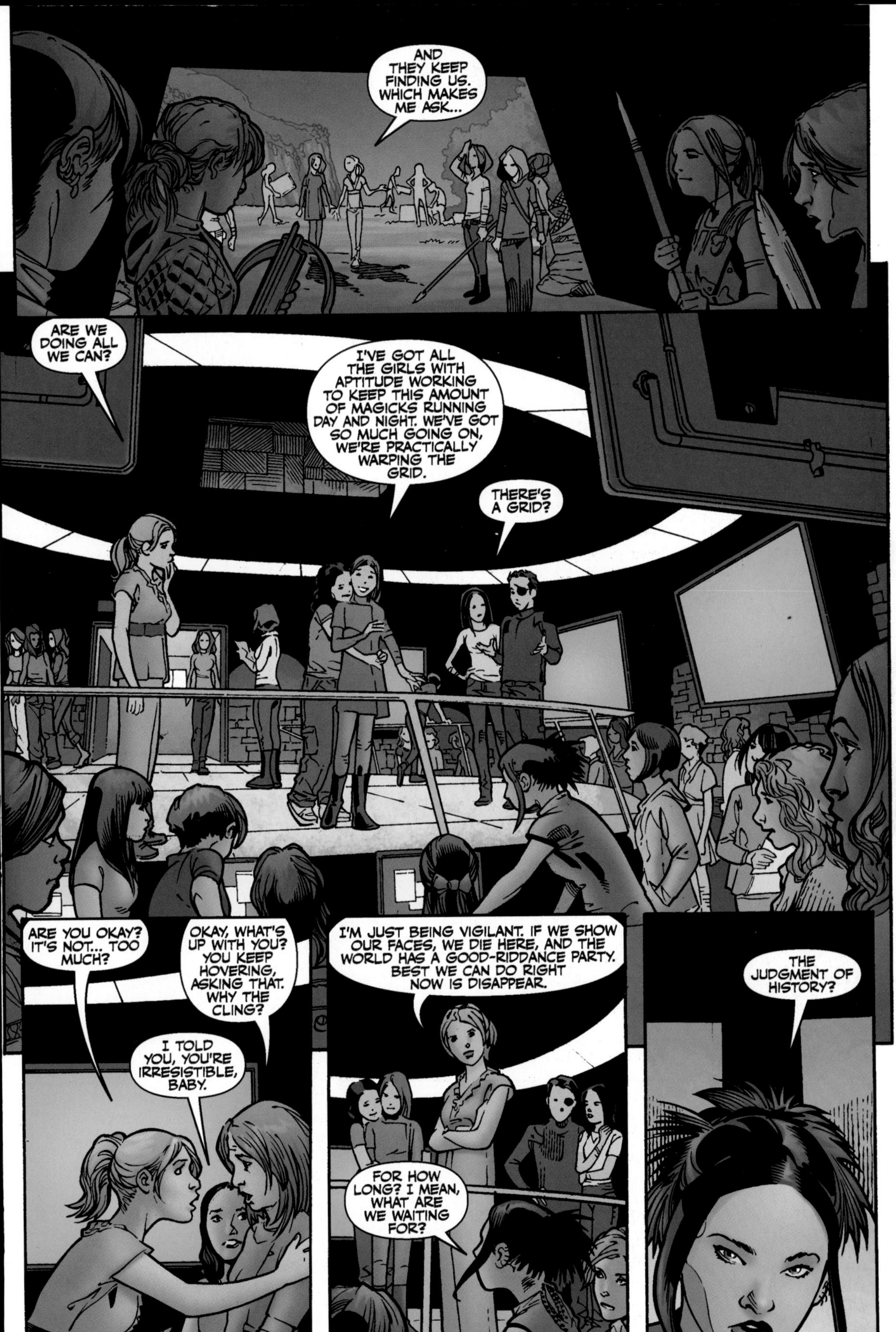
AND THEY KEEP FINDING US. WHICH MAKES ME ASK...
ARE WE DOING ALL WE CAN?
I'VE GOT ALL THE GIRLS WITH APTITUDE WORKING TO KEEP THIS AMOUNT OF MAGICKS RUNNING DAY AND NIGHT. WE'VE GOT SO MUCH GOING ON, WE'RE PRACTICALLY WARPING THE GRID.
THERE'S A GRID?
ARE YOU OKAY? IT'S NOT... TOO MUCH?
OKAY, WHAT'S UP WITH YOU? YOU KEEP HOVERING, ASKING THAT. WHY THE CLING?
I TOLD YOU, YOU'RE IRRESISTIBLE, BABY.
I'M JUST BEING VIGILANT. IF WE SHOW OUR FACES, WE DIE HERE, AND THE WORLD HAS A GOOD-RIDDANCE PARTY. BEST WE CAN DO RIGHT NOW IS DISAPPEAR.
FOR HOW LONG? I MEAN, WHAT ARE WE WAITING FOR?
THE JUDGMENT OF HISTORY?

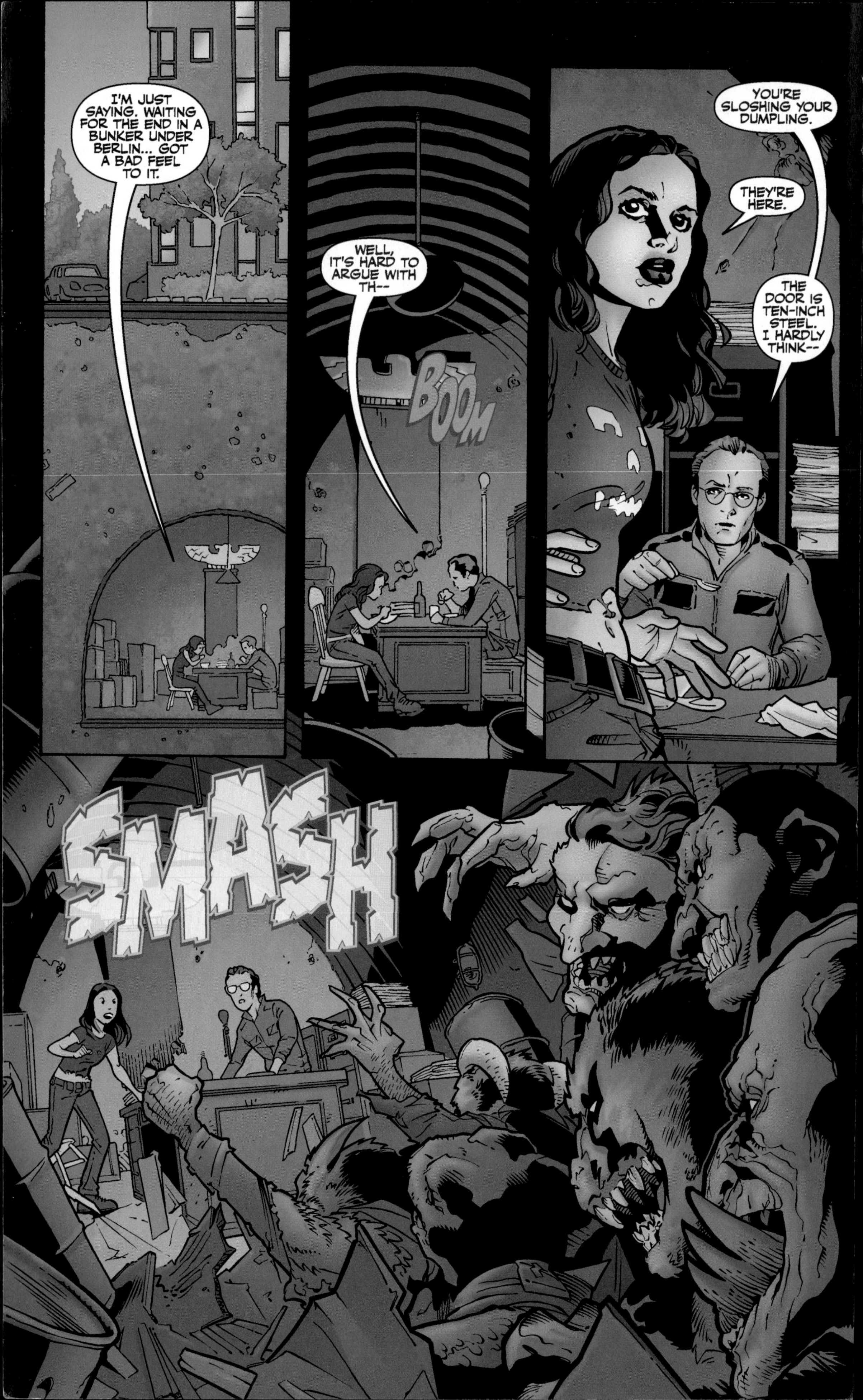
I'M JUST SAYING. WAITING FOR THE END IN A BUNKER UNDER BERLIN... GOT A BAD FEEL TO IT.
WELL, IT'S HARD TO ARGUE WITH TH--
BOOM
YOU'RE SLOSHING YOUR DUMPLING.
THEY'RE HERE.
THE DOOR IS TEN-INCH STEEL. I HARDLY THINK--
SMASH

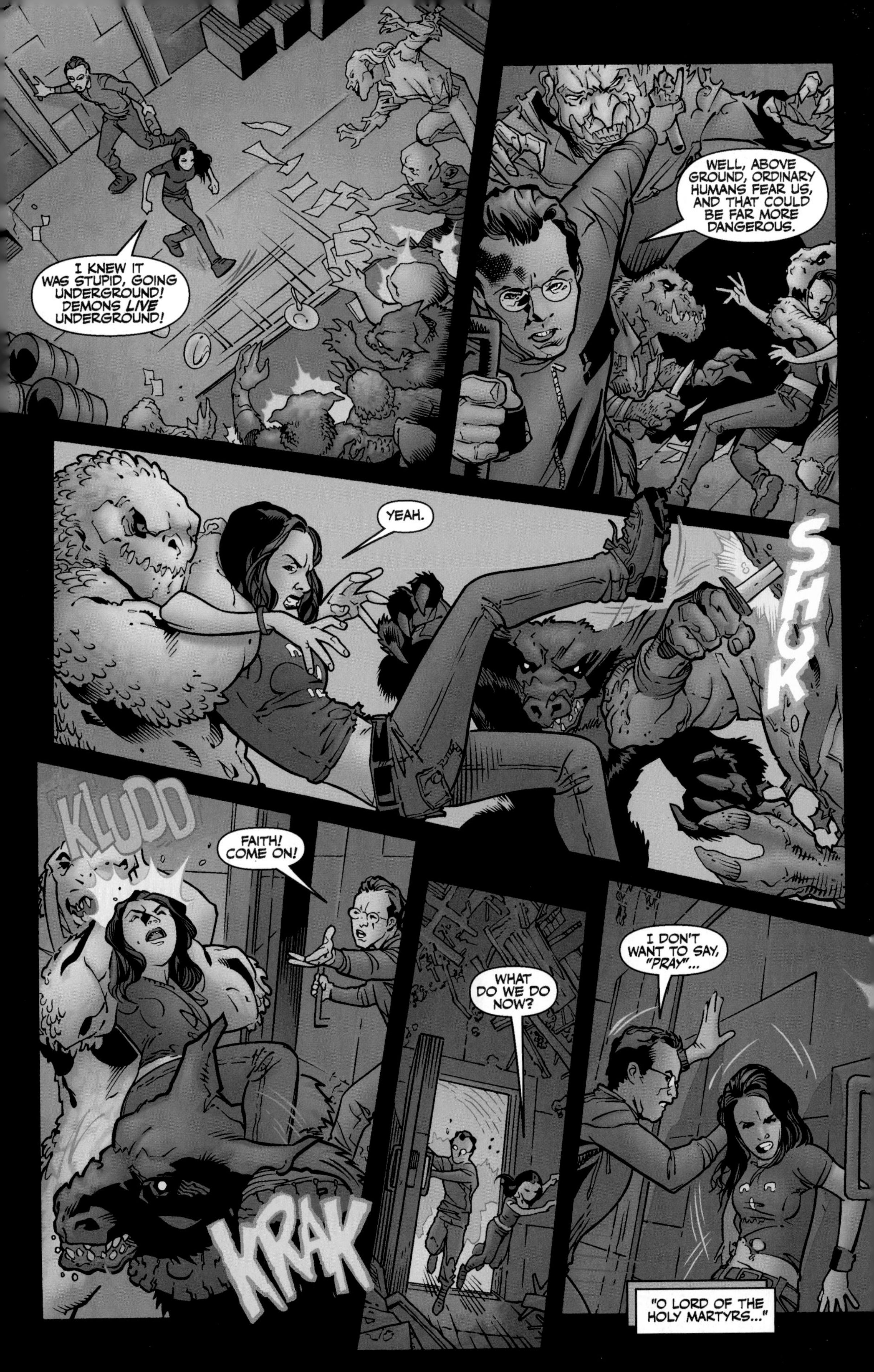
I KNEW IT WAS STUPID, GOING UNDERGROUND! DEMONS *LIVE* UNDERGROUND!
WELL, ABOVE GROUND, ORDINARY HUMANS FEAR US, AND THAT COULD BE FAR MORE DANGEROUS.
YEAH.
SHUK
KLUDD
FAITH! COME ON!
KRAK
WHAT DO WE DO NOW?
I DON'T WANT TO SAY, "*PRAY*"...
"O LORD OF THE HOLY MARTYRS..."

"O LORD OF THE HOLY MARTYRS AND SAINT HELEN, SAVE YOUR SERVANTS..." WHAT DOES IT MEAN?

POSEY KNOWS LATIN.

EE-MAY OO-TAY.

IT'S GRAFFITI. FROM THE EARLY CHRISTIAN MARTYRS. A LOT OF WHAT'S DOWN HERE UNDER ROME IS THEIRS. THE GRAFFITI, THE ART, THE...

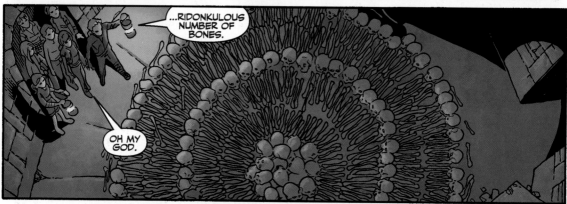

...RIDONKULOUS NUMBER OF BONES.

OH MY GOD.

WHEN YOU START USING BONES IN YOUR DECORATING, YOU'VE GOT TOO MANY BONES.

SCRABBB

WHAT'S THAT?

DID THEY FIND US? ARE PEOPLE HUNTING US DOWN HERE?

I'LL GO FIND OUT.

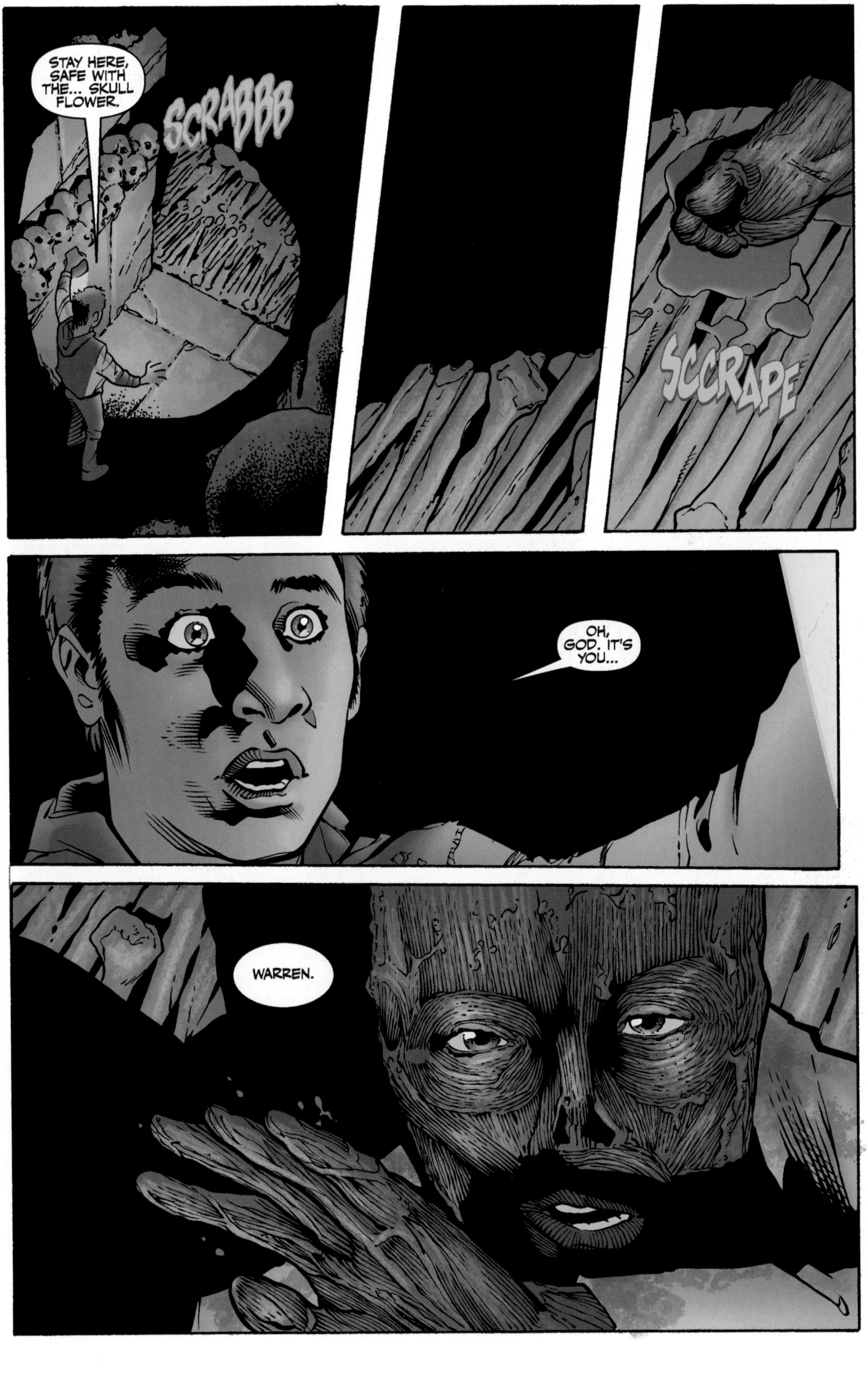
STAY HERE, SAFE WITH THE... SKULL FLOWER.
SCRABBB
SCCRAPE
OH, GOD. IT'S YOU...
WARREN.

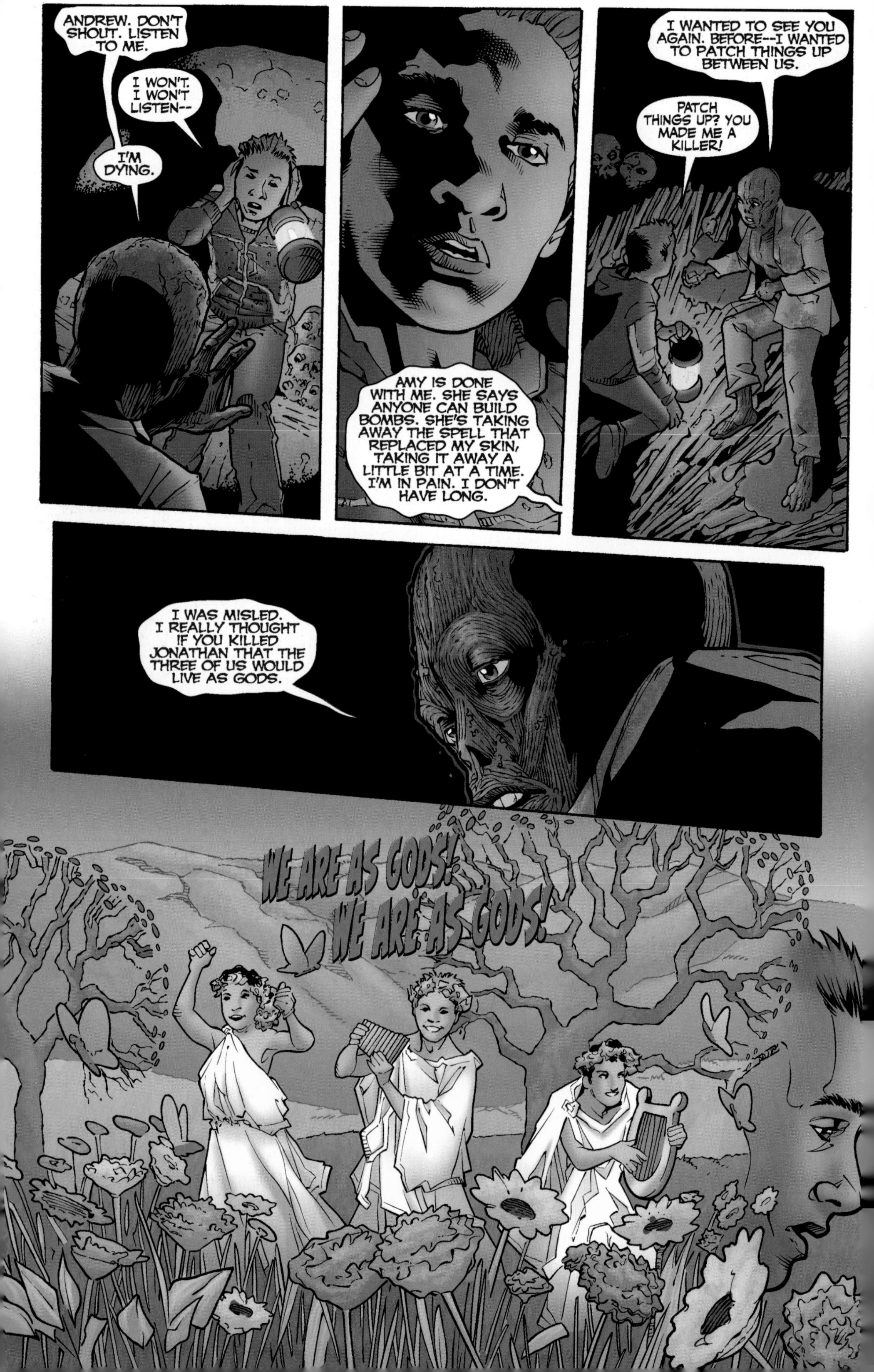

ANDREW. DON'T SHOUT. LISTEN TO ME.
I WON'T. I WON'T LISTEN--
I'M DYING.
AMY IS DONE WITH ME. SHE SAYS ANYONE CAN BUILD BOMBS. SHE'S TAKING AWAY THE SPELL THAT REPLACED MY SKIN, TAKING IT AWAY A LITTLE BIT AT A TIME. I'M IN PAIN. I DON'T HAVE LONG.
I WANTED TO SEE YOU AGAIN. BEFORE--I WANTED TO PATCH THINGS UP BETWEEN US.
PATCH THINGS UP? YOU MADE ME A KILLER!
I WAS MISLED. I REALLY THOUGHT IF YOU KILLED JONATHAN THAT THE THREE OF US WOULD LIVE AS GODS.
WE ARE AS GODS!
WE ARE AS GODS!

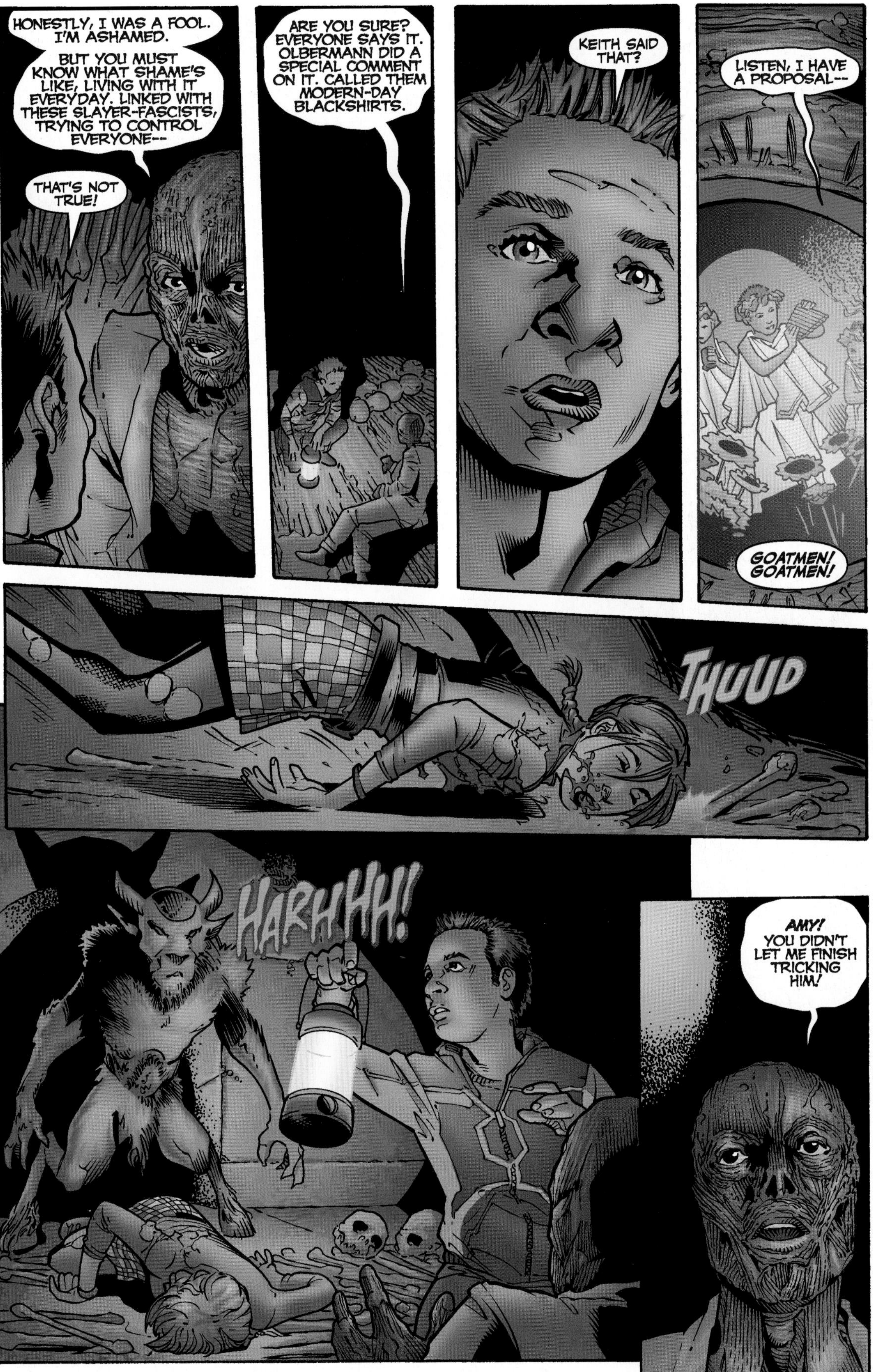
HONESTLY, I WAS A FOOL. I'M ASHAMED.
BUT YOU MUST KNOW WHAT SHAME'S LIKE, LIVING WITH IT EVERYDAY. LINKED WITH THESE SLAYER-FASCISTS, TRYING TO CONTROL EVERYONE--
THAT'S NOT TRUE!
ARE YOU SURE? EVERYONE SAYS IT. OLBERMANN DID A SPECIAL COMMENT ON IT. CALLED THEM MODERN-DAY BLACKSHIRTS.
KEITH SAID THAT?
LISTEN, I HAVE A PROPOSAL--
GOATMEN! GOATMEN!
THUUD
HARHHH!
AMY! YOU DIDN'T LET ME FINISH TRICKING HIM!

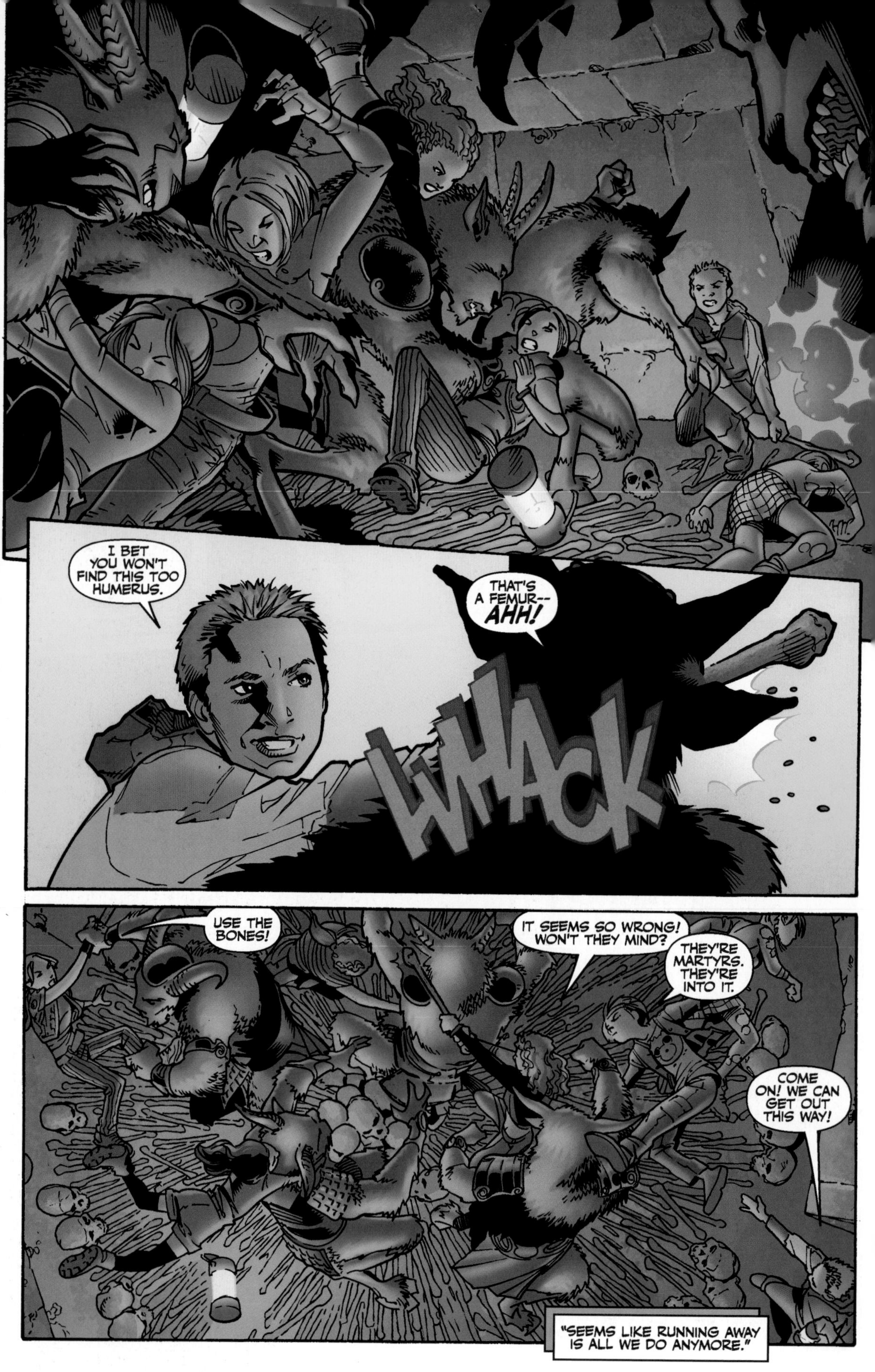

I BET YOU WON'T FIND THIS TOO HUMERUS.
THAT'S A FEMUR-- AHH!
WHACK
USE THE BONES!
IT SEEMS SO WRONG! WON'T THEY MIND?
THEY'RE MARTYRS. THEY'RE INTO IT.
COME ON! WE CAN GET OUT THIS WAY!
"SEEMS LIKE RUNNING AWAY IS ALL WE DO ANYMORE."

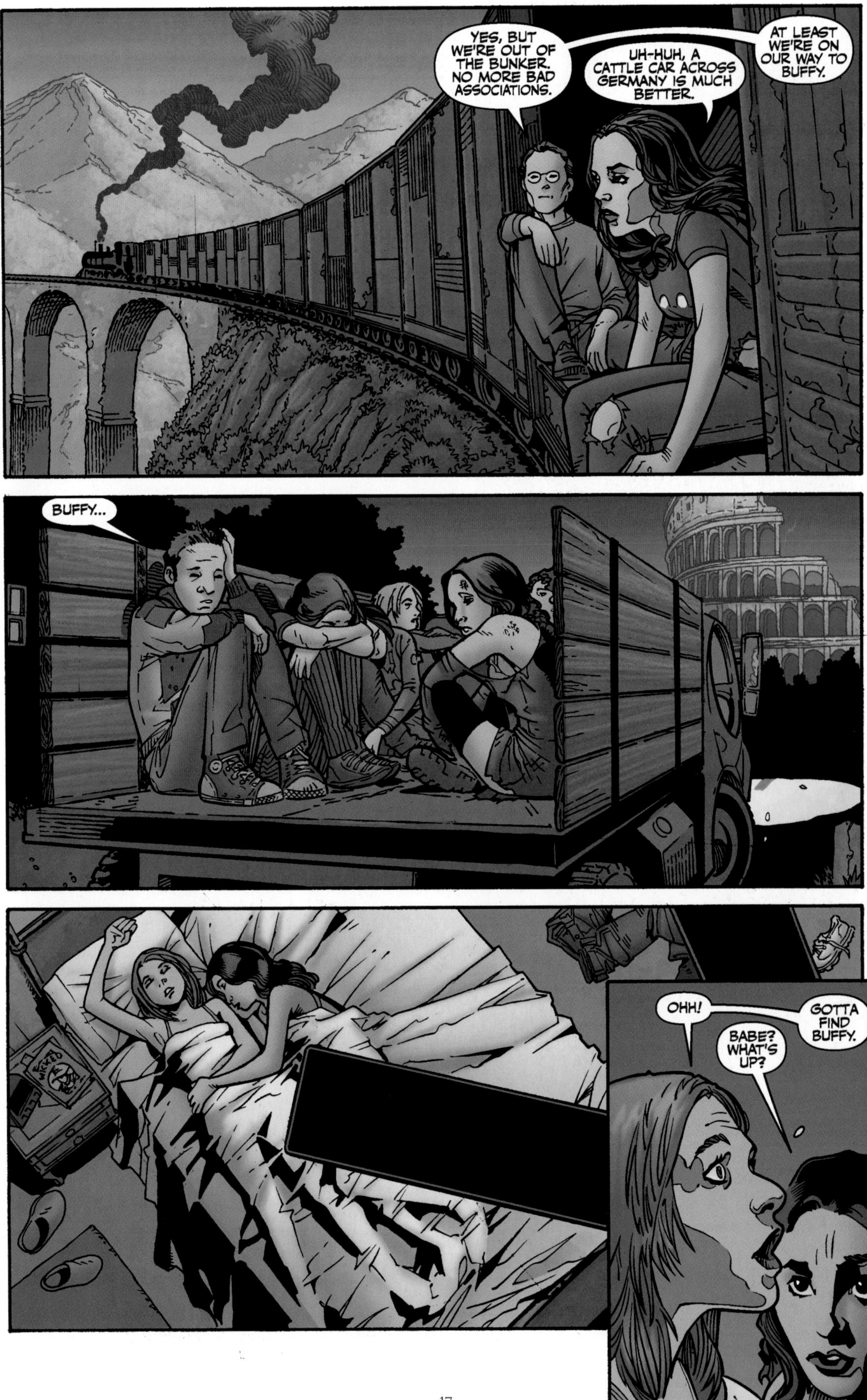
YES, BUT WE'RE OUT OF THE BUNKER. NO MORE BAD ASSOCIATIONS.
UH-HUH, A CATTLE CAR ACROSS GERMANY IS MUCH BETTER.
AT LEAST WE'RE ON OUR WAY TO BUFFY.
BUFFY...
OHH!
BABE? WHAT'S UP?
GOTTA FIND BUFFY.

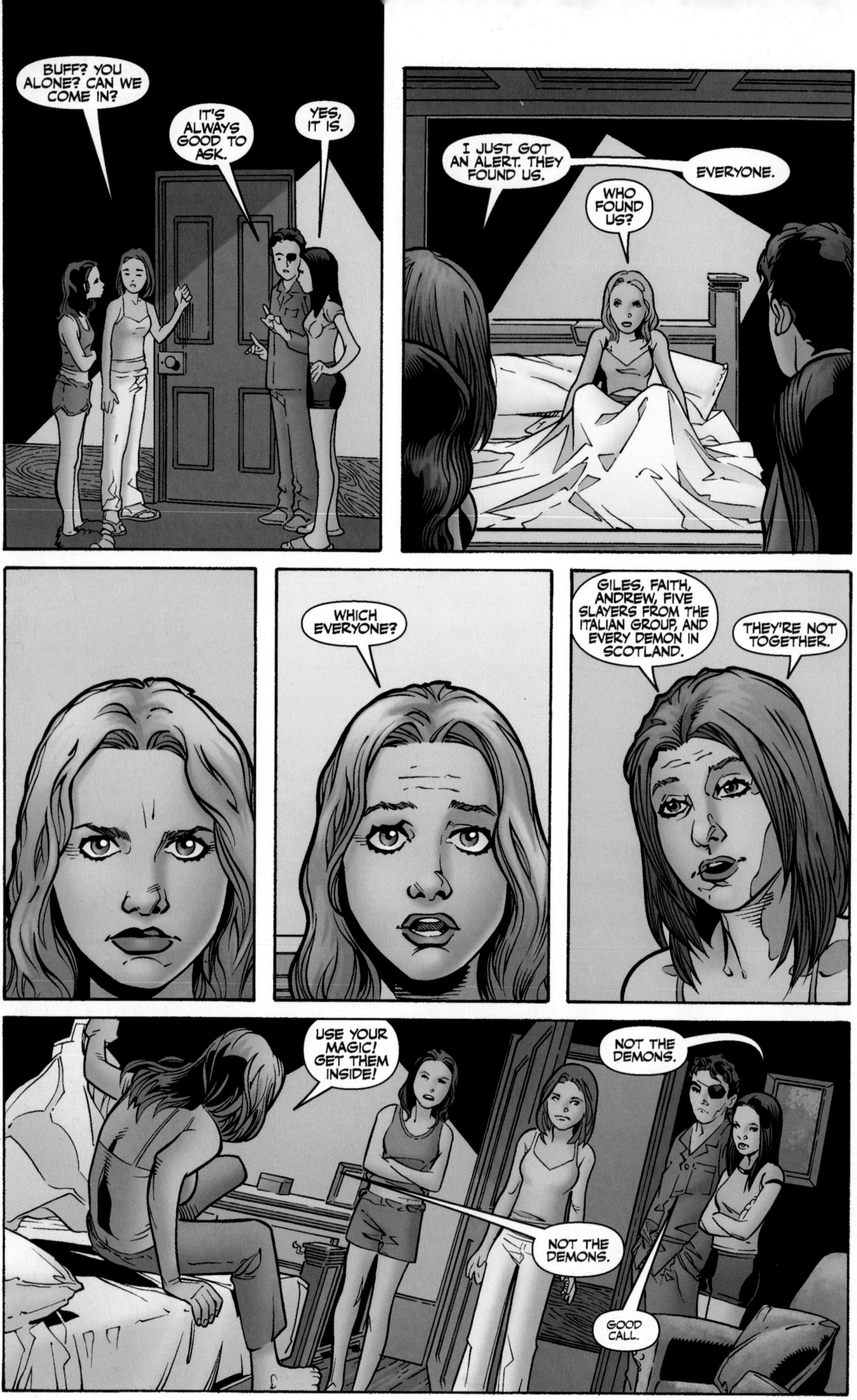
BUFF? YOU ALONE? CAN WE COME IN?
IT'S ALWAYS GOOD TO ASK.
YES, IT IS.
I JUST GOT AN ALERT. THEY FOUND US.
EVERYONE.
WHO FOUND US?
WHICH EVERYONE?
GILES, FAITH, ANDREW, FIVE SLAYERS FROM THE ITALIAN GROUP, AND EVERY DEMON IN SCOTLAND.
THEY'RE NOT TOGETHER.
USE YOUR MAGIC! GET THEM INSIDE!
NOT THE DEMONS.
NOT THE DEMONS.
GOOD CALL.

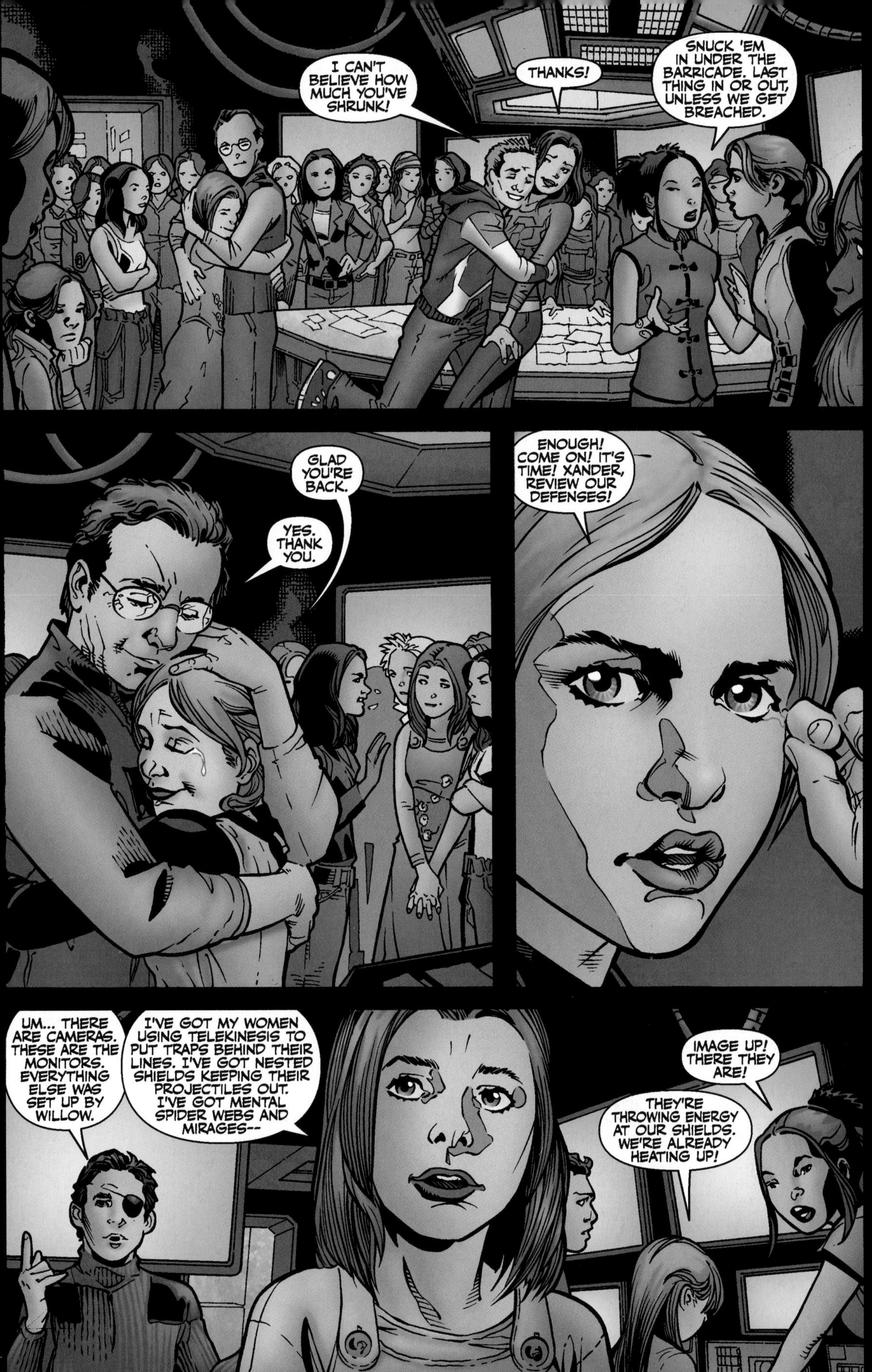
I CAN'T BELIEVE HOW MUCH YOU'VE SHRUNK!
THANKS!
SNUCK 'EM IN UNDER THE BARRICADE. LAST THING IN OR OUT, UNLESS WE GET BREACHED.
GLAD YOU'RE BACK.
YES. THANK YOU.
ENOUGH! COME ON! IT'S TIME! XANDER, REVIEW OUR DEFENSES!
UM... THERE ARE CAMERAS. THESE ARE THE MONITORS. EVERYTHING ELSE WAS SET UP BY WILLOW.
I'VE GOT MY WOMEN USING TELEKINESIS TO PUT TRAPS BEHIND THEIR LINES. I'VE GOT NESTED SHIELDS KEEPING THEIR PROJECTILES OUT. I'VE GOT MENTAL SPIDER WEBS AND MIRAGES--
IMAGE UP! THERE THEY ARE!
THEY'RE THROWING ENERGY AT OUR SHIELDS. WE'RE ALREADY HEATING UP!

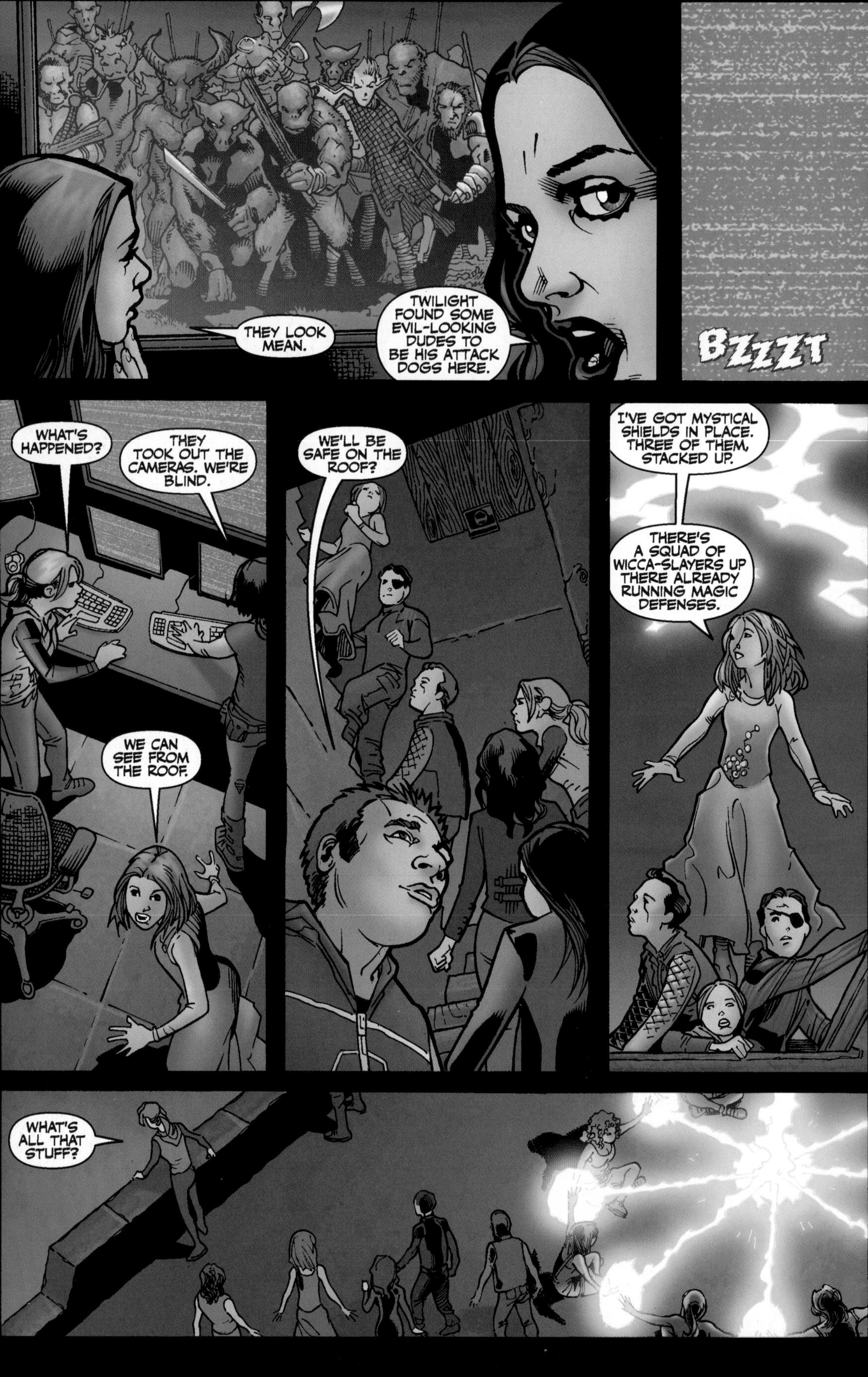
THEY LOOK MEAN.
TWILIGHT FOUND SOME EVIL-LOOKING DUDES TO BE HIS ATTACK DOGS HERE.
BZZZT
WHAT'S HAPPENED?
THEY TOOK OUT THE CAMERAS. WE'RE BLIND.
WE CAN SEE FROM THE ROOF.
WE'LL BE SAFE ON THE ROOF?
I'VE GOT MYSTICAL SHIELDS IN PLACE. THREE OF THEM, STACKED UP.
THERE'S A SQUAD OF WICCA-SLAYERS UP THERE ALREADY RUNNING MAGIC DEFENSES.
WHAT'S ALL THAT STUFF?

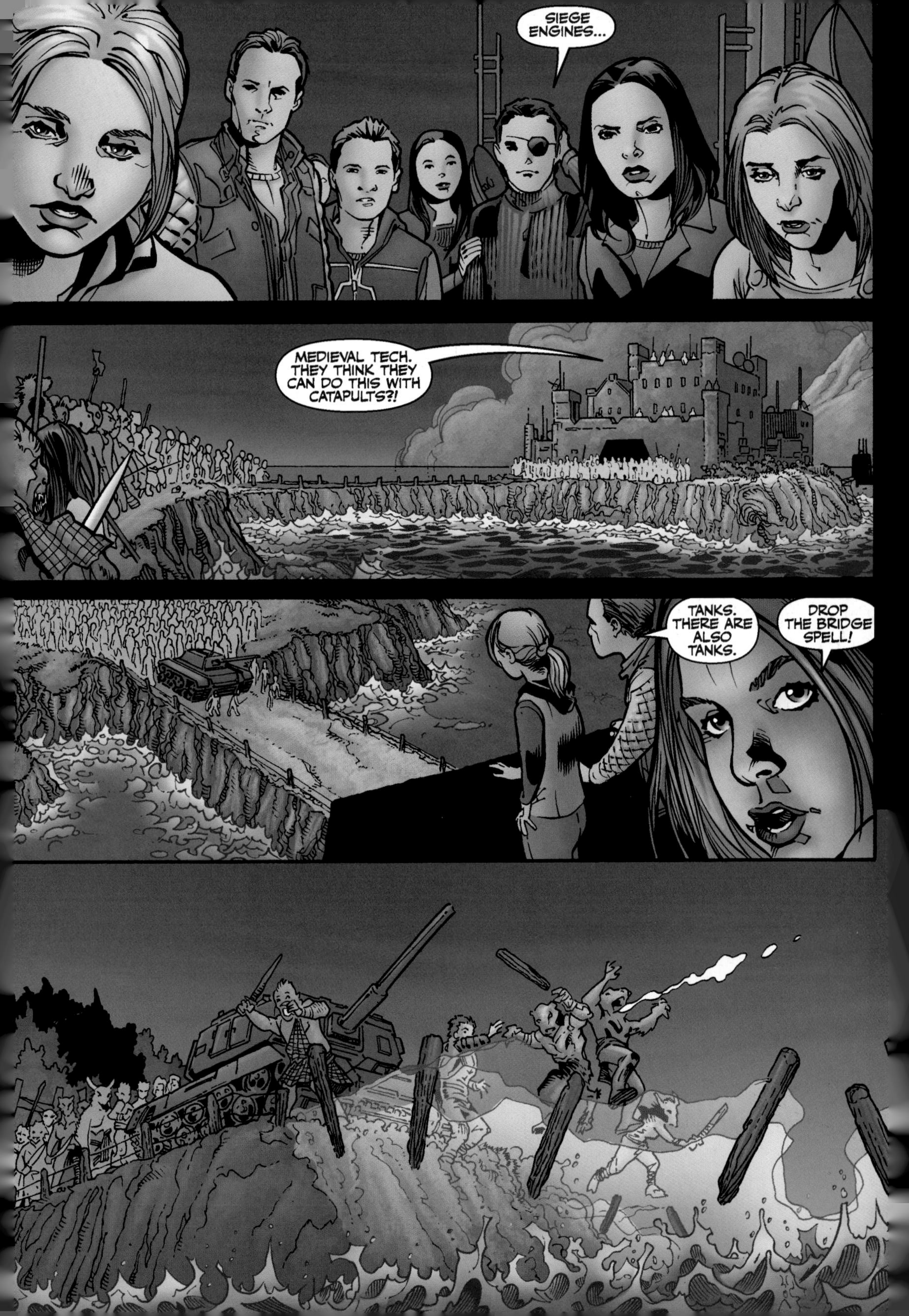
SIEGE ENGINES...
MEDIEVAL TECH. THEY THINK THEY CAN DO THIS WITH CATAPULTS?!
TANKS. THERE ARE ALSO TANKS.
DROP THE BRIDGE SPELL!

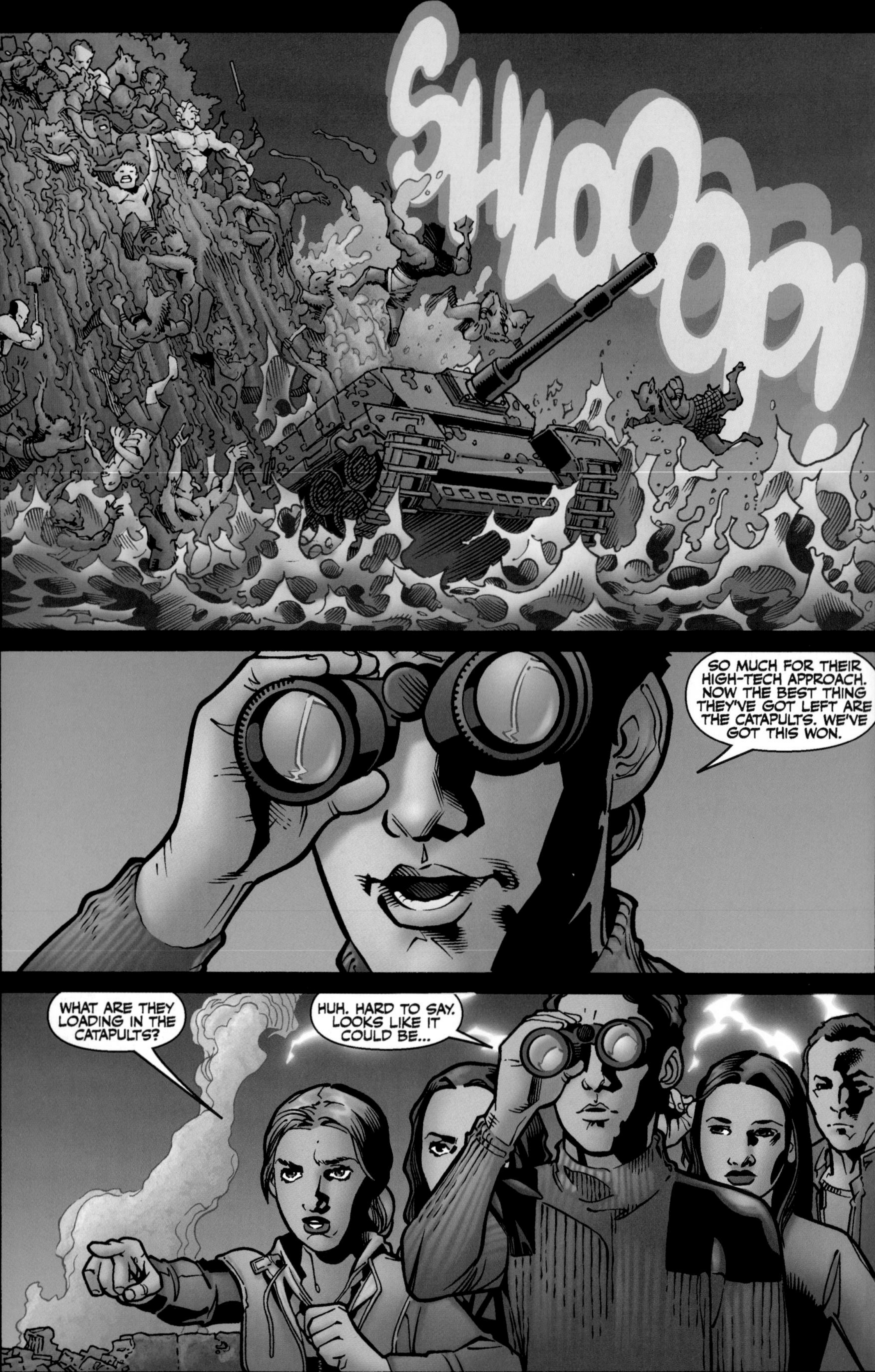
SHLOOOOP!
SO MUCH FOR THEIR HIGH-TECH APPROACH. NOW THE BEST THING THEY'VE GOT LEFT ARE THE CATAPULTS. WE'VE GOT THIS WON.
WHAT ARE THEY LOADING IN THE CATAPULTS?
HUH. HARD TO SAY. LOOKS LIKE IT COULD BE...

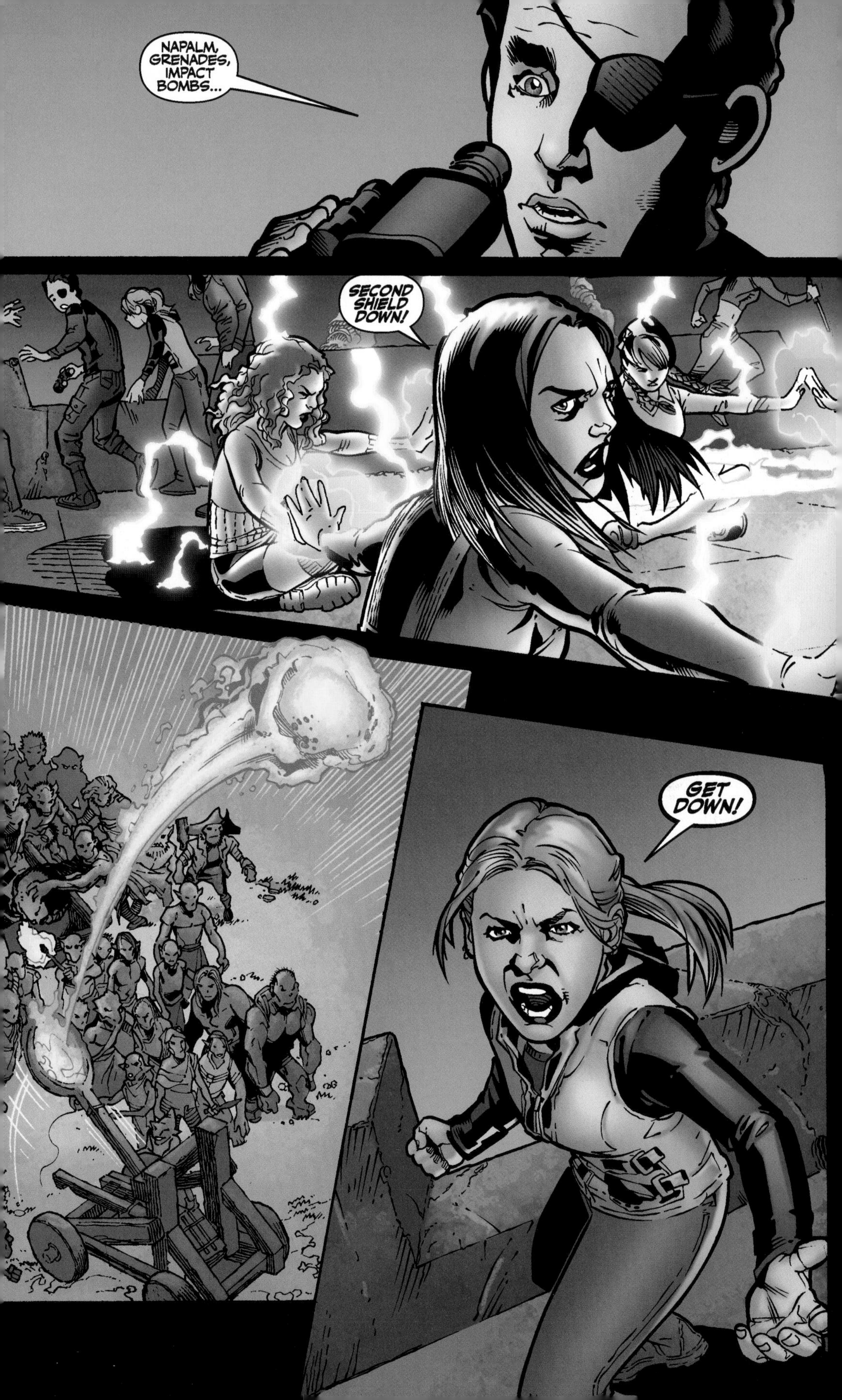
NAPALM, GRENADES, IMPACT BOMBS...
SECOND SHIELD DOWN!
GET DOWN!

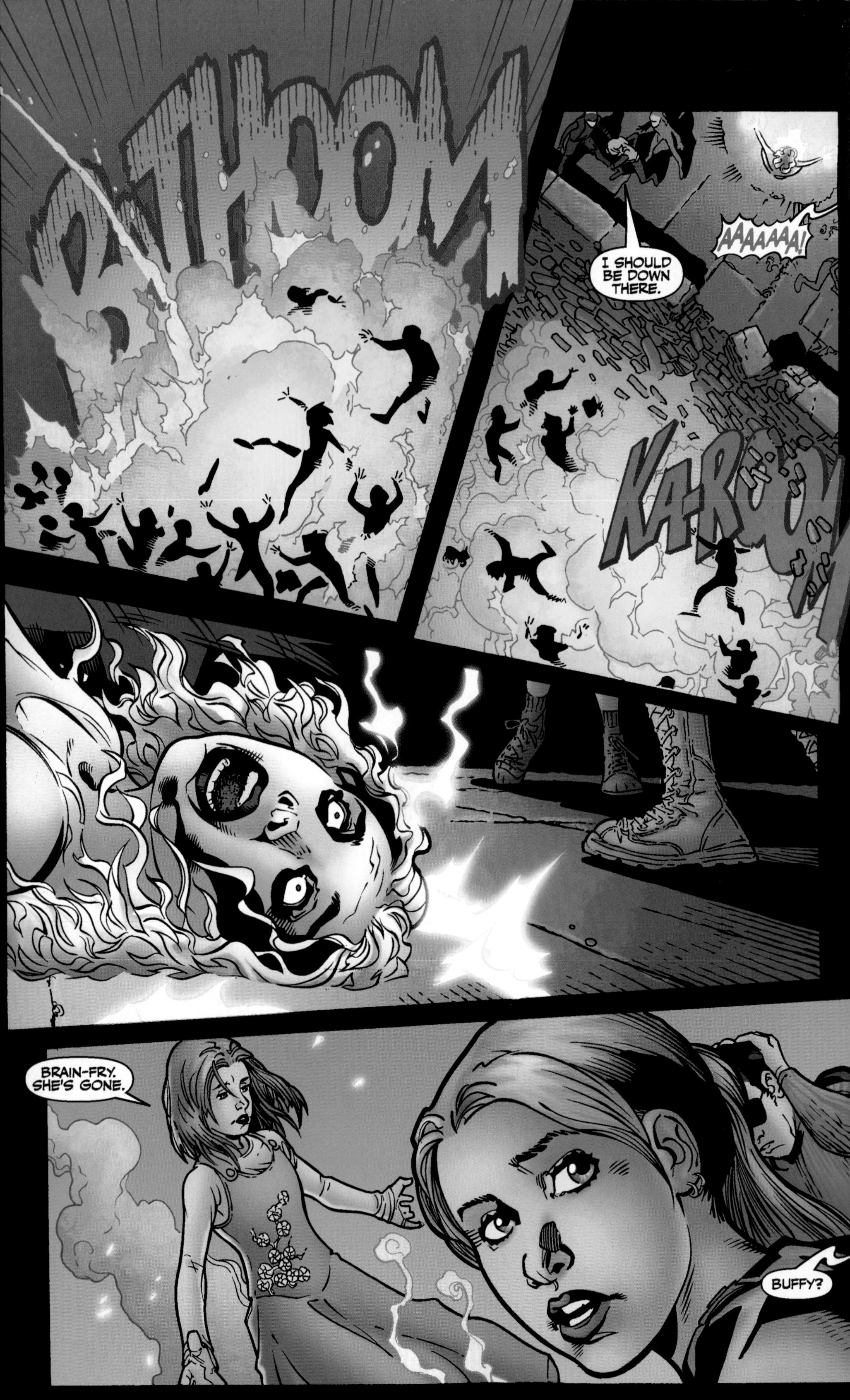
BATHOOM
I SHOULD BE DOWN THERE.
AAAAAAA!
KA-ROOM
BRAIN-FRY. SHE'S GONE.
BUFFY?

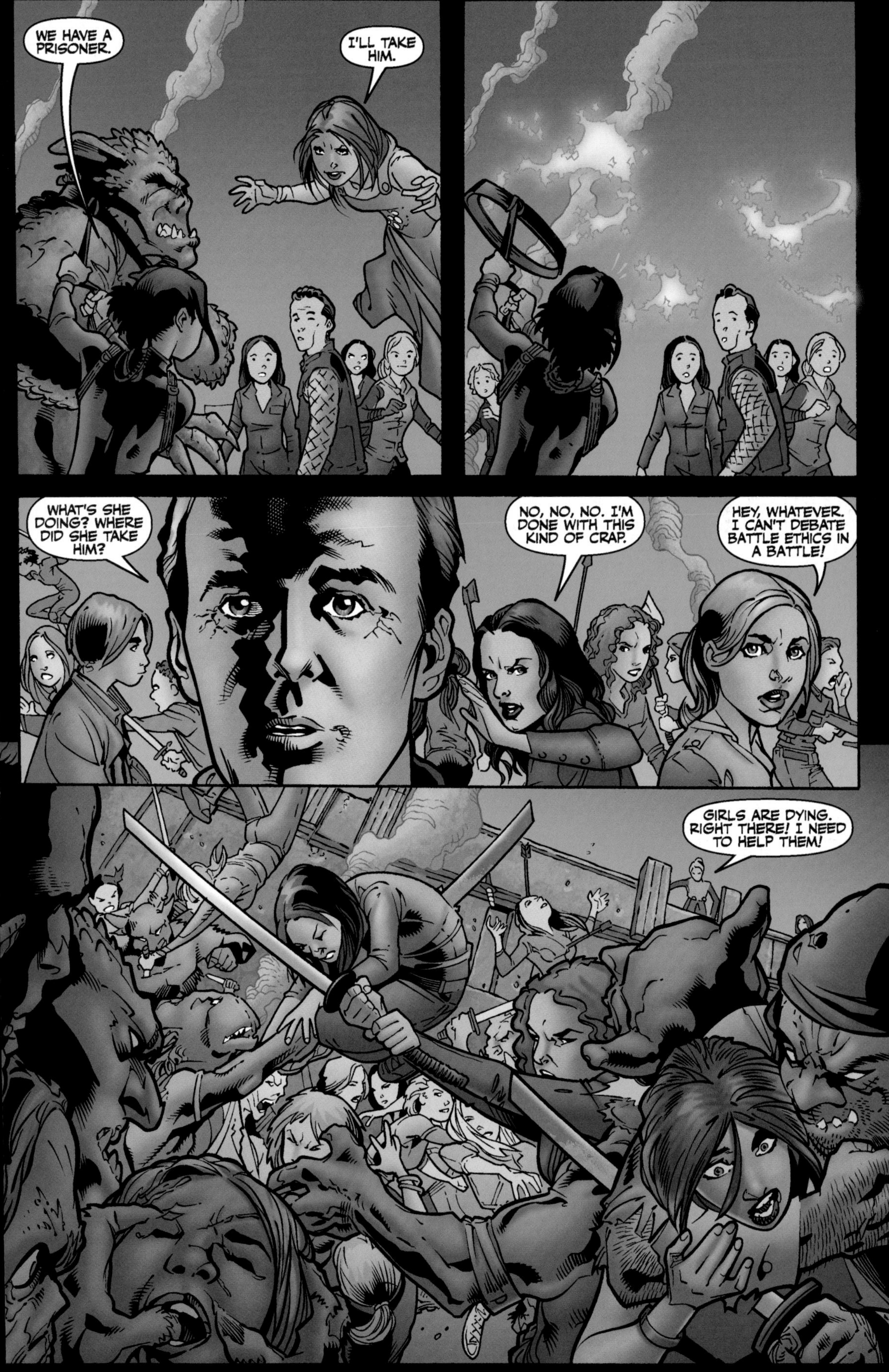
WE HAVE A PRISONER.
I'LL TAKE HIM.
WHAT'S SHE DOING? WHERE DID SHE TAKE HIM?
NO, NO, NO. I'M DONE WITH THIS KIND OF CRAP.
HEY, WHATEVER. I CAN'T DEBATE BATTLE ETHICS IN A BATTLE!
GIRLS ARE DYING. RIGHT THERE! I NEED TO HELP THEM!

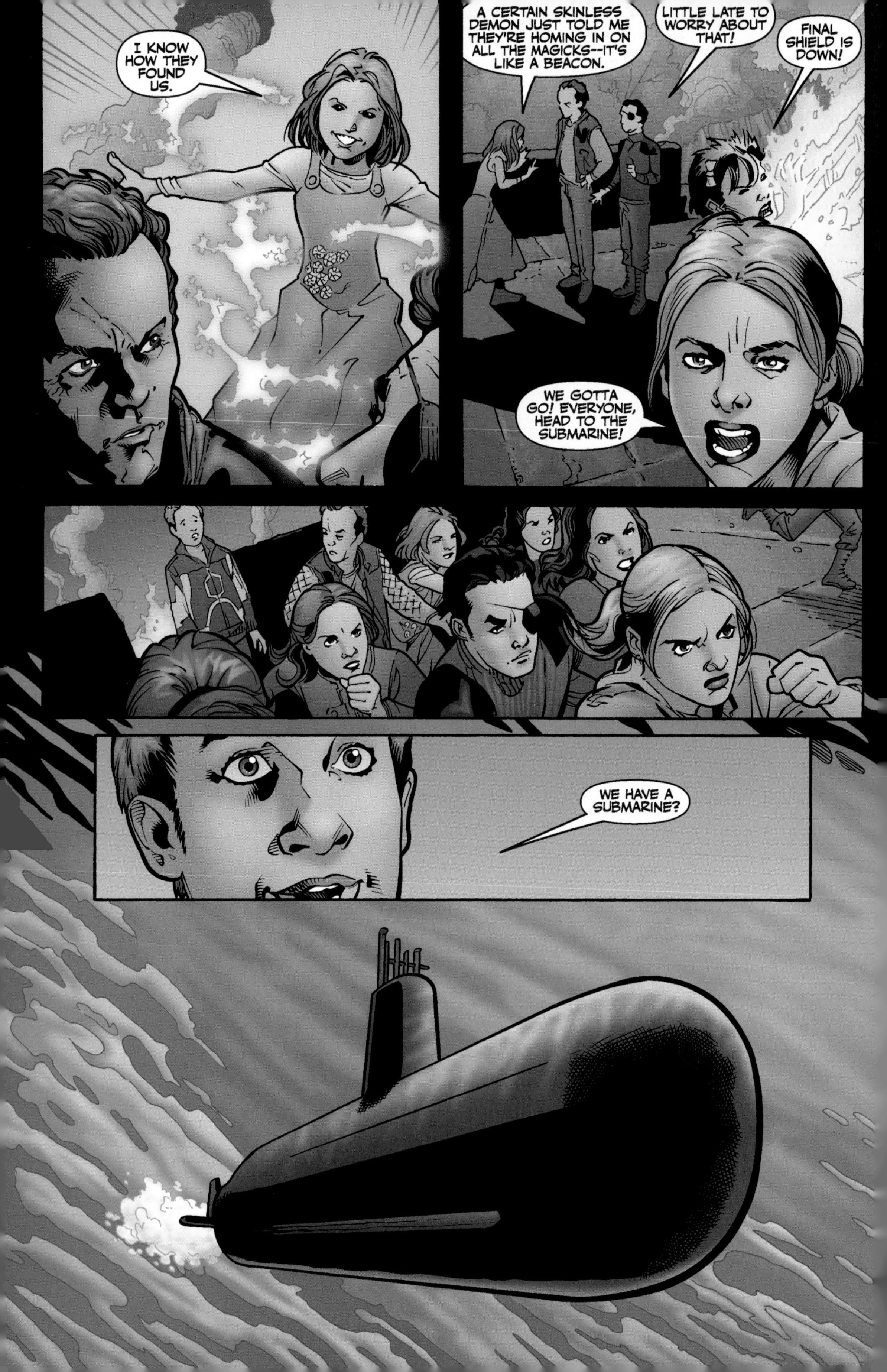
I KNOW HOW THEY FOUND US.
A CERTAIN SKINLESS DEMON JUST TOLD ME THEY'RE HOMING IN ON ALL THE MAGICKS--IT'S LIKE A BEACON.
LITTLE LATE TO WORRY ABOUT THAT!
FINAL SHIELD IS DOWN!
WE GOTTA GO! EVERYONE, HEAD TO THE SUBMARINE!
WE HAVE A SUBMARINE?

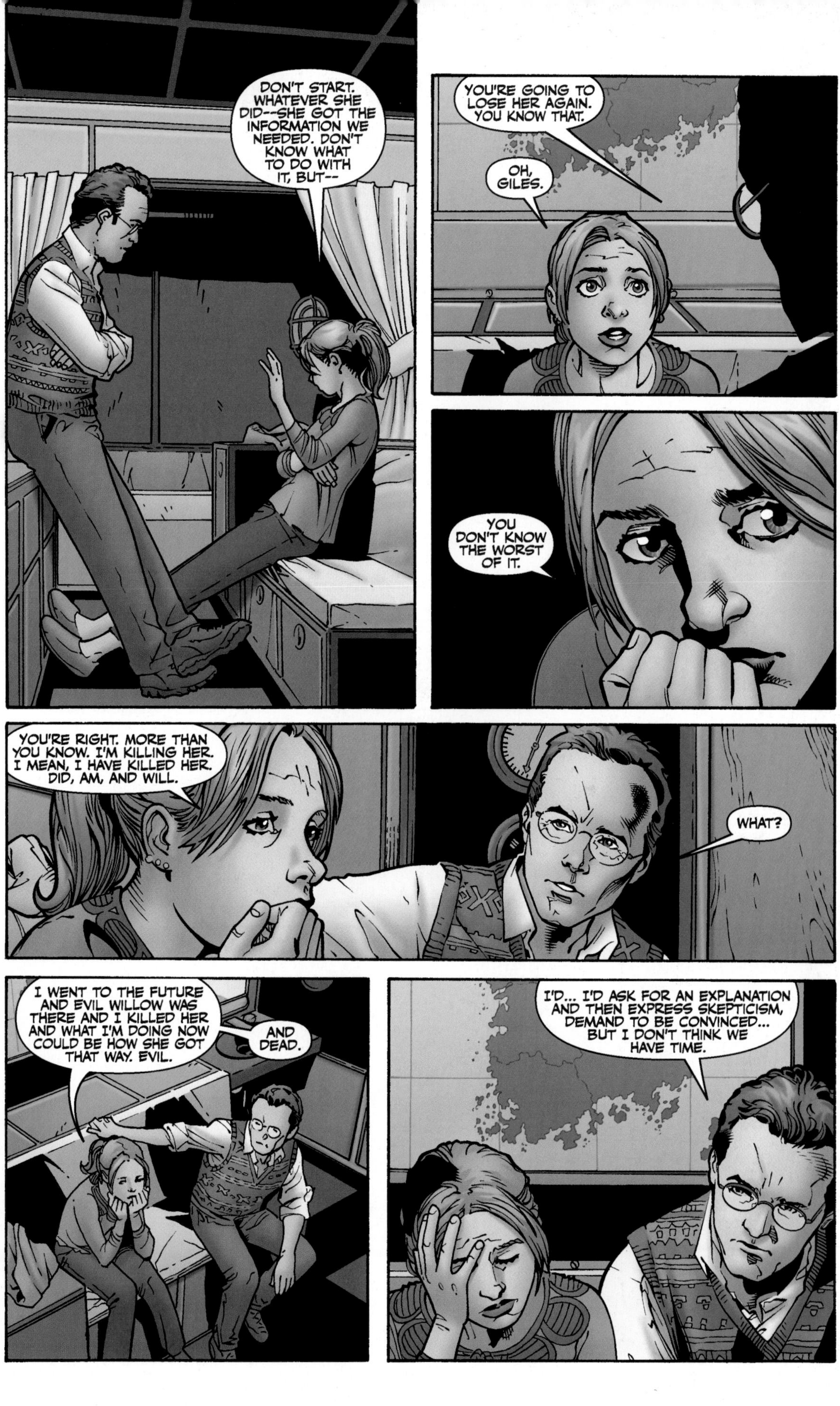
DON'T START. WHATEVER SHE DID--SHE GOT THE INFORMATION WE NEEDED. DON'T KNOW WHAT TO DO WITH IT, BUT--
YOU'RE GOING TO LOSE HER AGAIN. YOU KNOW THAT.
OH, GILES.
YOU DON'T KNOW THE WORST OF IT.
YOU'RE RIGHT. MORE THAN YOU KNOW. I'M KILLING HER. I MEAN, I HAVE KILLED HER. DID, AM, AND WILL.
WHAT?
I WENT TO THE FUTURE AND EVIL WILLOW WAS THERE AND I KILLED HER AND WHAT I'M DOING NOW COULD BE HOW SHE GOT THAT WAY. EVIL.
AND DEAD.
I'D... I'D ASK FOR AN EXPLANATION AND THEN EXPRESS SKEPTICISM, DEMAND TO BE CONVINCED... BUT I DON'T THINK WE HAVE TIME.

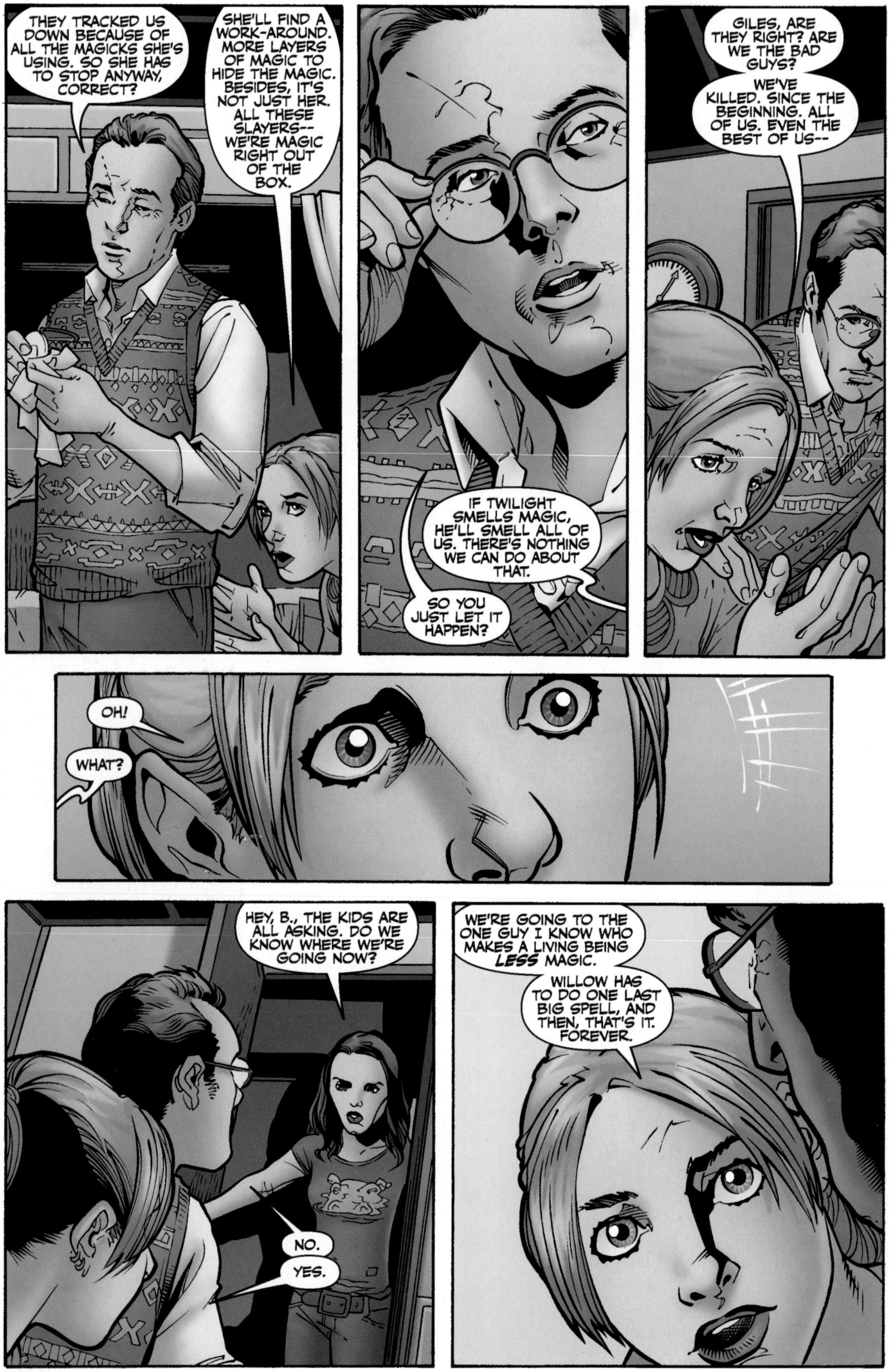
THEY TRACKED US DOWN BECAUSE OF ALL THE MAGICKS SHE'S USING. SO SHE HAS TO STOP ANYWAY, CORRECT?
SHE'LL FIND A WORK-AROUND. MORE LAYERS OF MAGIC TO HIDE THE MAGIC. BESIDES, IT'S NOT JUST HER. ALL THESE SLAYERS-- WE'RE MAGIC RIGHT OUT OF THE BOX.
IF TWILIGHT SMELLS MAGIC, HE'LL SMELL ALL OF US. THERE'S NOTHING WE CAN DO ABOUT THAT.
SO YOU JUST LET IT HAPPEN?
GILES, ARE THEY RIGHT? ARE WE THE BAD GUYS?
WE'VE KILLED. SINCE THE BEGINNING. ALL OF US. EVEN THE BEST OF US--
OH!
WHAT?
HEY, B., THE KIDS ARE ALL ASKING. DO WE KNOW WHERE WE'RE GOING NOW?
NO.
YES.
WE'RE GOING TO THE ONE GUY I KNOW WHO MAKES A LIVING BEING *LESS* MAGIC.
WILLOW HAS TO DO ONE LAST BIG SPELL, AND THEN, THAT'S IT. FOREVER.

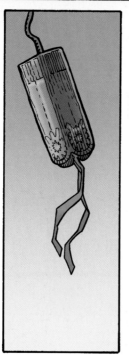

ting

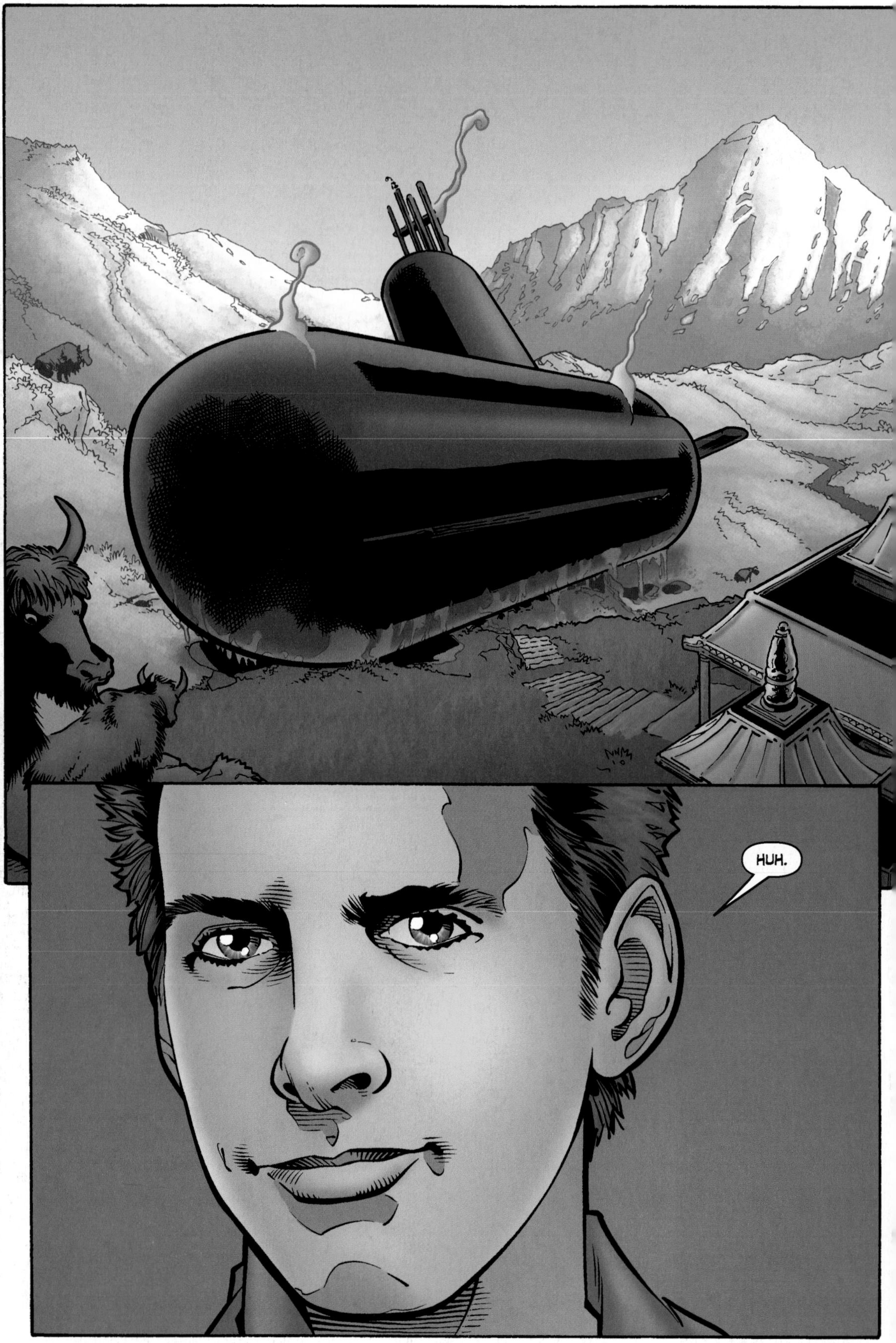
HUH.

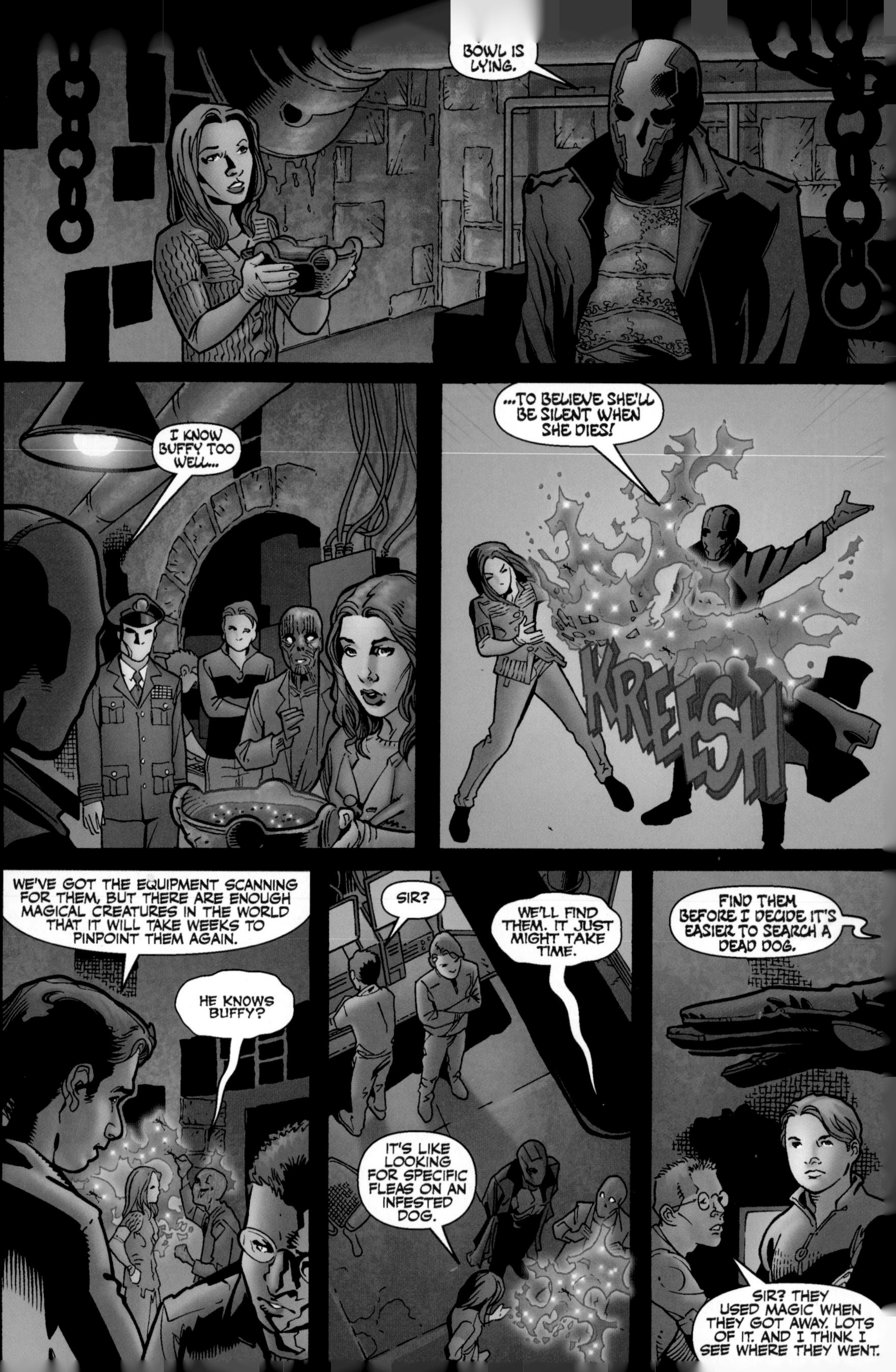
BOWL IS LYING.
I KNOW BUFFY TOO WELL...
...TO BELIEVE SHE'LL BE SILENT WHEN SHE DIES!
KREESH
WE'VE GOT THE EQUIPMENT SCANNING FOR THEM, BUT THERE ARE ENOUGH MAGICAL CREATURES IN THE WORLD THAT IT WILL TAKE WEEKS TO PINPOINT THEM AGAIN.
HE KNOWS BUFFY?
SIR?
WE'LL FIND THEM. IT JUST MIGHT TAKE TIME.
IT'S LIKE LOOKING FOR SPECIFIC FLEAS ON AN INFESTED DOG.
FIND THEM BEFORE I DECIDE IT'S EASIER TO SEARCH A DEAD DOG.
SIR? THEY USED MAGIC WHEN THEY GOT AWAY. LOTS OF IT. AND I THINK I SEE WHERE THEY WENT.

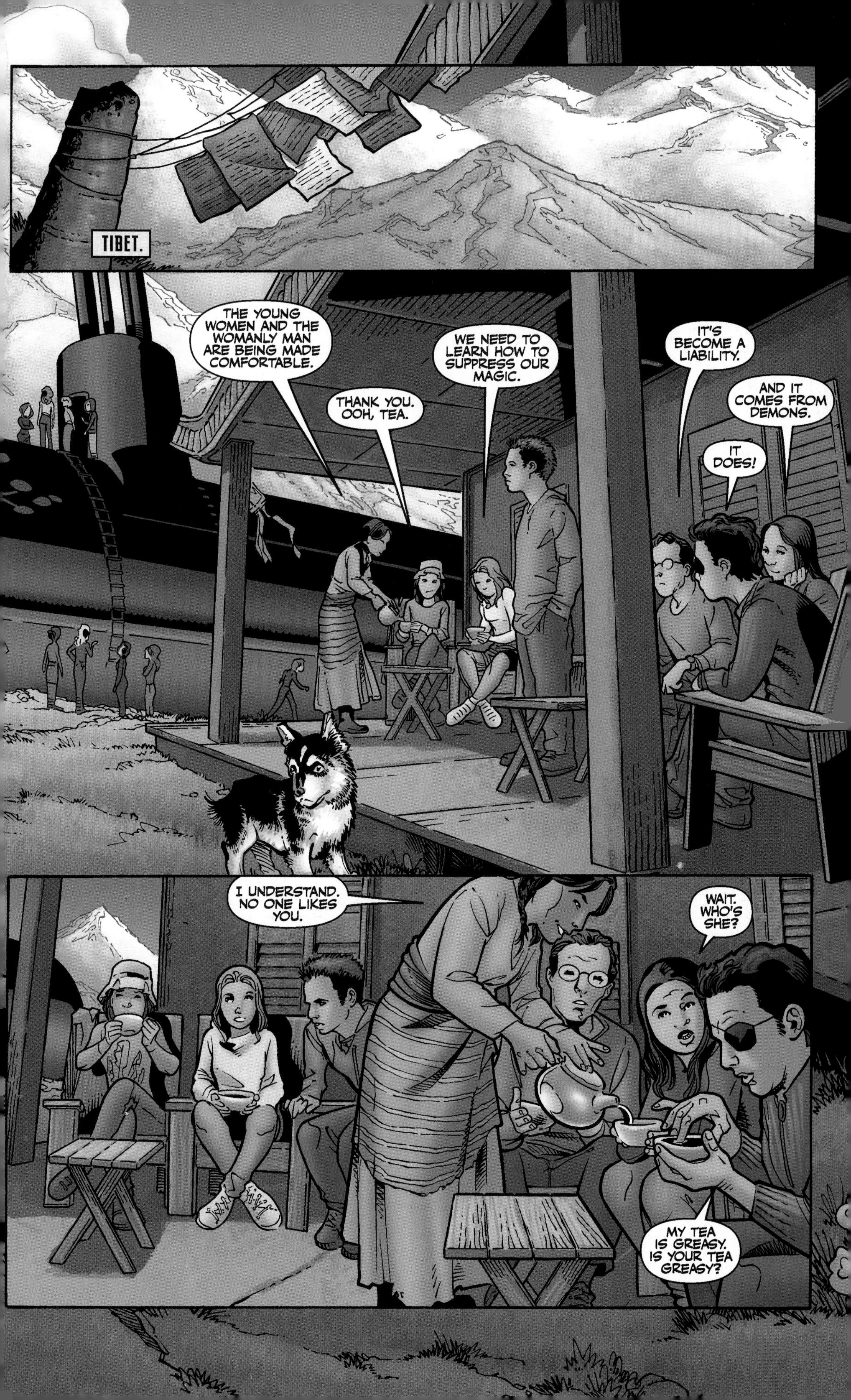
TIBET.
THE YOUNG WOMEN AND THE WOMANLY MAN ARE BEING MADE COMFORTABLE.
THANK YOU. OOH, TEA.
WE NEED TO LEARN HOW TO SUPPRESS OUR MAGIC.
IT'S BECOME A LIABILITY.
AND IT COMES FROM DEMONS.
IT DOES!
I UNDERSTAND. NO ONE LIKES YOU.
WAIT. WHO'S SHE?
MY TEA IS GREASY. IS YOUR TEA GREASY?

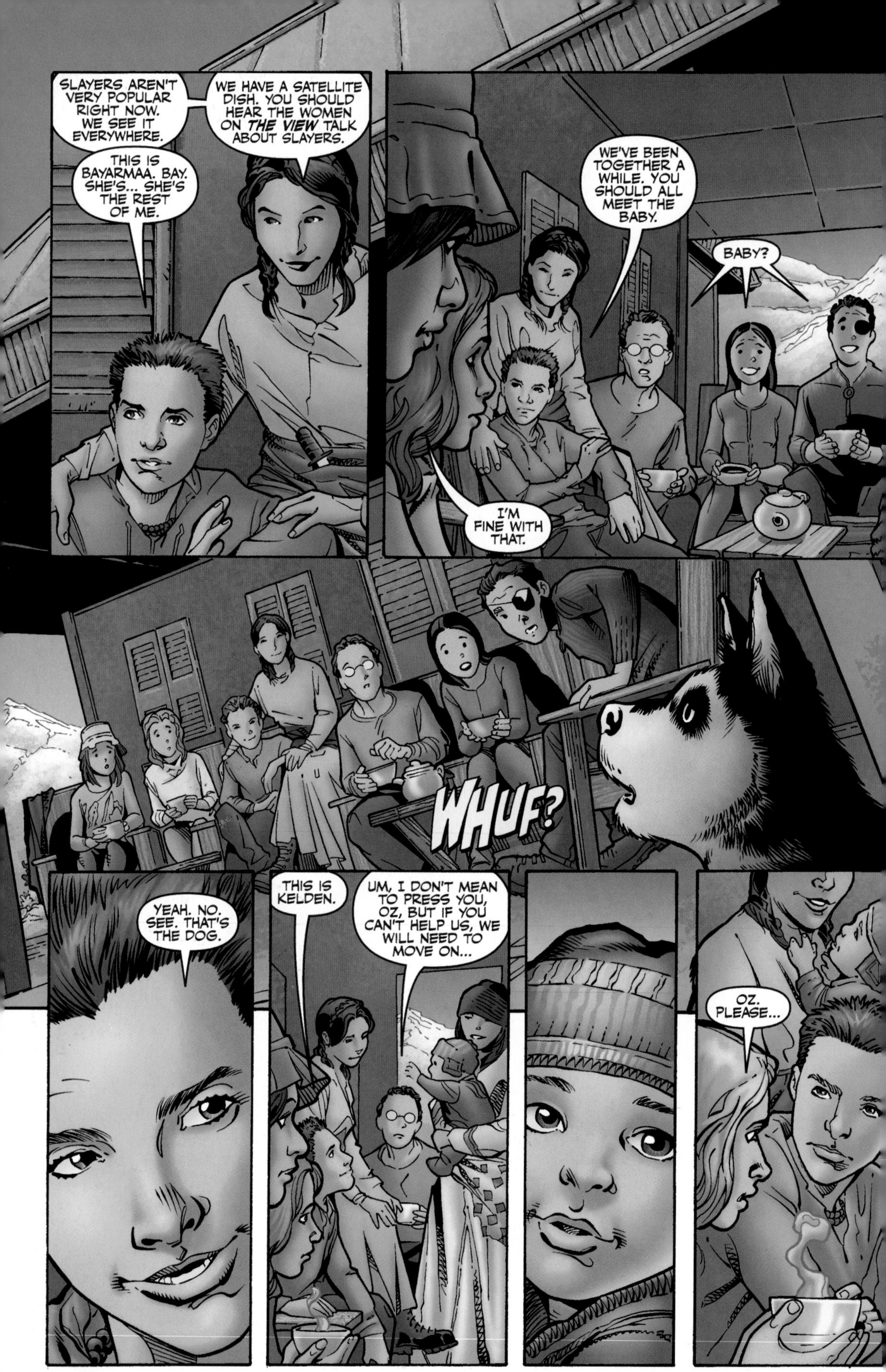

SLAYERS AREN'T VERY POPULAR RIGHT NOW. WE SEE IT EVERYWHERE.
WE HAVE A SATELLITE DISH. YOU SHOULD HEAR THE WOMEN ON *THE VIEW* TALK ABOUT SLAYERS.
THIS IS BAYARMAA. BAY. SHE'S... SHE'S THE REST OF ME.
WE'VE BEEN TOGETHER A WHILE. YOU SHOULD ALL MEET THE BABY.
BABY?
I'M FINE WITH THAT.
WHUF?
YEAH. NO. SEE. THAT'S THE DOG.
THIS IS KELDEN.
UM, I DON'T MEAN TO PRESS YOU, OZ, BUT IF YOU CAN'T HELP US, WE WILL NEED TO MOVE ON...
OZ. PLEASE...

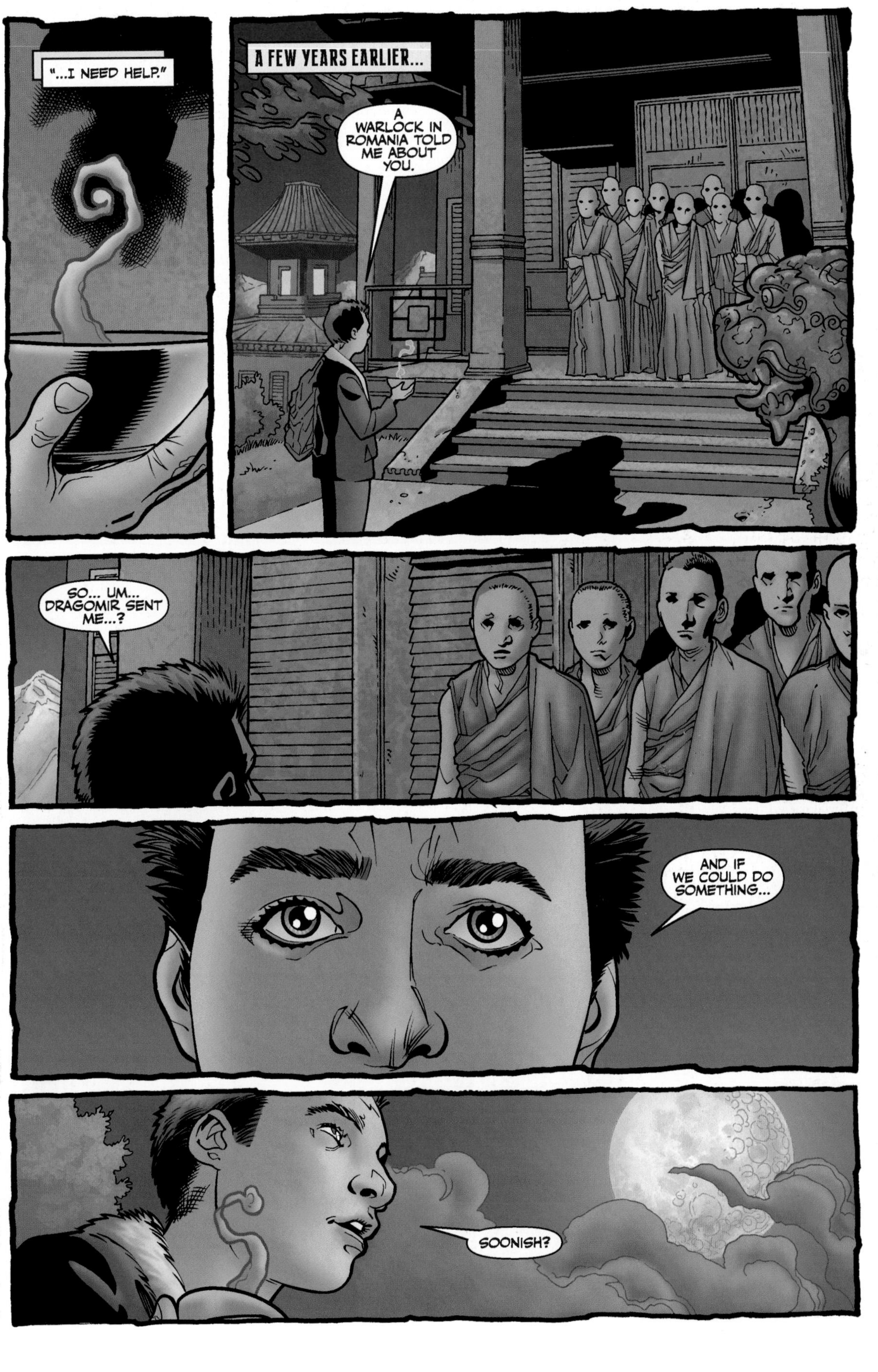
"...I NEED HELP."
A FEW YEARS EARLIER...
A WARLOCK IN ROMANIA TOLD ME ABOUT YOU.
SO... UM... DRAGOMIR SENT ME...?
AND IF WE COULD DO SOMETHING...
SOONISH?

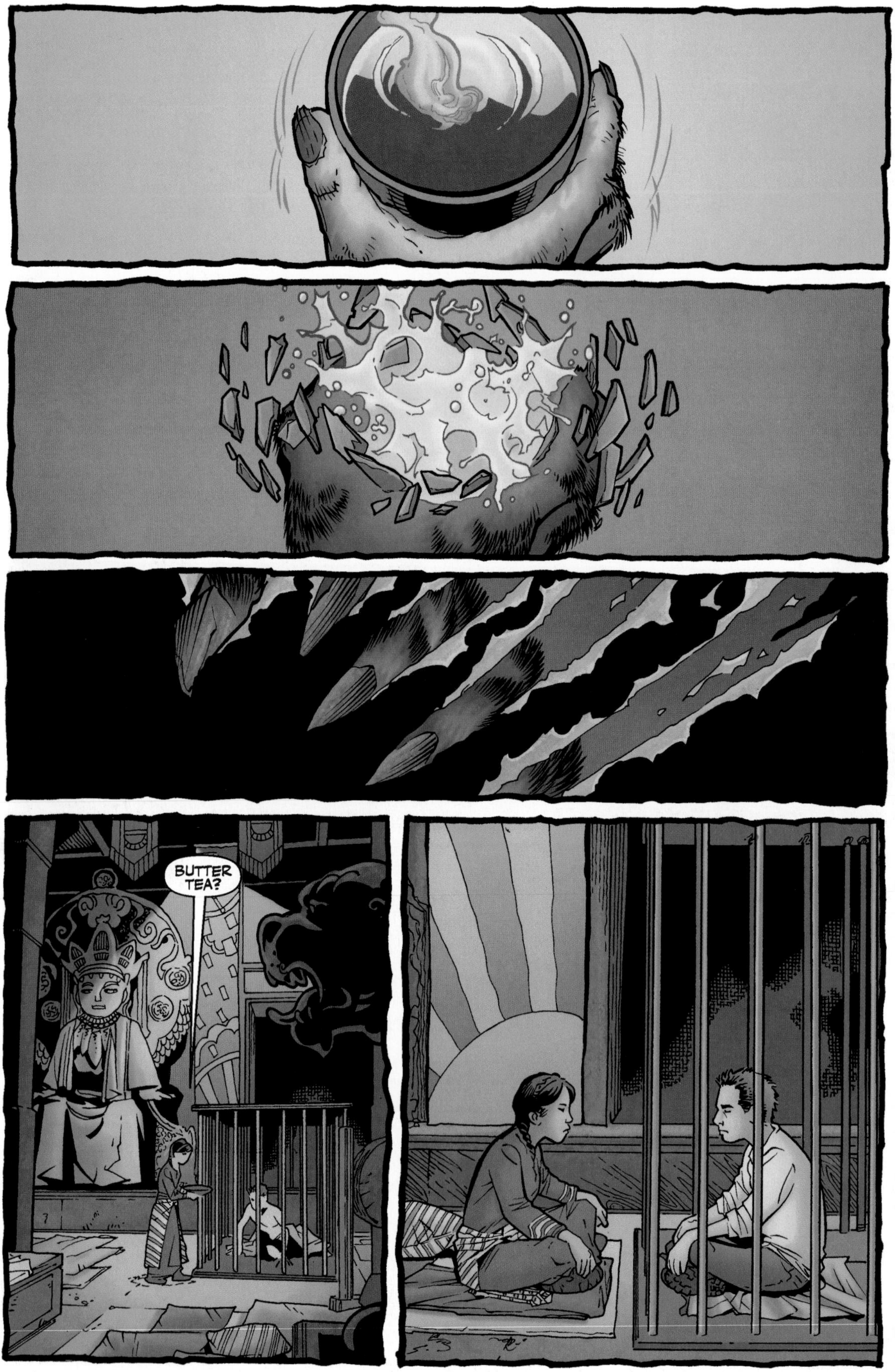
BUTTER TEA?

"THEY TAUGHT ME.

"THEY GAVE ME HERBS...

"...AND CHARMS."

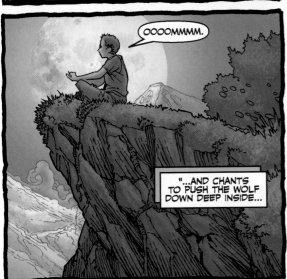

OOOOMMMM.

"...AND CHANTS TO PUSH THE WOLF DOWN DEEP INSIDE...

"I SLIPPED ONCE OR TWICE. BUT I WAS GETTING BETTER.

"I THOUGHT I COULD GO BACK."

RUN.

"I WASN'T SO MUCH RIGHT."

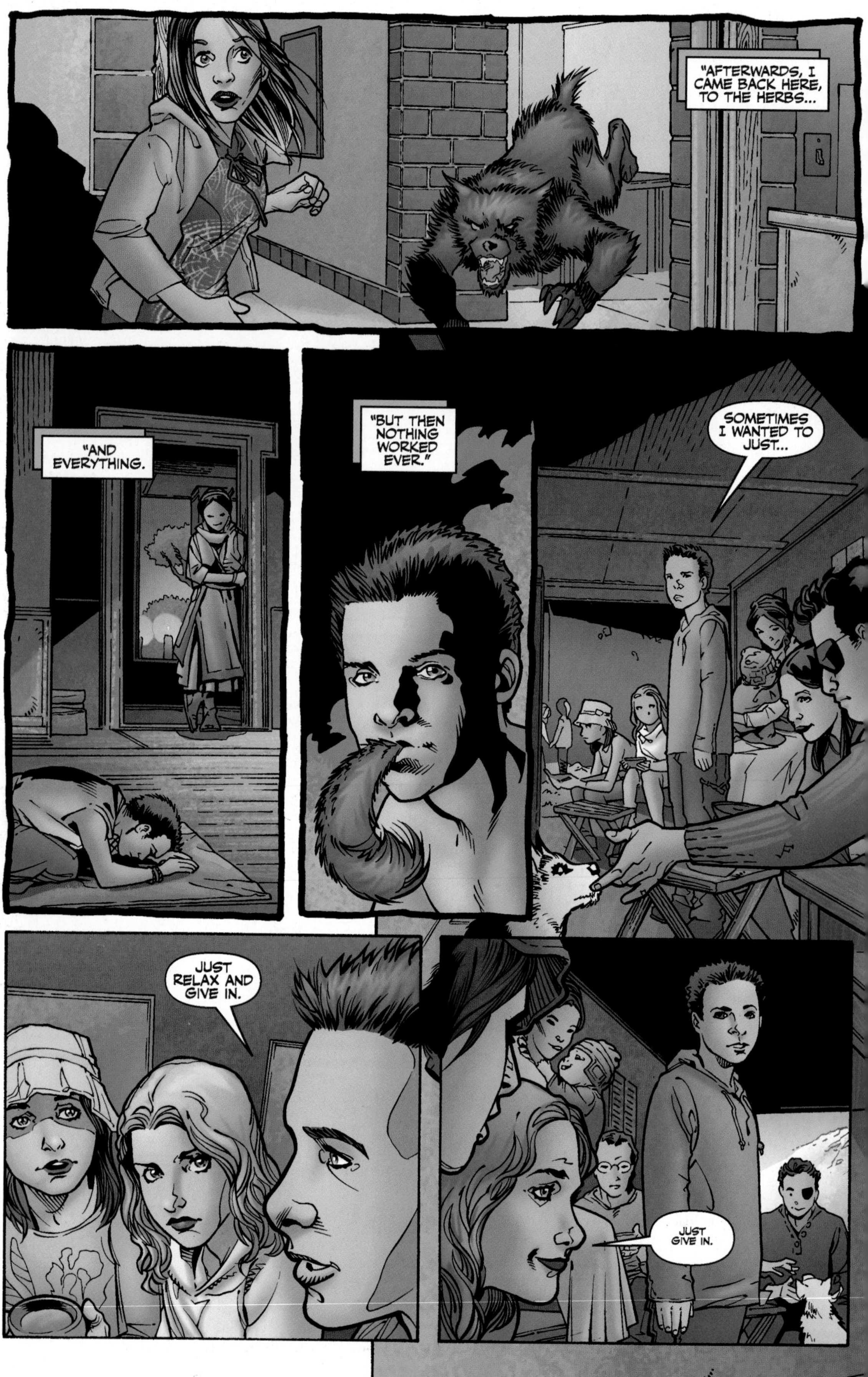
"AFTERWARDS, I CAME BACK HERE, TO THE HERBS...
"AND EVERYTHING.
"BUT THEN NOTHING WORKED EVER."
SOMETIMES I WANTED TO JUST...
JUST RELAX AND GIVE IN.
JUST GIVE IN.

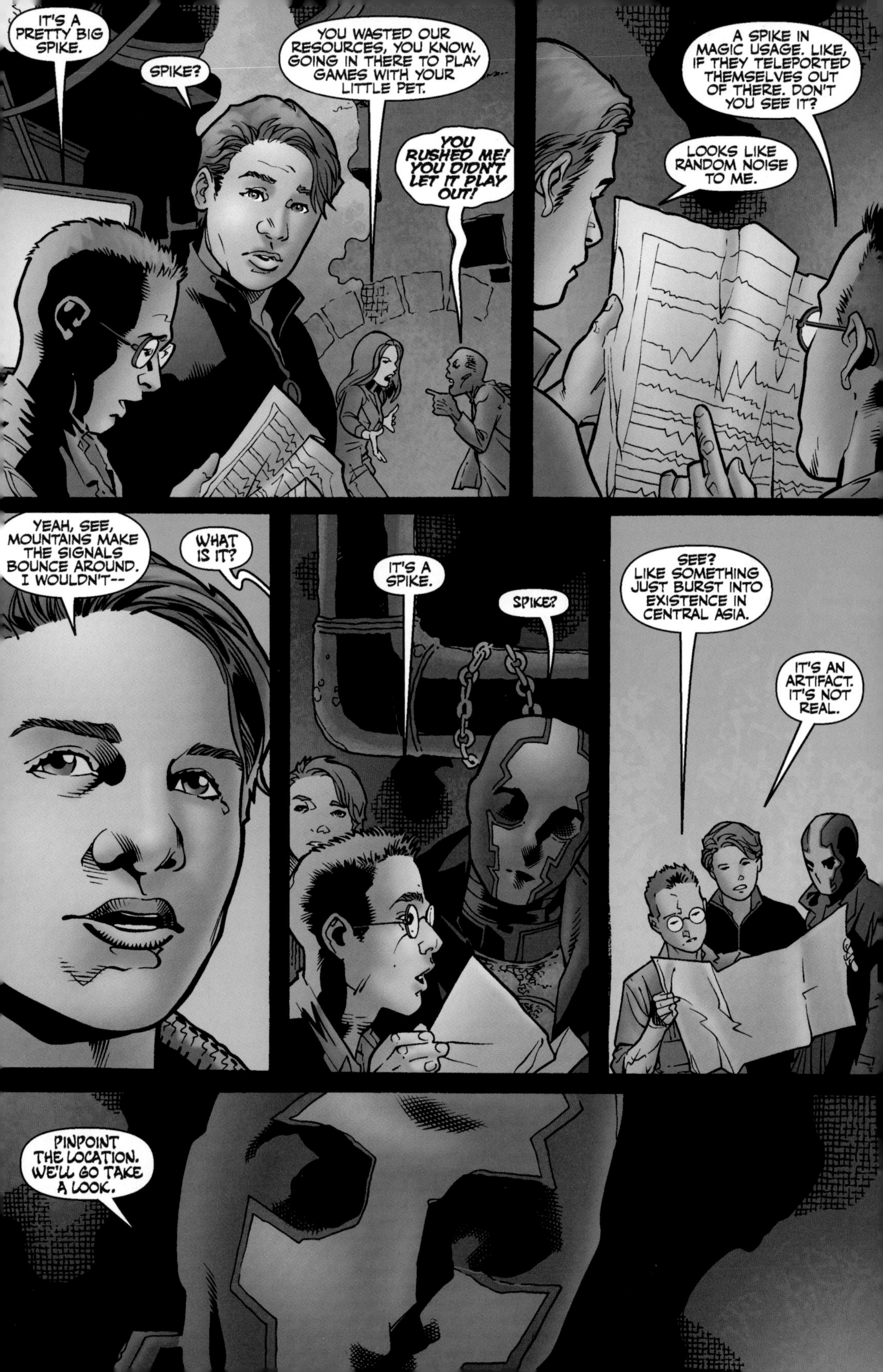
IT'S A PRETTY BIG SPIKE.
SPIKE?
YOU WASTED OUR RESOURCES, YOU KNOW. GOING IN THERE TO PLAY GAMES WITH YOUR LITTLE PET.
YOU RUSHED ME! YOU DIDN'T LET IT PLAY OUT!
A SPIKE IN MAGIC USAGE. LIKE, IF THEY TELEPORTED THEMSELVES OUT OF THERE. DON'T YOU SEE IT?
LOOKS LIKE RANDOM NOISE TO ME.
YEAH, SEE, MOUNTAINS MAKE THE SIGNALS BOUNCE AROUND. I WOULDN'T--
WHAT IS IT?
IT'S A SPIKE.
SPIKE?
SEE? LIKE SOMETHING JUST BURST INTO EXISTENCE IN CENTRAL ASIA.
IT'S AN ARTIFACT. IT'S NOT REAL.
PINPOINT THE LOCATION. WE'LL GO TAKE A LOOK.

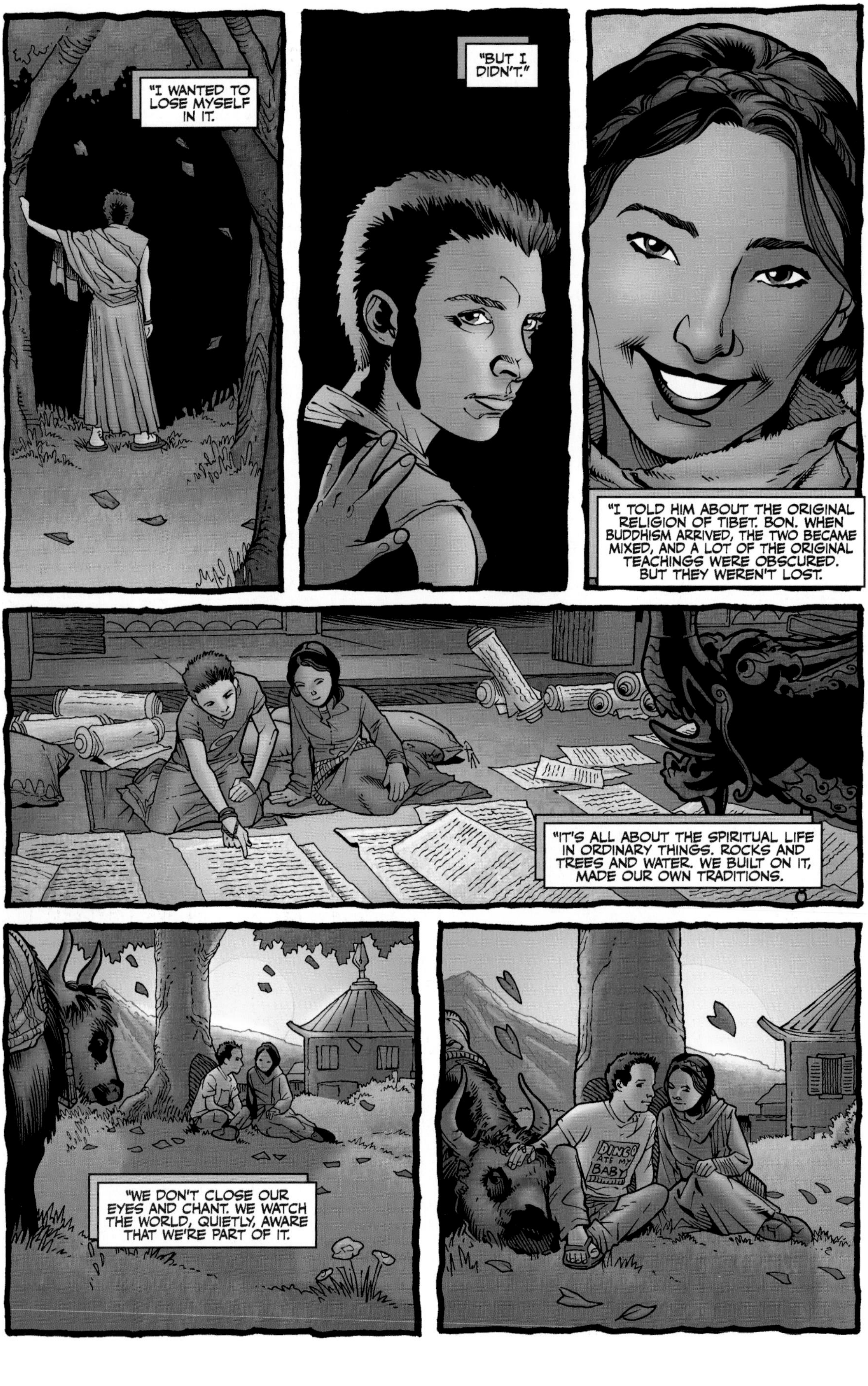
"I WANTED TO LOSE MYSELF IN IT.
"BUT I DIDN'T."
"I TOLD HIM ABOUT THE ORIGINAL RELIGION OF TIBET. BON. WHEN BUDDHISM ARRIVED, THE TWO BECAME MIXED, AND A LOT OF THE ORIGINAL TEACHINGS WERE OBSCURED. BUT THEY WEREN'T LOST.
"IT'S ALL ABOUT THE SPIRITUAL LIFE IN ORDINARY THINGS. ROCKS AND TREES AND WATER. WE BUILT ON IT, MADE OUR OWN TRADITIONS.
"WE DON'T CLOSE OUR EYES AND CHANT. WE WATCH THE WORLD, QUIETLY, AWARE THAT WE'RE PART OF IT.
DINGO ATE MY BABY

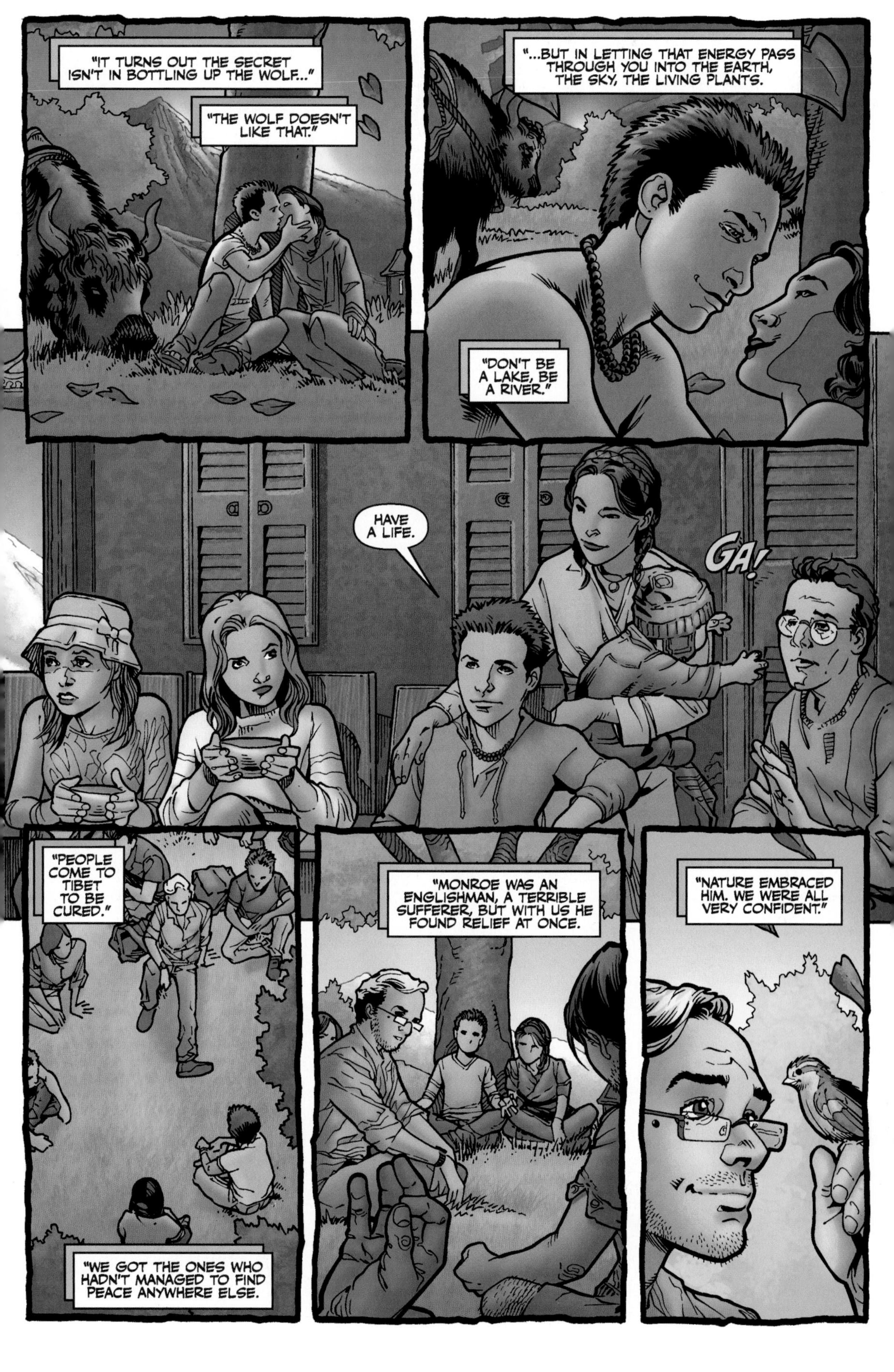
"IT TURNS OUT THE SECRET ISN'T IN BOTTLING UP THE WOLF..."
"THE WOLF DOESN'T LIKE THAT."
"...BUT IN LETTING THAT ENERGY PASS THROUGH YOU INTO THE EARTH, THE SKY, THE LIVING PLANTS.
"DON'T BE A LAKE, BE A RIVER."
HAVE A LIFE.
GA!
"PEOPLE COME TO TIBET TO BE CURED."
"WE GOT THE ONES WHO HADN'T MANAGED TO FIND PEACE ANYWHERE ELSE.
"MONROE WAS AN ENGLISHMAN, A TERRIBLE SUFFERER, BUT WITH US HE FOUND RELIEF AT ONCE.
"NATURE EMBRACED HIM. WE WERE ALL VERY CONFIDENT."

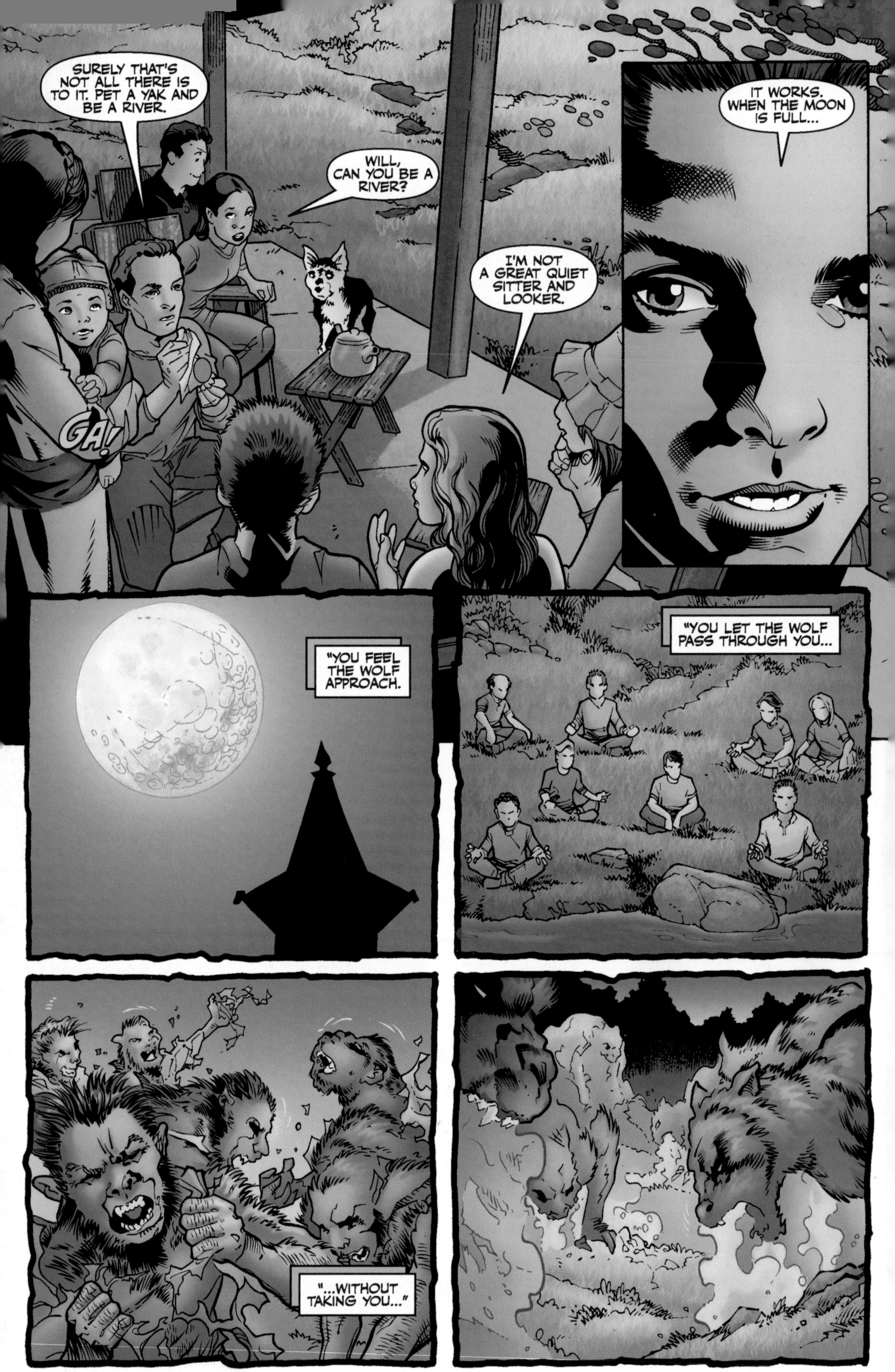
SURELY THAT'S NOT ALL THERE IS TO IT. PET A YAK AND BE A RIVER.
WILL, CAN YOU BE A RIVER?
GA!
I'M NOT A GREAT QUIET SITTER AND LOOKER.
IT WORKS. WHEN THE MOON IS FULL...
"YOU FEEL THE WOLF APPROACH.
"YOU LET THE WOLF PASS THROUGH YOU...
"...WITHOUT TAKING YOU..."

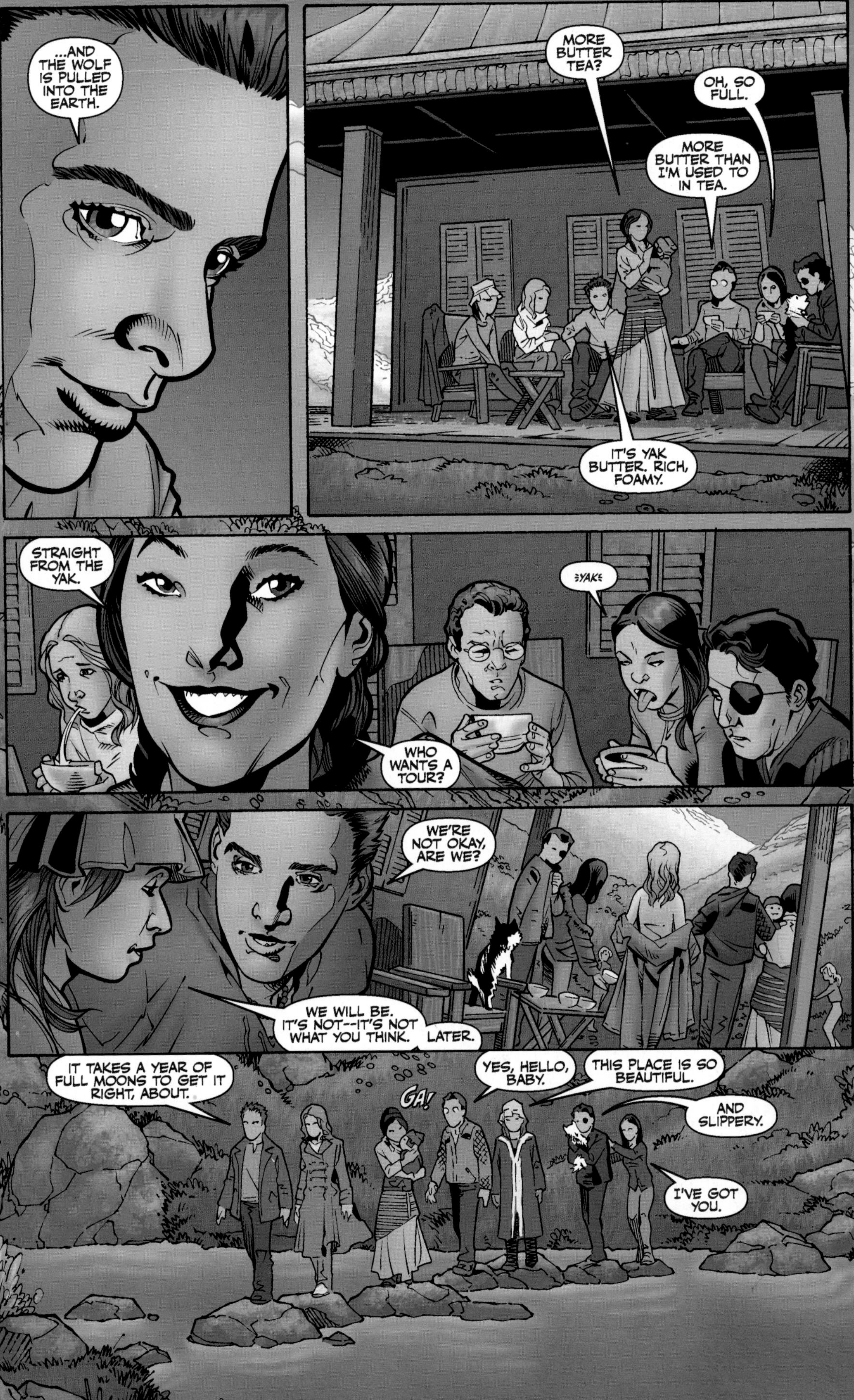

...AND THE WOLF IS PULLED INTO THE EARTH.
MORE BUTTER TEA?
OH, SO FULL.
MORE BUTTER THAN I'M USED TO IN TEA.
IT'S YAK BUTTER. RICH, FOAMY.
STRAIGHT FROM THE YAK.
WHO WANTS A TOUR?
ƎYAK€
WE'RE NOT OKAY, ARE WE?
WE WILL BE. IT'S NOT--IT'S NOT WHAT YOU THINK.
LATER.
IT TAKES A YEAR OF FULL MOONS TO GET IT RIGHT, ABOUT.
GA!
YES, HELLO, BABY.
THIS PLACE IS SO BEAUTIFUL.
AND SLIPPERY.
I'VE GOT YOU.

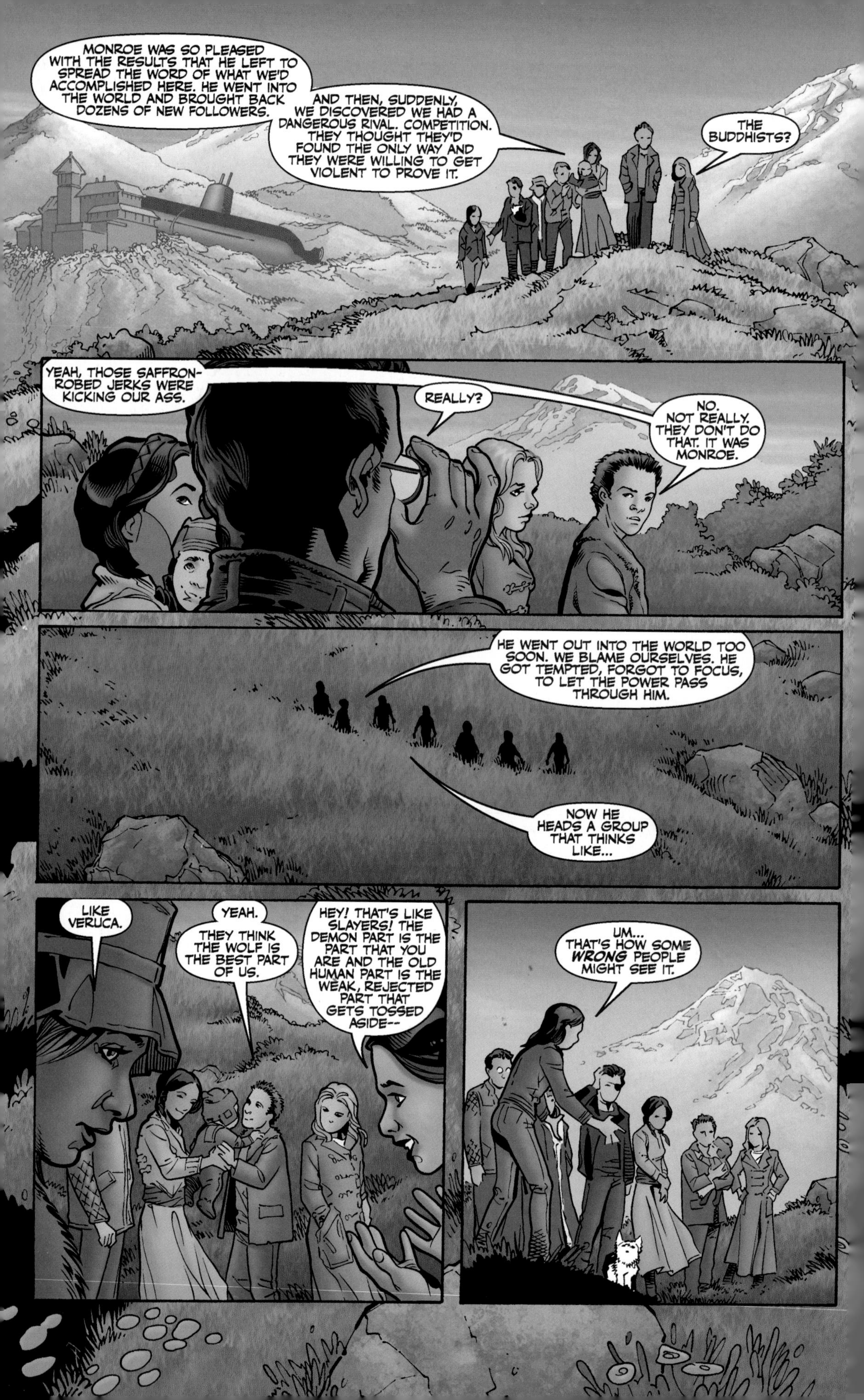
MONROE WAS SO PLEASED WITH THE RESULTS THAT HE LEFT TO SPREAD THE WORD OF WHAT WE'D ACCOMPLISHED HERE. HE WENT INTO THE WORLD AND BROUGHT BACK DOZENS OF NEW FOLLOWERS.
AND THEN, SUDDENLY, WE DISCOVERED WE HAD A DANGEROUS RIVAL. COMPETITION. THEY THOUGHT THEY'D FOUND THE ONLY WAY AND THEY WERE WILLING TO GET VIOLENT TO PROVE IT.
THE BUDDHISTS?
YEAH, THOSE SAFFRON-ROBED JERKS WERE KICKING OUR ASS.
REALLY?
NO. NOT REALLY. THEY DON'T DO THAT. IT WAS MONROE.
HE WENT OUT INTO THE WORLD TOO SOON. WE BLAME OURSELVES. HE GOT TEMPTED, FORGOT TO FOCUS, TO LET THE POWER PASS THROUGH HIM.
NOW HE HEADS A GROUP THAT THINKS LIKE...
LIKE VERUCA.
YEAH.
THEY THINK THE WOLF IS THE BEST PART OF US.
HEY! THAT'S LIKE SLAYERS! THE DEMON PART IS THE PART THAT YOU ARE AND THE OLD HUMAN PART IS THE WEAK, REJECTED PART THAT GETS TOSSED ASIDE--
UM... THAT'S HOW SOME WRONG PEOPLE MIGHT SEE IT.

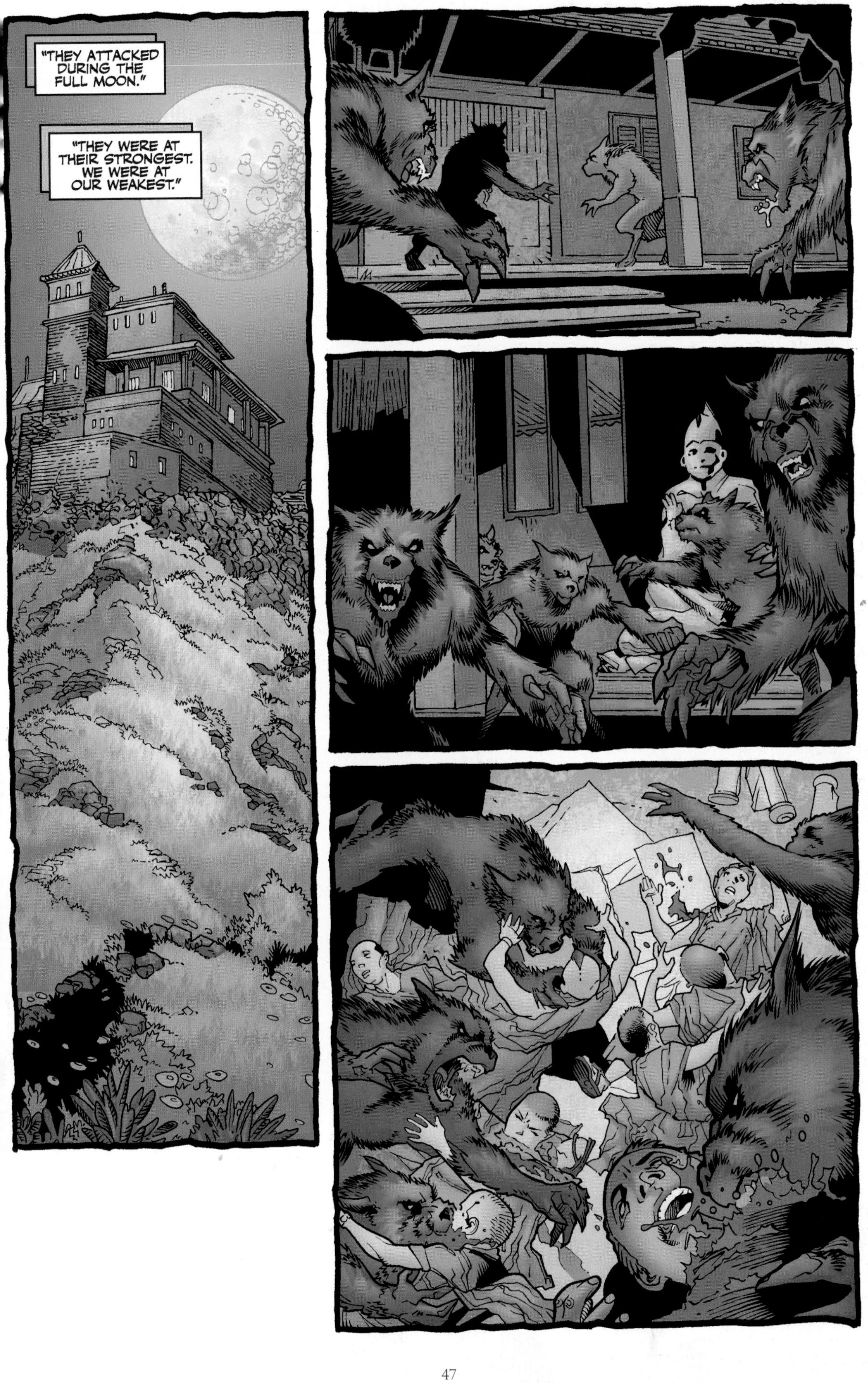
"THEY ATTACKED DURING THE FULL MOON."
"THEY WERE AT THEIR STRONGEST. WE WERE AT OUR WEAKEST."

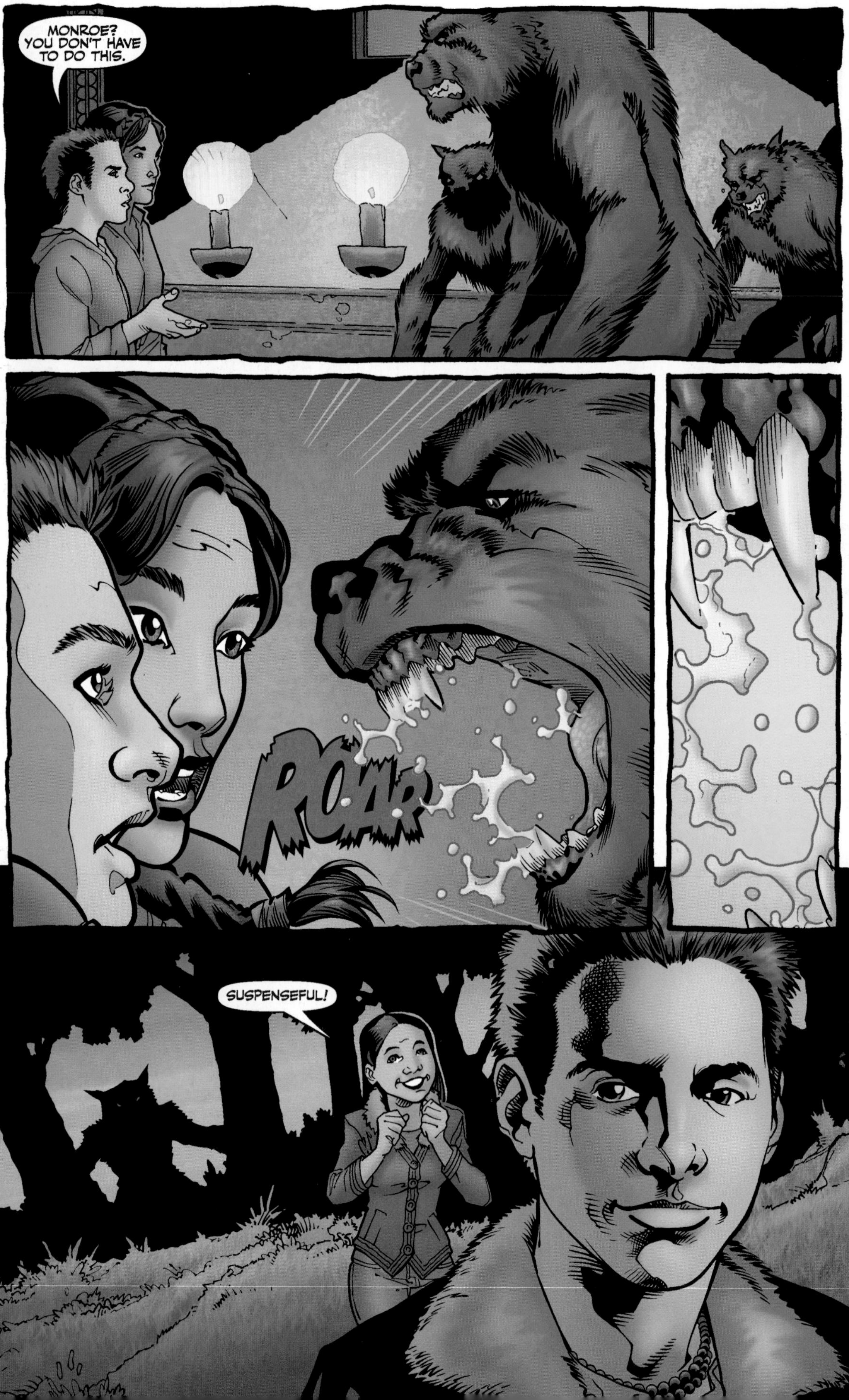
MONROE? YOU DON'T HAVE TO DO THIS.
ROAR
SUSPENSEFUL!

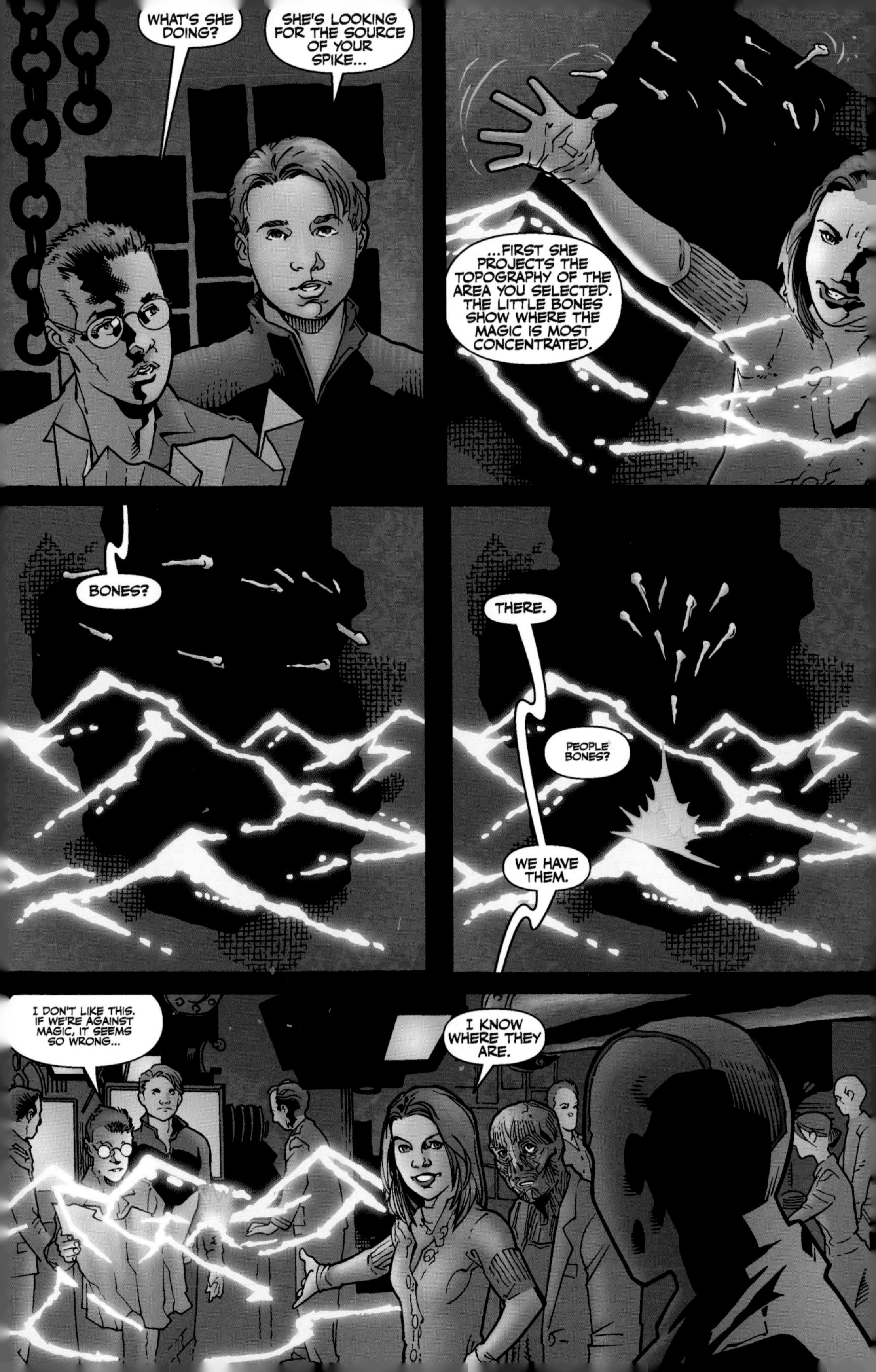
WHAT'S SHE DOING?
SHE'S LOOKING FOR THE SOURCE OF YOUR SPIKE...
...FIRST SHE PROJECTS THE TOPOGRAPHY OF THE AREA YOU SELECTED. THE LITTLE BONES SHOW WHERE THE MAGIC IS MOST CONCENTRATED.
BONES?
THERE.
PEOPLE BONES?
WE HAVE THEM.
I DON'T LIKE THIS. IF WE'RE AGAINST MAGIC, IT SEEMS SO WRONG...
I KNOW WHERE THEY ARE.

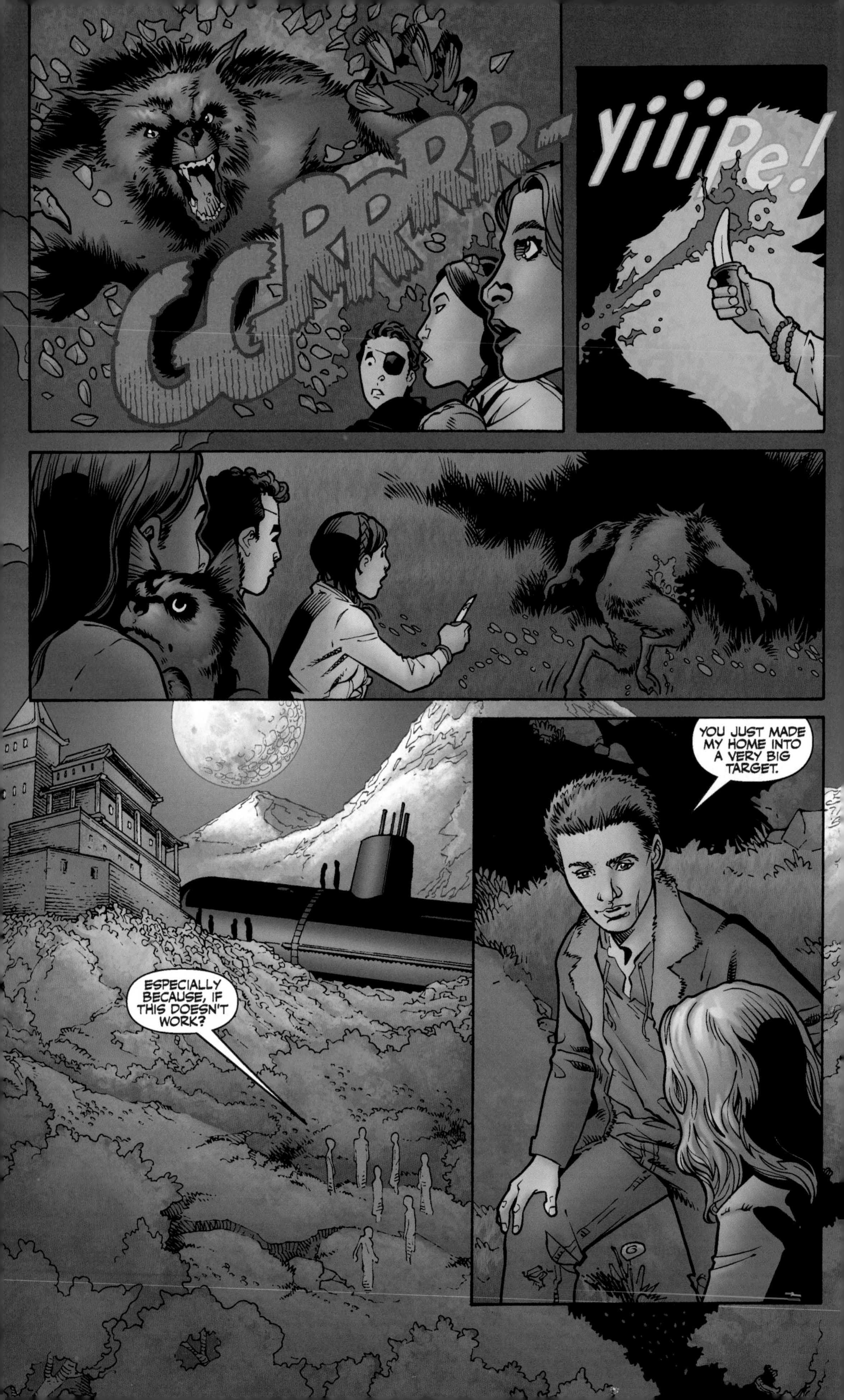
GGRRRRR-
YIIIPE!
YOU JUST MADE MY HOME INTO A VERY BIG TARGET.
ESPECIALLY BECAUSE, IF THIS DOESN'T WORK?

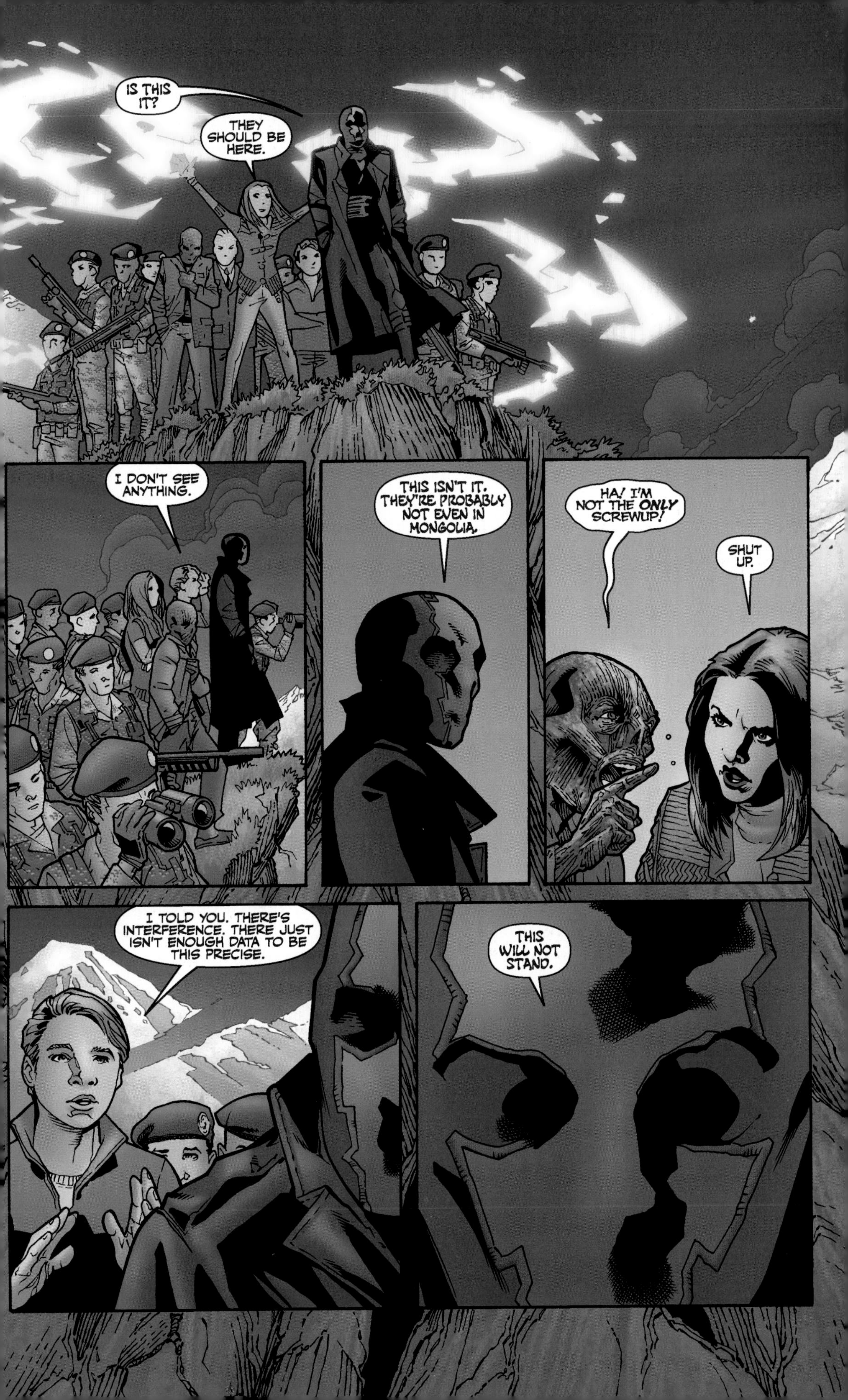
IS THIS IT?
THEY SHOULD BE HERE.
I DON'T SEE ANYTHING.
THIS ISN'T IT. THEY'RE PROBABLY NOT EVEN IN MONGOLIA.
HA! I'M NOT THE ONLY SCREWUP!
SHUT UP.
I TOLD YOU. THERE'S INTERFERENCE. THERE JUST ISN'T ENOUGH DATA TO BE THIS PRECISE.
THIS WILL NOT STAND.

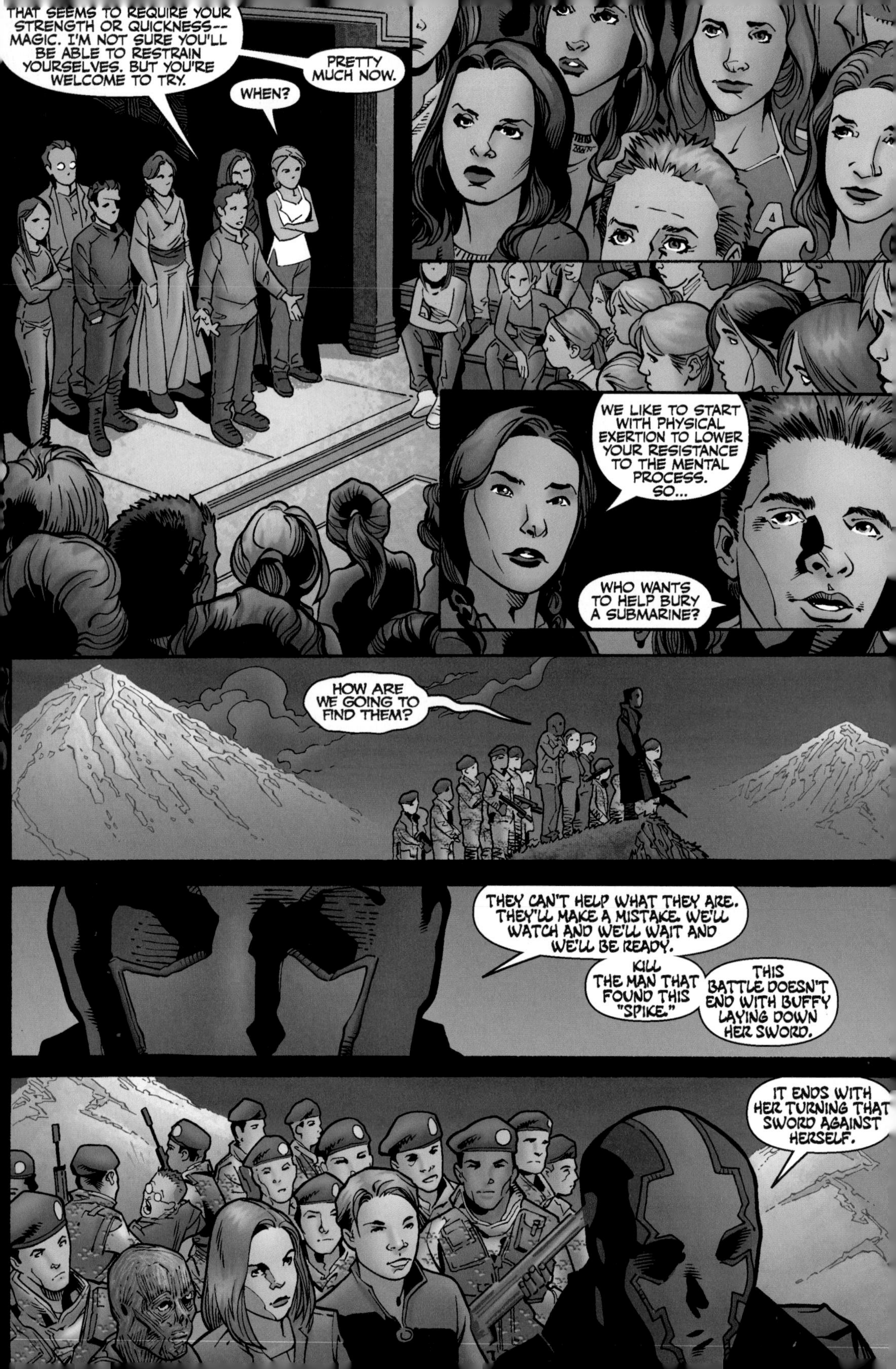
THAT SEEMS TO REQUIRE YOUR STRENGTH OR QUICKNESS-- MAGIC. I'M NOT SURE YOU'LL BE ABLE TO RESTRAIN YOURSELVES. BUT YOU'RE WELCOME TO TRY.
WHEN?
PRETTY MUCH NOW.
WE LIKE TO START WITH PHYSICAL EXERTION TO LOWER YOUR RESISTANCE TO THE MENTAL PROCESS. SO...
WHO WANTS TO HELP BURY A SUBMARINE?
HOW ARE WE GOING TO FIND THEM?
THEY CAN'T HELP WHAT THEY ARE. THEY'LL MAKE A MISTAKE. WE'LL WATCH AND WE'LL WAIT AND WE'LL BE READY.
KILL THE MAN THAT FOUND THIS "SPIKE."
THIS BATTLE DOESN'T END WITH BUFFY LAYING DOWN HER SWORD.
IT ENDS WITH HER TURNING THAT SWORD AGAINST HERSELF.

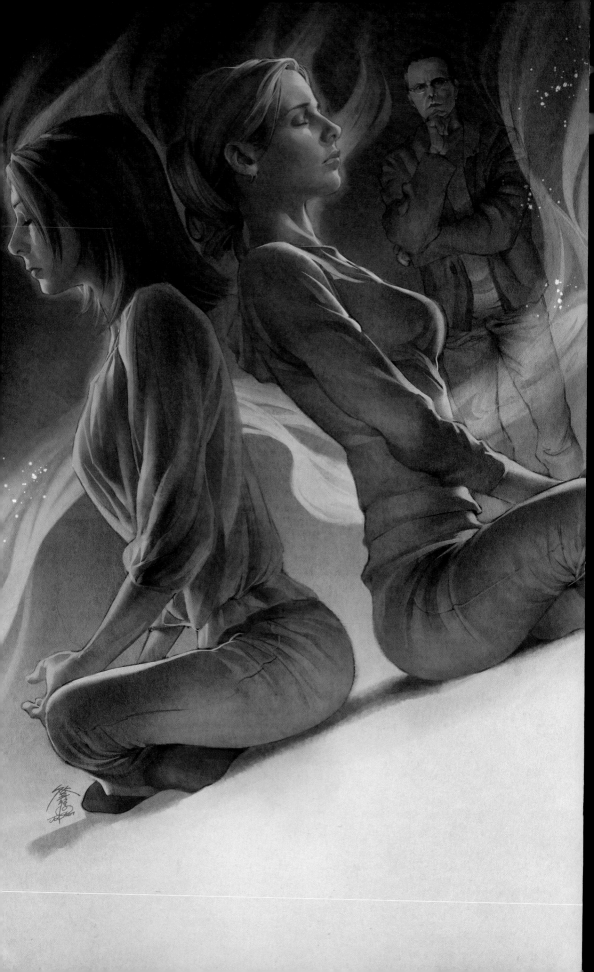

RETREAT

PART THREE

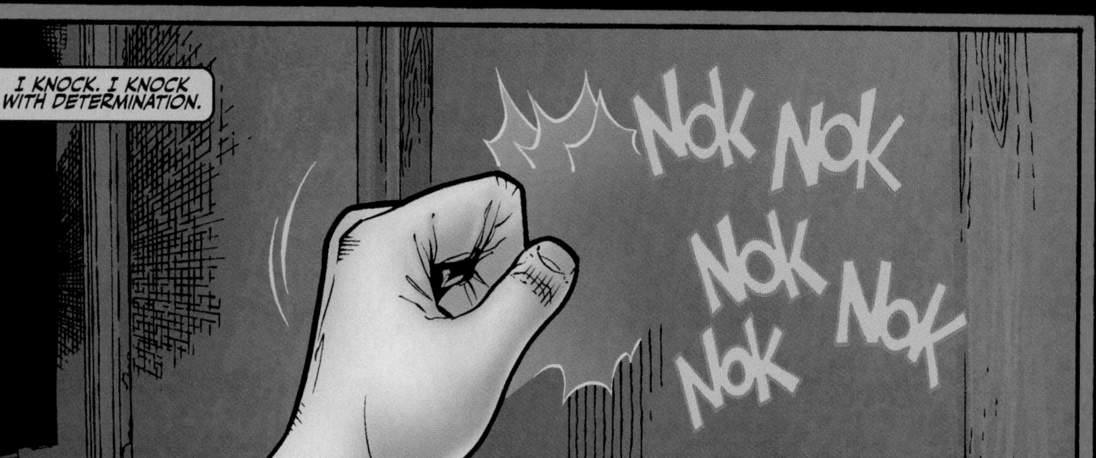

I KNOCK. I KNOCK WITH DETERMINATION.
NOK NOK
NOK
NOK
NOK

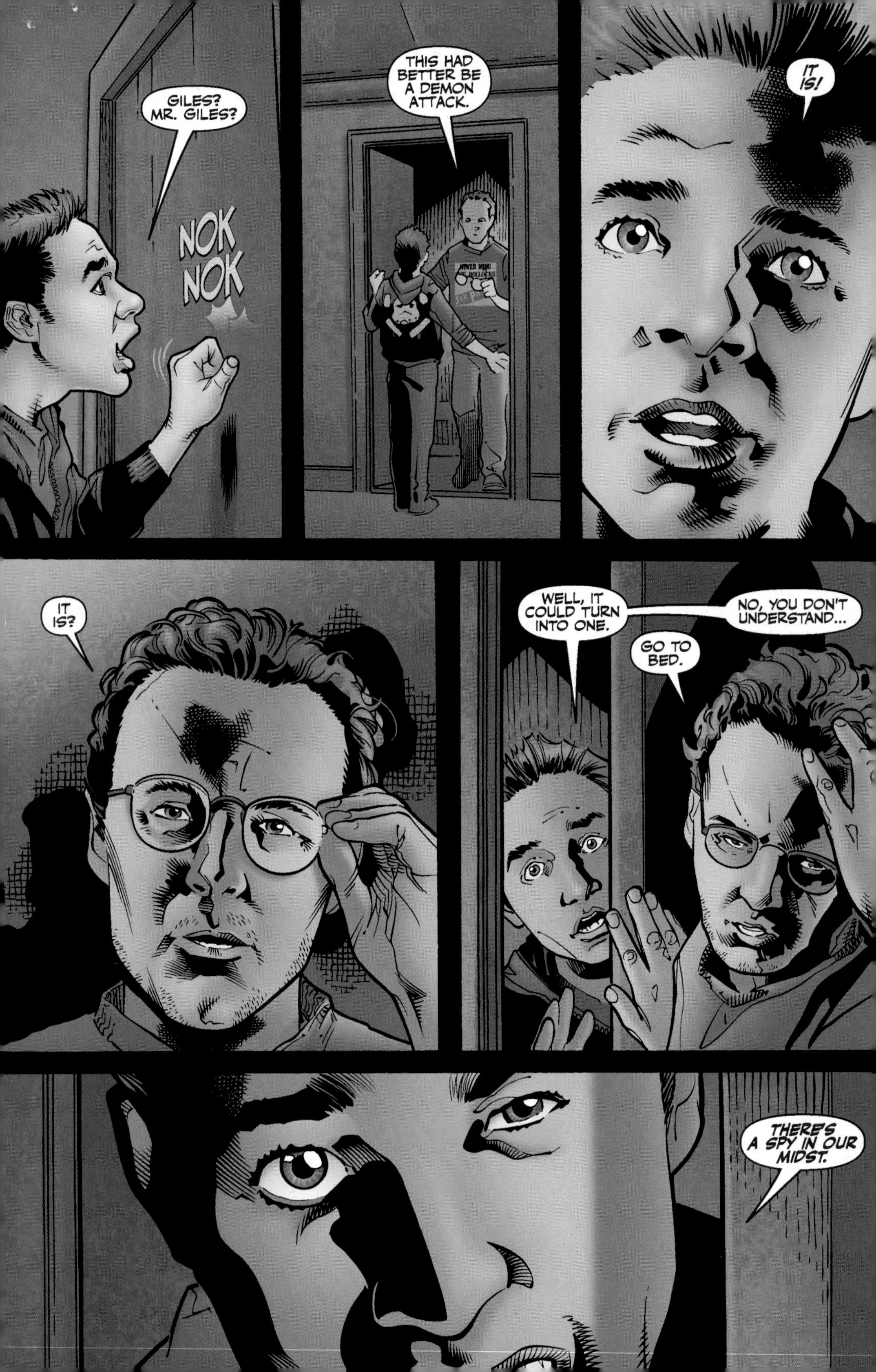
GILES? MR. GILES?
NOK NOK
THIS HAD BETTER BE A DEMON ATTACK.
IT IS!
IT IS?
WELL, IT COULD TURN INTO ONE.
NO, YOU DON'T UNDERSTAND...
GO TO BED.
THERE'S A SPY IN OUR MIDST.

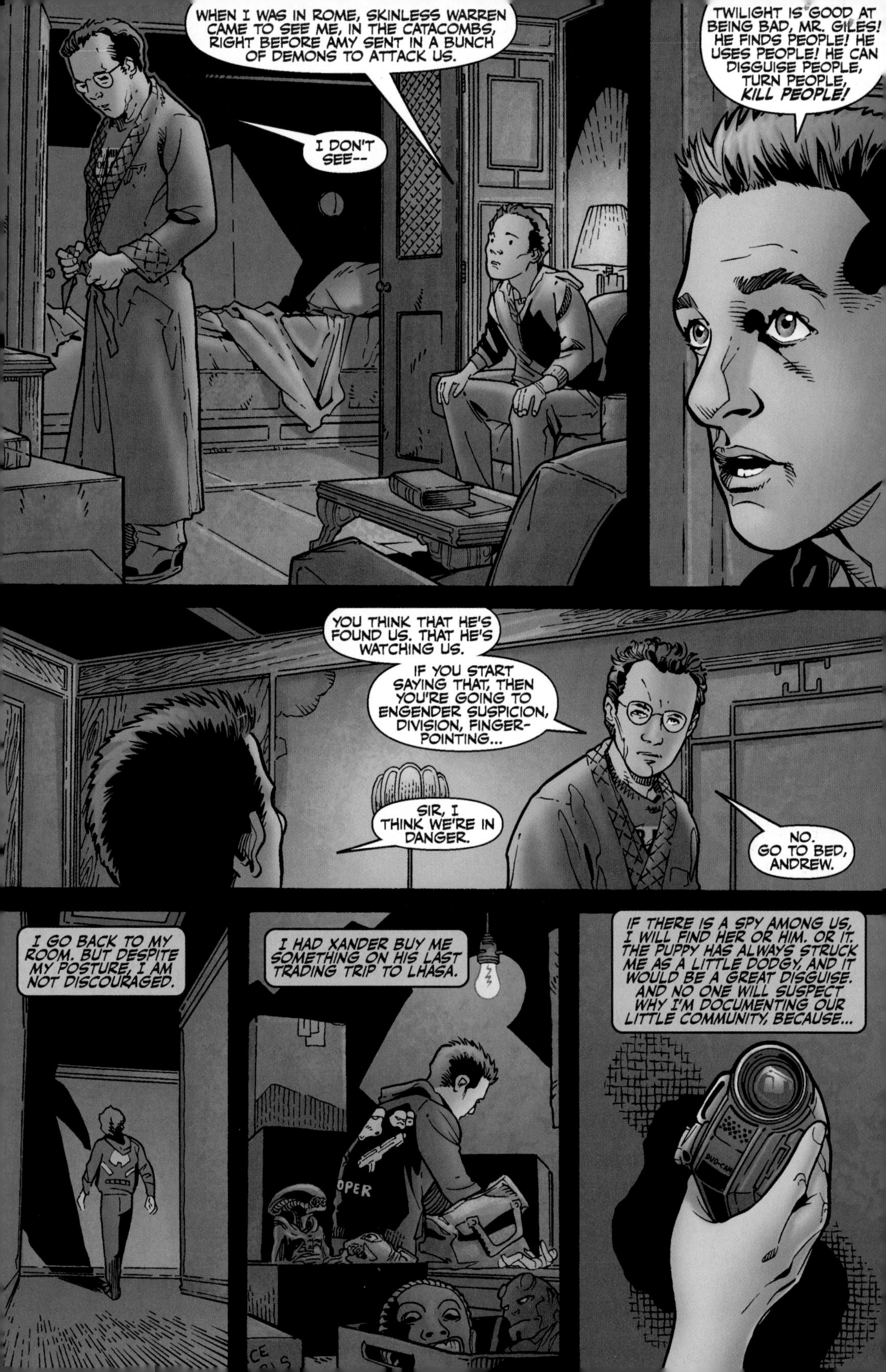

WHEN I WAS IN ROME, SKINLESS WARREN CAME TO SEE ME, IN THE CATACOMBS, RIGHT BEFORE AMY SENT IN A BUNCH OF DEMONS TO ATTACK US.
I DON'T SEE--
TWILIGHT IS GOOD AT BEING BAD, MR. GILES! HE FINDS PEOPLE! HE USES PEOPLE! HE CAN DISGUISE PEOPLE, TURN PEOPLE, KILL PEOPLE!
YOU THINK THAT HE'S FOUND US. THAT HE'S WATCHING US.
IF YOU START SAYING THAT, THEN YOU'RE GOING TO ENGENDER SUSPICION, DIVISION, FINGER-POINTING...
SIR, I THINK WE'RE IN DANGER.
NO. GO TO BED, ANDREW.
I GO BACK TO MY ROOM. BUT DESPITE MY POSTURE, I AM NOT DISCOURAGED.
I HAD XANDER BUY ME SOMETHING ON HIS LAST TRADING TRIP TO LHASA.
IF THERE IS A SPY AMONG US, I WILL FIND HER OR HIM. OR IT. THE PUPPY HAS ALWAYS STRUCK ME AS A LITTLE DODGY, AND IT WOULD BE A GREAT DISGUISE. AND NO ONE WILL SUSPECT WHY I'M DOCUMENTING OUR LITTLE COMMUNITY, BECAUSE...

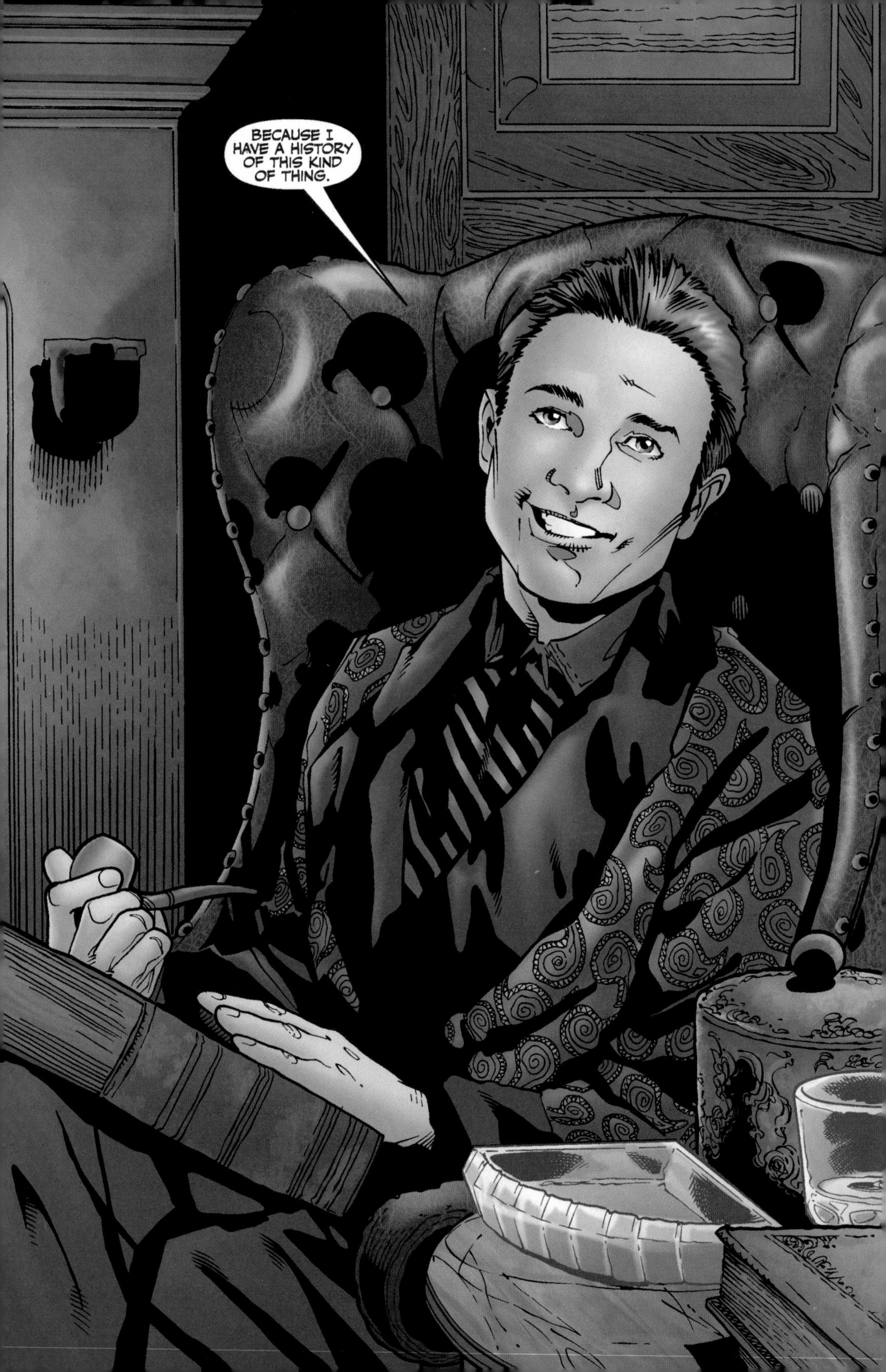
BECAUSE I HAVE A HISTORY OF THIS KIND OF THING.

I WILL BEGIN WITH A LITTLE TOUR. AND A LITTLE EXAMINATION OF A CERTAIN STRANGER WHO IS SUDDENLY ALL UP IN OUR MIDST.

TELL US ABOUT THE GIVING UP OF MAGICKS, OZ'S EXOTIC MATE, BAYARMAA.

IT'S NOT ABOUT "GIVING UP" THE MAGIC. IT'S ABOUT REDIRECTING THE ENERGY INTO THE EARTH INSTEAD OF HOLDING ON TO IT. IF YOU ARE REALLY AT PEACE, THE BOUNDARY BETWEEN YOU AND EARTH MELTS AWAY.

SO IT IS AS IF YOU'RE DECOMPOSING?

NOT AT ALL.

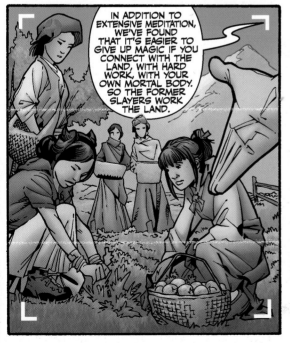

IN ADDITION TO EXTENSIVE MEDITATION, WE'VE FOUND THAT IT'S EASIER TO GIVE UP MAGIC IF YOU CONNECT WITH THE LAND, WITH HARD WORK, WITH YOUR OWN MORTAL BODY. SO THE FORMER SLAYERS WORK THE LAND.

THEY WEAVE. THEY CHURN. IT'S HARD WORK.

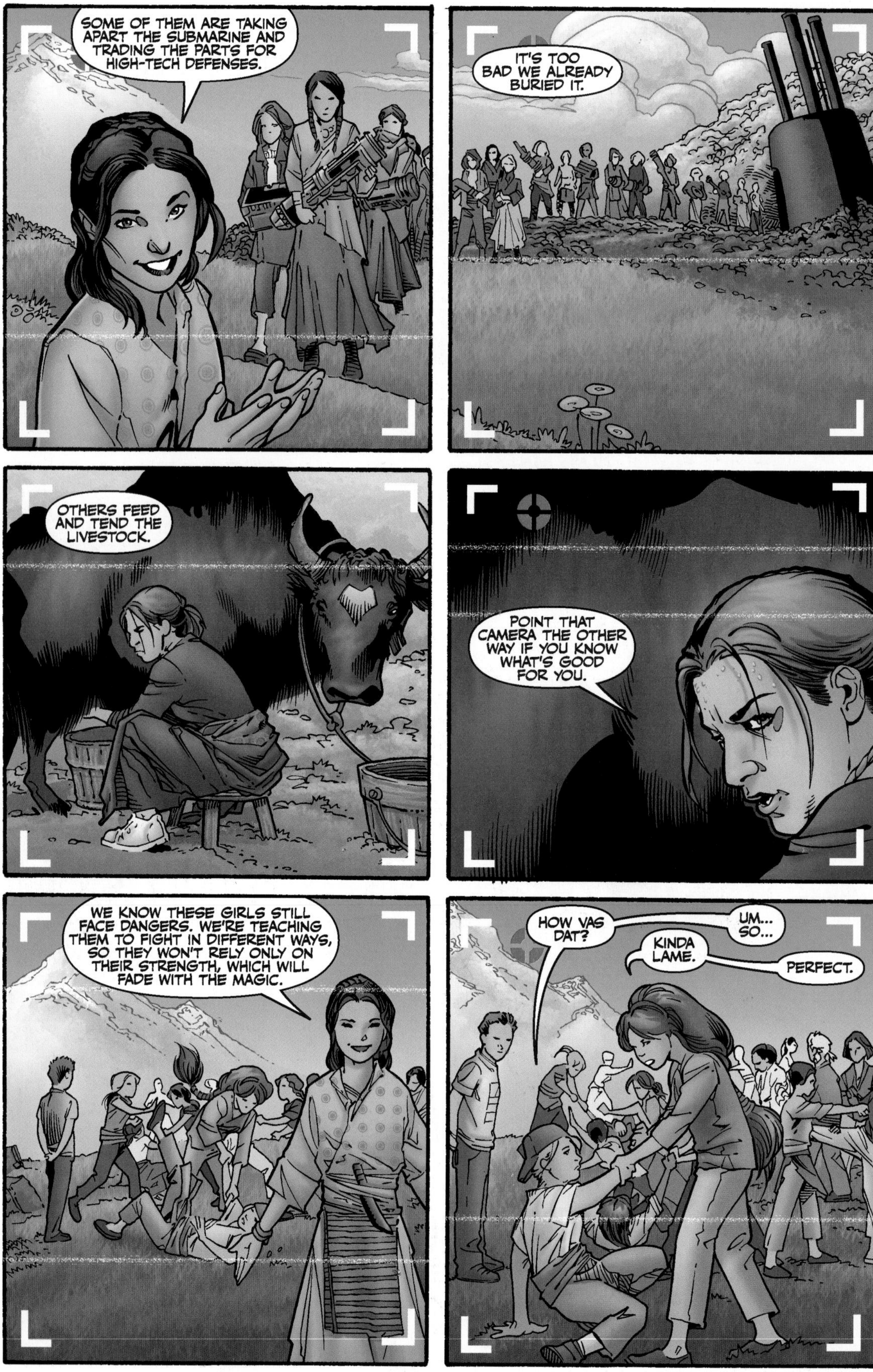
SOME OF THEM ARE TAKING APART THE SUBMARINE AND TRADING THE PARTS FOR HIGH-TECH DEFENSES.
IT'S TOO BAD WE ALREADY BURIED IT.
OTHERS FEED AND TEND THE LIVESTOCK.
POINT THAT CAMERA THE OTHER WAY IF YOU KNOW WHAT'S GOOD FOR YOU.
WE KNOW THESE GIRLS STILL FACE DANGERS. WE'RE TEACHING THEM TO FIGHT IN DIFFERENT WAYS, SO THEY WON'T RELY ONLY ON THEIR STRENGTH, WHICH WILL FADE WITH THE MAGIC.
HOW VAS DAT?
UM... SO...
KINDA LAME.
PERFECT.

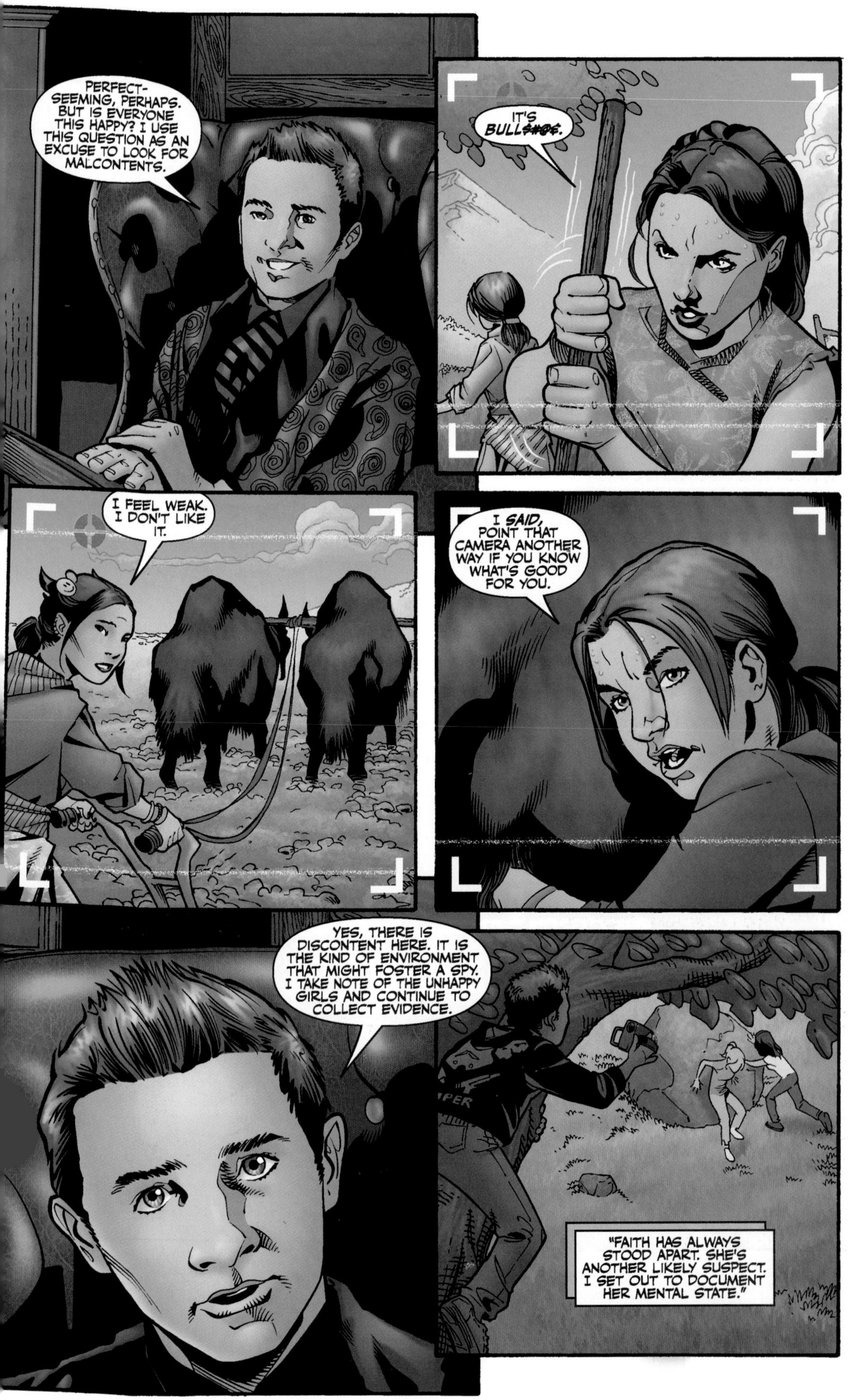
PERFECT-SEEMING, PERHAPS. BUT IS EVERYONE THIS HAPPY? I USE THIS QUESTION AS AN EXCUSE TO LOOK FOR MALCONTENTS.
IT'S BULL$#@¢.
I FEEL WEAK. I DON'T LIKE IT.
I SAID, POINT THAT CAMERA ANOTHER WAY IF YOU KNOW WHAT'S GOOD FOR YOU.
YES, THERE IS DISCONTENT HERE. IT IS THE KIND OF ENVIRONMENT THAT MIGHT FOSTER A SPY. I TAKE NOTE OF THE UNHAPPY GIRLS AND CONTINUE TO COLLECT EVIDENCE.
"FAITH HAS ALWAYS STOOD APART. SHE'S ANOTHER LIKELY SUSPECT. I SET OUT TO DOCUMENT HER MENTAL STATE."

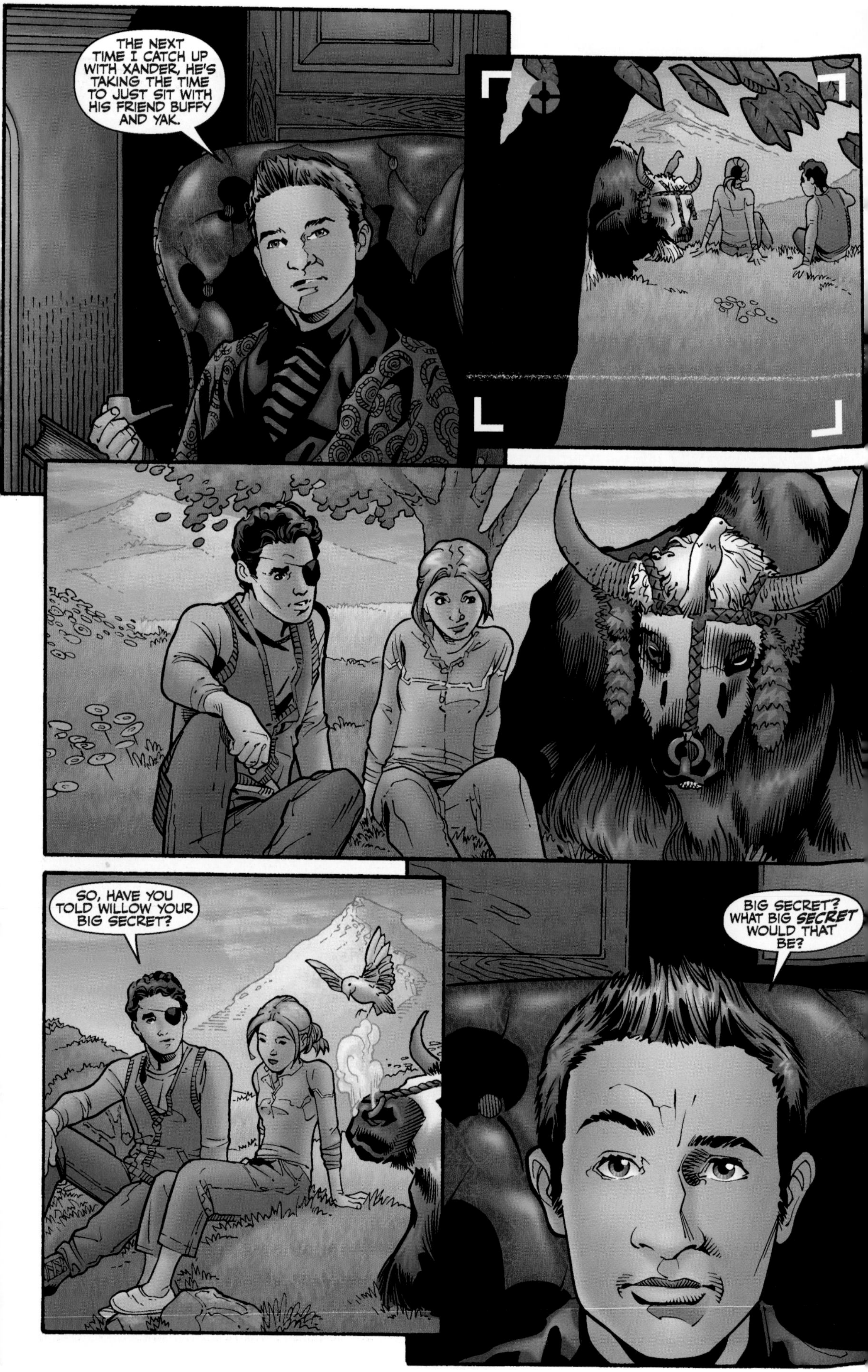
THE NEXT TIME I CATCH UP WITH XANDER, HE'S TAKING THE TIME TO JUST SIT WITH HIS FRIEND BUFFY AND YAK.
SO, HAVE YOU TOLD WILLOW YOUR BIG SECRET?
BIG SECRET? WHAT BIG SECRET WOULD THAT BE?

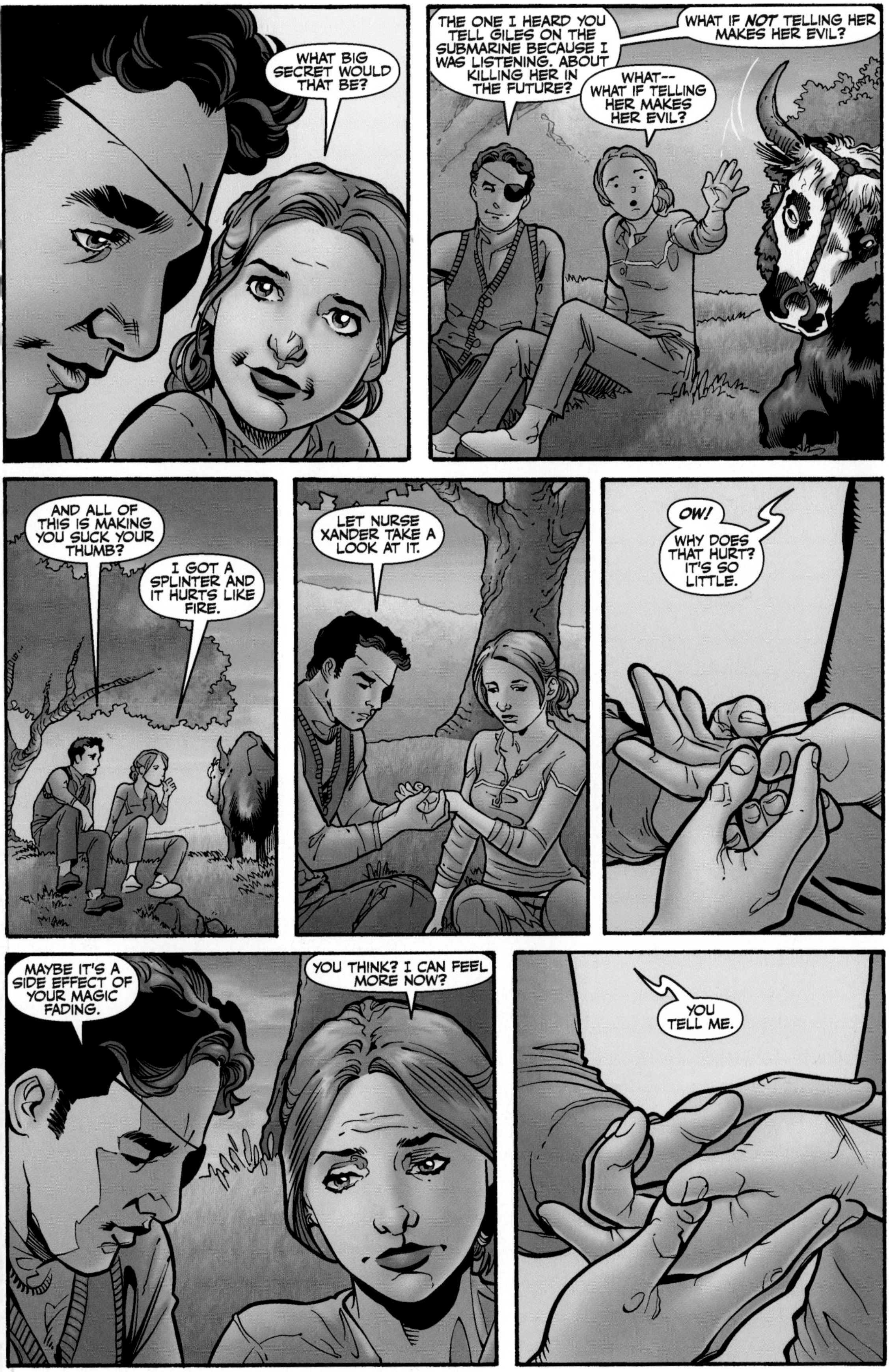
WHAT BIG SECRET WOULD THAT BE?
THE ONE I HEARD YOU TELL GILES ON THE SUBMARINE BECAUSE I WAS LISTENING. ABOUT KILLING HER IN THE FUTURE?
WHAT-- WHAT IF TELLING HER MAKES HER EVIL?
WHAT IF NOT TELLING HER MAKES HER EVIL?
AND ALL OF THIS IS MAKING YOU SUCK YOUR THUMB?
I GOT A SPLINTER AND IT HURTS LIKE FIRE.
LET NURSE XANDER TAKE A LOOK AT IT.
OW!
WHY DOES THAT HURT? IT'S SO LITTLE.
MAYBE IT'S A SIDE EFFECT OF YOUR MAGIC FADING.
YOU THINK? I CAN FEEL MORE NOW?
YOU TELL ME.

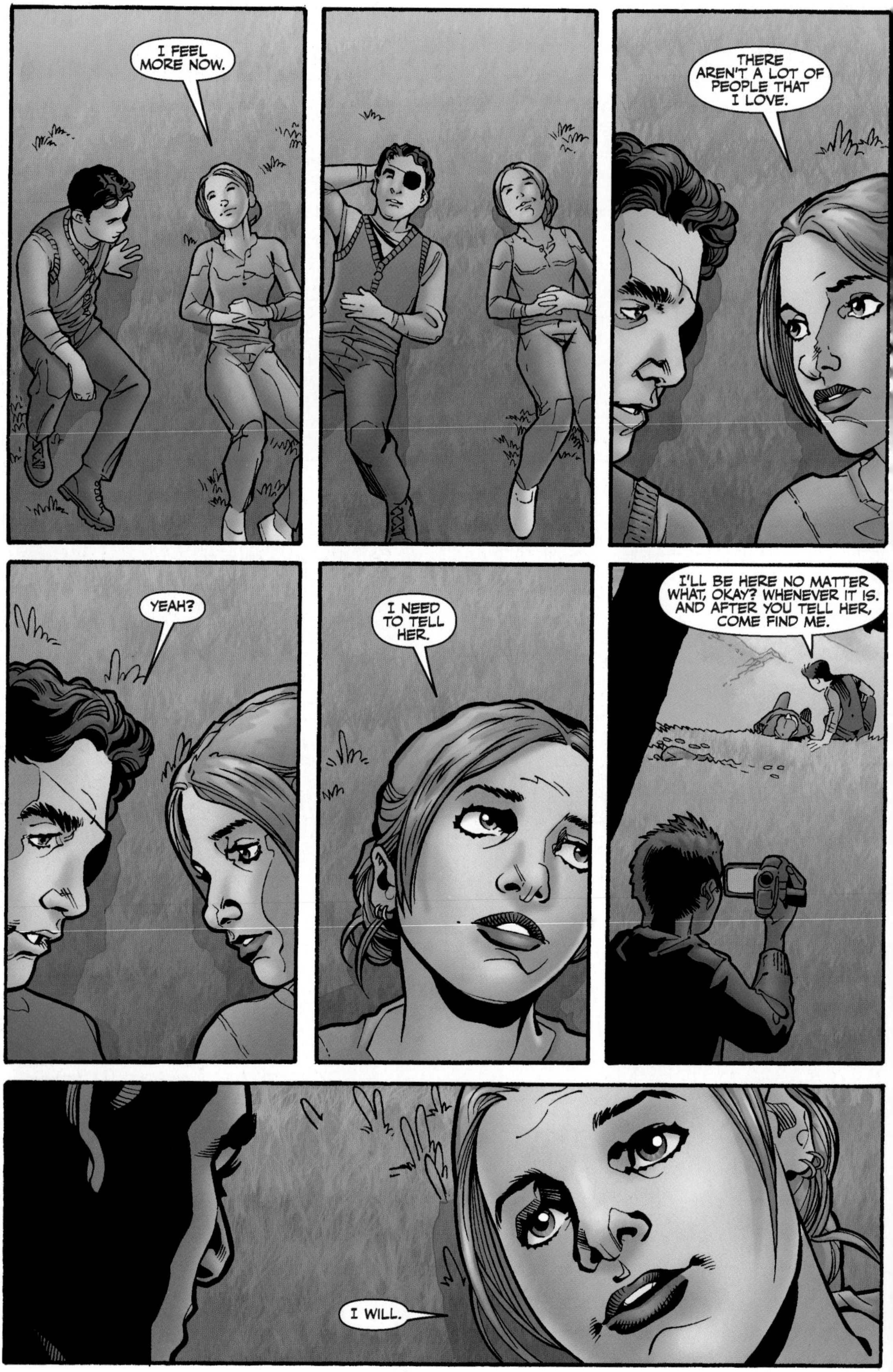
I FEEL MORE NOW.
THERE AREN'T A LOT OF PEOPLE THAT I LOVE.
YEAH?
I NEED TO TELL HER.
I'LL BE HERE NO MATTER WHAT, OKAY? WHENEVER IT IS. AND AFTER YOU TELL HER, COME FIND ME.
I WILL.

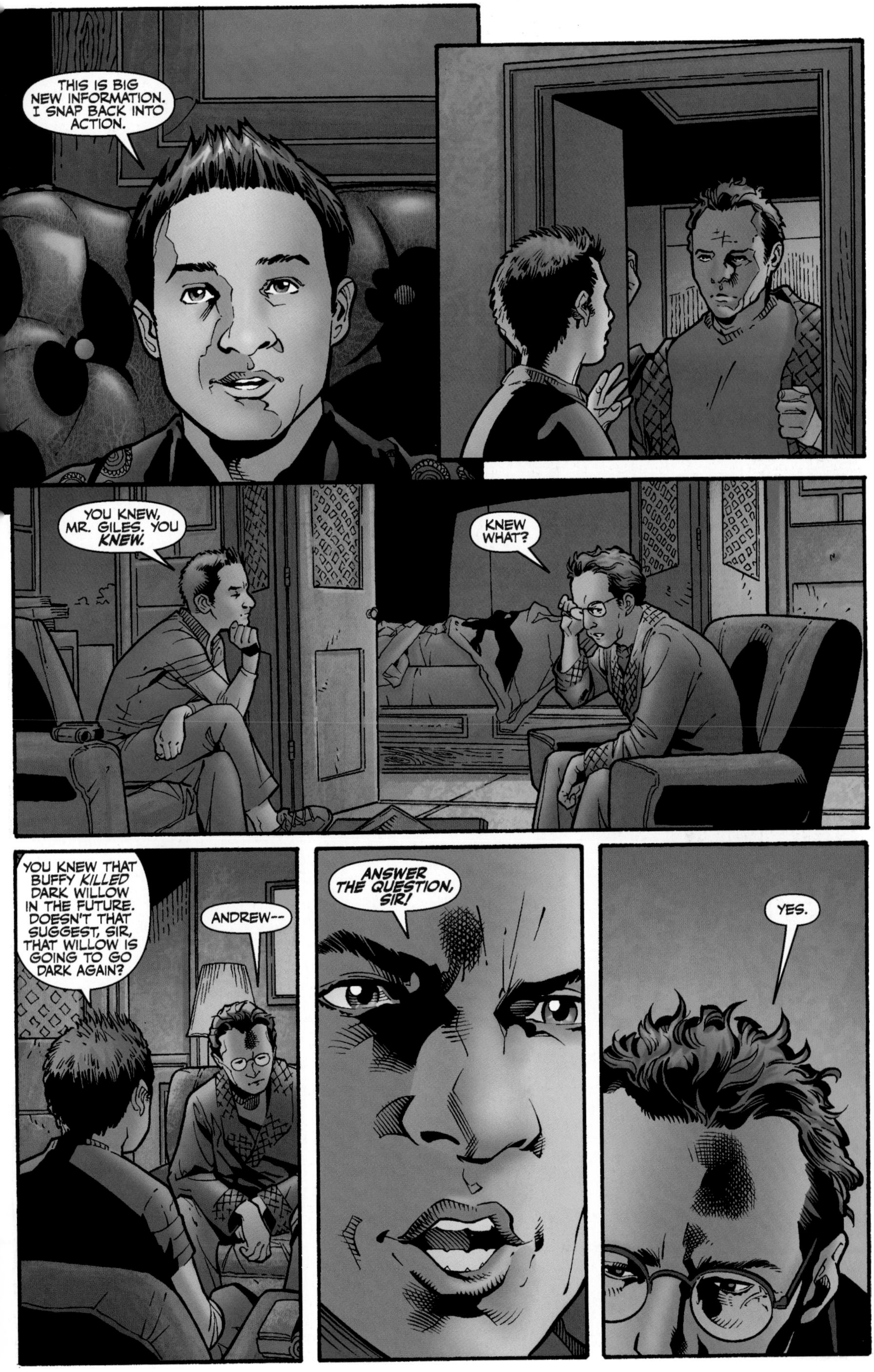
THIS IS BIG NEW INFORMATION. I SNAP BACK INTO ACTION.
YOU KNEW, MR. GILES. YOU *KNEW.*
KNEW WHAT?
YOU KNEW THAT BUFFY *KILLED* DARK WILLOW IN THE FUTURE. DOESN'T THAT SUGGEST, SIR, THAT WILLOW IS GOING TO GO DARK AGAIN?
ANDREW--
ANSWER THE QUESTION, SIR!
YES.

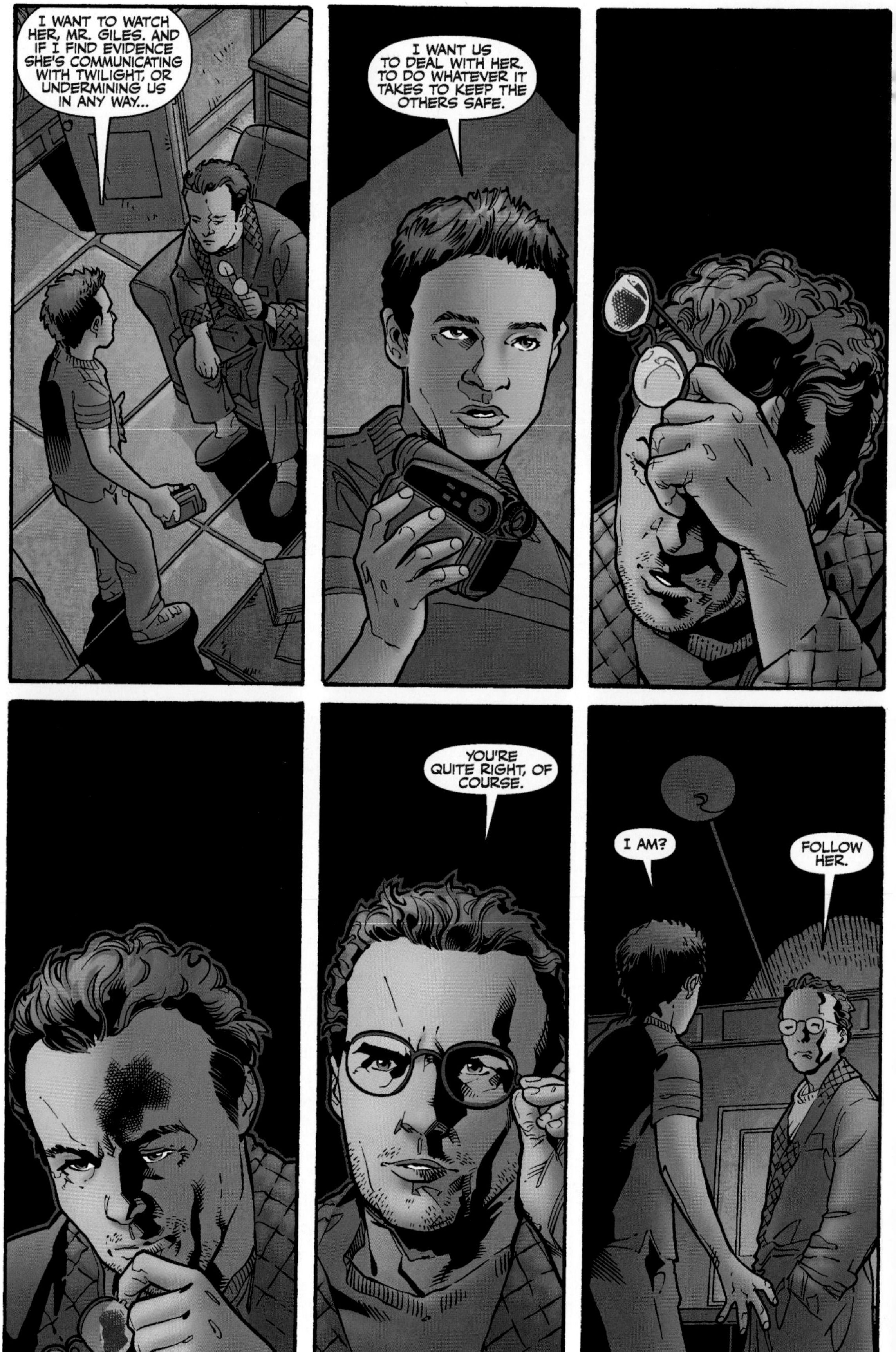
I WANT TO WATCH HER, MR. GILES. AND IF I FIND EVIDENCE SHE'S COMMUNICATING WITH TWILIGHT, OR UNDERMINING US IN ANY WAY...
I WANT US TO DEAL WITH HER. TO DO WHATEVER IT TAKES TO KEEP THE OTHERS SAFE.
YOU'RE QUITE RIGHT, OF COURSE.
I AM?
FOLLOW HER.

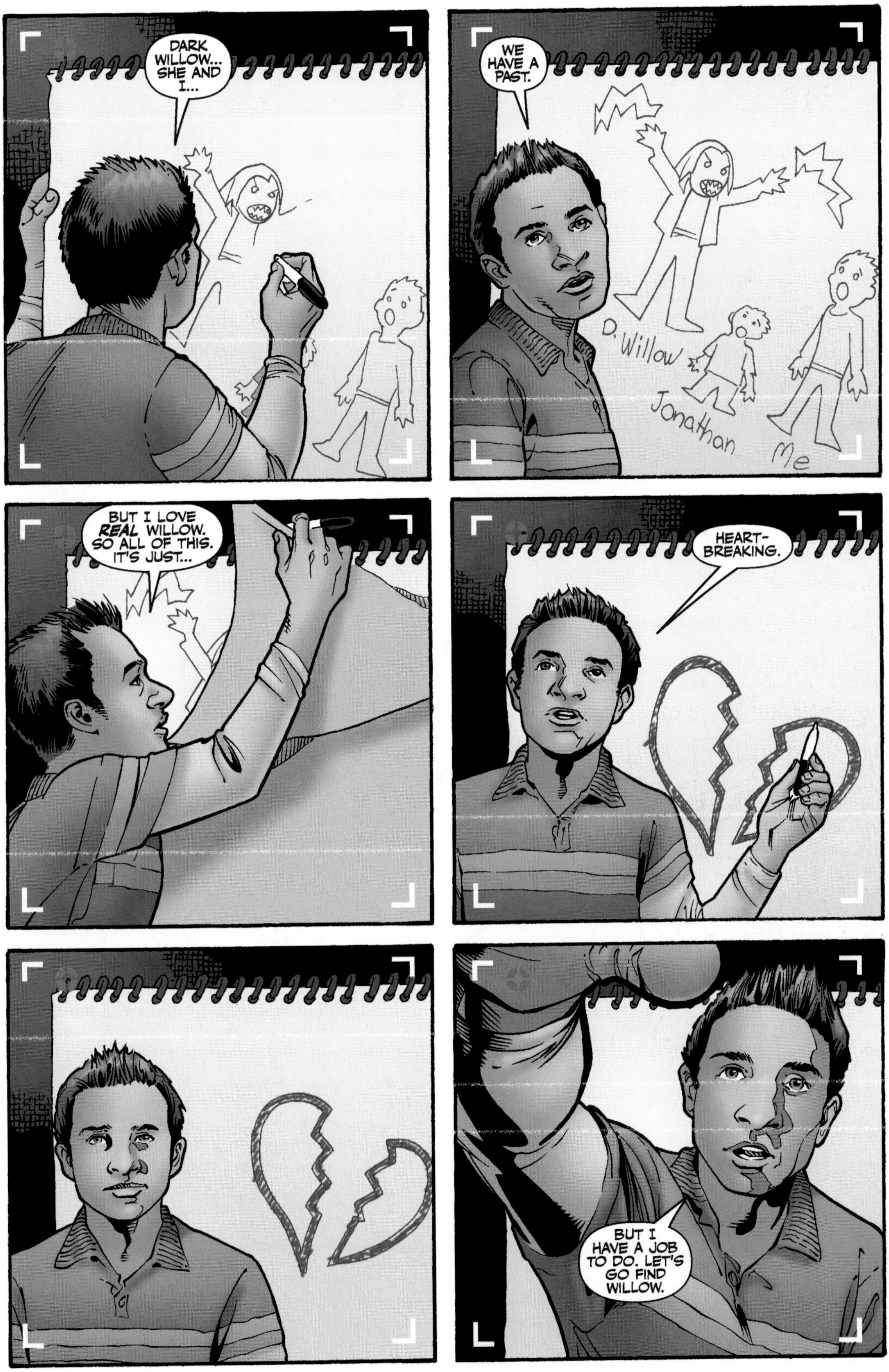
DARK WILLOW... SHE AND I...
WE HAVE A PAST.
D. Willow
Jonathan
Me
BUT I LOVE REAL WILLOW. SO ALL OF THIS. IT'S JUST...
HEART-BREAKING.
BUT I HAVE A JOB TO DO. LET'S GO FIND WILLOW.

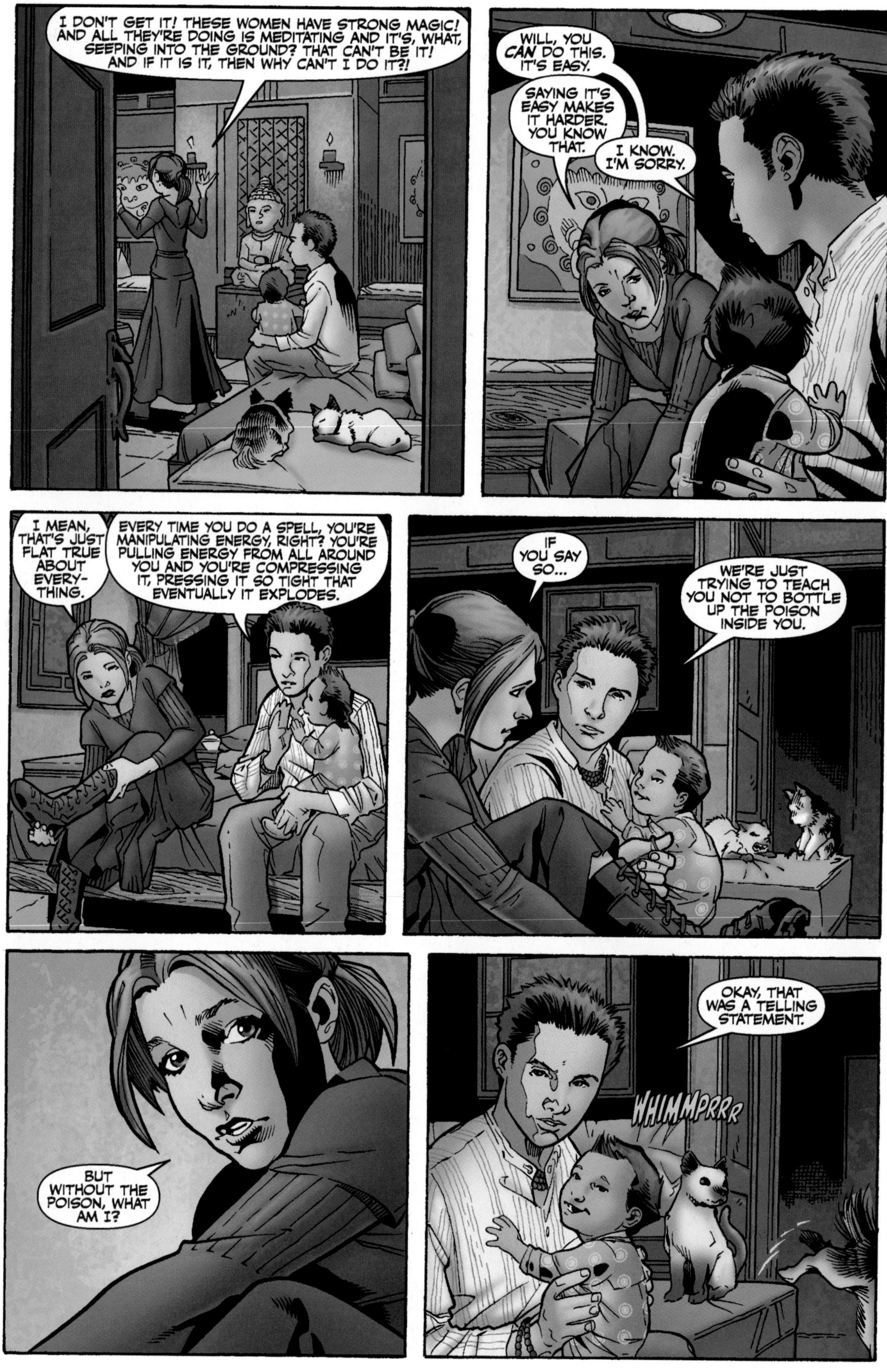

I DON'T GET IT! THESE WOMEN HAVE STRONG MAGIC! AND ALL THEY'RE DOING IS MEDITATING AND IT'S, WHAT, SEEPING INTO THE GROUND? THAT CAN'T BE IT! AND IF IT IS IT, THEN WHY CAN'T I DO IT?!
WILL, YOU CAN DO THIS. IT'S EASY.
SAYING IT'S EASY MAKES IT HARDER. YOU KNOW THAT.
I KNOW. I'M SORRY.
I MEAN, THAT'S JUST FLAT TRUE ABOUT EVERY-THING.
EVERY TIME YOU DO A SPELL, YOU'RE MANIPULATING ENERGY, RIGHT? YOU'RE PULLING ENERGY FROM ALL AROUND YOU AND YOU'RE COMPRESSING IT, PRESSING IT SO TIGHT THAT EVENTUALLY IT EXPLODES.
IF YOU SAY SO...
WE'RE JUST TRYING TO TEACH YOU NOT TO BOTTLE UP THE POISON INSIDE YOU.
BUT WITHOUT THE POISON, WHAT AM I?
OKAY, THAT WAS A TELLING STATEMENT.
WHIMMPRRR

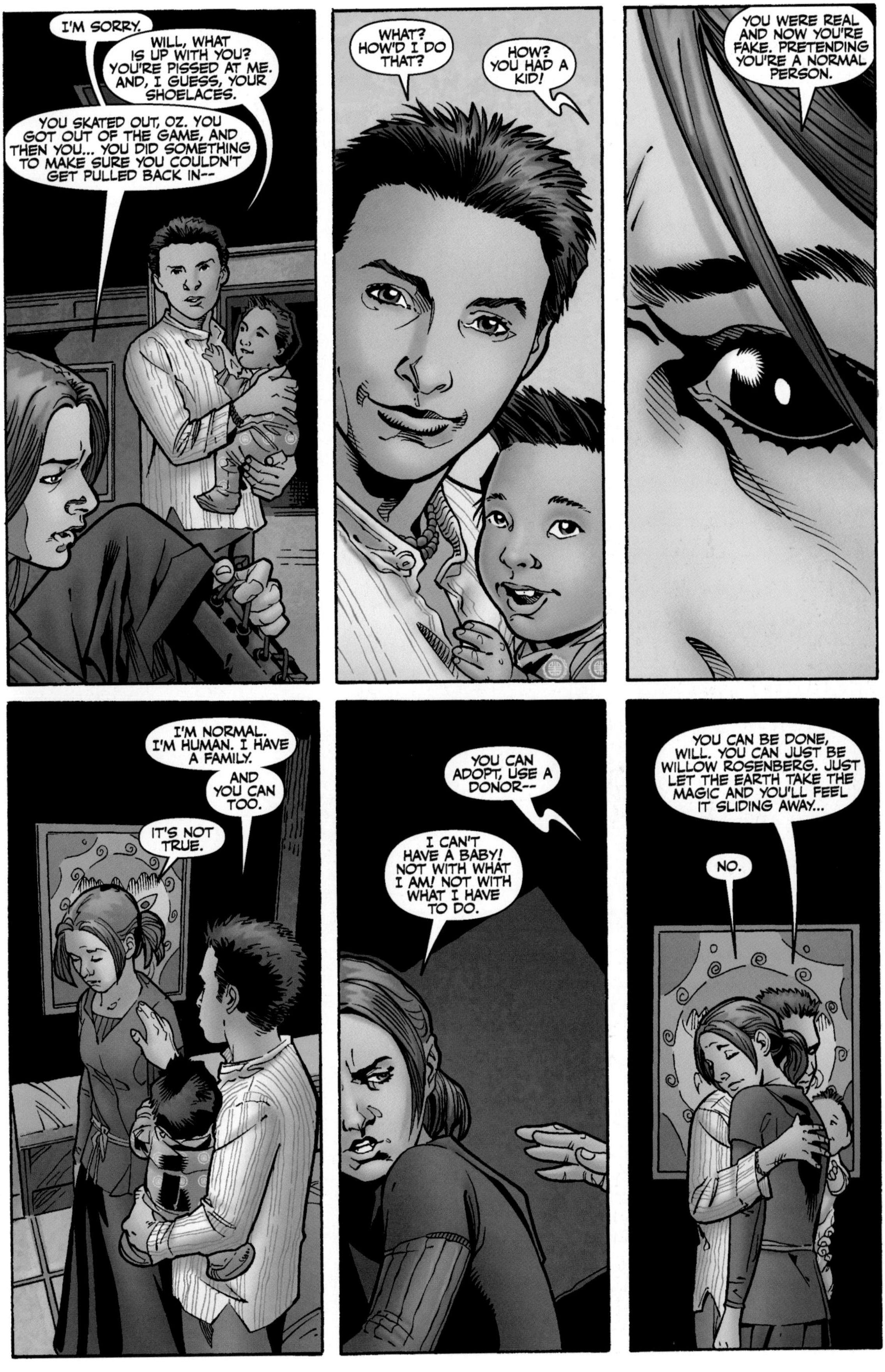
I'M SORRY.
WILL, WHAT IS UP WITH YOU? YOU'RE PISSED AT ME. AND, I GUESS, YOUR SHOELACES.
YOU SKATED OUT, OZ. YOU GOT OUT OF THE GAME, AND THEN YOU... YOU DID SOMETHING TO MAKE SURE YOU COULDN'T GET PULLED BACK IN--
WHAT? HOW'D I DO THAT?
HOW? YOU HAD A KID!
YOU WERE REAL AND NOW YOU'RE FAKE. PRETENDING YOU'RE A NORMAL PERSON.
I'M NORMAL. I'M HUMAN. I HAVE A FAMILY.
AND YOU CAN TOO.
IT'S NOT TRUE.
YOU CAN ADOPT, USE A DONOR--
I CAN'T HAVE A BABY! NOT WITH WHAT I AM! NOT WITH WHAT I HAVE TO DO.
YOU CAN BE DONE, WILL. YOU CAN JUST BE WILLOW ROSENBERG. JUST LET THE EARTH TAKE THE MAGIC AND YOU'LL FEEL IT SLIDING AWAY...
NO.

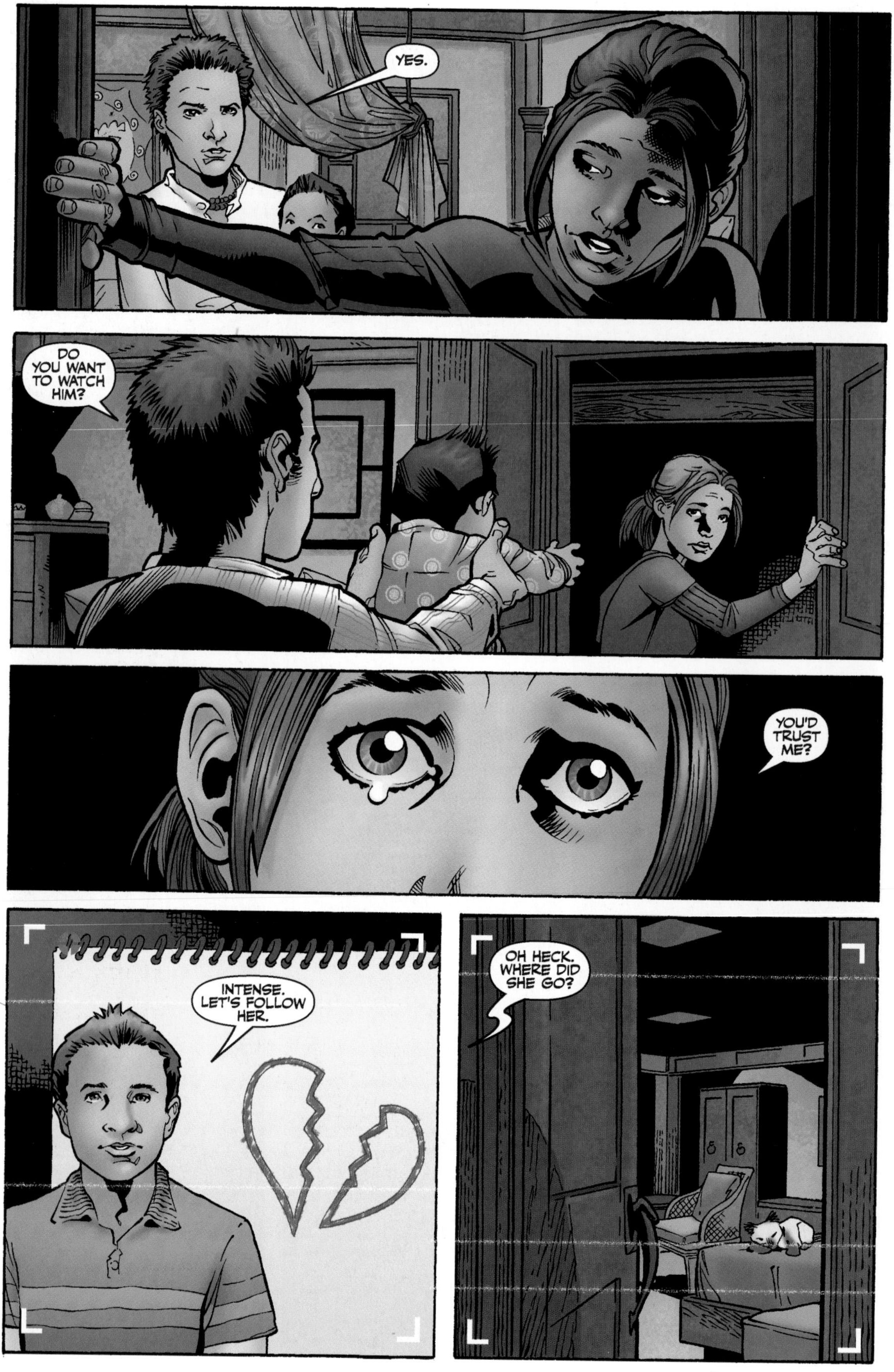
YES.
DO YOU WANT TO WATCH HIM?
YOU'D TRUST ME?
INTENSE. LET'S FOLLOW HER.
OH HECK. WHERE DID SHE GO?

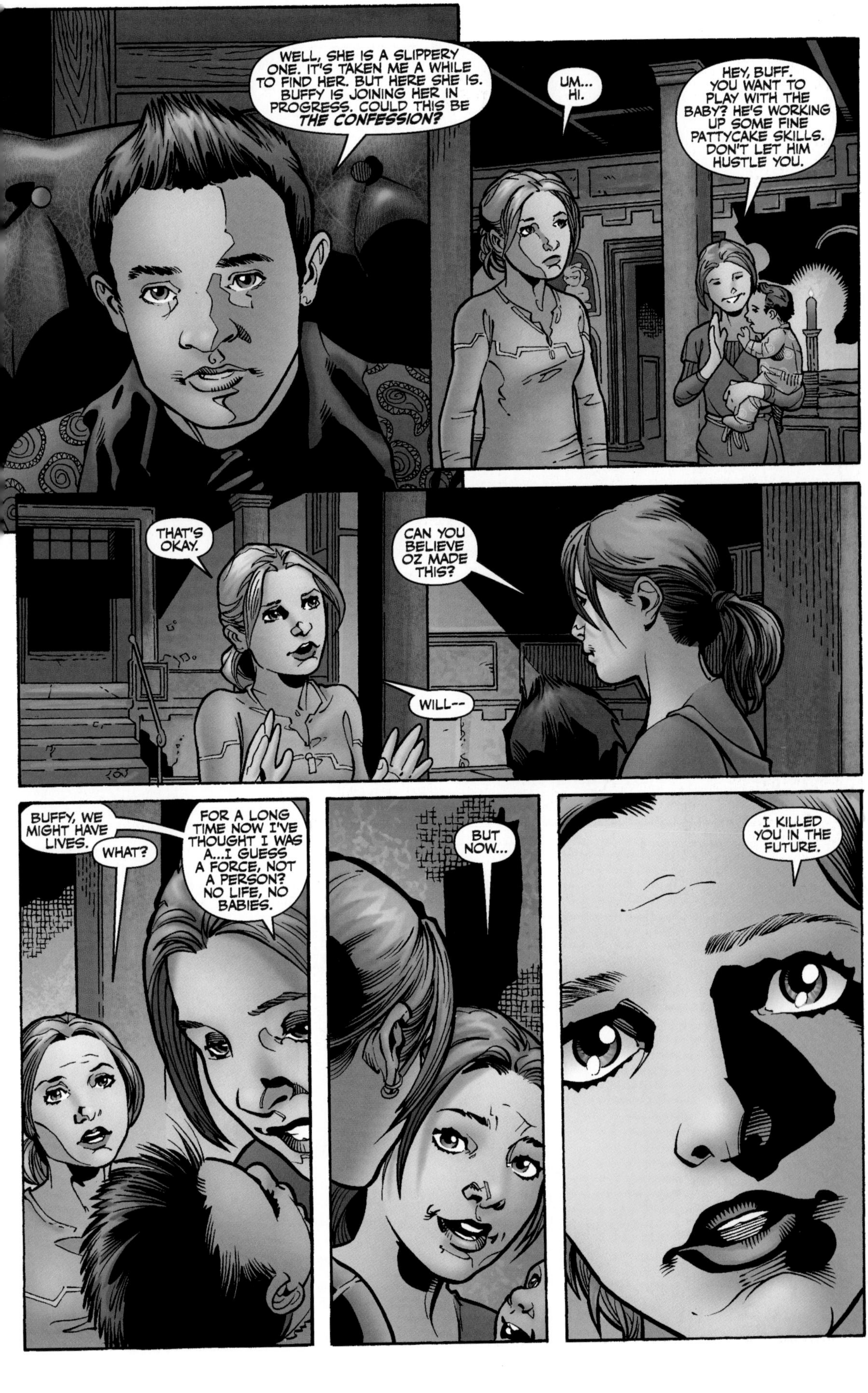
WELL, SHE IS A SLIPPERY ONE. IT'S TAKEN ME A WHILE TO FIND HER. BUT HERE SHE IS. BUFFY IS JOINING HER IN PROGRESS. COULD THIS BE THE CONFESSION?
UM... HI.
HEY, BUFF. YOU WANT TO PLAY WITH THE BABY? HE'S WORKING UP SOME FINE PATTYCAKE SKILLS. DON'T LET HIM HUSTLE YOU.
THAT'S OKAY.
CAN YOU BELIEVE OZ MADE THIS?
WILL--
BUFFY, WE MIGHT HAVE LIVES.
WHAT?
FOR A LONG TIME NOW I'VE THOUGHT I WAS A...I GUESS A FORCE, NOT A PERSON? NO LIFE, NO BABIES.
BUT NOW...
I KILLED YOU IN THE FUTURE.

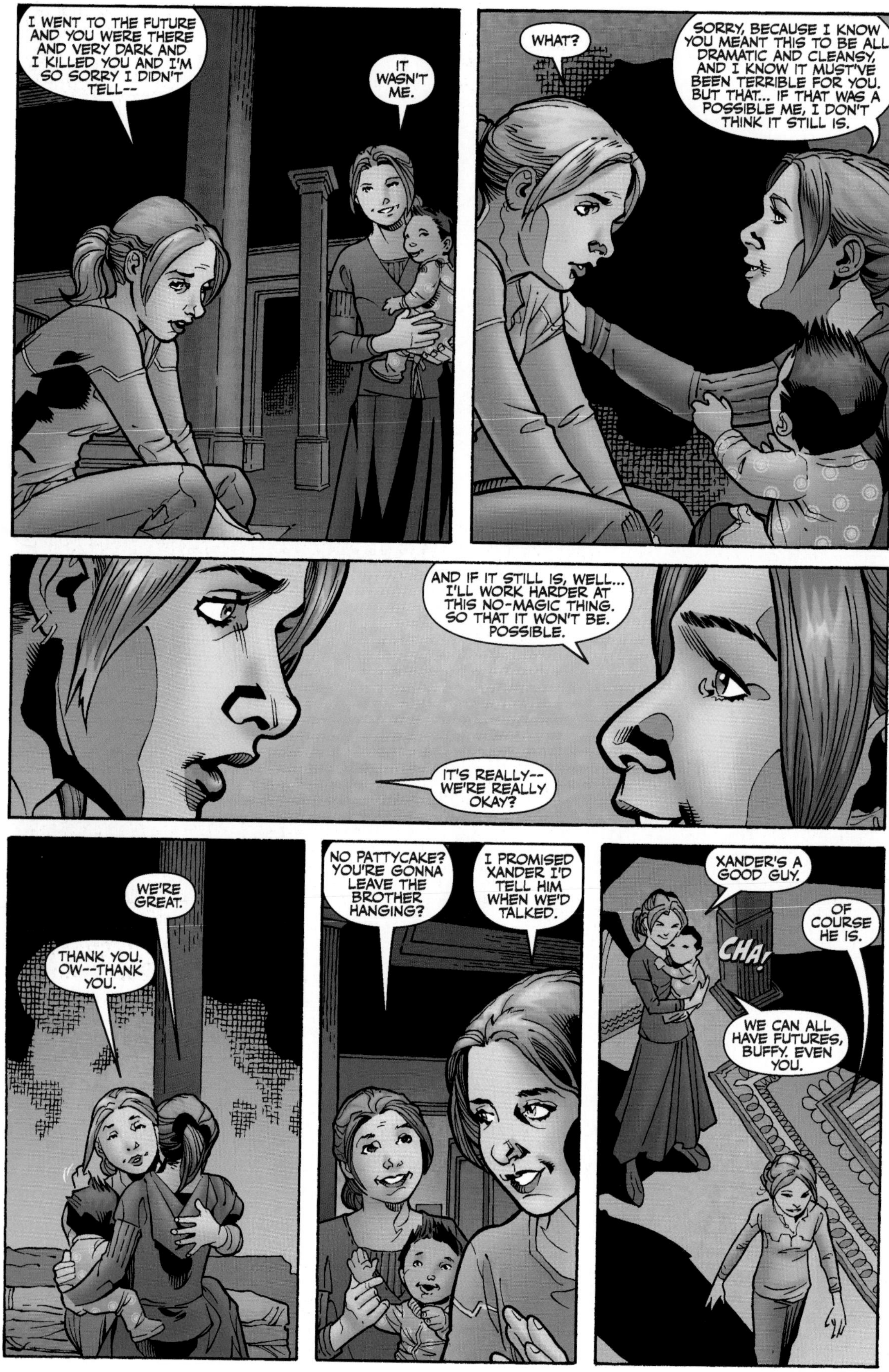
I WENT TO THE FUTURE AND YOU WERE THERE AND VERY DARK AND I KILLED YOU AND I'M SO SORRY I DIDN'T TELL--
IT WASN'T ME.
WHAT?
SORRY, BECAUSE I KNOW YOU MEANT THIS TO BE ALL DRAMATIC AND CLEANSY, AND I KNOW IT MUST'VE BEEN TERRIBLE FOR YOU. BUT THAT... IF THAT WAS A POSSIBLE ME, I DON'T THINK IT STILL IS.
AND IF IT STILL IS, WELL... I'LL WORK HARDER AT THIS NO-MAGIC THING. SO THAT IT WON'T BE. POSSIBLE.
IT'S REALLY-- WE'RE REALLY OKAY?
WE'RE GREAT.
THANK YOU. OW--THANK YOU.
NO PATTYCAKE? YOU'RE GONNA LEAVE THE BROTHER HANGING?
I PROMISED XANDER I'D TELL HIM WHEN WE'D TALKED.
XANDER'S A GOOD GUY.
OF COURSE HE IS.
CHA!
WE CAN ALL HAVE FUTURES, BUFFY. EVEN YOU.

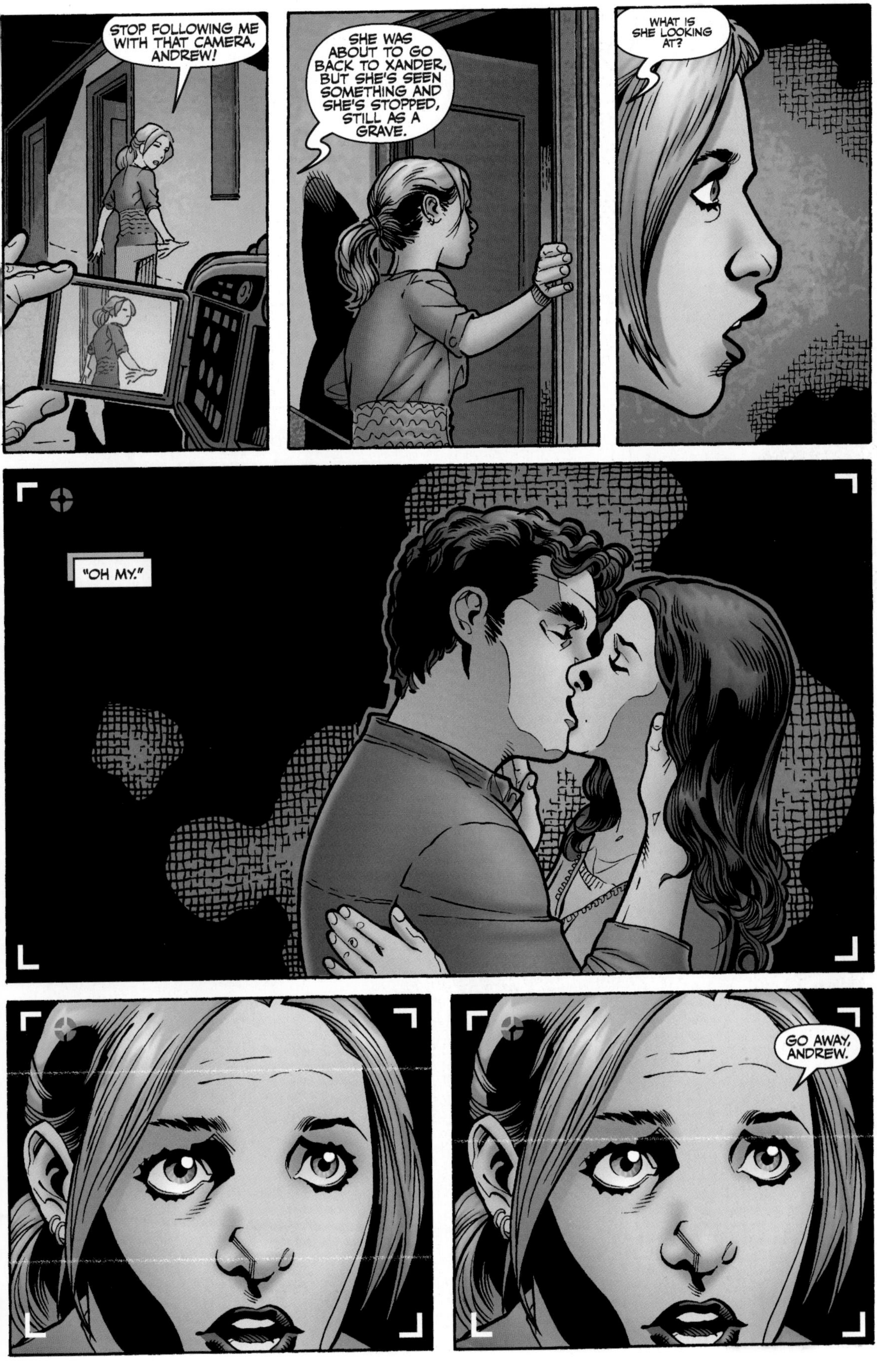
STOP FOLLOWING ME WITH THAT CAMERA, ANDREW!
SHE WAS ABOUT TO GO BACK TO XANDER, BUT SHE'S SEEN SOMETHING AND SHE'S STOPPED, STILL AS A GRAVE.
WHAT IS SHE LOOKING AT?
"OH MY."
GO AWAY, ANDREW.

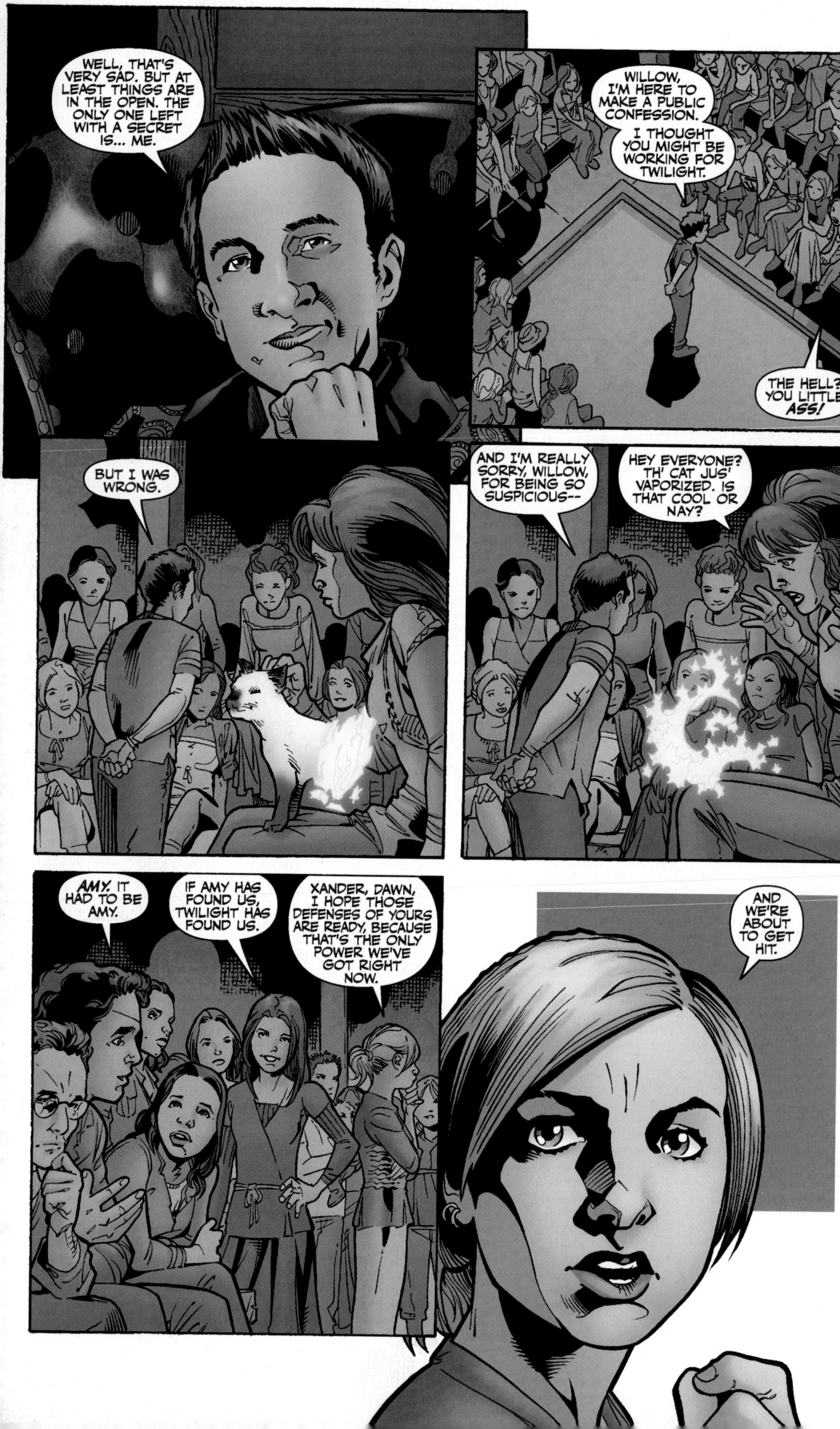

WELL, THAT'S VERY SAD. BUT AT LEAST THINGS ARE IN THE OPEN. THE ONLY ONE LEFT WITH A SECRET IS... ME.
WILLOW, I'M HERE TO MAKE A PUBLIC CONFESSION.
I THOUGHT YOU MIGHT BE WORKING FOR TWILIGHT.
THE HELL? YOU LITTLE ASS!
BUT I WAS WRONG.
AND I'M REALLY SORRY, WILLOW, FOR BEING SO SUSPICIOUS--
HEY EVERYONE? TH' CAT JUS' VAPORIZED. IS THAT COOL OR NAY?
AMY. IT HAD TO BE AMY.
IF AMY HAS FOUND US, TWILIGHT HAS FOUND US.
XANDER, DAWN, I HOPE THOSE DEFENSES OF YOURS ARE READY, BECAUSE THAT'S THE ONLY POWER WE'VE GOT RIGHT NOW.
AND WE'RE ABOUT TO GET HIT.

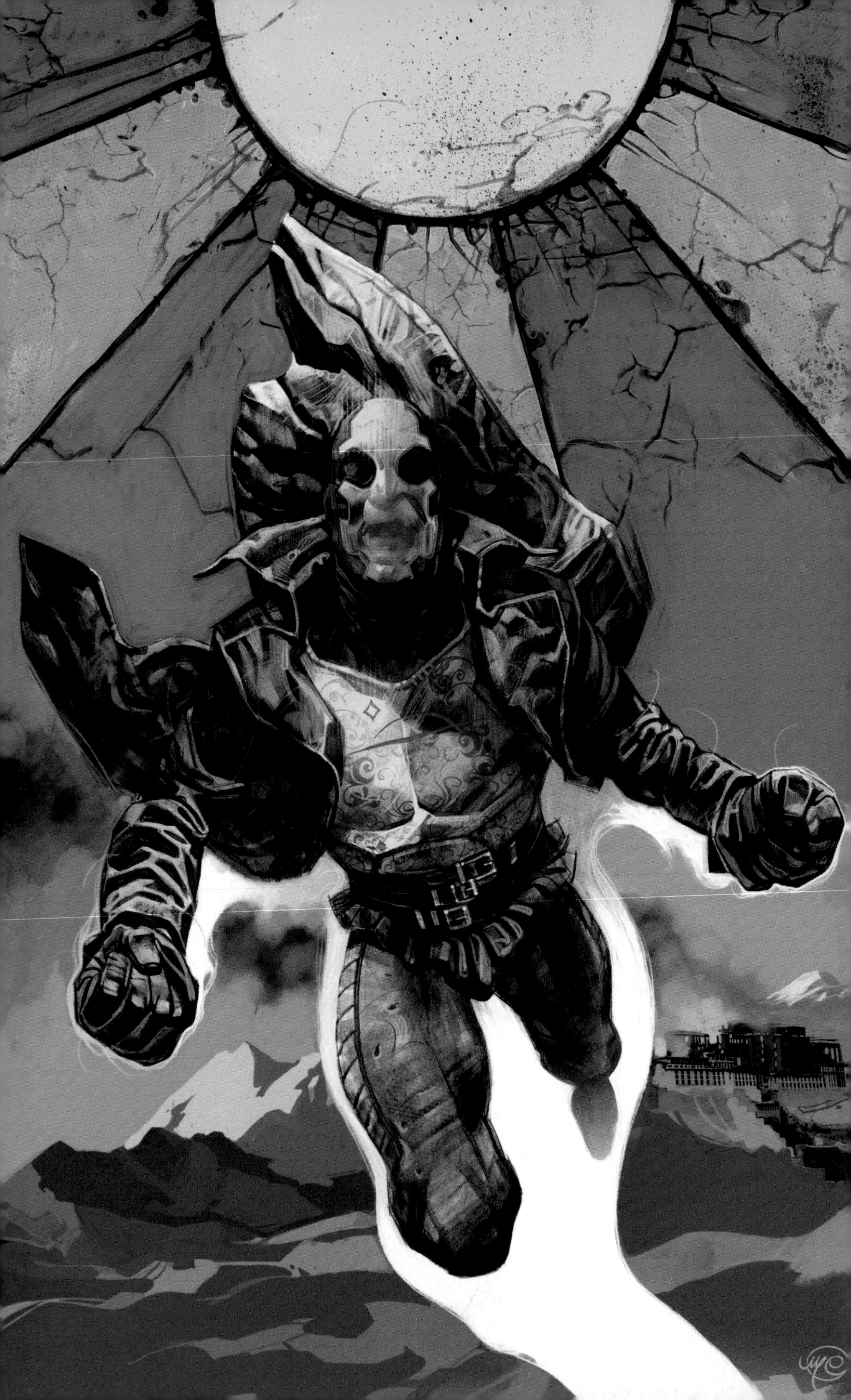

RETREAT

PART FOUR

"BELIEVE IT OR NOT..."

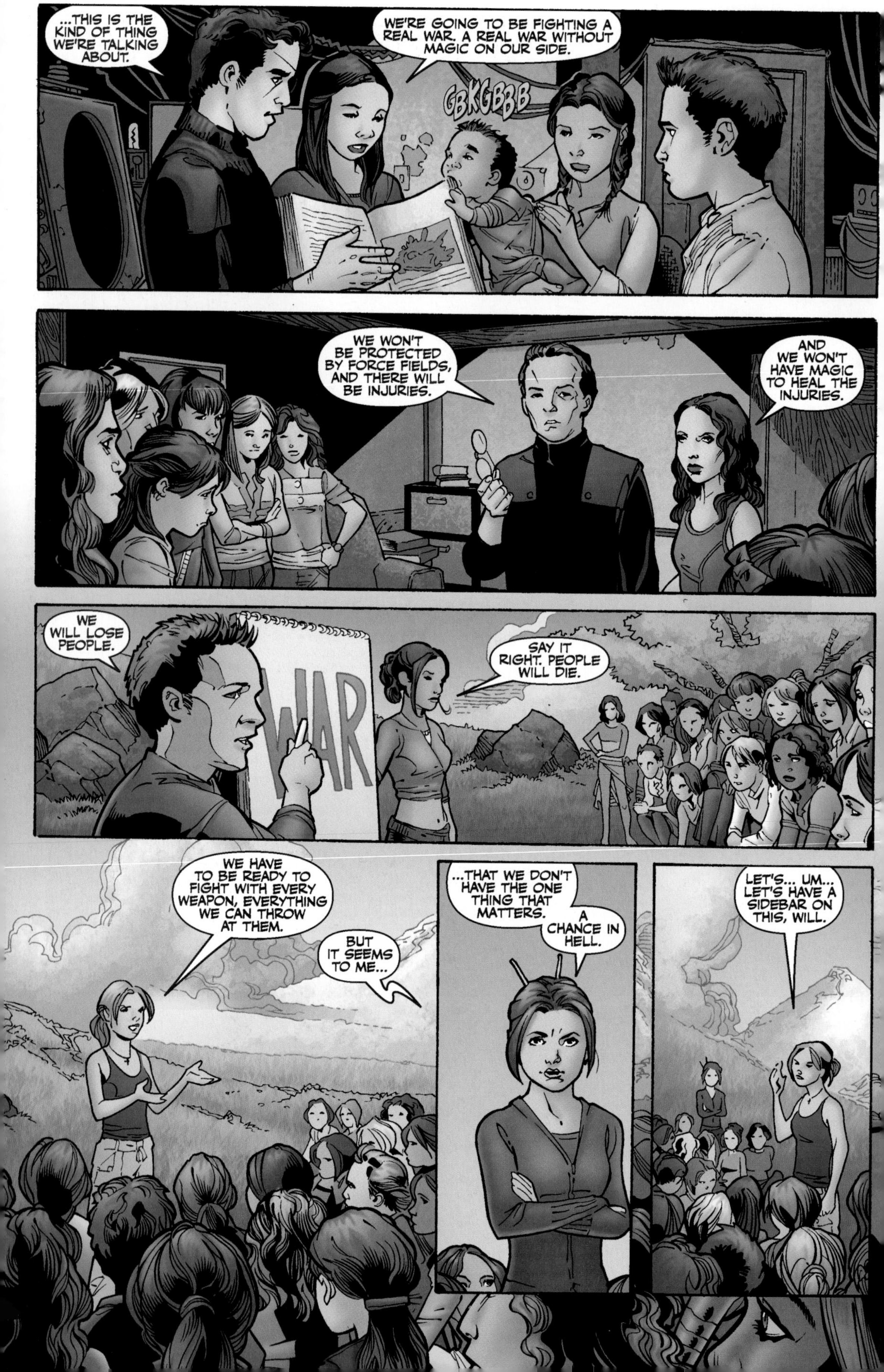
...THIS IS THE KIND OF THING WE'RE TALKING ABOUT.
WE'RE GOING TO BE FIGHTING A REAL WAR. A REAL WAR WITHOUT MAGIC ON OUR SIDE.
GBKGBBB
WE WON'T BE PROTECTED BY FORCE FIELDS, AND THERE WILL BE INJURIES.
AND WE WON'T HAVE MAGIC TO HEAL THE INJURIES.
WE WILL LOSE PEOPLE.
WAR
SAY IT RIGHT. PEOPLE WILL DIE.
WE HAVE TO BE READY TO FIGHT WITH EVERY WEAPON, EVERYTHING WE CAN THROW AT THEM.
BUT IT SEEMS TO ME...
...THAT WE DON'T HAVE THE ONE THING THAT MATTERS.
A CHANCE IN HELL.
LET'S... UM... LET'S HAVE A SIDEBAR ON THIS, WILL.

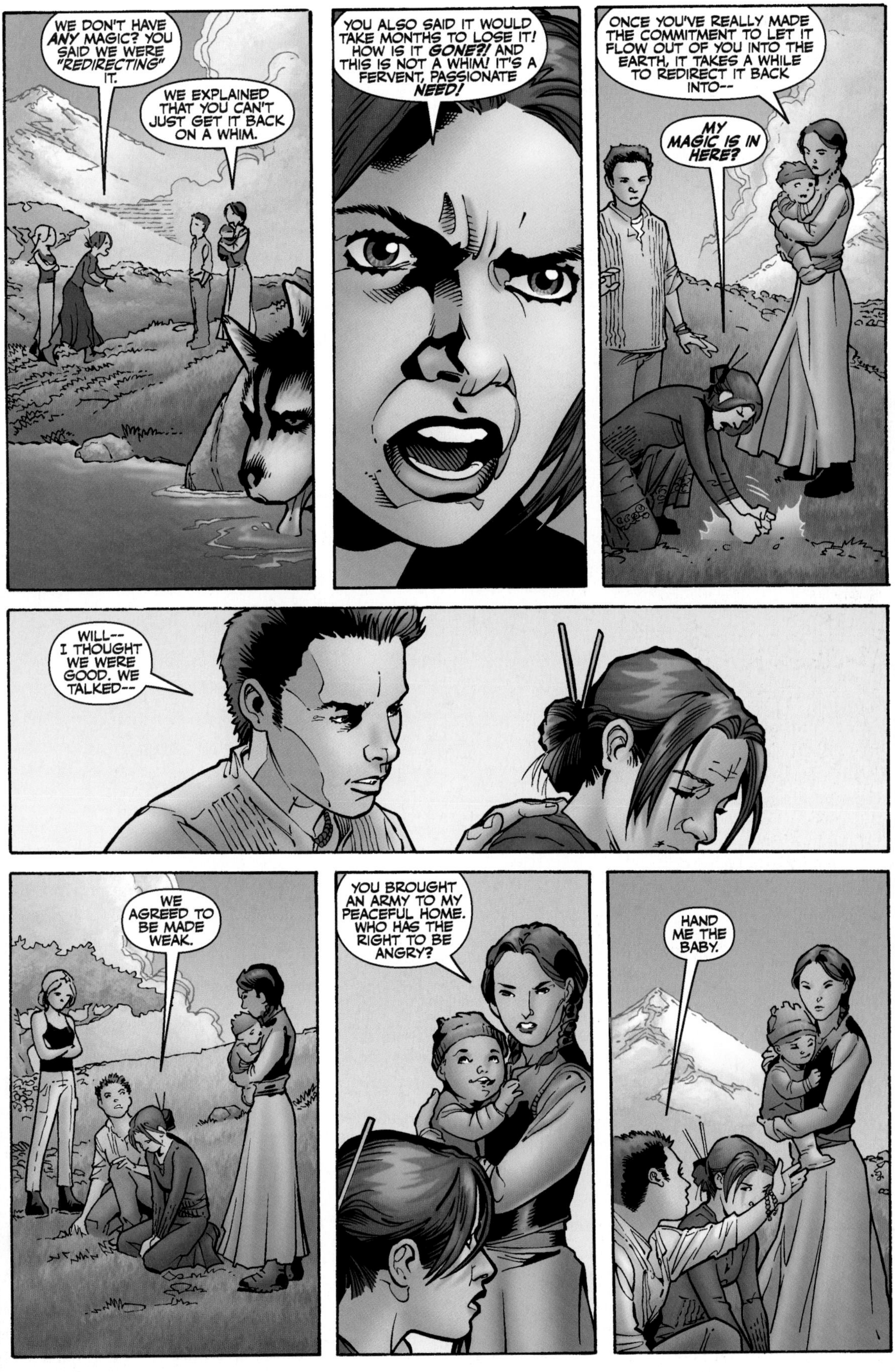
WE DON'T HAVE ANY MAGIC? YOU SAID WE WERE "REDIRECTING" IT.
WE EXPLAINED THAT YOU CAN'T JUST GET IT BACK ON A WHIM.
YOU ALSO SAID IT WOULD TAKE MONTHS TO LOSE IT! HOW IS IT GONE?! AND THIS IS NOT A WHIM! IT'S A FERVENT, PASSIONATE NEED!
ONCE YOU'VE REALLY MADE THE COMMITMENT TO LET IT FLOW OUT OF YOU INTO THE EARTH, IT TAKES A WHILE TO REDIRECT IT BACK INTO--
MY MAGIC IS IN HERE?
WILL-- I THOUGHT WE WERE GOOD. WE TALKED--
WE AGREED TO BE MADE WEAK.
YOU BROUGHT AN ARMY TO MY PEACEFUL HOME. WHO HAS THE RIGHT TO BE ANGRY?
HAND ME THE BABY.

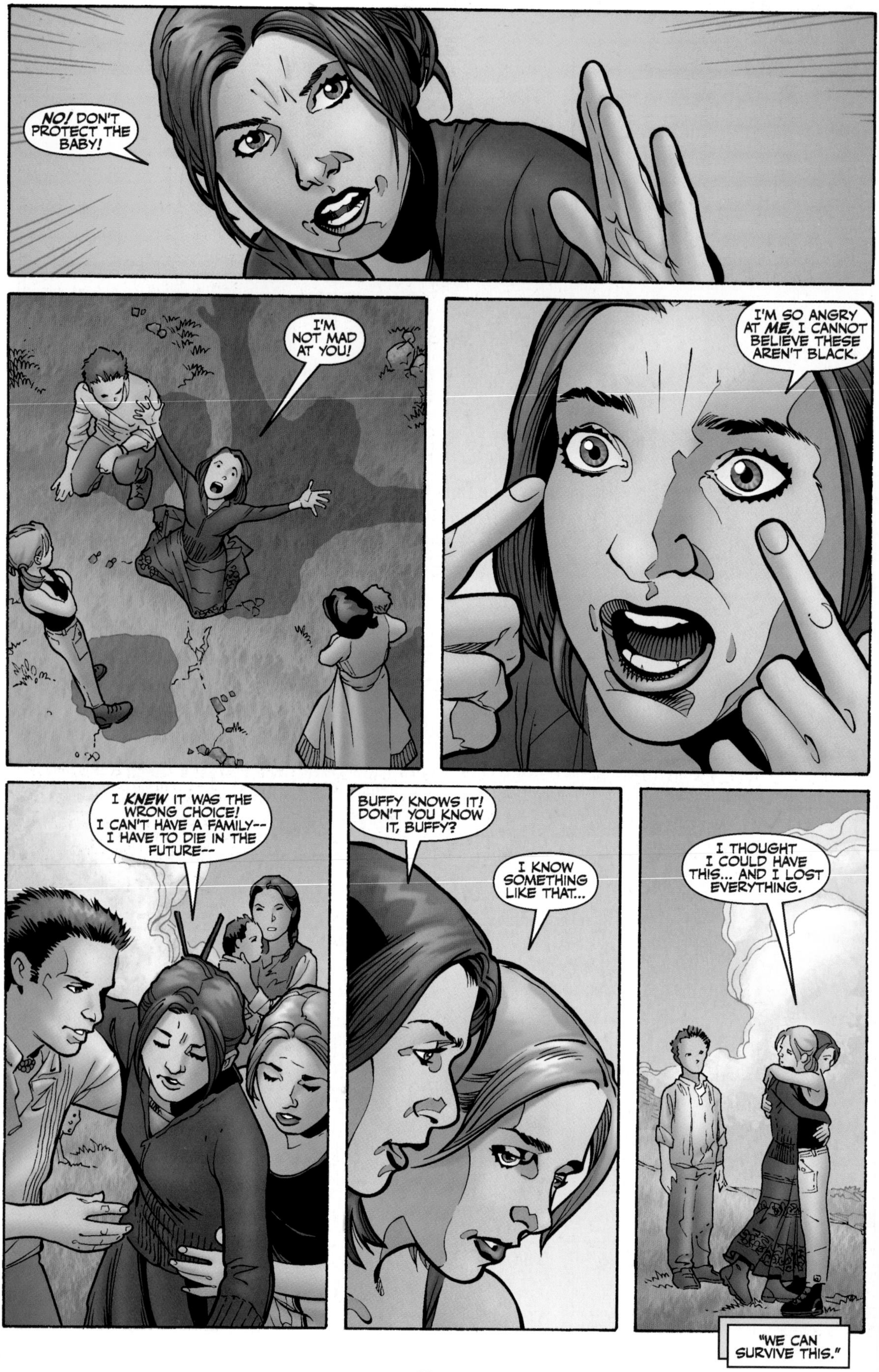
NO! DON'T PROTECT THE BABY!
I'M NOT MAD AT YOU!
I'M SO ANGRY AT ME, I CANNOT BELIEVE THESE AREN'T BLACK.
I KNEW IT WAS THE WRONG CHOICE! I CAN'T HAVE A FAMILY-- I HAVE TO DIE IN THE FUTURE--
BUFFY KNOWS IT! DON'T YOU KNOW IT, BUFFY?
I KNOW SOMETHING LIKE THAT...
I THOUGHT I COULD HAVE THIS... AND I LOST EVERYTHING.
"WE CAN SURVIVE THIS."

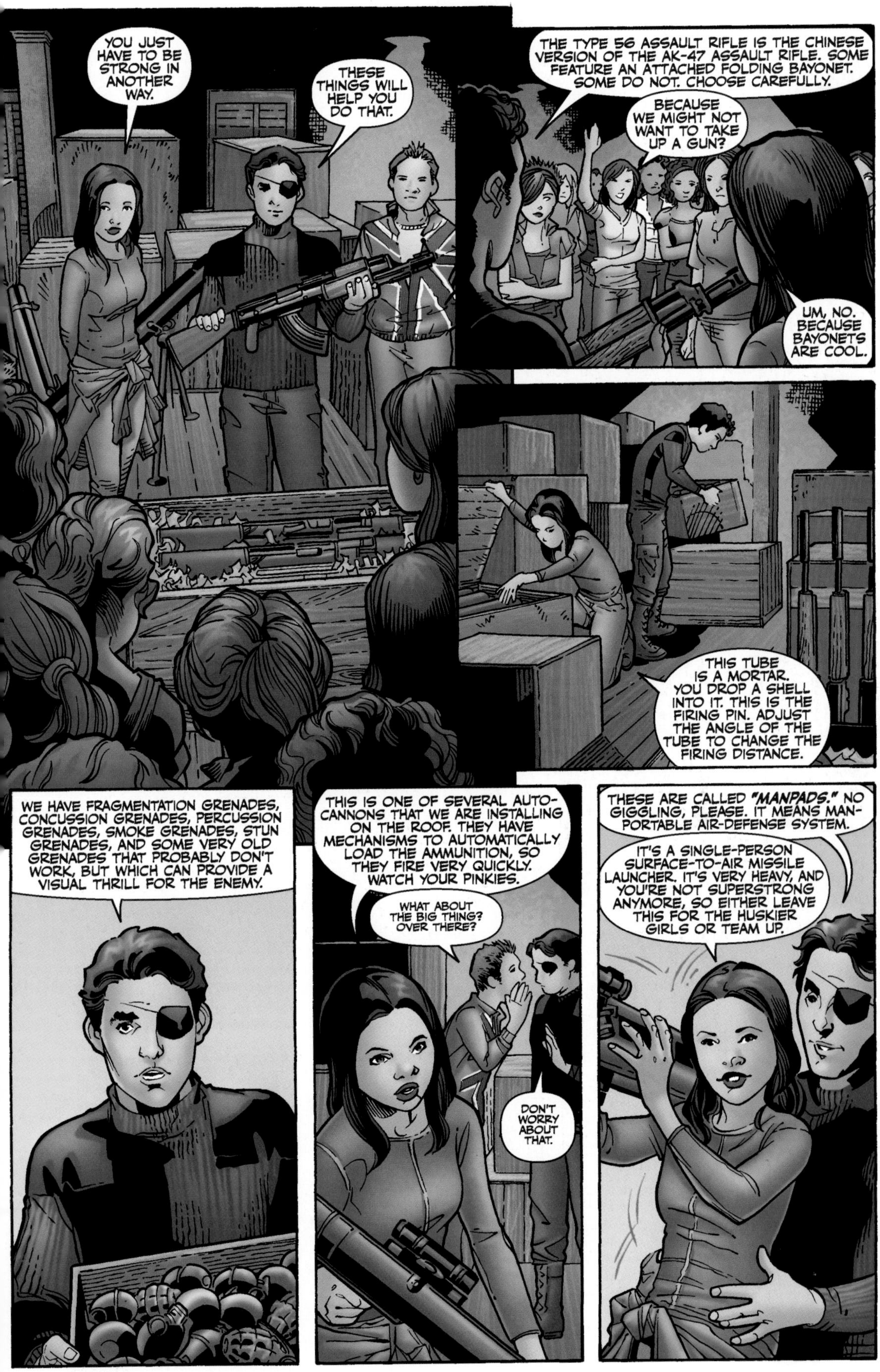
YOU JUST HAVE TO BE STRONG IN ANOTHER WAY.
THESE THINGS WILL HELP YOU DO THAT.
THE TYPE 56 ASSAULT RIFLE IS THE CHINESE VERSION OF THE AK-47 ASSAULT RIFLE. SOME FEATURE AN ATTACHED FOLDING BAYONET. SOME DO NOT. CHOOSE CAREFULLY.
BECAUSE WE MIGHT NOT WANT TO TAKE UP A GUN?
UM, NO. BECAUSE BAYONETS ARE COOL.
THIS TUBE IS A MORTAR. YOU DROP A SHELL INTO IT. THIS IS THE FIRING PIN. ADJUST THE ANGLE OF THE TUBE TO CHANGE THE FIRING DISTANCE.
WE HAVE FRAGMENTATION GRENADES, CONCUSSION GRENADES, PERCUSSION GRENADES, SMOKE GRENADES, STUN GRENADES, AND SOME VERY OLD GRENADES THAT PROBABLY DON'T WORK, BUT WHICH CAN PROVIDE A VISUAL THRILL FOR THE ENEMY.
THIS IS ONE OF SEVERAL AUTO-CANNONS THAT WE ARE INSTALLING ON THE ROOF. THEY HAVE MECHANISMS TO AUTOMATICALLY LOAD THE AMMUNITION, SO THEY FIRE VERY QUICKLY. WATCH YOUR PINKIES.
WHAT ABOUT THE BIG THING? OVER THERE?
DON'T WORRY ABOUT THAT.
THESE ARE CALLED "MANPADS." NO GIGGLING, PLEASE. IT MEANS MAN-PORTABLE AIR-DEFENSE SYSTEM.
IT'S A SINGLE-PERSON SURFACE-TO-AIR MISSILE LAUNCHER. IT'S VERY HEAVY, AND YOU'RE NOT SUPERSTRONG ANYMORE, SO EITHER LEAVE THIS FOR THE HUSKIER GIRLS OR TEAM UP.

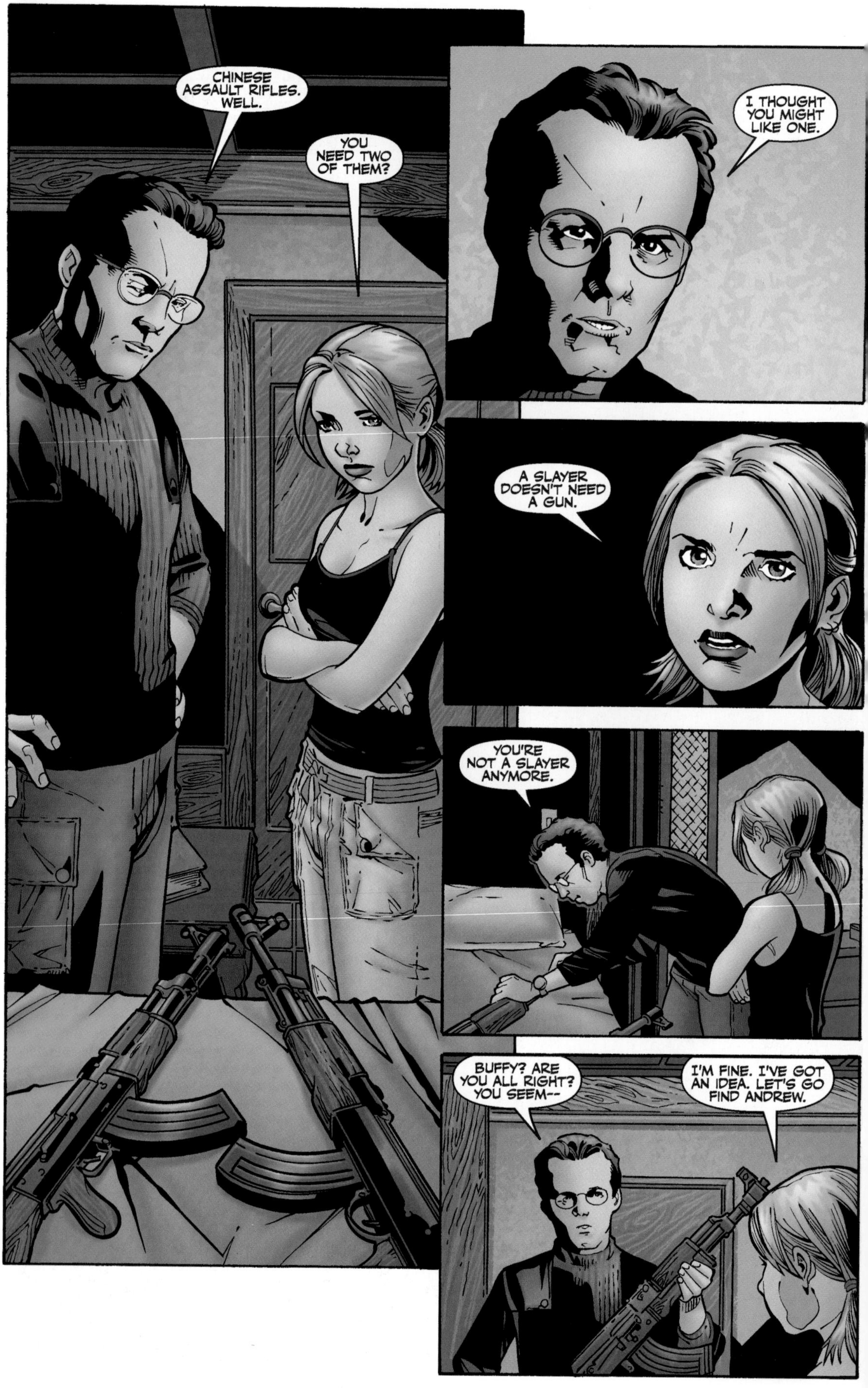
CHINESE ASSAULT RIFLES. WELL.
YOU NEED TWO OF THEM?
I THOUGHT YOU MIGHT LIKE ONE.
A SLAYER DOESN'T NEED A GUN.
YOU'RE NOT A SLAYER ANYMORE.
BUFFY? ARE YOU ALL RIGHT? YOU SEEM--
I'M FINE. I'VE GOT AN IDEA. LET'S GO FIND ANDREW.

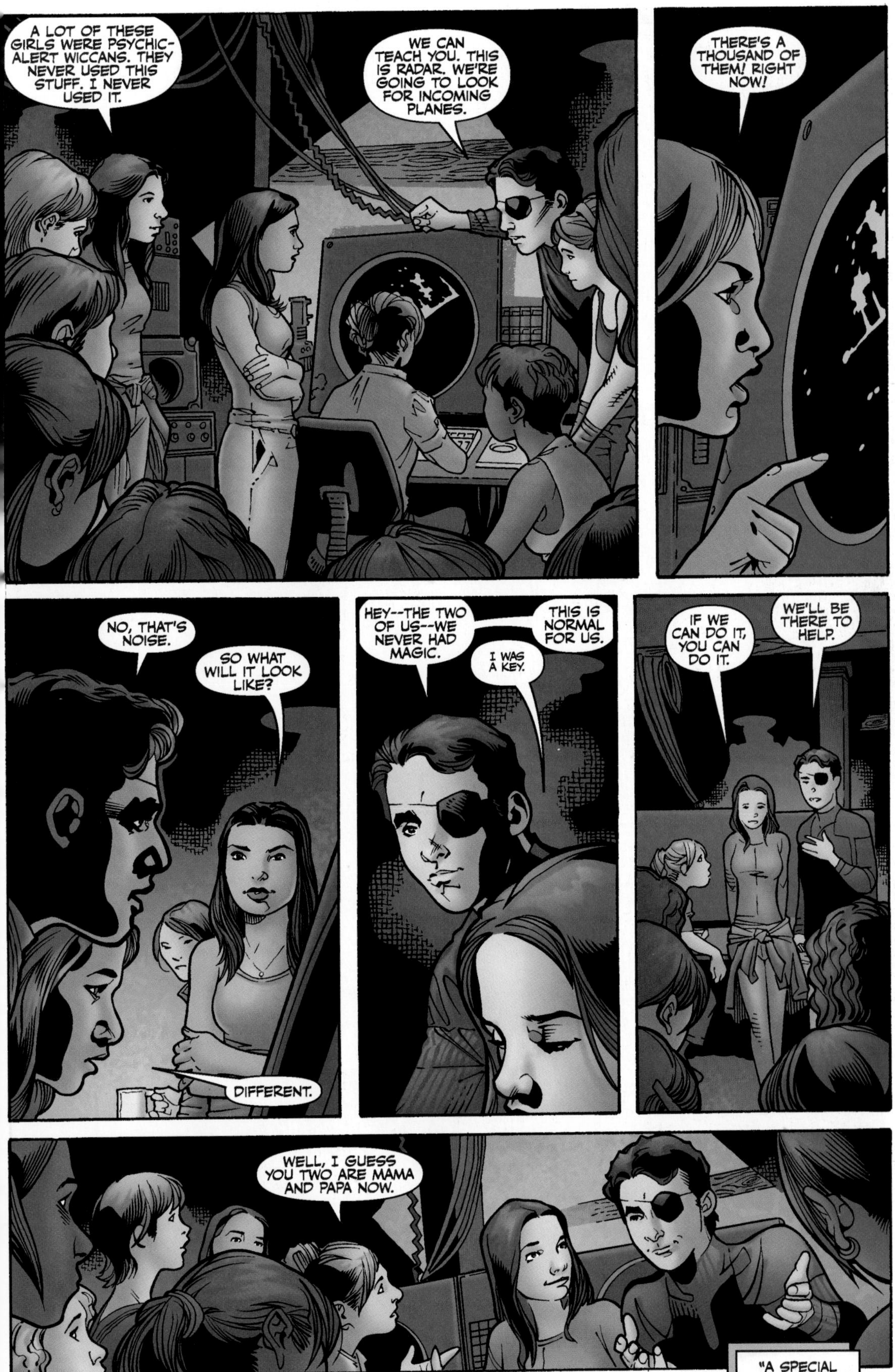
A LOT OF THESE GIRLS WERE PSYCHIC-ALERT WICCANS. THEY NEVER USED THIS STUFF. I NEVER USED IT.
WE CAN TEACH YOU. THIS IS RADAR. WE'RE GOING TO LOOK FOR INCOMING PLANES.
THERE'S A THOUSAND OF THEM! RIGHT NOW!
NO, THAT'S NOISE.
SO WHAT WILL IT LOOK LIKE?
DIFFERENT.
HEY--THE TWO OF US--WE NEVER HAD MAGIC.
THIS IS NORMAL FOR US.
I WAS A KEY.
IF WE CAN DO IT, YOU CAN DO IT.
WE'LL BE THERE TO HELP.
WELL, I GUESS YOU TWO ARE MAMA AND PAPA NOW.
"A SPECIAL ASSIGNMENT?"

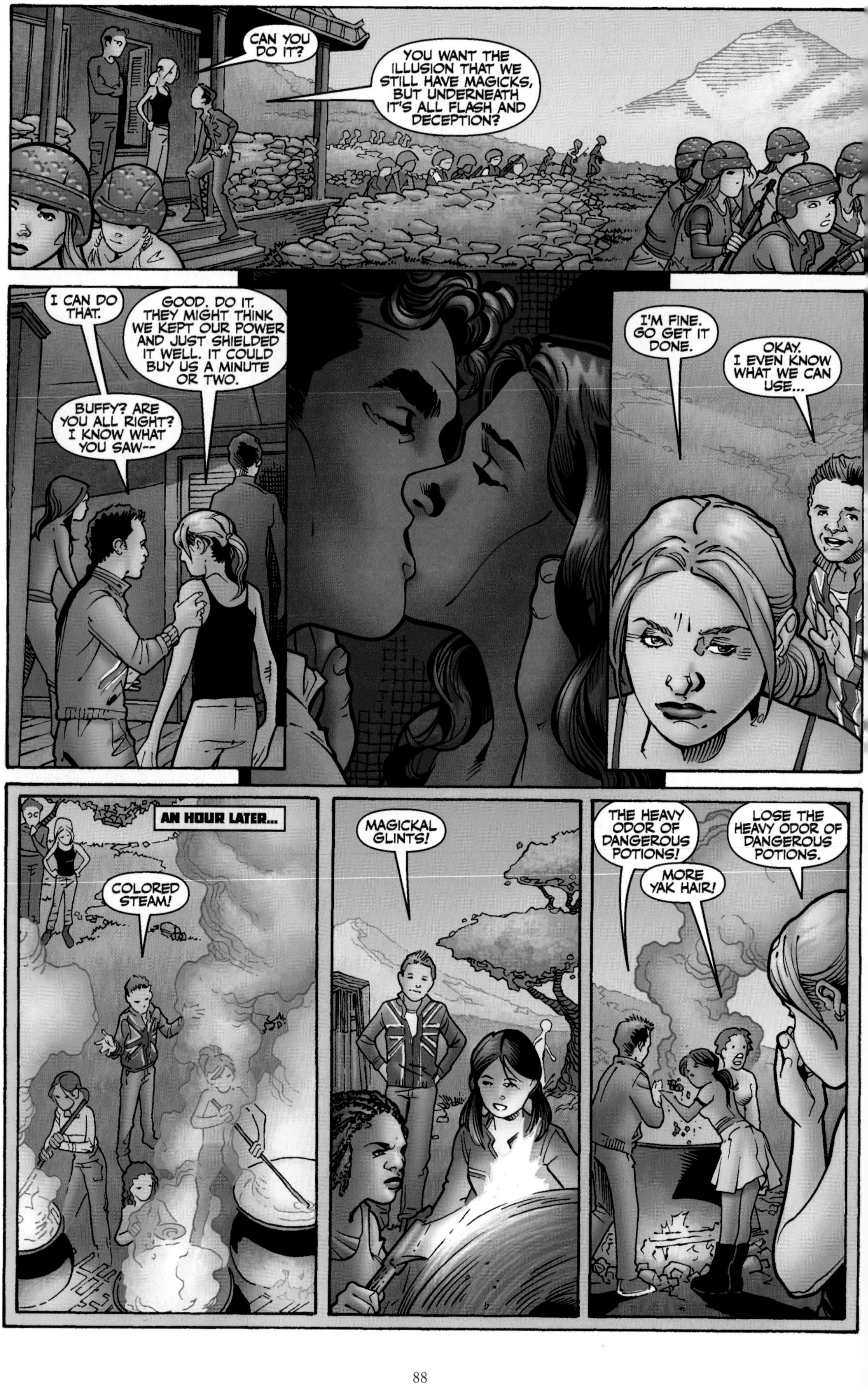
CAN YOU DO IT?
YOU WANT THE ILLUSION THAT WE STILL HAVE MAGICKS, BUT UNDERNEATH IT'S ALL FLASH AND DECEPTION?
I CAN DO THAT.
GOOD. DO IT. THEY MIGHT THINK WE KEPT OUR POWER AND JUST SHIELDED IT WELL. IT COULD BUY US A MINUTE OR TWO.
BUFFY? ARE YOU ALL RIGHT? I KNOW WHAT YOU SAW--
I'M FINE. GO GET IT DONE.
OKAY. I EVEN KNOW WHAT WE CAN USE...
AN HOUR LATER...
COLORED STEAM!
MAGICKAL GLINTS!
THE HEAVY ODOR OF DANGEROUS POTIONS!
MORE YAK HAIR!
LOSE THE HEAVY ODOR OF DANGEROUS POTIONS.

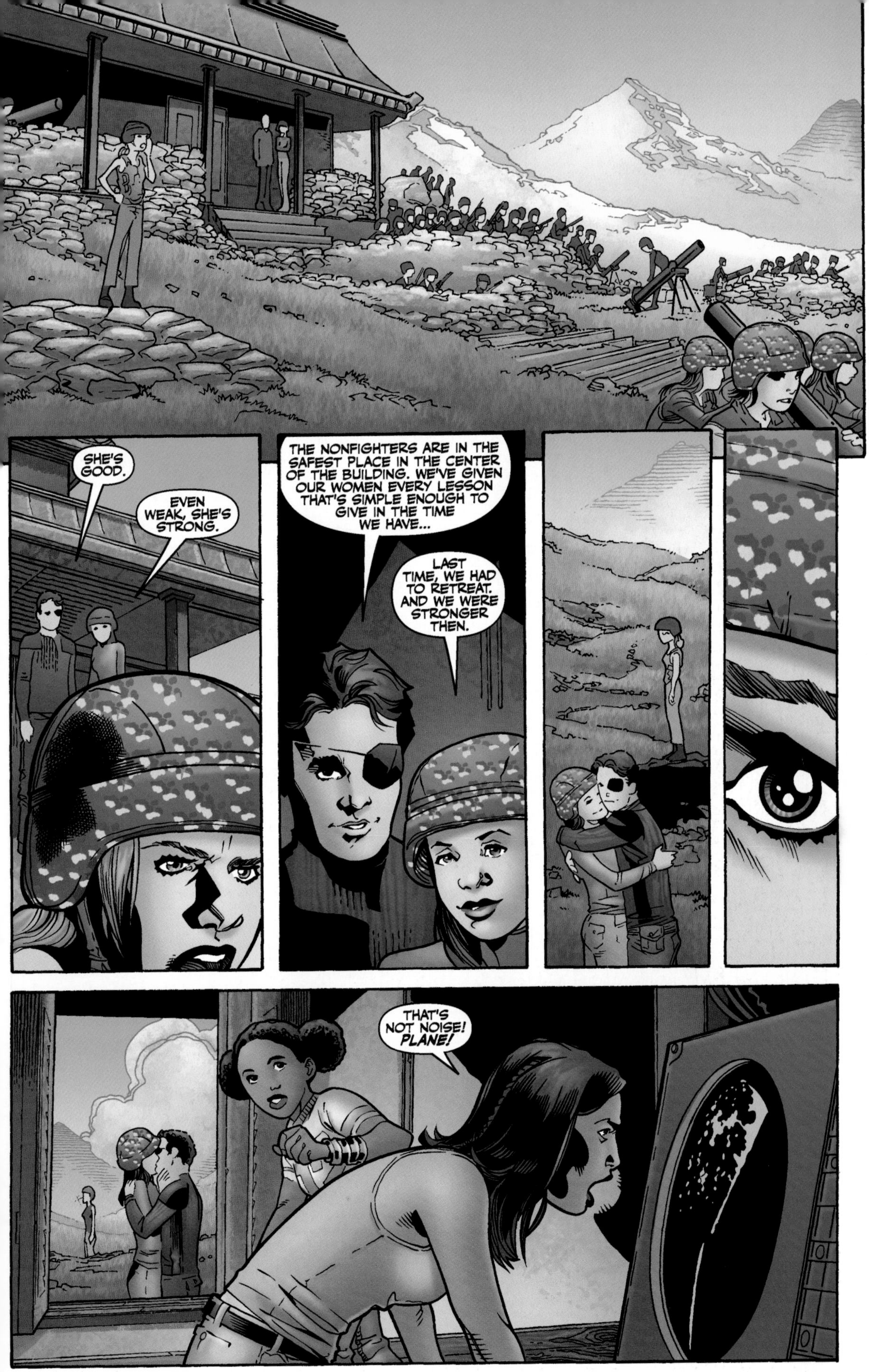
SHE'S GOOD.
EVEN WEAK, SHE'S STRONG.
THE NONFIGHTERS ARE IN THE SAFEST PLACE IN THE CENTER OF THE BUILDING. WE'VE GIVEN OUR WOMEN EVERY LESSON THAT'S SIMPLE ENOUGH TO GIVE IN THE TIME WE HAVE...
LAST TIME, WE HAD TO RETREAT. AND WE WERE STRONGER THEN.
THAT'S NOT NOISE! *PLANE!*

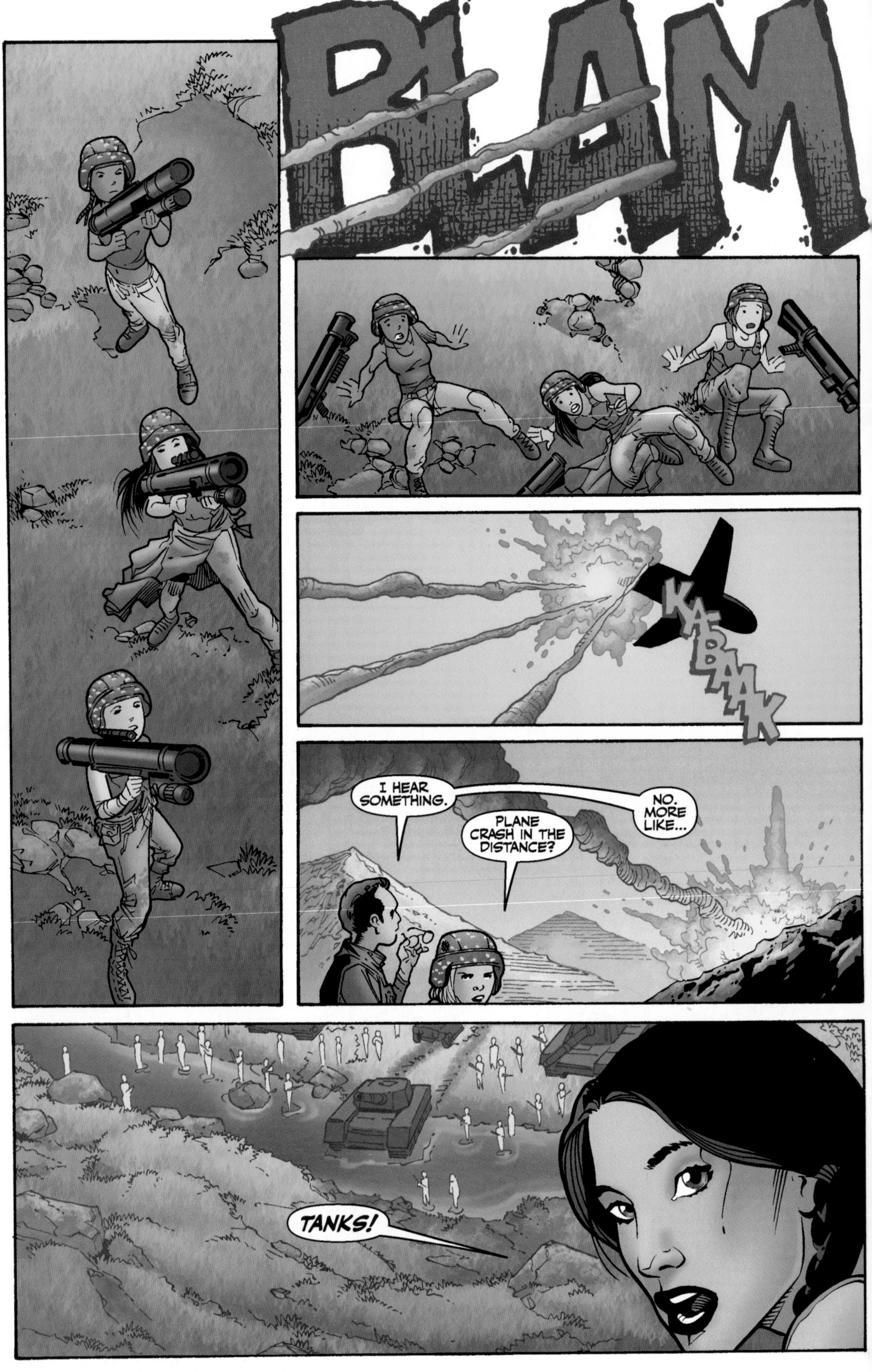
BLAM
KABAAAK
I HEAR SOMETHING.
PLANE CRASH IN THE DISTANCE?
NO. MORE LIKE...
TANKS!

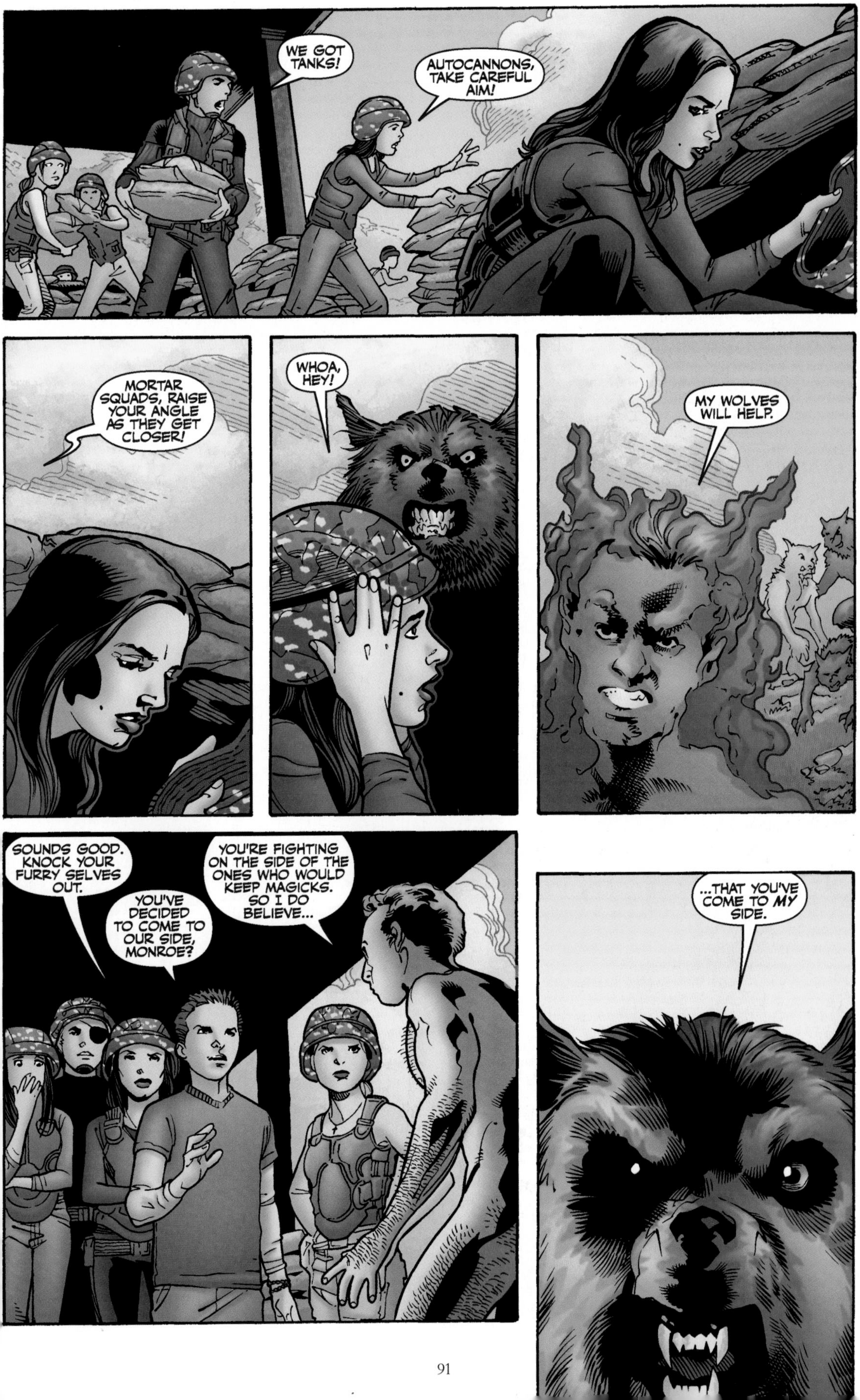
WE GOT TANKS!
AUTOCANNONS, TAKE CAREFUL AIM!
MORTAR SQUADS, RAISE YOUR ANGLE AS THEY GET CLOSER!
WHOA, HEY!
MY WOLVES WILL HELP.
SOUNDS GOOD. KNOCK YOUR FURRY SELVES OUT.
YOU'VE DECIDED TO COME TO OUR SIDE, MONROE?
YOU'RE FIGHTING ON THE SIDE OF THE ONES WHO WOULD KEEP MAGICKS. SO I DO BELIEVE...
...THAT YOU'VE COME TO *MY* SIDE.

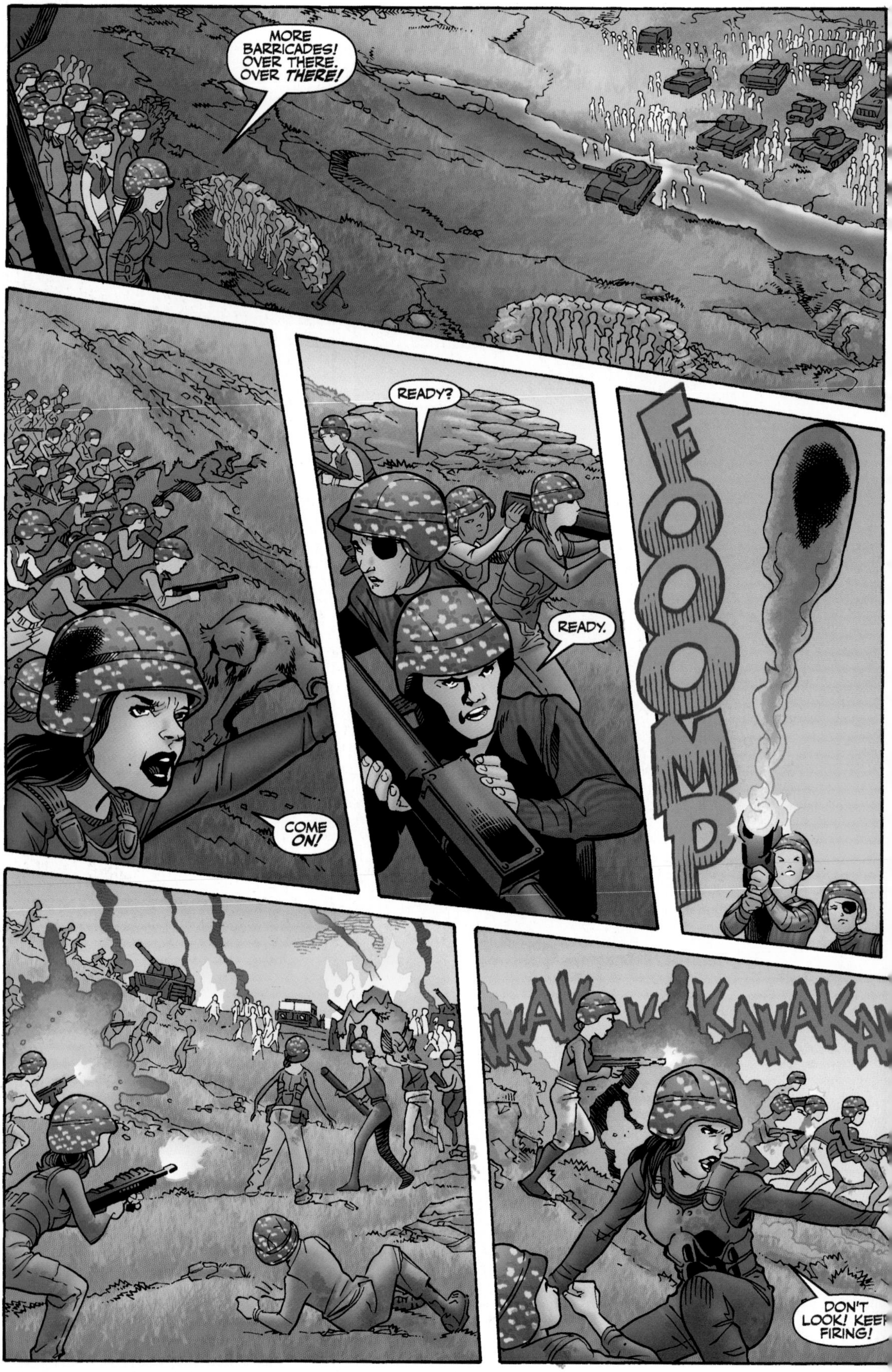
MORE BARRICADES! OVER THERE. OVER THERE!
COME ON!
READY?
READY.
FOOOOMP
KAKAKAKAKAKA
DON'T LOOK! KEEP FIRING!

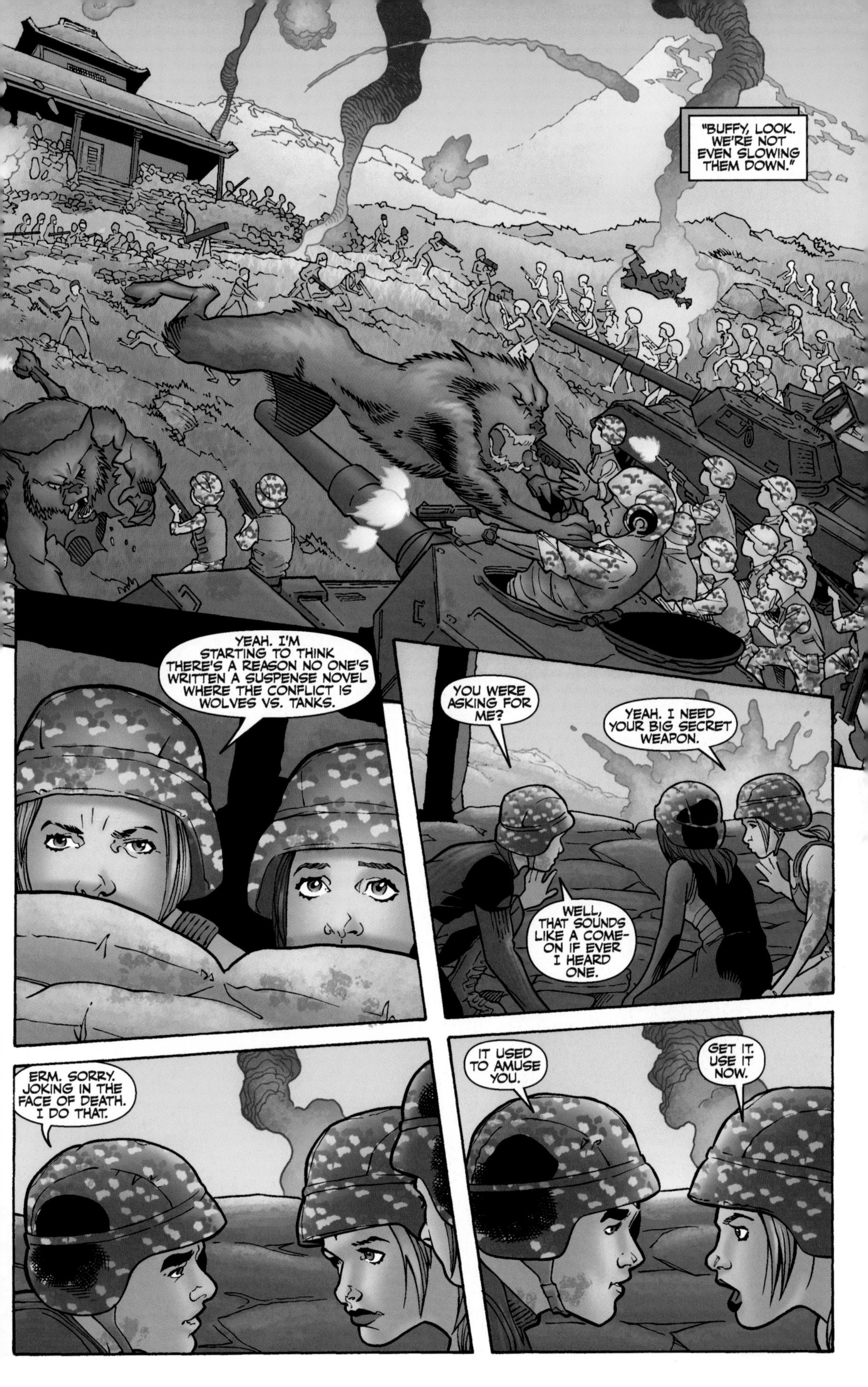
"BUFFY, LOOK. WE'RE NOT EVEN SLOWING THEM DOWN."
YEAH. I'M STARTING TO THINK THERE'S A REASON NO ONE'S WRITTEN A SUSPENSE NOVEL WHERE THE CONFLICT IS WOLVES VS. TANKS.
YOU WERE ASKING FOR ME?
YEAH. I NEED YOUR BIG SECRET WEAPON.
WELL, THAT SOUNDS LIKE A COME-ON IF EVER I HEARD ONE.
ERM. SORRY. JOKING IN THE FACE OF DEATH. I DO THAT.
IT USED TO AMUSE YOU.
GET IT. USE IT NOW.

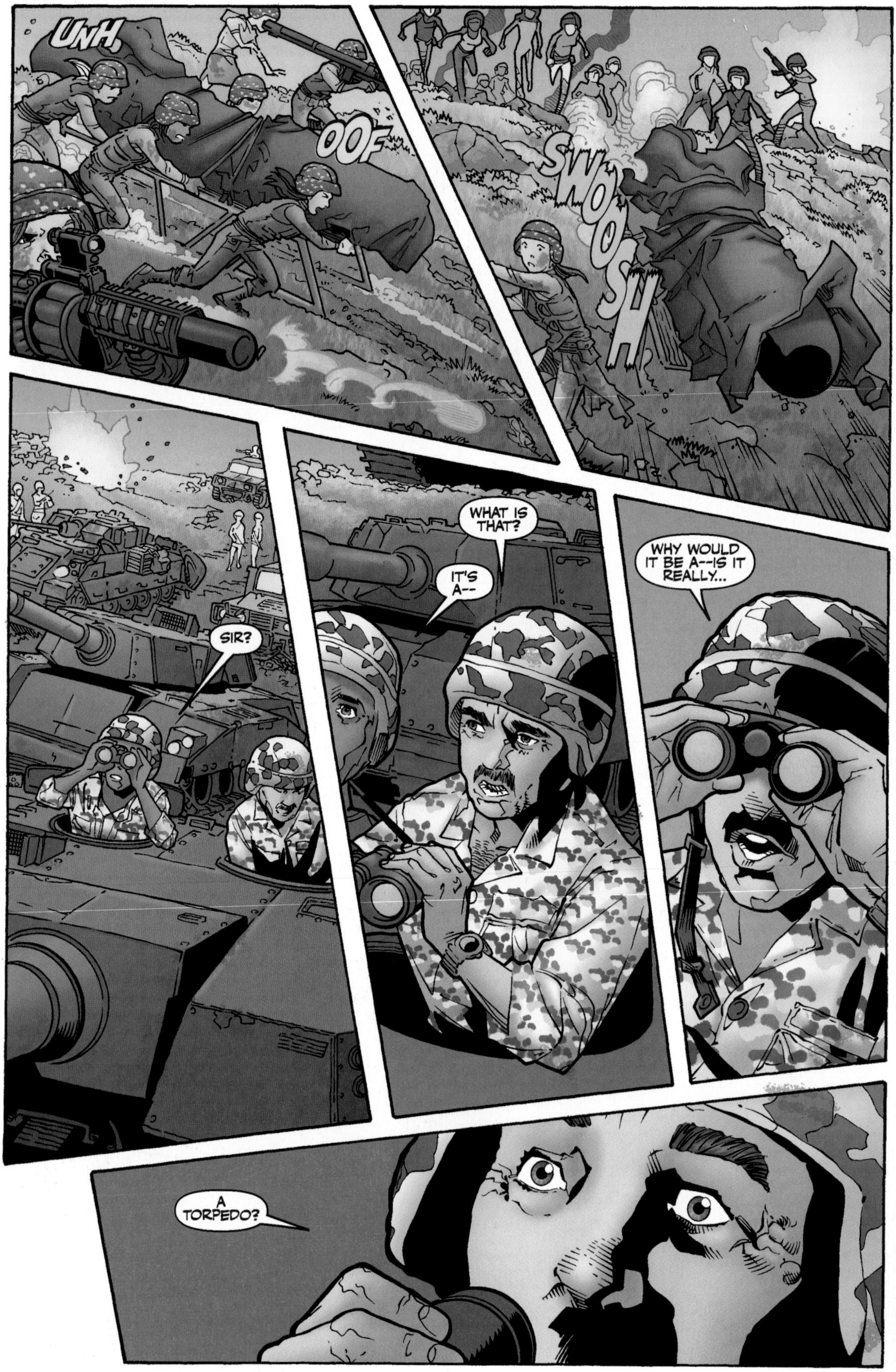
UNH
OOF
SWOOSH
SIR?
WHAT IS THAT?
IT'S A--
WHY WOULD IT BE A--IS IT REALLY...
A TORPEDO?

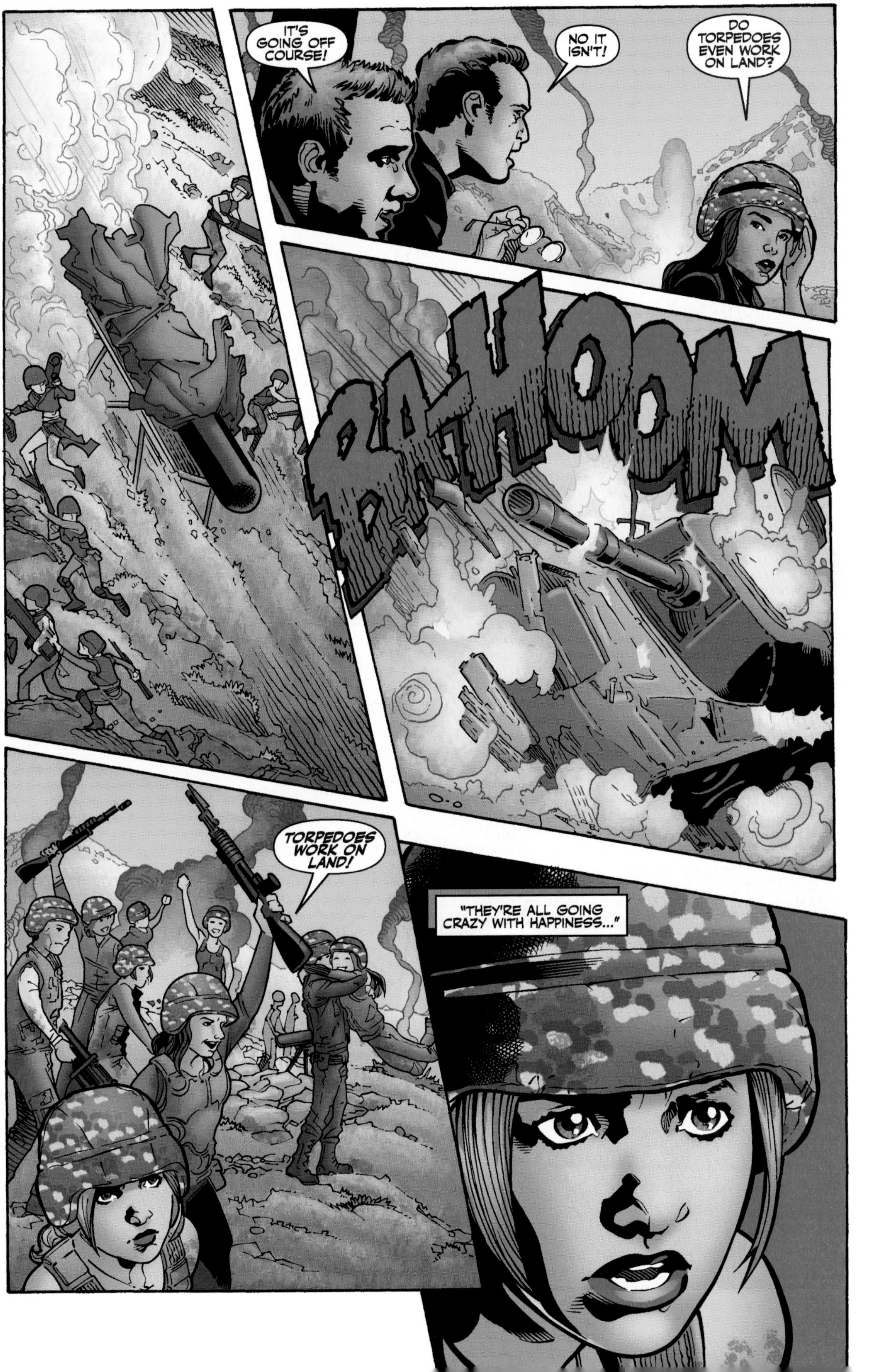
IT'S GOING OFF COURSE!
NO IT ISN'T!
DO TORPEDOES EVEN WORK ON LAND?
BA-HOOM
TORPEDOES WORK ON LAND!
"THEY'RE ALL GOING CRAZY WITH HAPPINESS..."

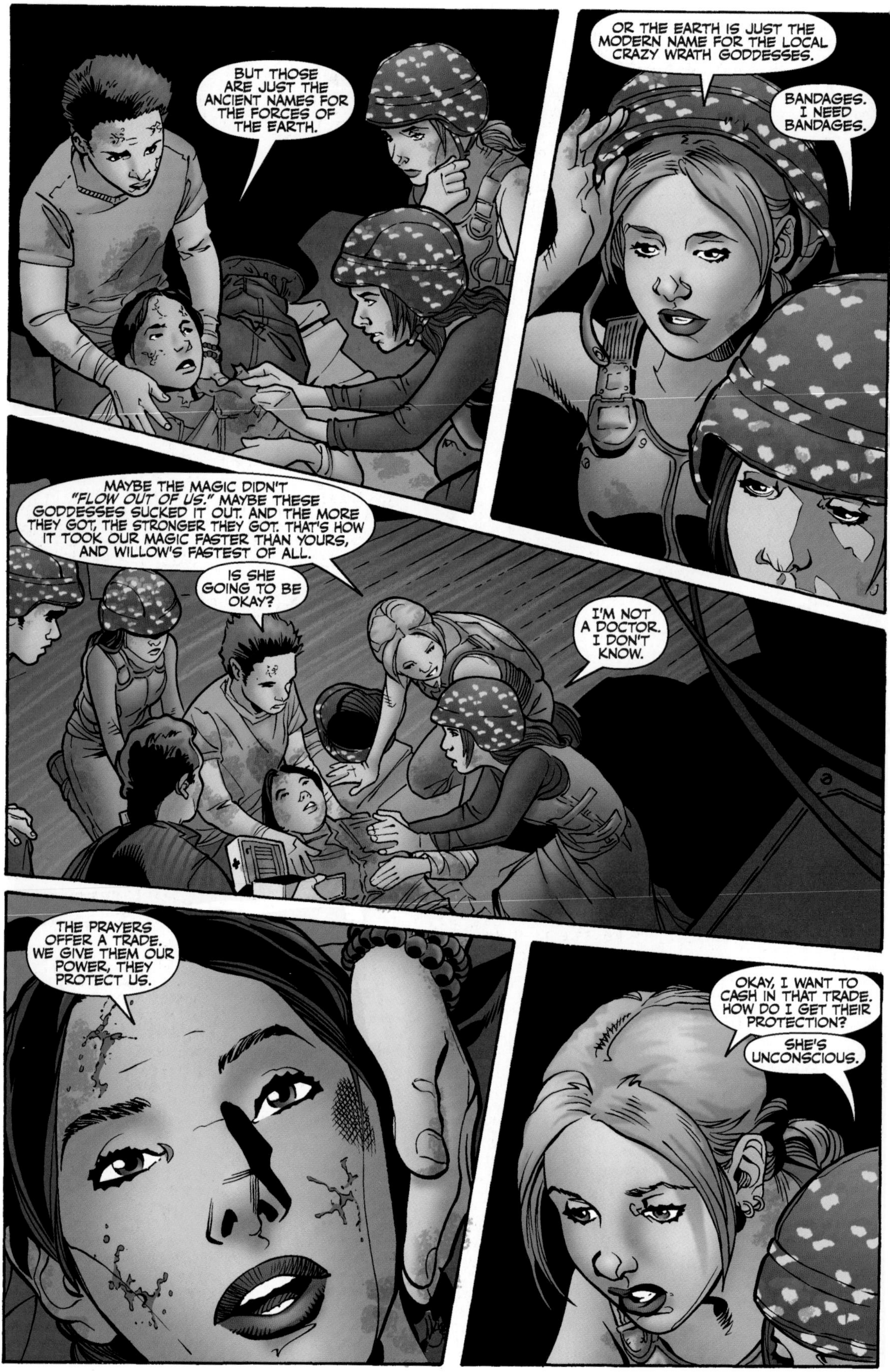
BUT THOSE ARE JUST THE ANCIENT NAMES FOR THE FORCES OF THE EARTH.
OR THE EARTH IS JUST THE MODERN NAME FOR THE LOCAL CRAZY WRATH GODDESSES.
BANDAGES. I NEED BANDAGES.
MAYBE THE MAGIC DIDN'T *"FLOW OUT OF US."* MAYBE THESE GODDESSES SUCKED IT OUT. AND THE MORE THEY GOT, THE STRONGER THEY GOT. THAT'S HOW IT TOOK OUR MAGIC FASTER THAN YOURS, AND WILLOW'S FASTEST OF ALL.
IS SHE GOING TO BE OKAY?
I'M NOT A DOCTOR. I DON'T KNOW.
THE PRAYERS OFFER A TRADE. WE GIVE THEM OUR POWER, THEY PROTECT US.
OKAY, I WANT TO CASH IN THAT TRADE. HOW DO I GET THEIR PROTECTION?
SHE'S UNCONSCIOUS.

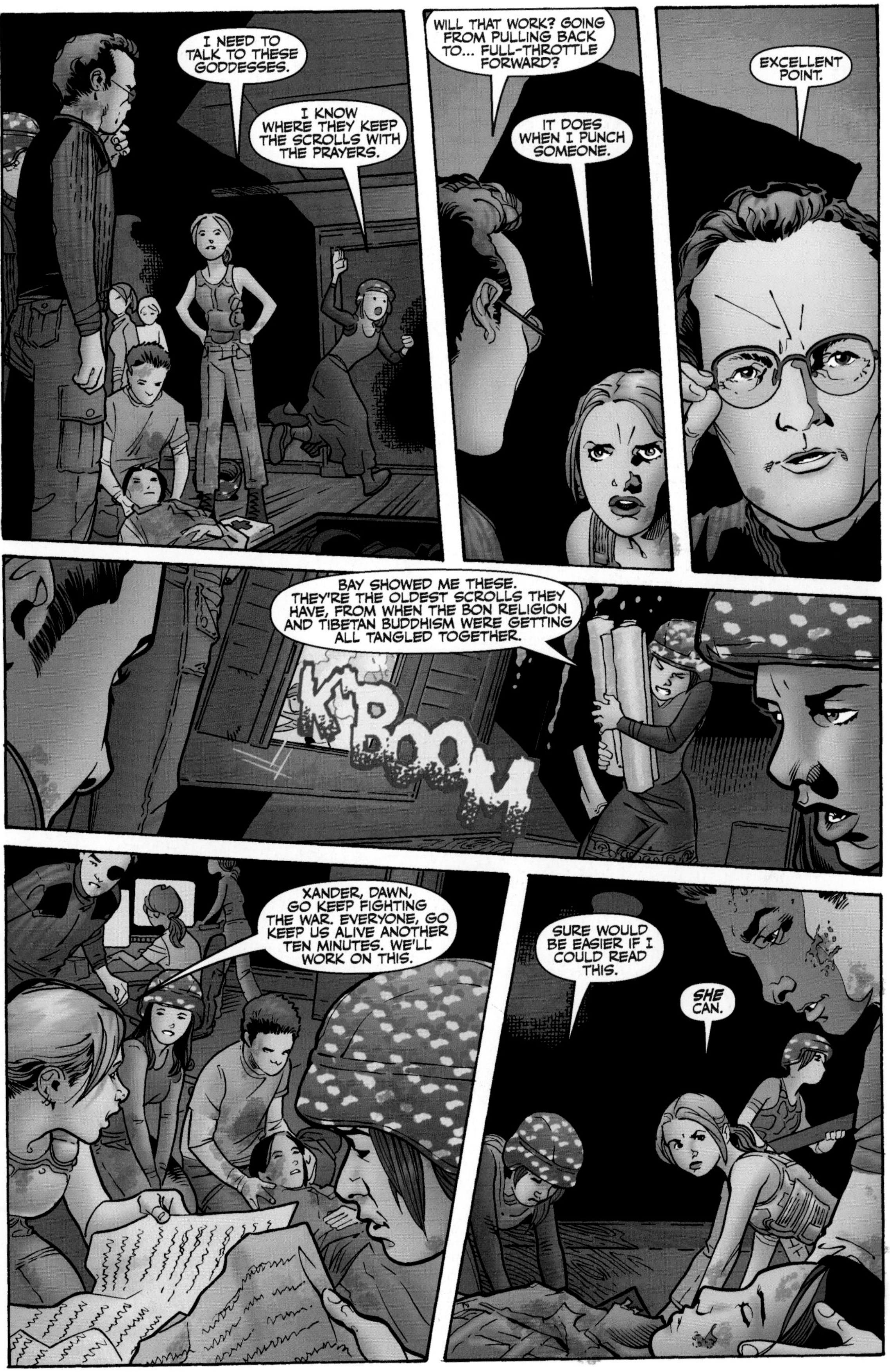
I NEED TO TALK TO THESE GODDESSES.
I KNOW WHERE THEY KEEP THE SCROLLS WITH THE PRAYERS.
WILL THAT WORK? GOING FROM PULLING BACK TO... FULL-THROTTLE FORWARD?
IT DOES WHEN I PUNCH SOMEONE.
EXCELLENT POINT.
BAY SHOWED ME THESE. THEY'RE THE OLDEST SCROLLS THEY HAVE, FROM WHEN THE BON RELIGION AND TIBETAN BUDDHISM WERE GETTING ALL TANGLED TOGETHER.
K*BOOM
XANDER, DAWN, GO KEEP FIGHTING THE WAR. EVERYONE, GO KEEP US ALIVE ANOTHER TEN MINUTES. WE'LL WORK ON THIS.
SURE WOULD BE EASIER IF I COULD READ THIS.
SHE CAN.

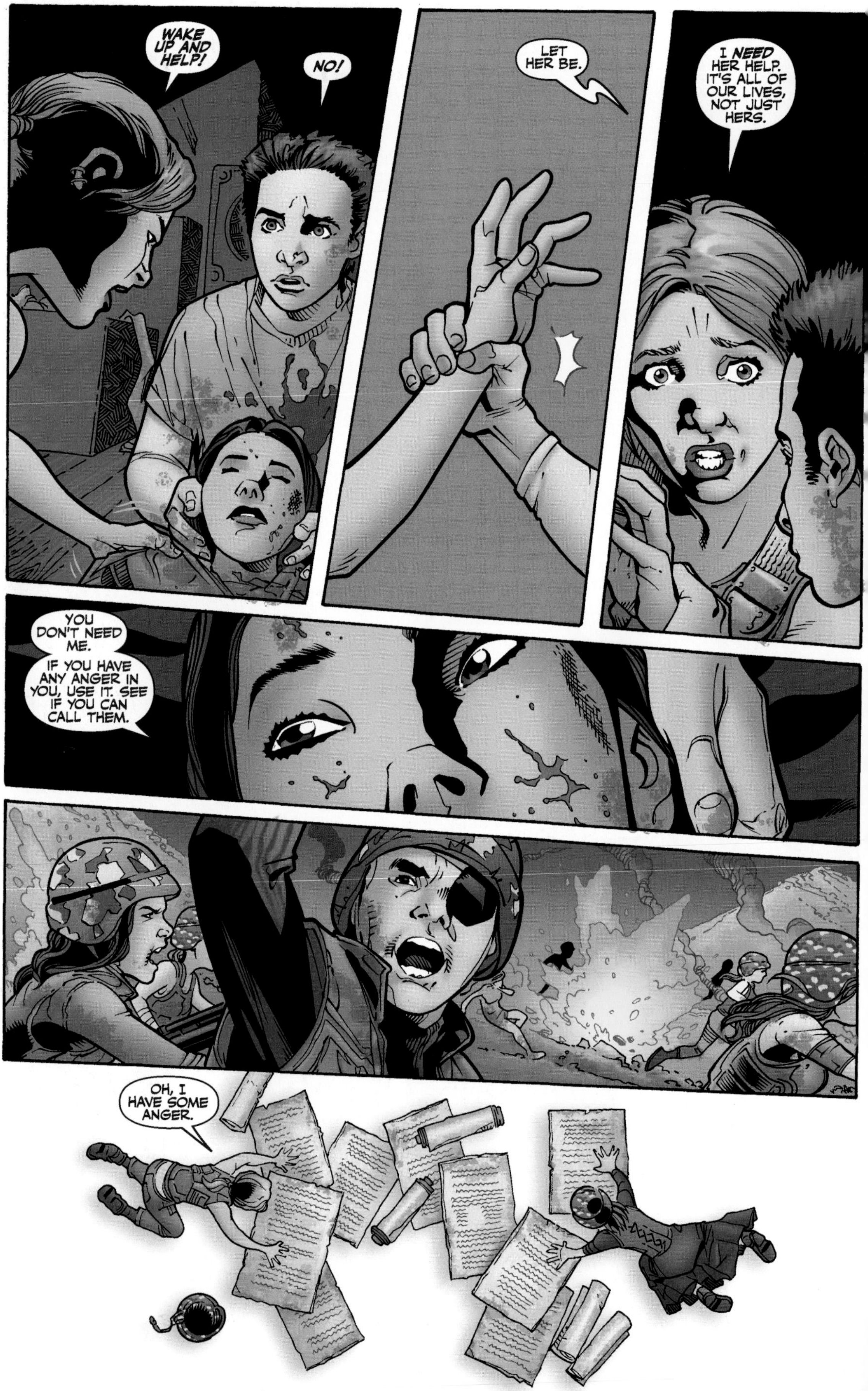
WAKE UP AND HELP!
NO!
LET HER BE.
I NEED HER HELP. IT'S ALL OF OUR LIVES, NOT JUST HERS.
YOU DON'T NEED ME.
IF YOU HAVE ANY ANGER IN YOU, USE IT. SEE IF YOU CAN CALL THEM.
OH, I HAVE SOME ANGER.

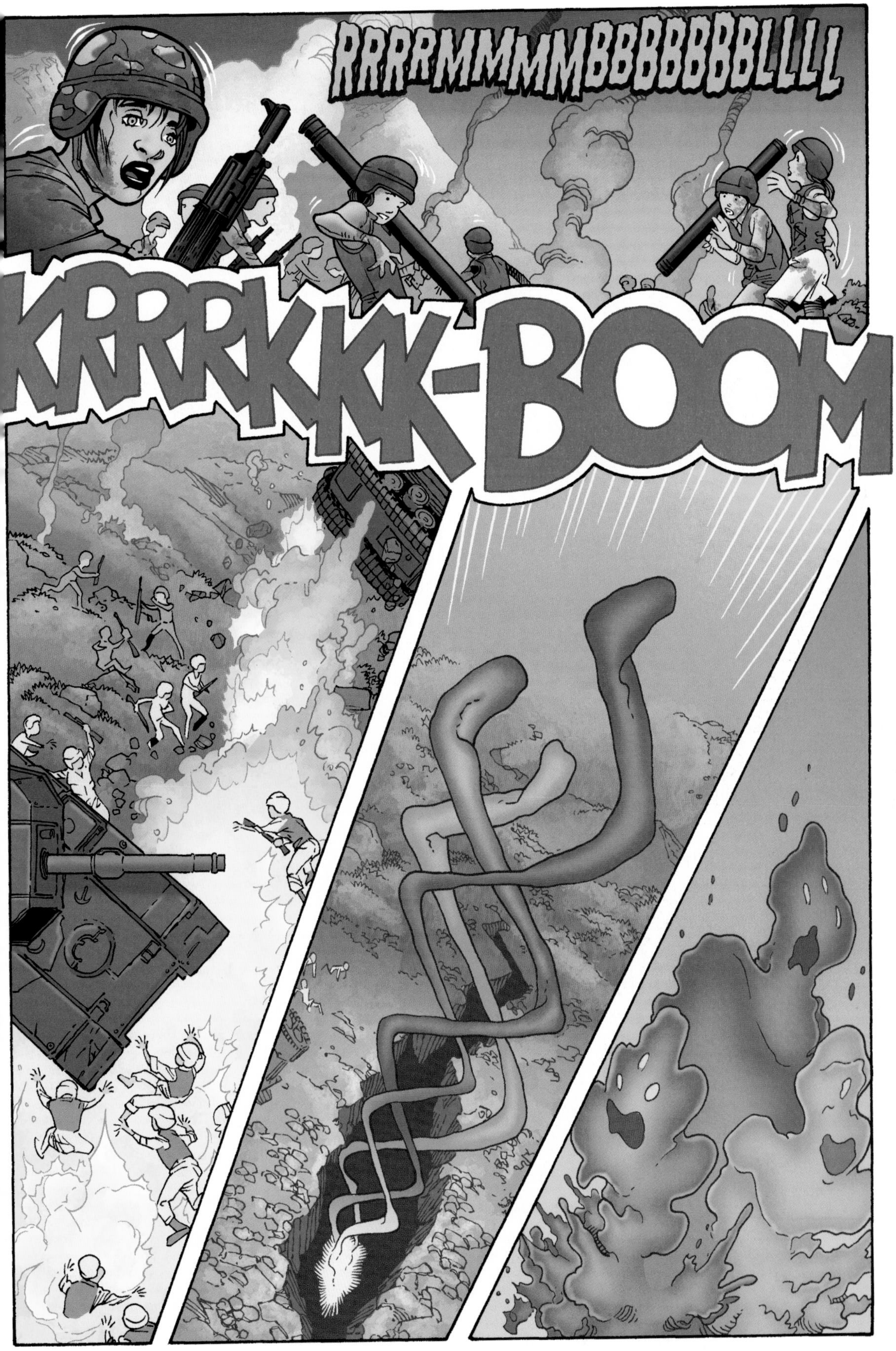
RRRRMMMMMBBBBBBBLLLL
KRRRKKK-BOOM

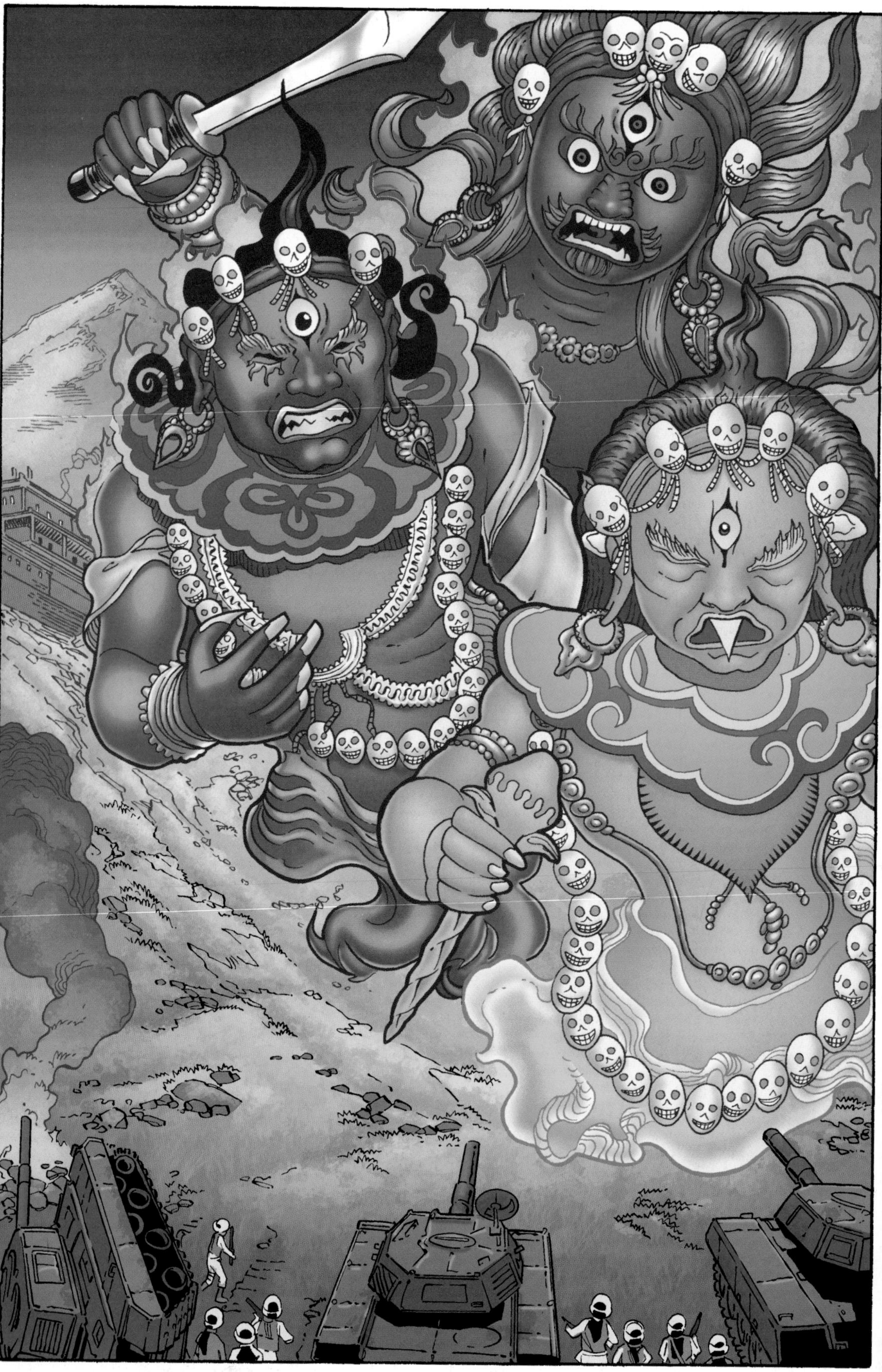

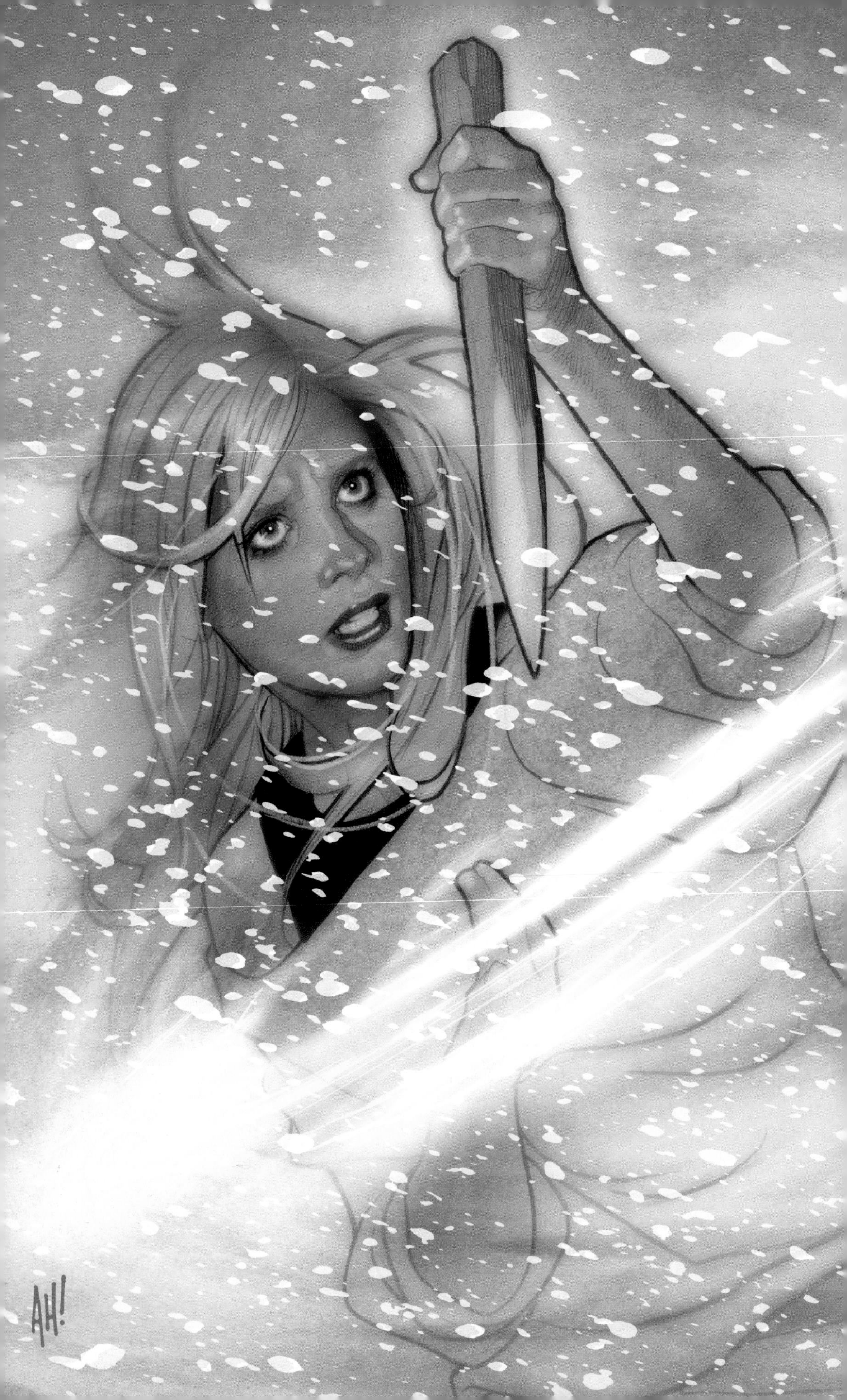
AH!

RETREAT

PART FIVE

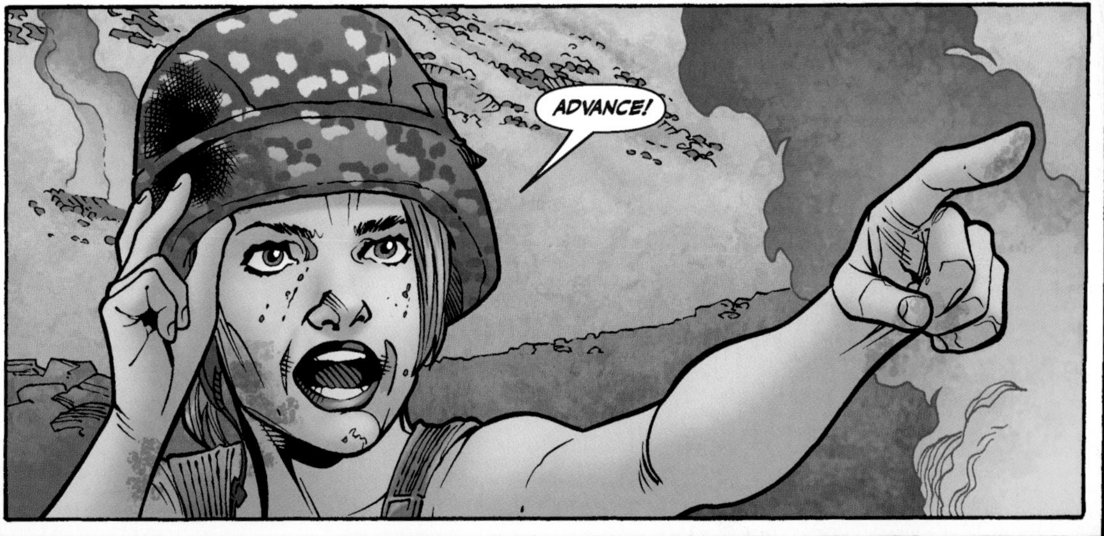
ADVANCE!

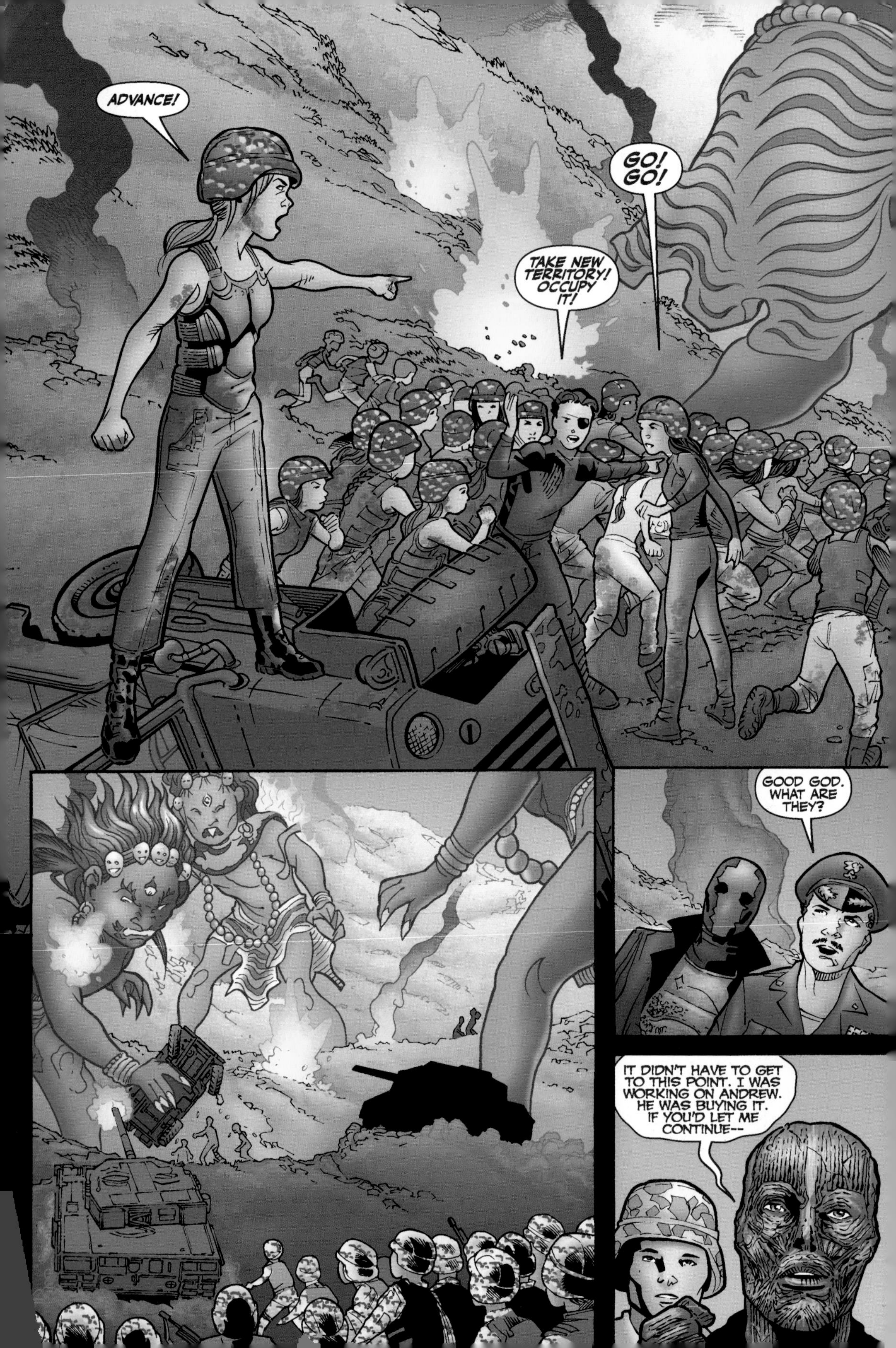
ADVANCE!
GO! GO!
TAKE NEW TERRITORY! OCCUPY IT!
GOOD GOD. WHAT ARE THEY?
IT DIDN'T HAVE TO GET TO THIS POINT. I WAS WORKING ON ANDREW. HE WAS BUYING IT. IF YOU'D LET ME CONTINUE--

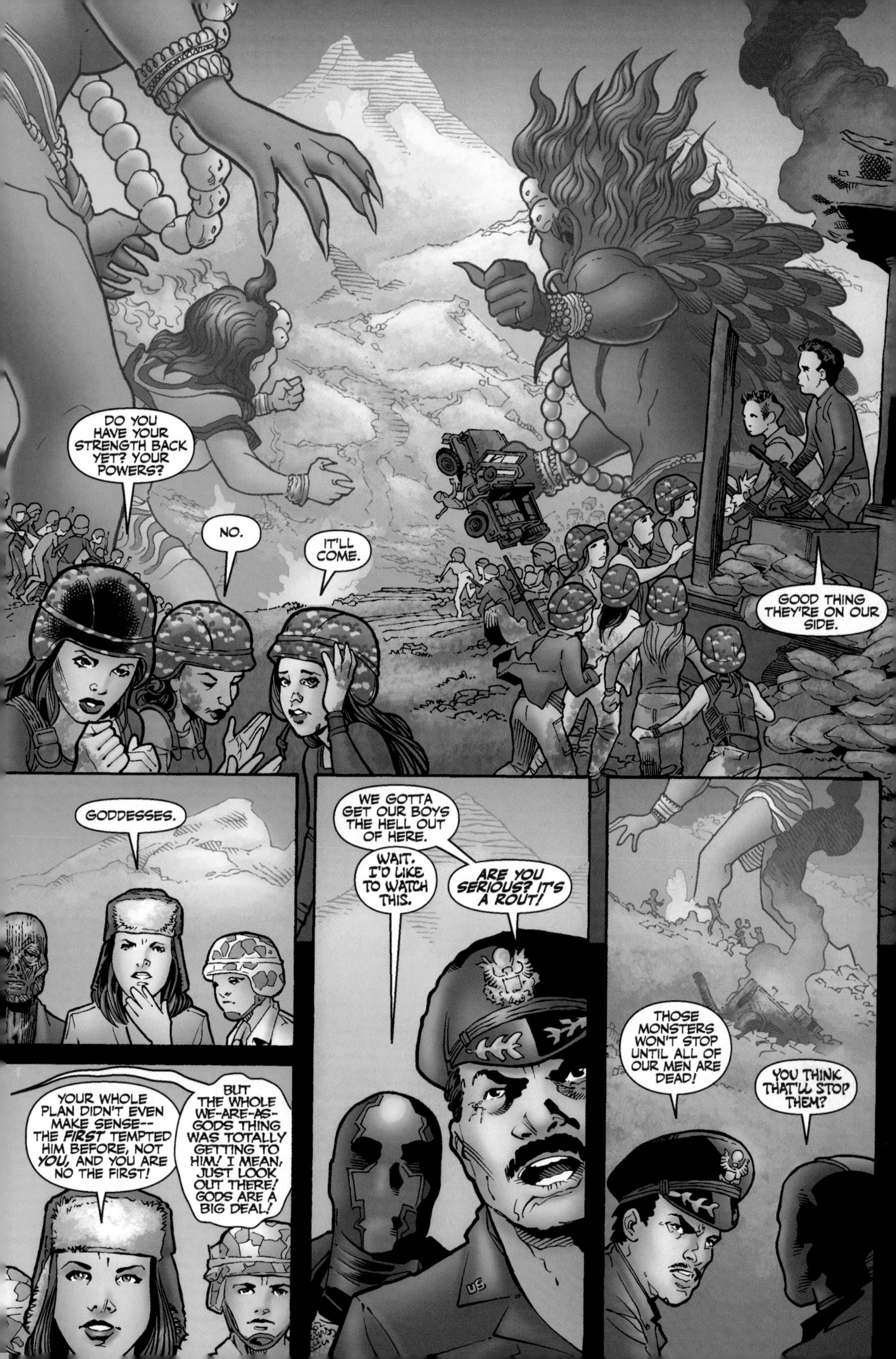
DO YOU HAVE YOUR STRENGTH BACK YET? YOUR POWERS?
NO.
IT'LL COME.
GOOD THING THEY'RE ON OUR SIDE.
GODDESSES.
WE GOTTA GET OUR BOYS THE HELL OUT OF HERE.
WAIT. I'D LIKE TO WATCH THIS.
ARE YOU SERIOUS? IT'S A ROUT!
YOUR WHOLE PLAN DIDN'T EVEN MAKE SENSE-- THE FIRST TEMPTED HIM BEFORE, NOT YOU, AND YOU ARE NO THE FIRST!
BUT THE WHOLE WE-ARE-AS-GODS THING WAS TOTALLY GETTING TO HIM! I MEAN, JUST LOOK OUT THERE! GODS ARE A BIG DEAL!
THOSE MONSTERS WON'T STOP UNTIL ALL OF OUR MEN ARE DEAD!
YOU THINK THAT'LL STOP THEM?

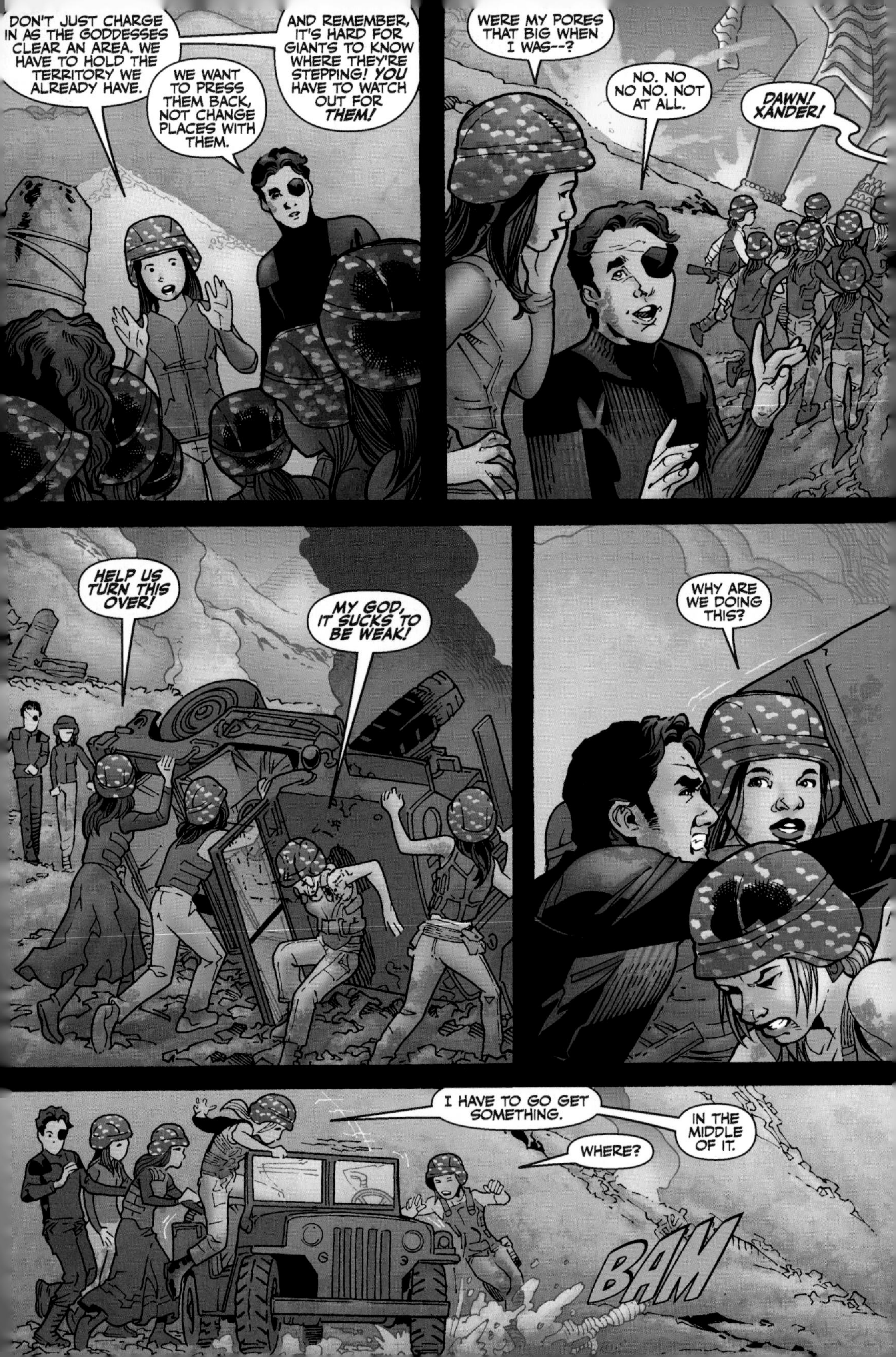
DON'T JUST CHARGE IN AS THE GODDESSES CLEAR AN AREA. WE HAVE TO HOLD THE TERRITORY WE ALREADY HAVE.
WE WANT TO PRESS THEM BACK, NOT CHANGE PLACES WITH THEM.
AND REMEMBER, IT'S HARD FOR GIANTS TO KNOW WHERE THEY'RE STEPPING! YOU HAVE TO WATCH OUT FOR THEM!
WERE MY PORES THAT BIG WHEN I WAS--?
NO. NO NO NO. NOT AT ALL.
DAWN! XANDER!
HELP US TURN THIS OVER!
MY GOD, IT SUCKS TO BE WEAK!
WHY ARE WE DOING THIS?
I HAVE TO GO GET SOMETHING.
WHERE?
IN THE MIDDLE OF IT.
BAM

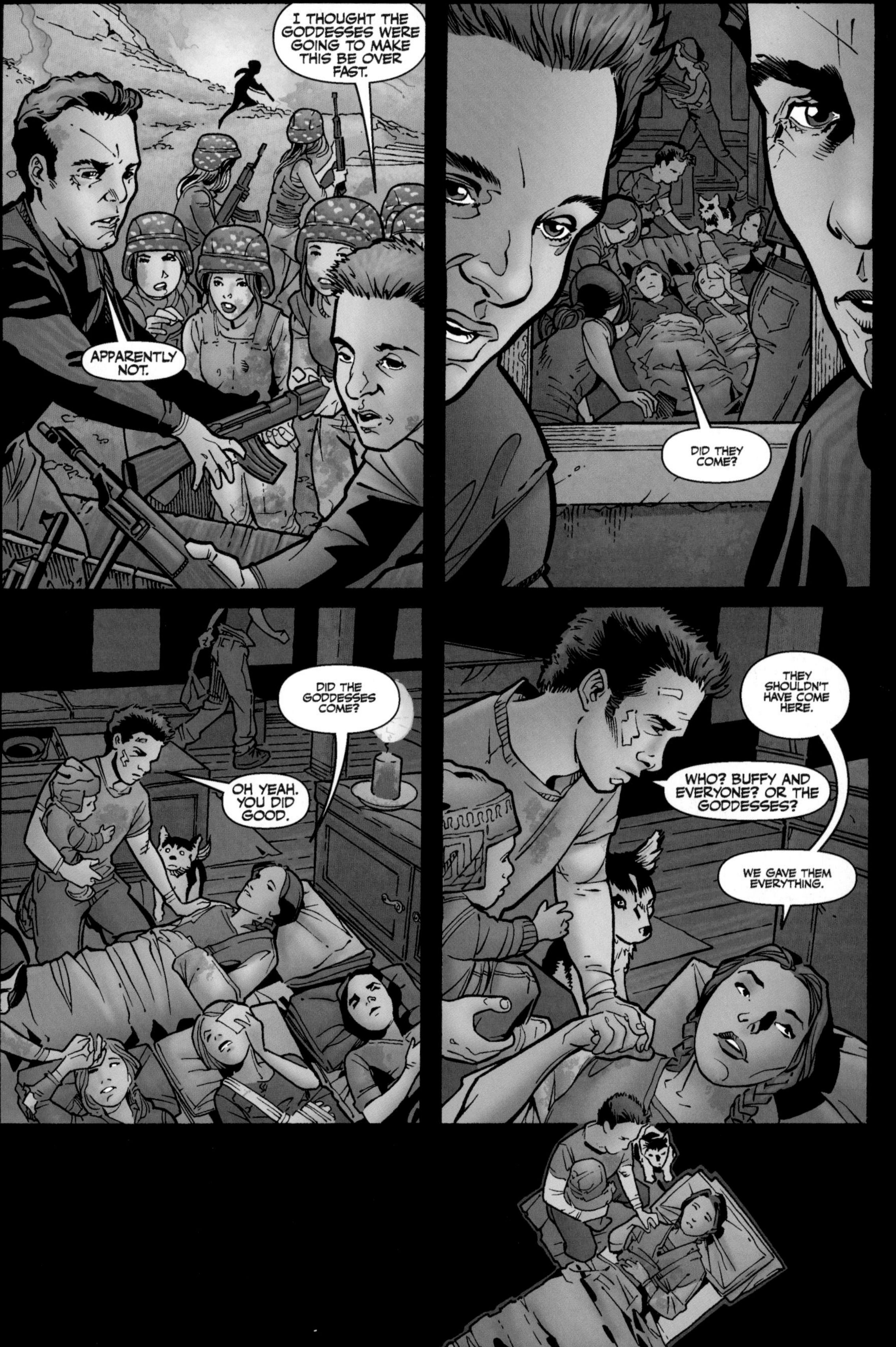
I THOUGHT THE GODDESSES WERE GOING TO MAKE THIS BE OVER FAST.
APPARENTLY NOT.
DID THEY COME?
DID THE GODDESSES COME?
OH YEAH. YOU DID GOOD.
THEY SHOULDN'T HAVE COME HERE.
WHO? BUFFY AND EVERYONE? OR THE GODDESSES?
WE GAVE THEM EVERYTHING.

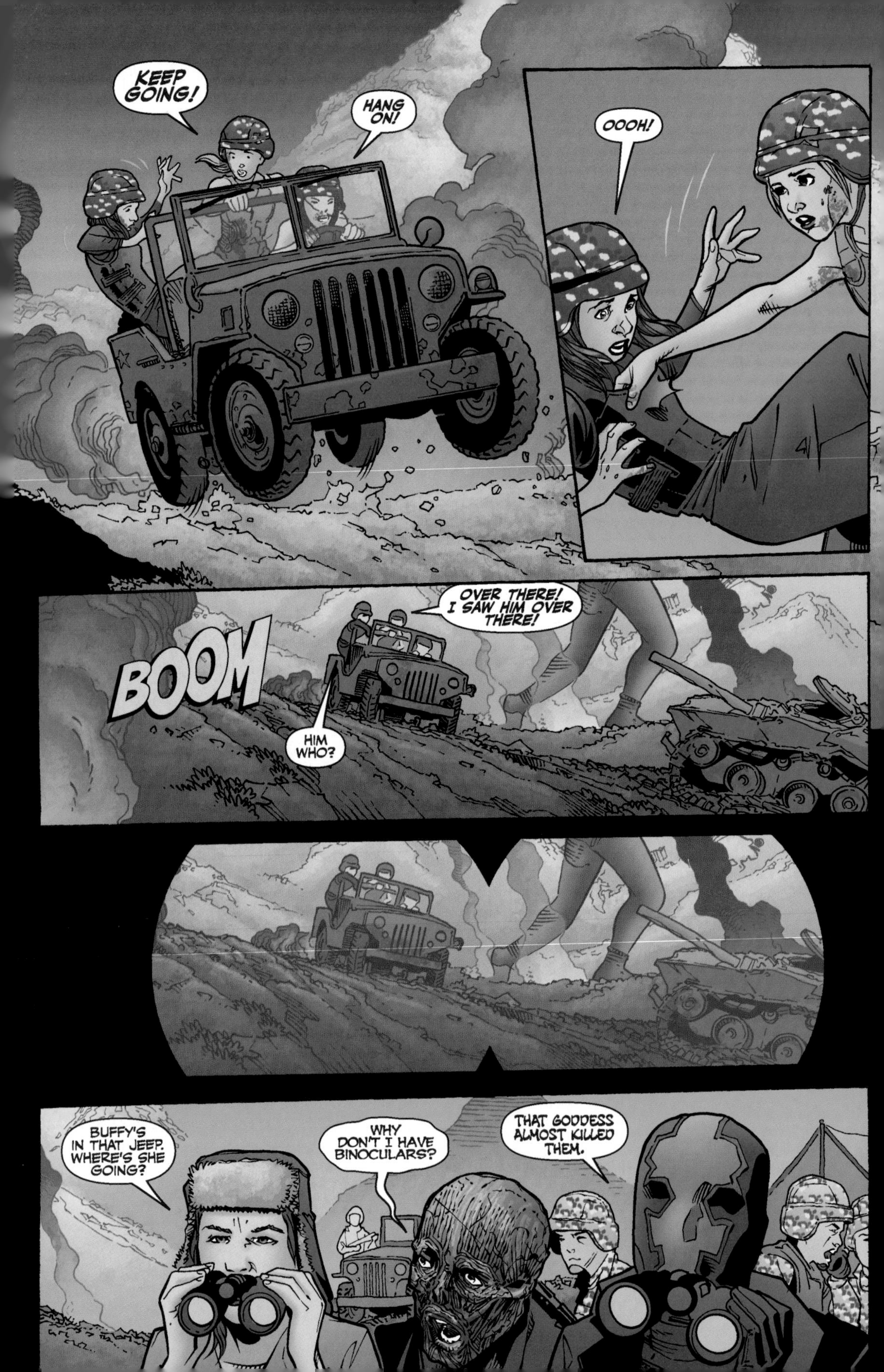
KEEP GOING!
HANG ON!
OOOH!
BOOM
OVER THERE! I SAW HIM OVER THERE!
HIM WHO?
BUFFY'S IN THAT JEEP. WHERE'S SHE GOING?
WHY DON'T I HAVE BINOCULARS?
THAT GODDESS ALMOST KILLED THEM.

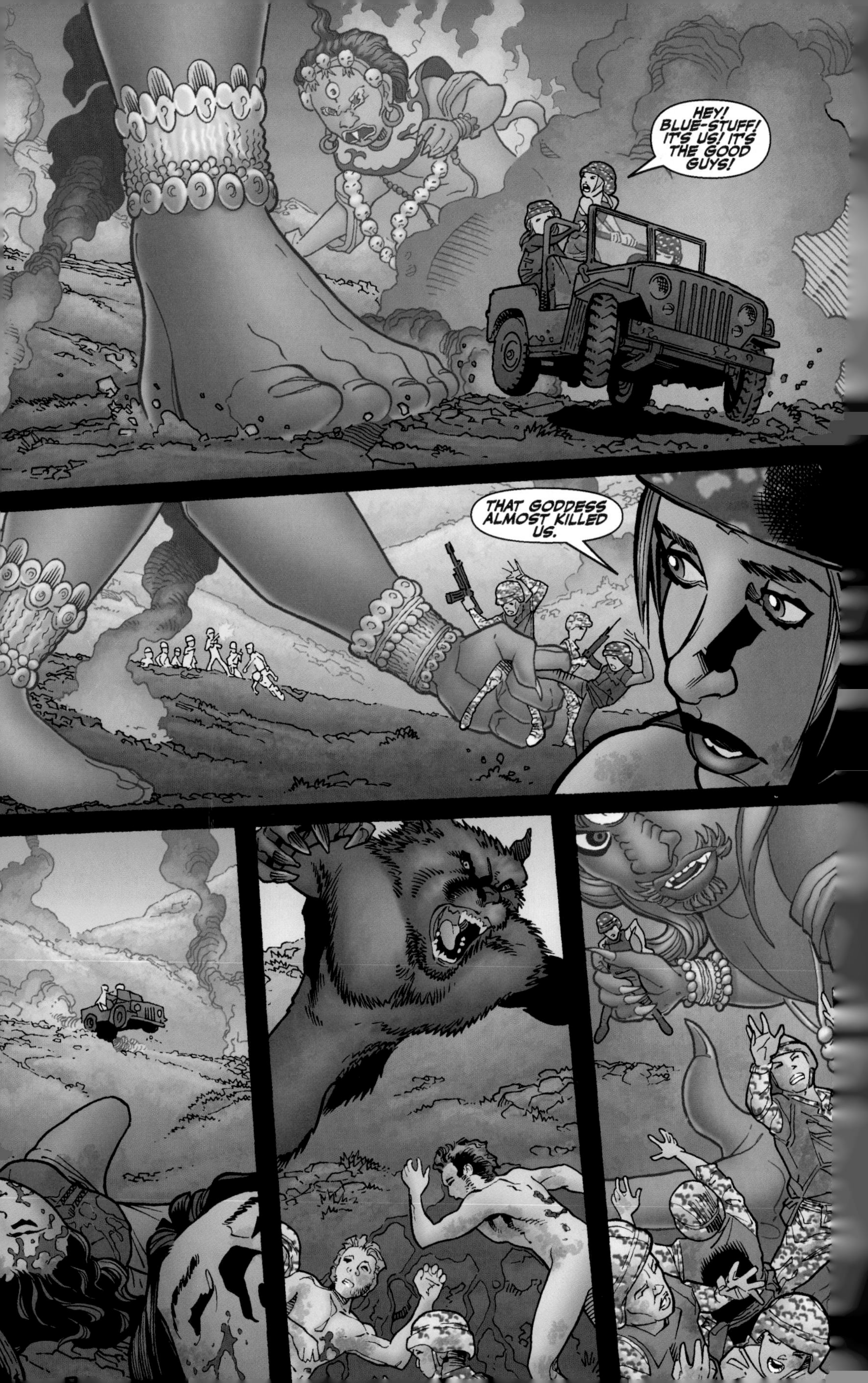
HEY! BLUE-STUFF! IT'S US! IT'S THE GOOD GUYS!
THAT GODDESS ALMOST KILLED US.

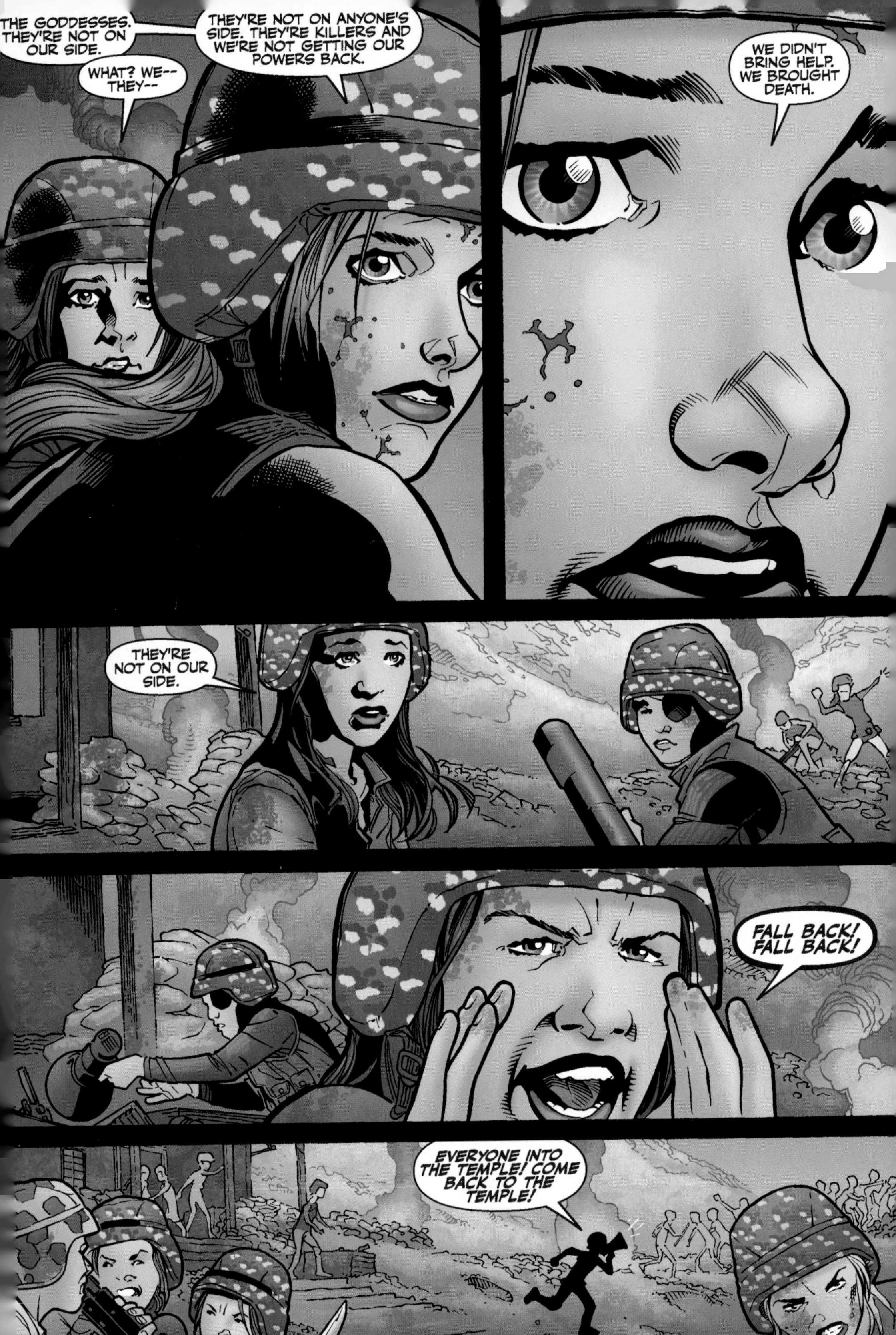
THE GODDESSES. THEY'RE NOT ON OUR SIDE.
WHAT? WE-- THEY--
THEY'RE NOT ON ANYONE'S SIDE. THEY'RE KILLERS AND WE'RE NOT GETTING OUR POWERS BACK.
WE DIDN'T BRING HELP. WE BROUGHT DEATH.
THEY'RE NOT ON OUR SIDE.
FALL BACK! FALL BACK!
EVERYONE INTO THE TEMPLE! COME BACK TO THE TEMPLE!

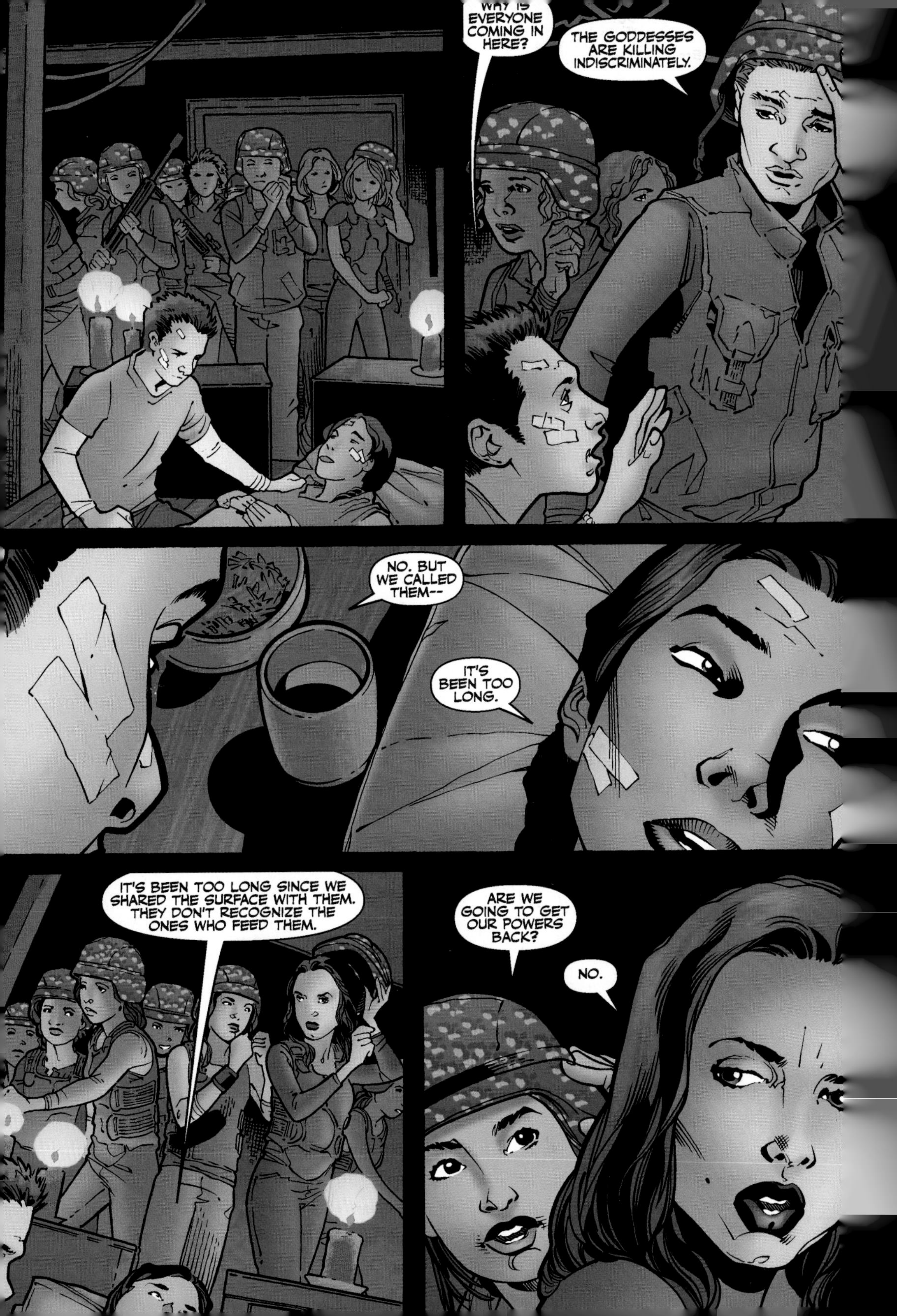
WHY IS EVERYONE COMING IN HERE?
THE GODDESSES ARE KILLING INDISCRIMINATELY.
NO. BUT WE CALLED THEM--
IT'S BEEN TOO LONG.
IT'S BEEN TOO LONG SINCE WE SHARED THE SURFACE WITH THEM. THEY DON'T RECOGNIZE THE ONES WHO FEED THEM.
ARE WE GOING TO GET OUR POWERS BACK?
NO.

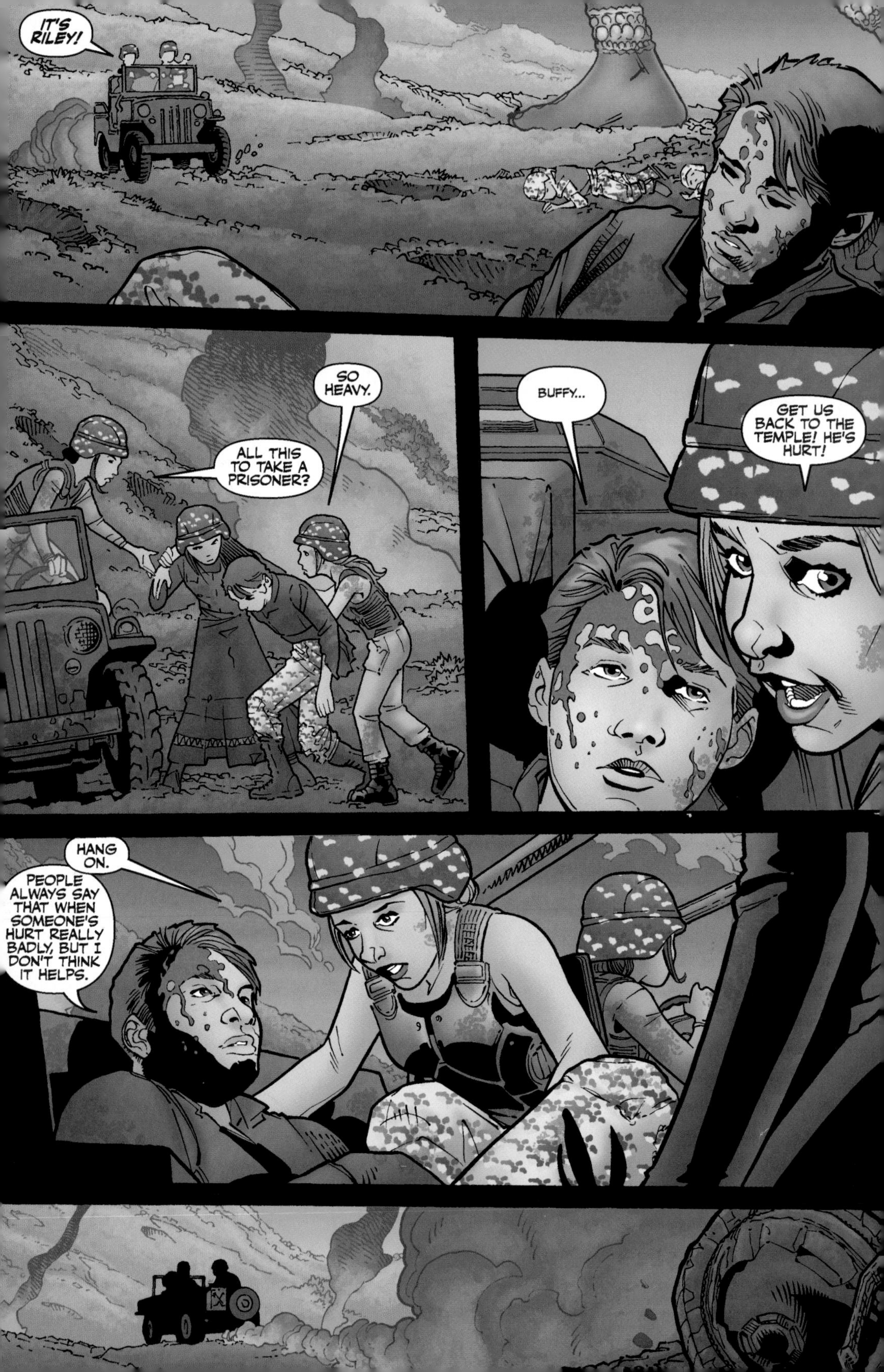
IT'S RILEY!
ALL THIS TO TAKE A PRISONER?
SO HEAVY.
BUFFY...
GET US BACK TO THE TEMPLE! HE'S HURT!
HANG ON.
PEOPLE ALWAYS SAY THAT WHEN SOMEONE'S HURT REALLY BADLY, BUT I DON'T THINK IT HELPS.

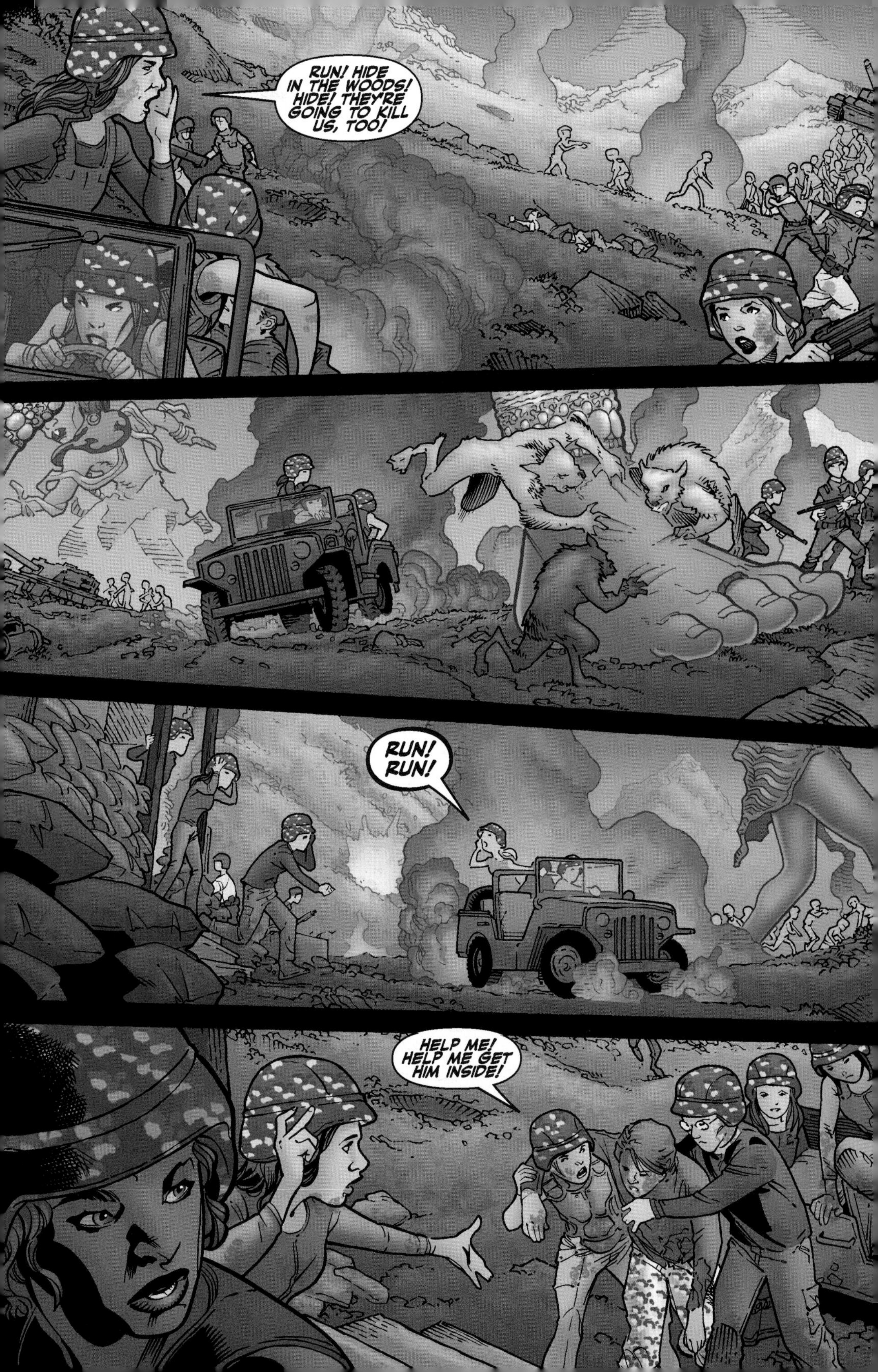
RUN! HIDE IN THE WOODS! HIDE! THEY'RE GOING TO KILL US, TOO!
RUN! RUN!
HELP ME! HELP ME GET HIM INSIDE!

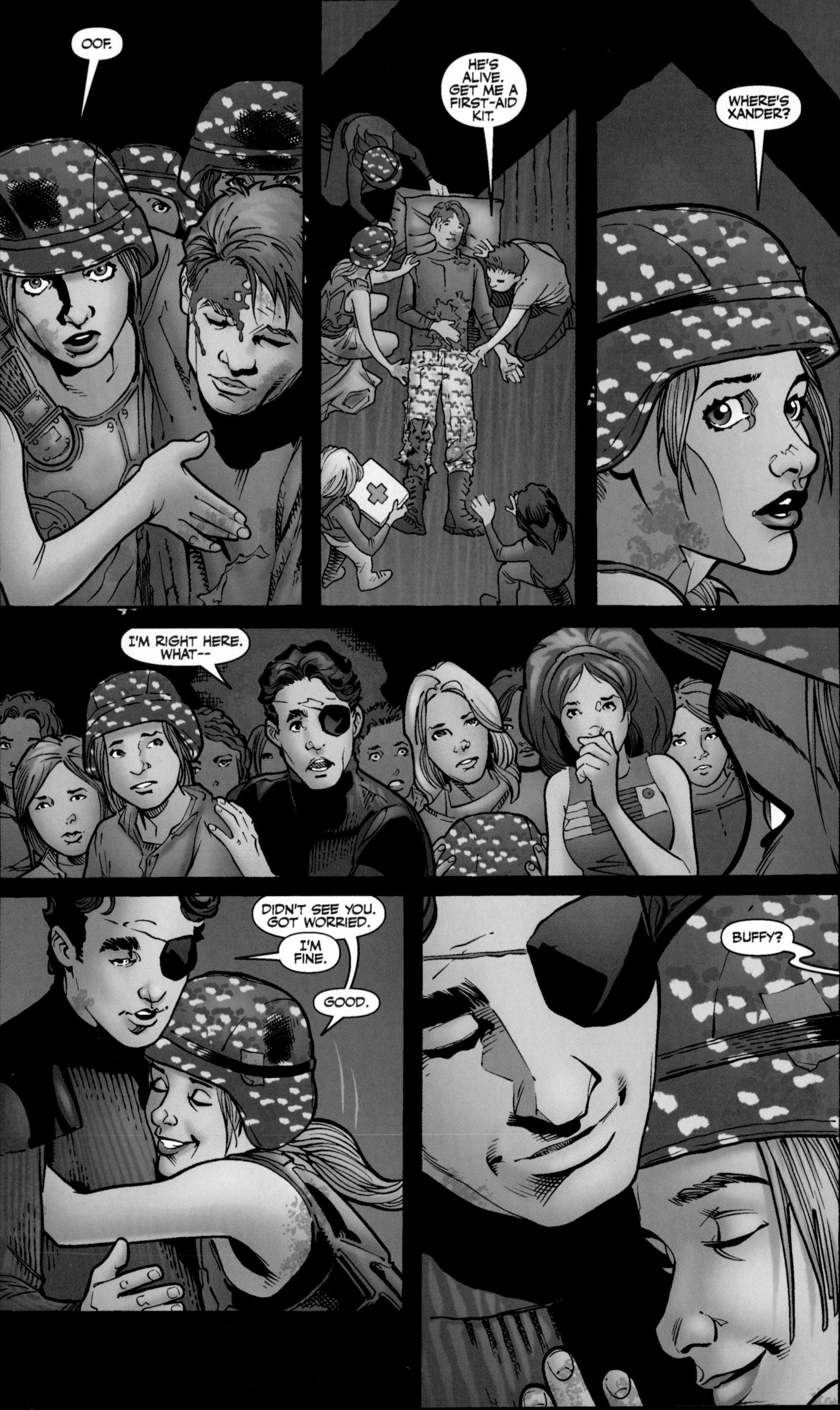
OOF.
HE'S ALIVE. GET ME A FIRST-AID KIT.
WHERE'S XANDER?
I'M RIGHT HERE. WHAT--
DIDN'T SEE YOU. GOT WORRIED.
I'M FINE.
GOOD.
BUFFY?

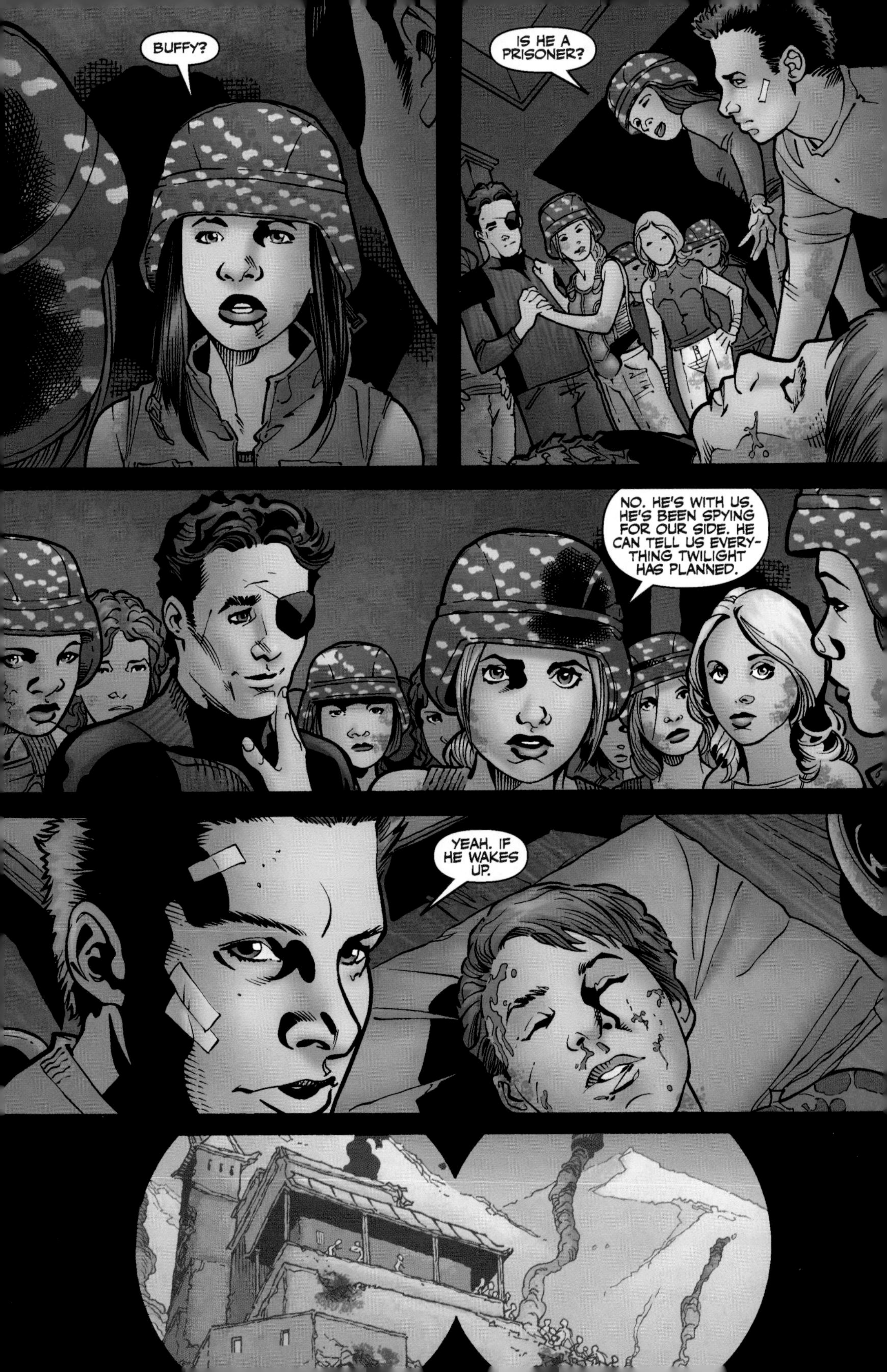
BUFFY?
IS HE A PRISONER?
NO. HE'S WITH US. HE'S BEEN SPYING FOR OUR SIDE. HE CAN TELL US EVERYTHING TWILIGHT HAS PLANNED.
YEAH. IF HE WAKES UP.

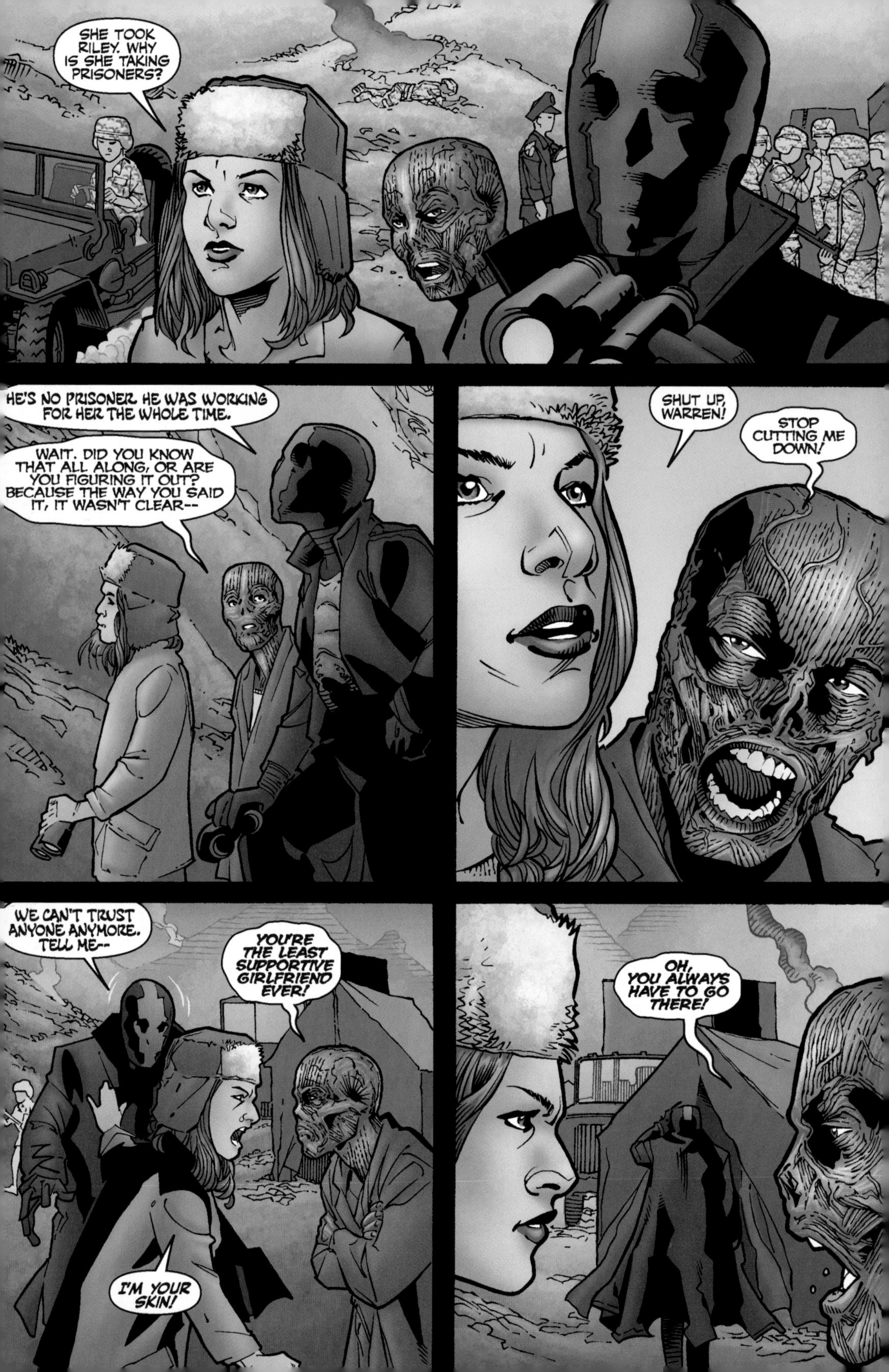
SHE TOOK RILEY. WHY IS SHE TAKING PRISONERS?
HE'S NO PRISONER HE WAS WORKING FOR HER THE WHOLE TIME.
WAIT. DID YOU KNOW THAT ALL ALONG, OR ARE YOU FIGURING IT OUT? BECAUSE THE WAY YOU SAID IT, IT WASN'T CLEAR--
SHUT UP, WARREN!
STOP CUTTING ME DOWN!
WE CAN'T TRUST ANYONE ANYMORE. TELL ME--
YOU'RE THE LEAST SUPPORTIVE GIRLFRIEND EVER!
I'M YOUR SKIN!
OH, YOU ALWAYS HAVE TO GO THERE!

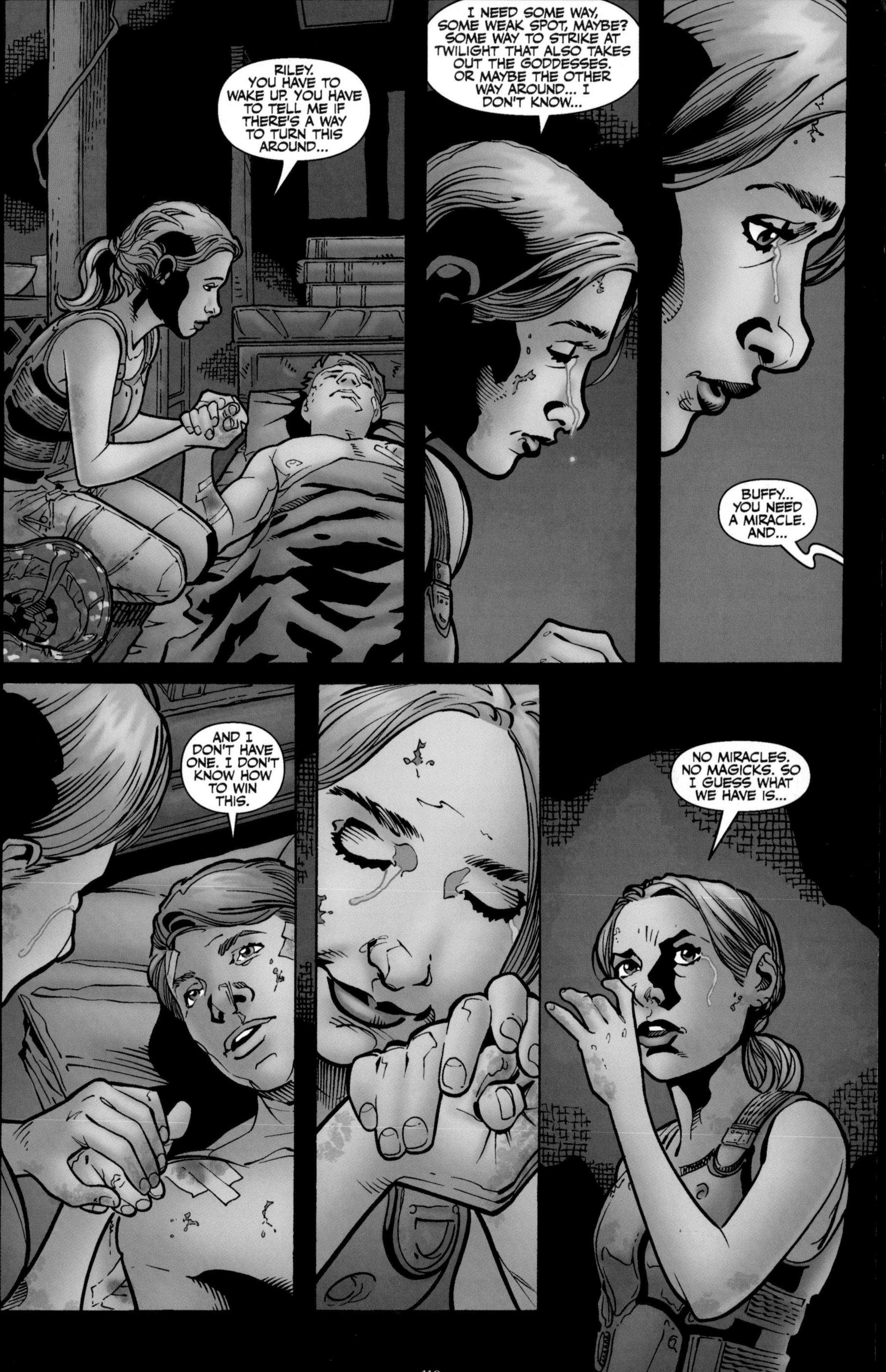

RILEY. YOU HAVE TO WAKE UP. YOU HAVE TO TELL ME IF THERE'S A WAY TO TURN THIS AROUND...
I NEED SOME WAY, SOME WEAK SPOT, MAYBE? SOME WAY TO STRIKE AT TWILIGHT THAT ALSO TAKES OUT THE GODDESSES. OR MAYBE THE OTHER WAY AROUND... I DON'T KNOW...
BUFFY... YOU NEED A MIRACLE. AND...
AND I DON'T HAVE ONE. I DON'T KNOW HOW TO WIN THIS.
NO MIRACLES. NO MAGICKS. SO I GUESS WHAT WE HAVE IS...

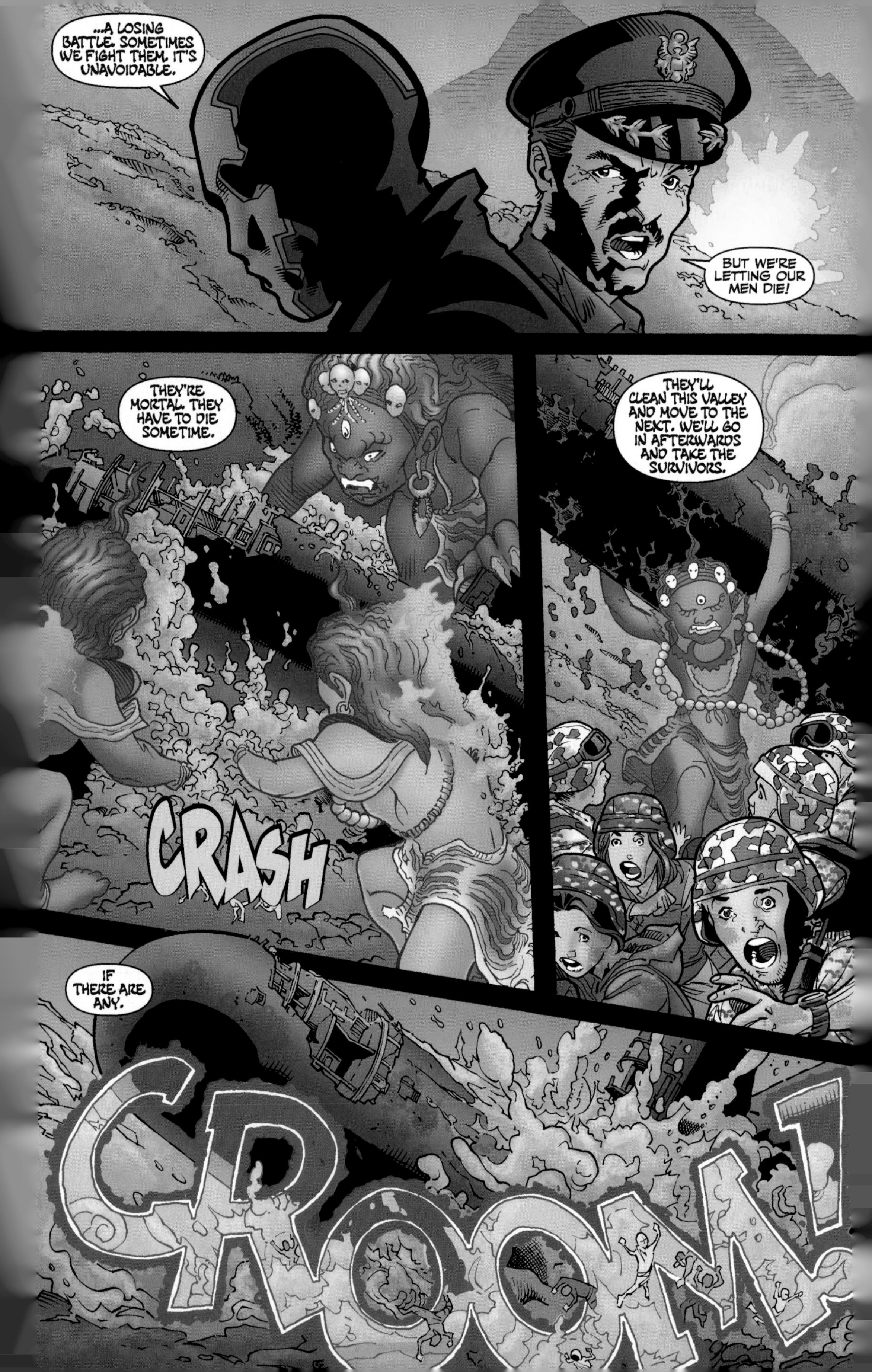
...A LOSING BATTLE. SOMETIMES WE FIGHT THEM. IT'S UNAVOIDABLE.
BUT WE'RE LETTING OUR MEN DIE!
THEY'RE MORTAL. THEY HAVE TO DIE SOMETIME.
CRASH
THEY'LL CLEAN THIS VALLEY AND MOVE TO THE NEXT. WE'LL GO IN AFTERWARDS AND TAKE THE SURVIVORS.
IF THERE ARE ANY.
CROOM!

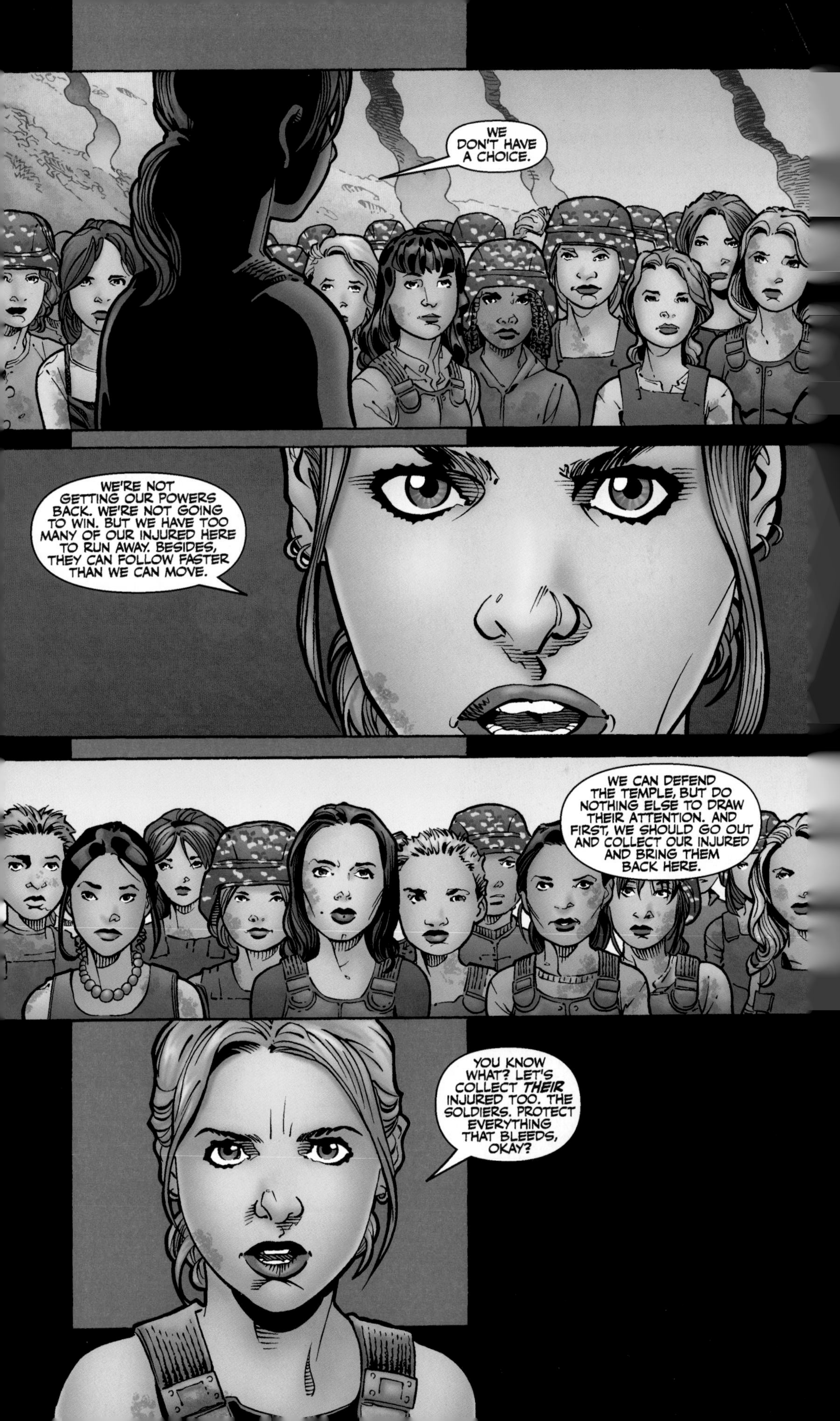
WE DON'T HAVE A CHOICE.
WE'RE NOT GETTING OUR POWERS BACK. WE'RE NOT GOING TO WIN. BUT WE HAVE TOO MANY OF OUR INJURED HERE TO RUN AWAY. BESIDES, THEY CAN FOLLOW FASTER THAN WE CAN MOVE.
WE CAN DEFEND THE TEMPLE, BUT DO NOTHING ELSE TO DRAW THEIR ATTENTION. AND FIRST, WE SHOULD GO OUT AND COLLECT OUR INJURED AND BRING THEM BACK HERE.
YOU KNOW WHAT? LET'S COLLECT *THEIR* INJURED TOO. THE SOLDIERS. PROTECT EVERYTHING THAT BLEEDS, OKAY?

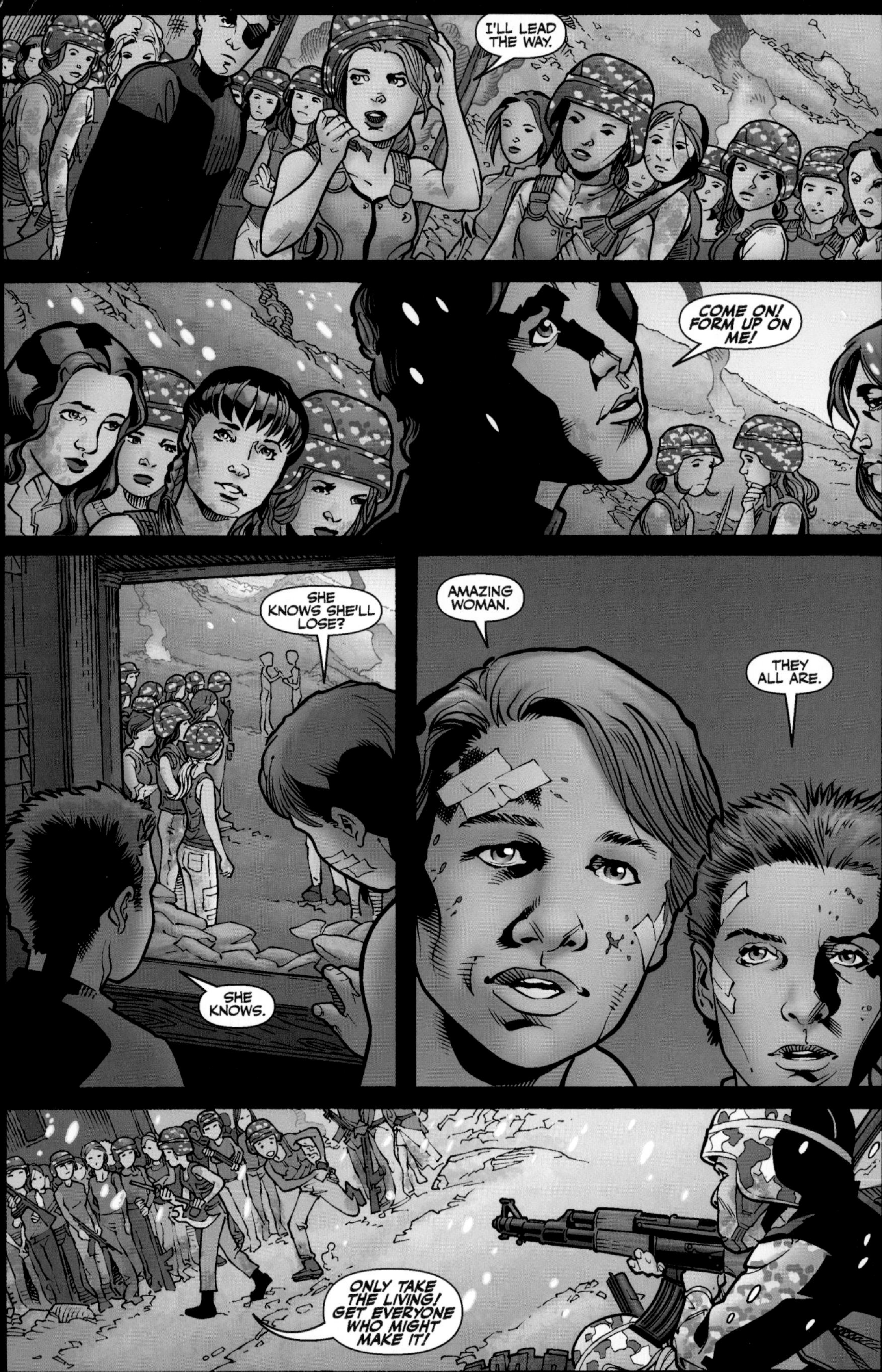
I'LL LEAD THE WAY.
COME ON! FORM UP ON ME!
SHE KNOWS SHE'LL LOSE?
SHE KNOWS.
AMAZING WOMAN.
THEY ALL ARE.
ONLY TAKE THE LIVING! GET EVERYONE WHO MIGHT MAKE IT!

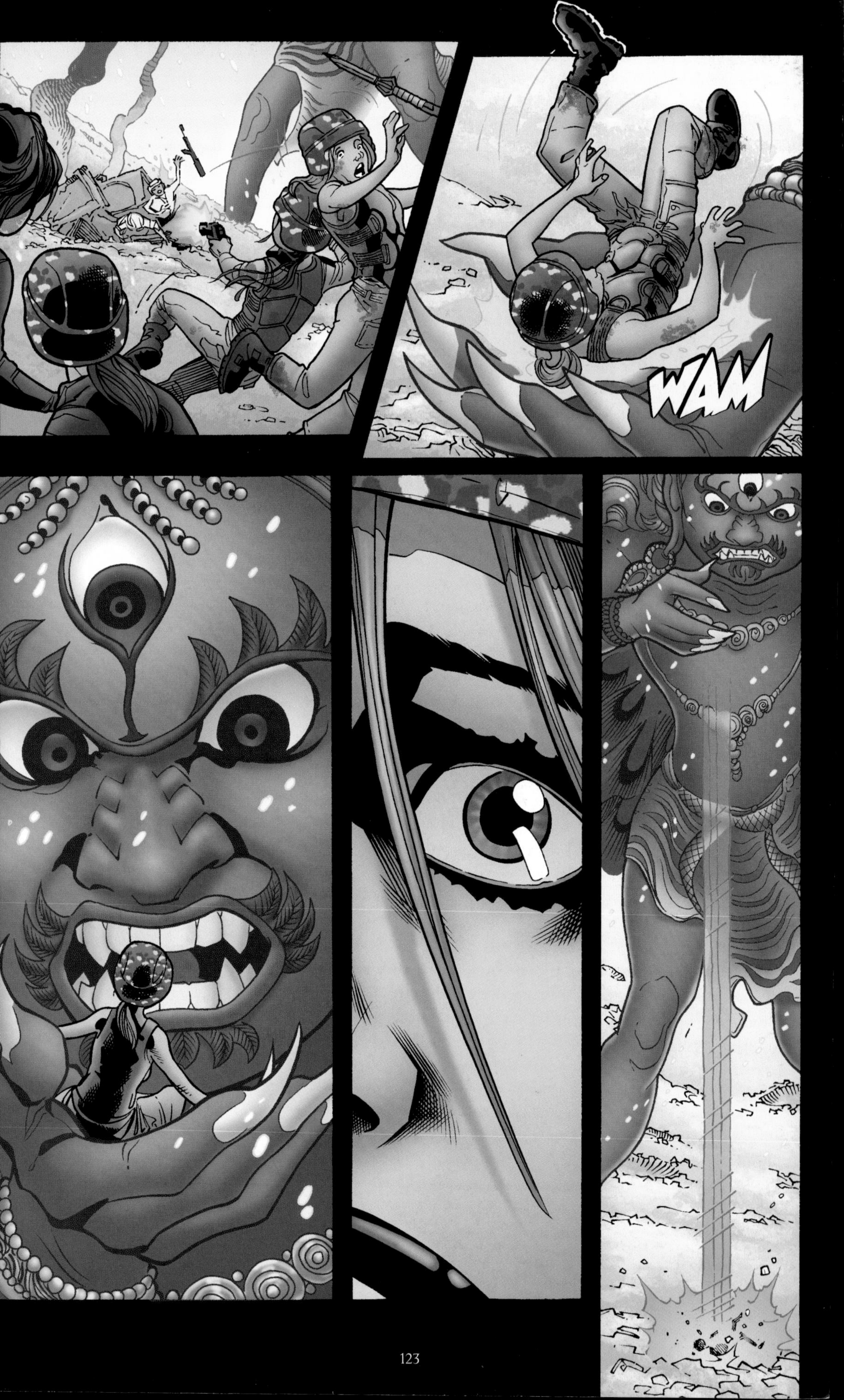
WAM

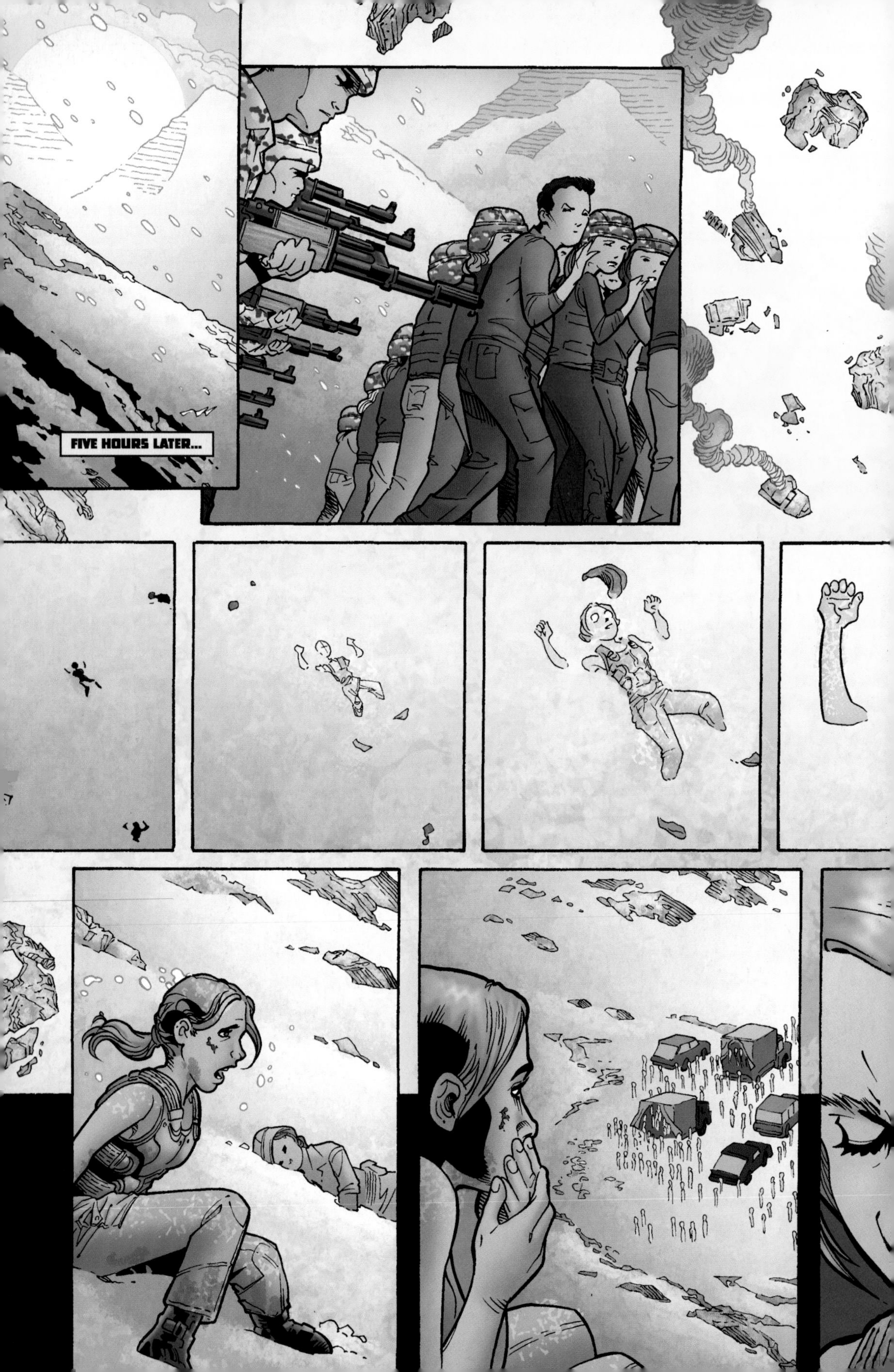
FIVE HOURS LATER...

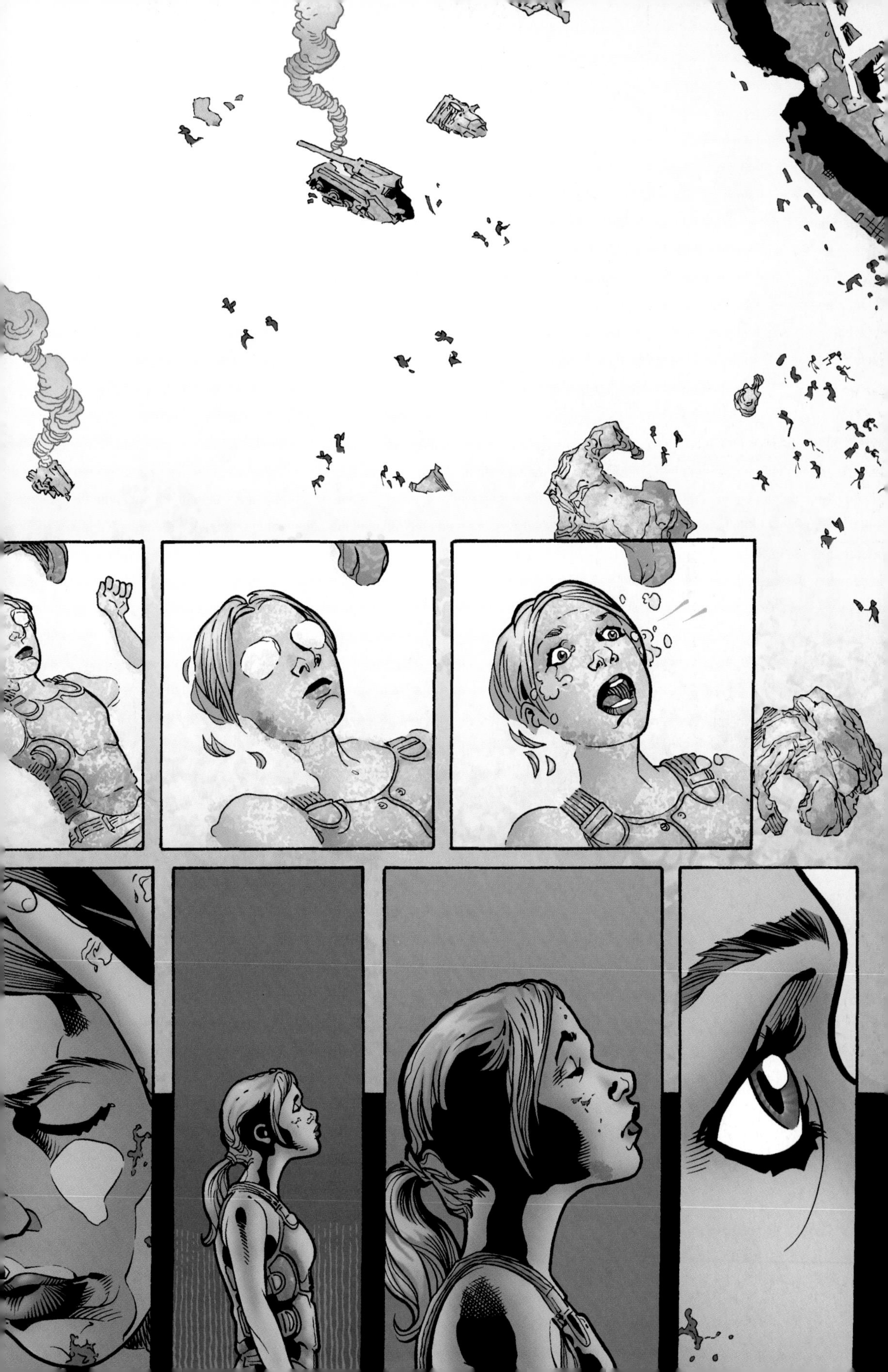

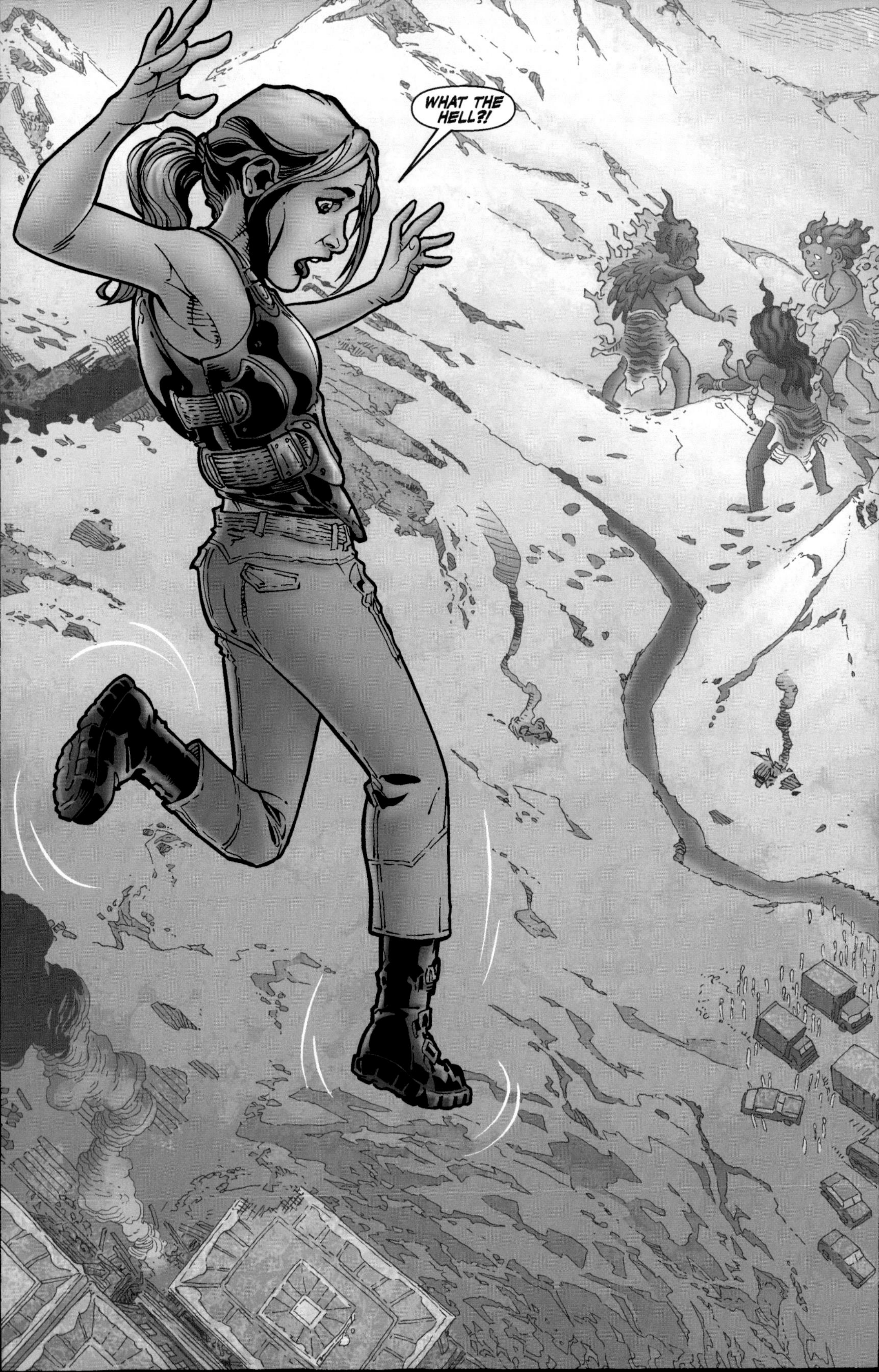
WHAT THE HELL?!

THE END

COVERS FROM

BUFFY THE VAMPIRE SLAYER

ISSUES #26–#28 & #30

By

GEORGES JEANTY

with

DEXTER VINES & MICHELLE MADSEN

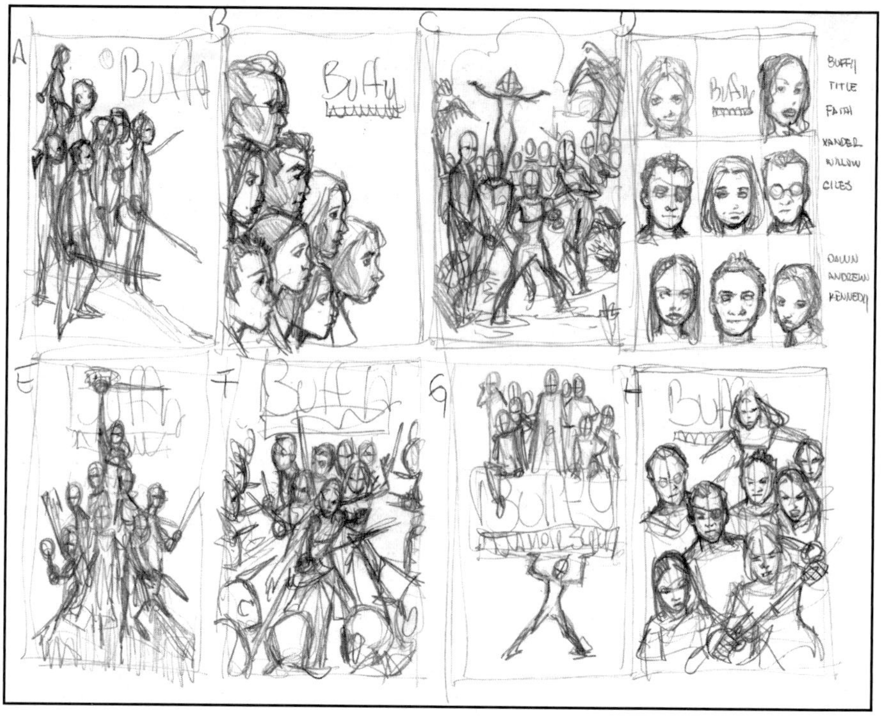
A
B
C
D
Buffy
BUFFY
TITLE
FAITH
XANDER
WILLOW
GILES
DAWN
ANDREW
KENNEDY
E
F
G
H

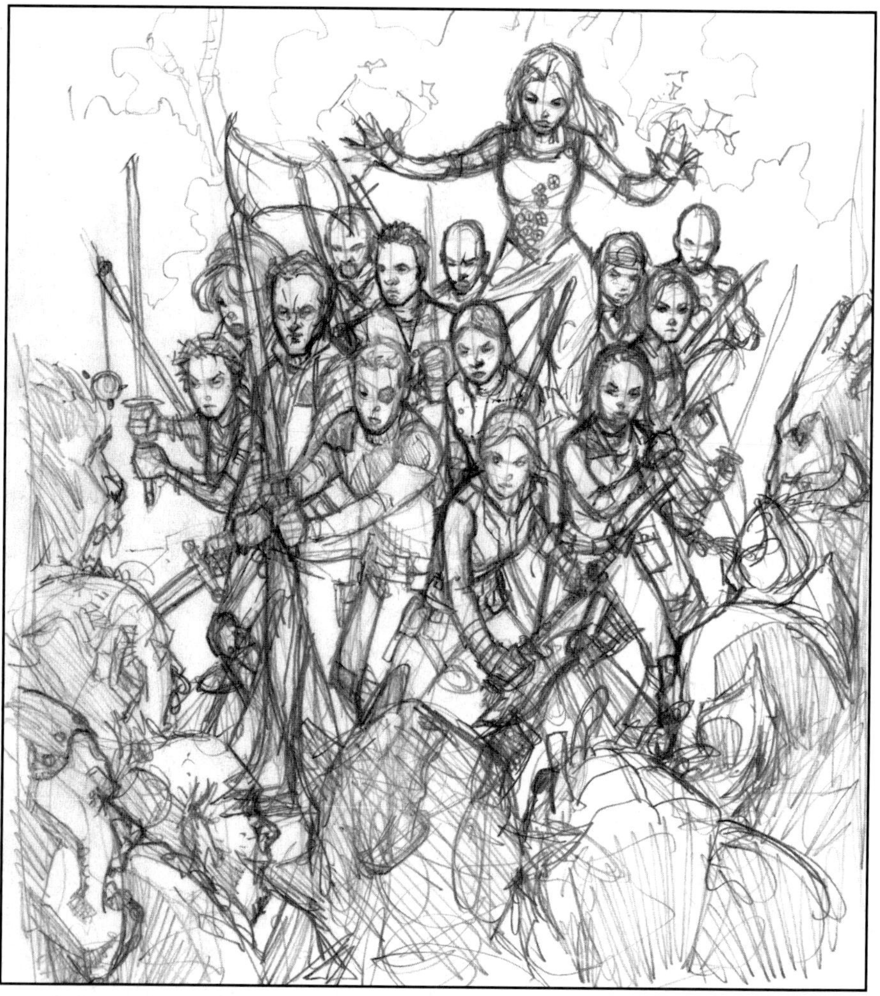

Georges provides multiple sketches (top) for each cover for Joss, the writer, and editors to pick from. Then he does a tighter sketch (bottom) where we can see more detail.

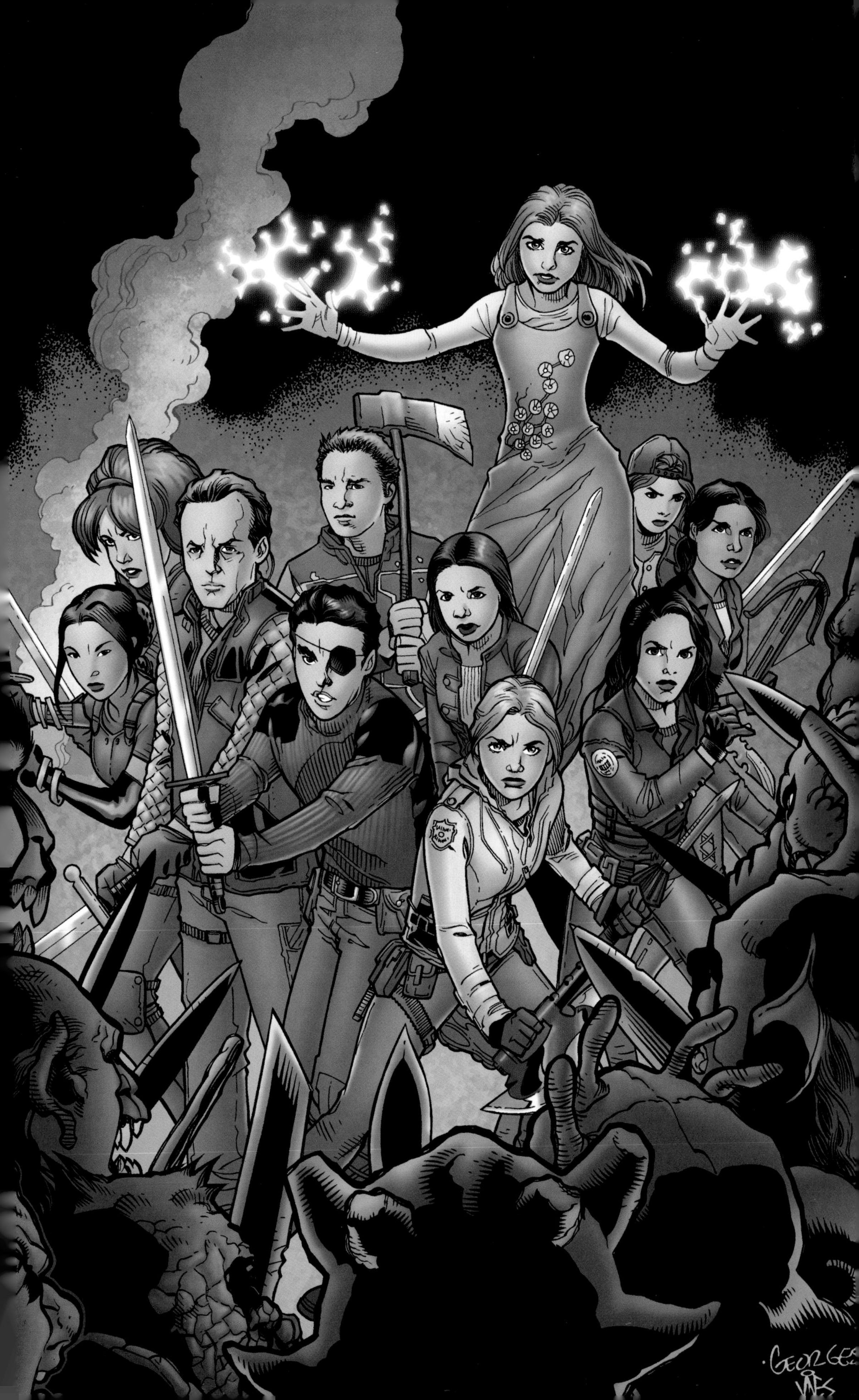

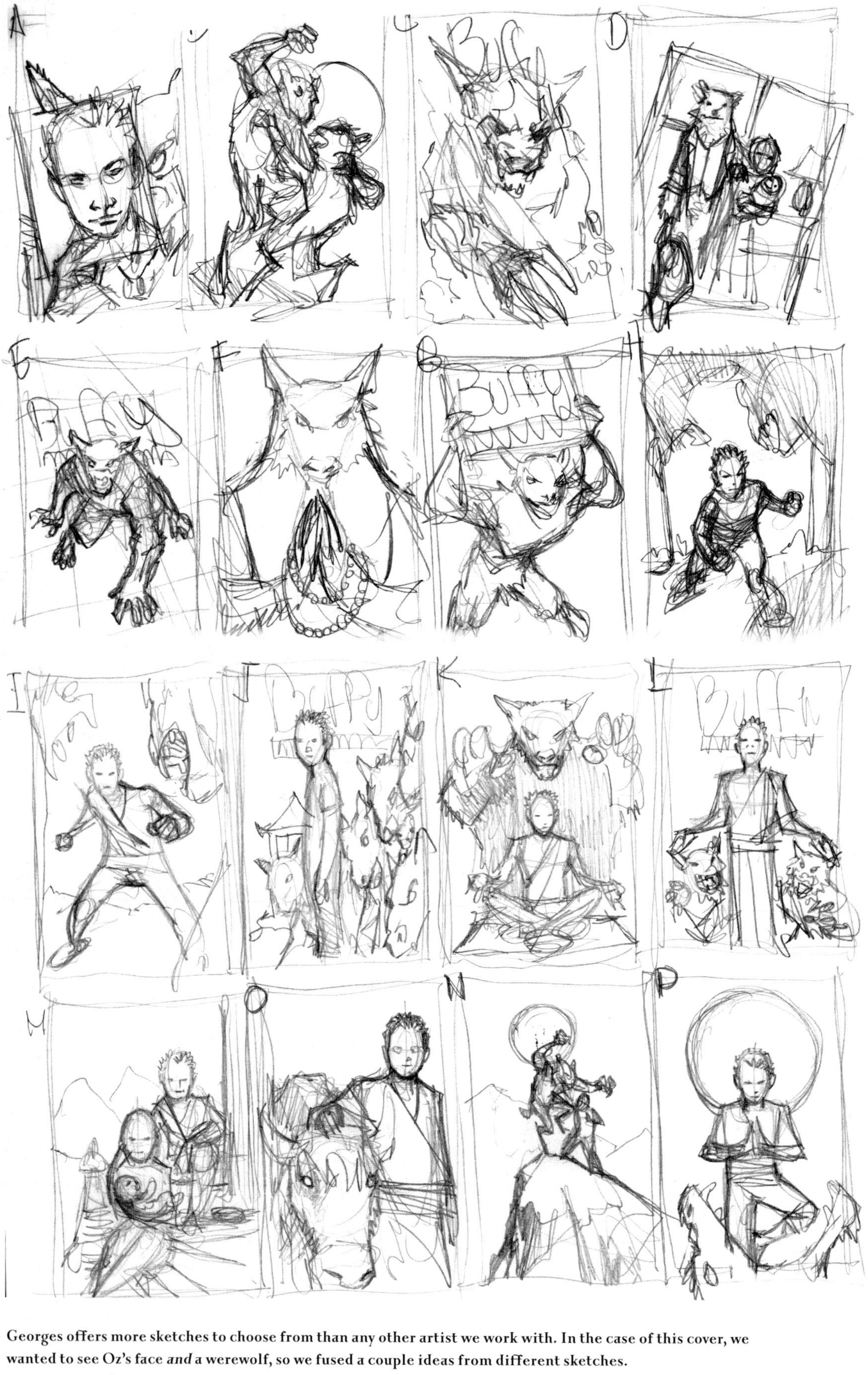

Georges offers more sketches to choose from than any other artist we work with. In the case of this cover, we wanted to see Oz's face *and* a werewolf, so we fused a couple ideas from different sketches.

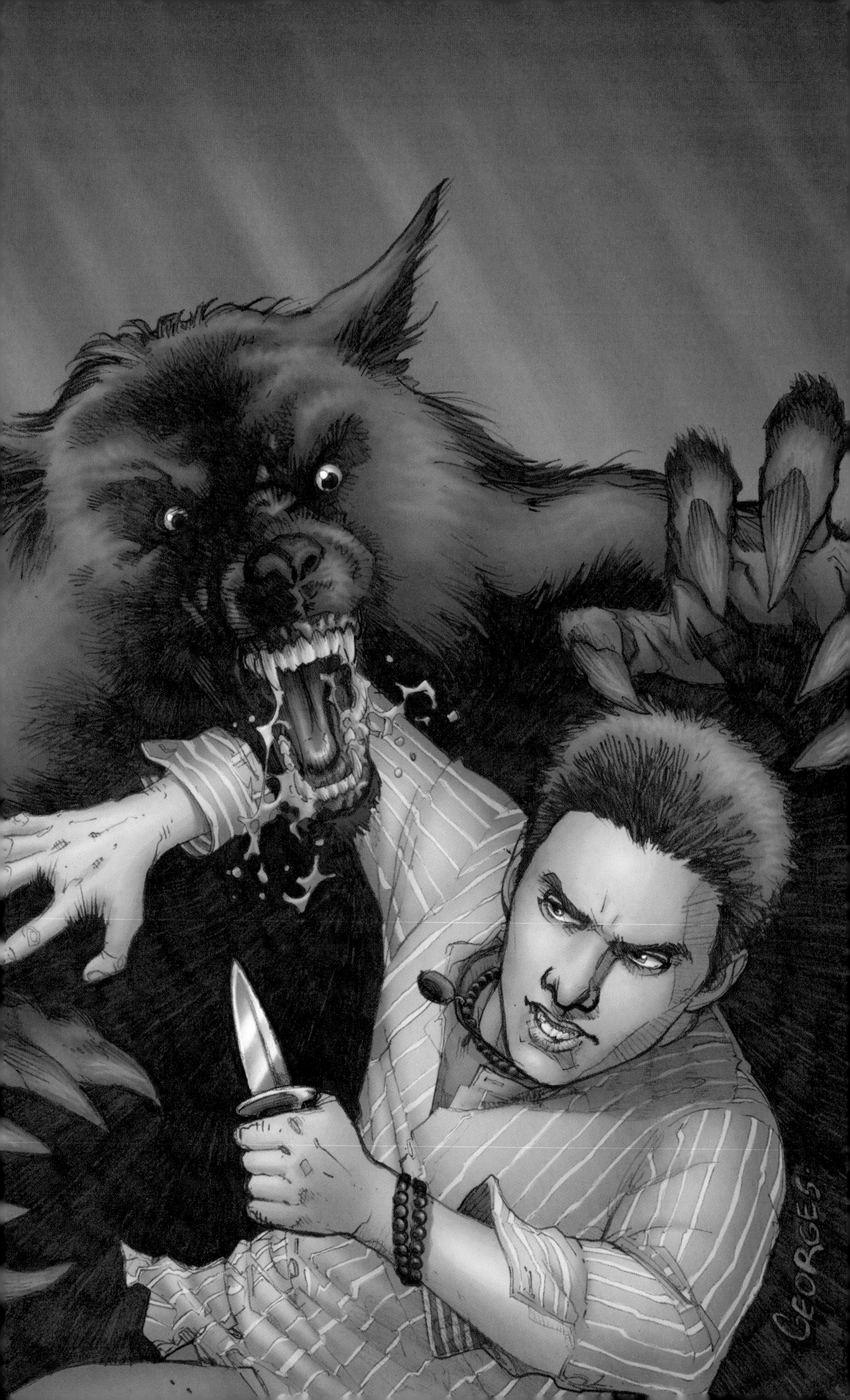
GEORGES.

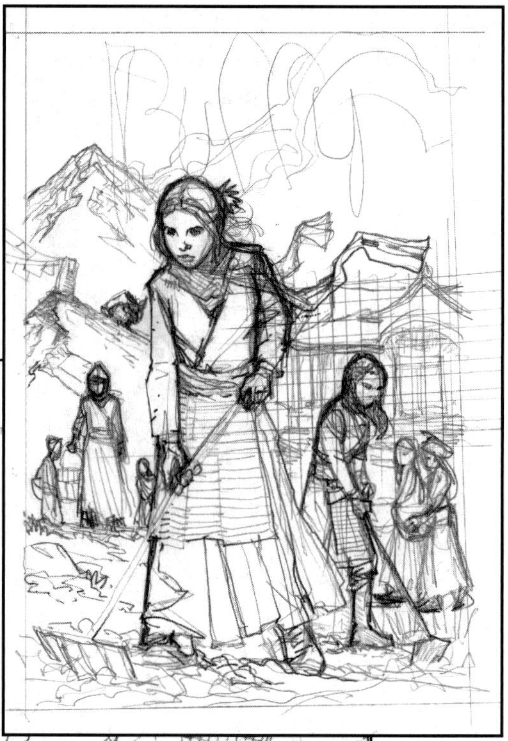

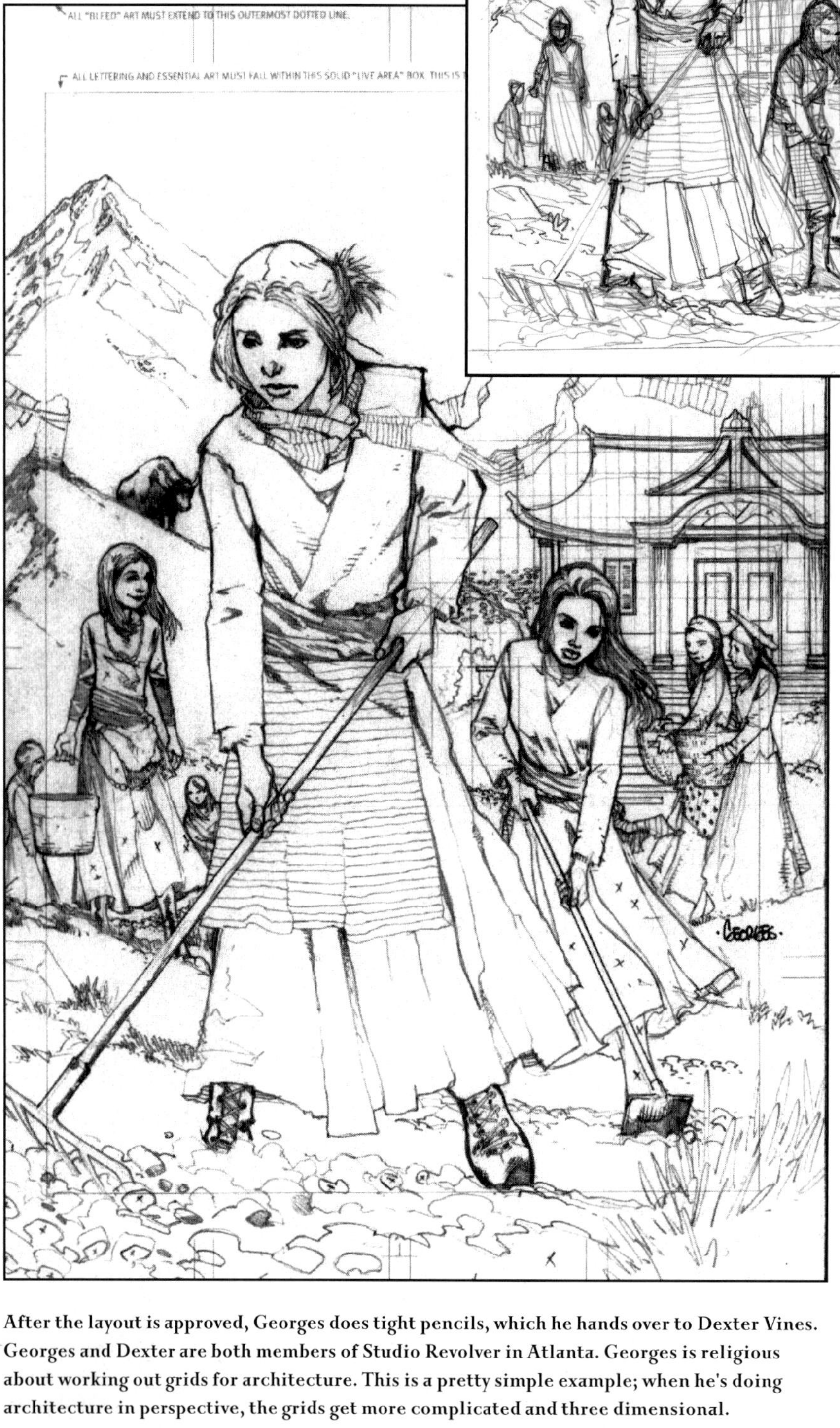
ALL "BLEED" ART MUST EXTEND TO THIS OUTERMOST DOTTED LINE.
ALL LETTERING AND ESSENTIAL ART MUST FALL WITHIN THIS SOLID "LIVE AREA" BOX.
GEORGES

After the layout is approved, Georges does tight pencils, which he hands over to Dexter Vines. Georges and Dexter are both members of Studio Revolver in Atlanta. Georges is religious about working out grids for architecture. This is a pretty simple example; when he's doing architecture in perspective, the grids get more complicated and three dimensional.

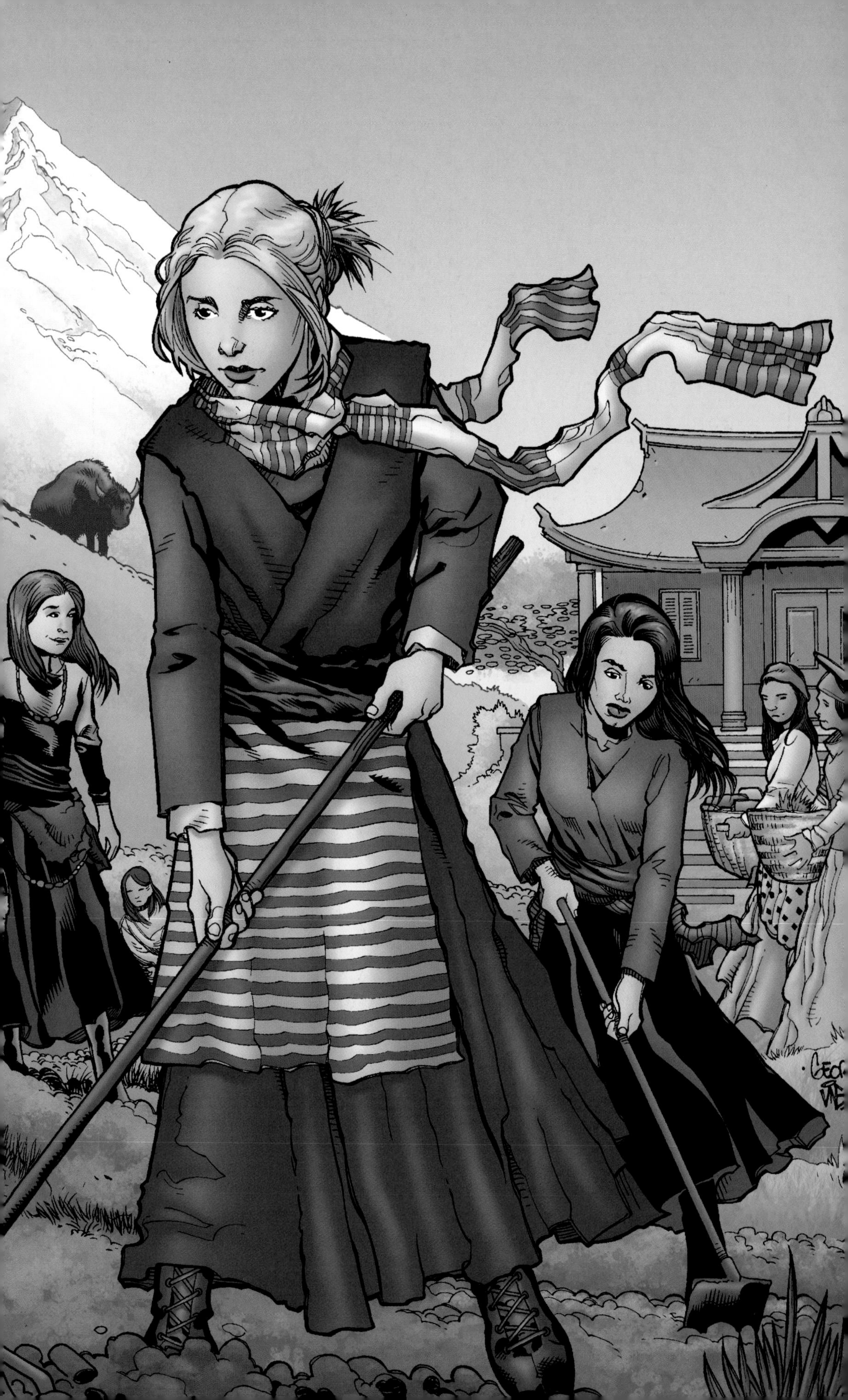

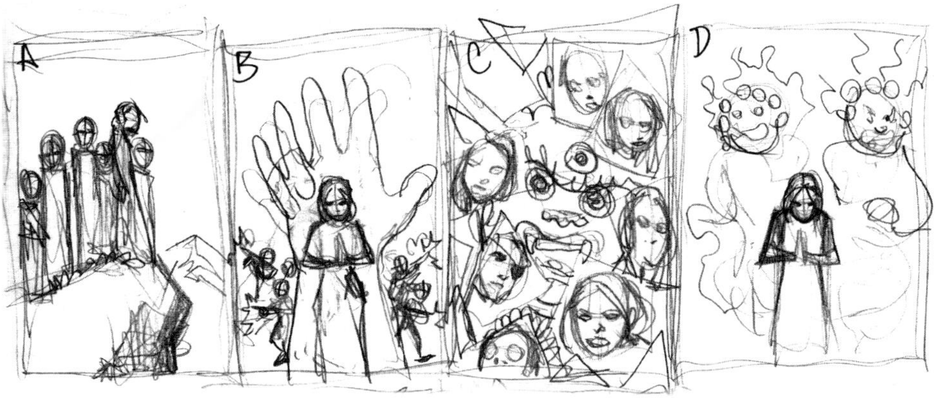
A
B
C
D

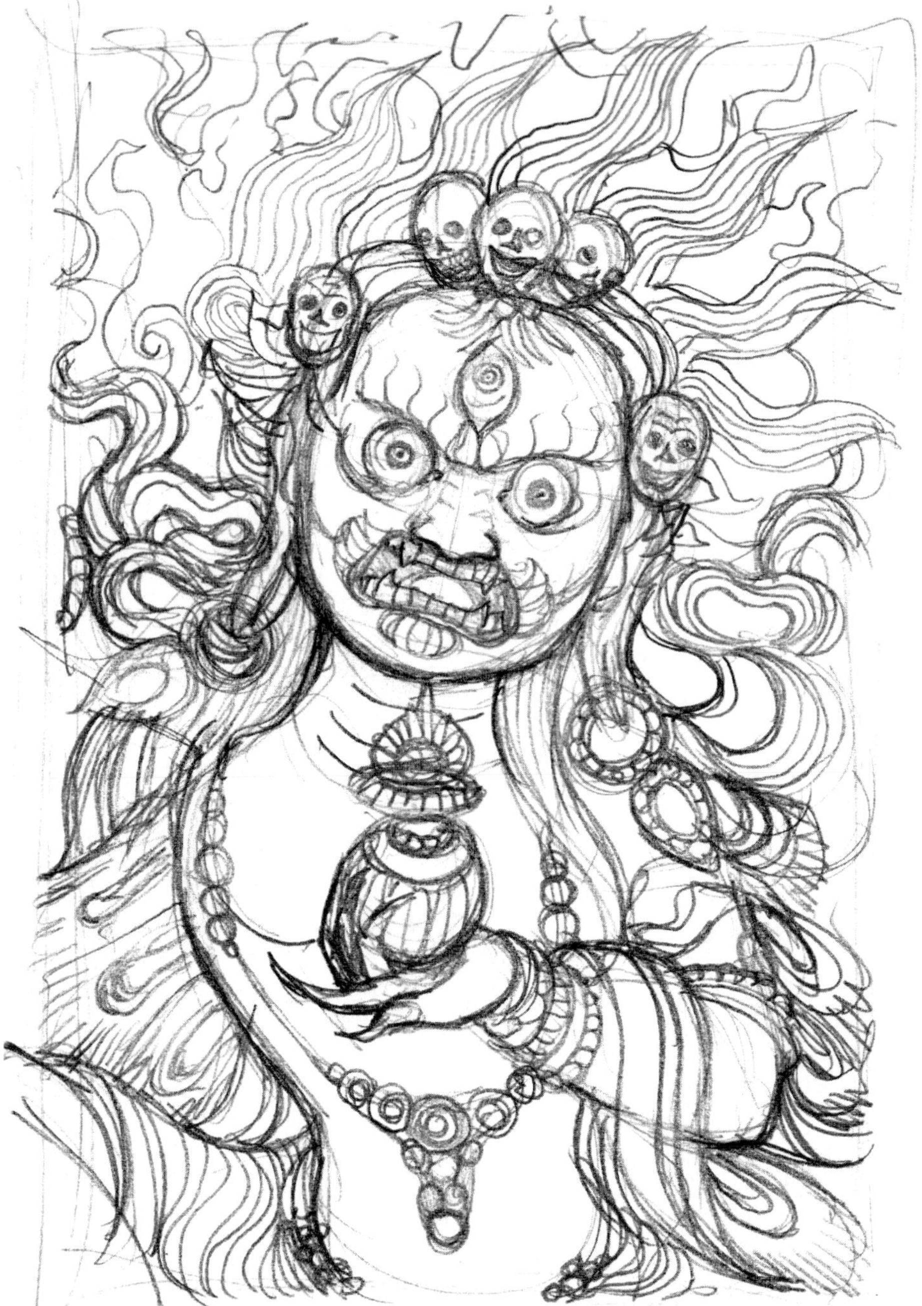

With a high-concept cover like this, sometimes the artist has to work it out in pieces. These are loose pencils for the background. Tighter details were worked out around the shattered mirror insets.

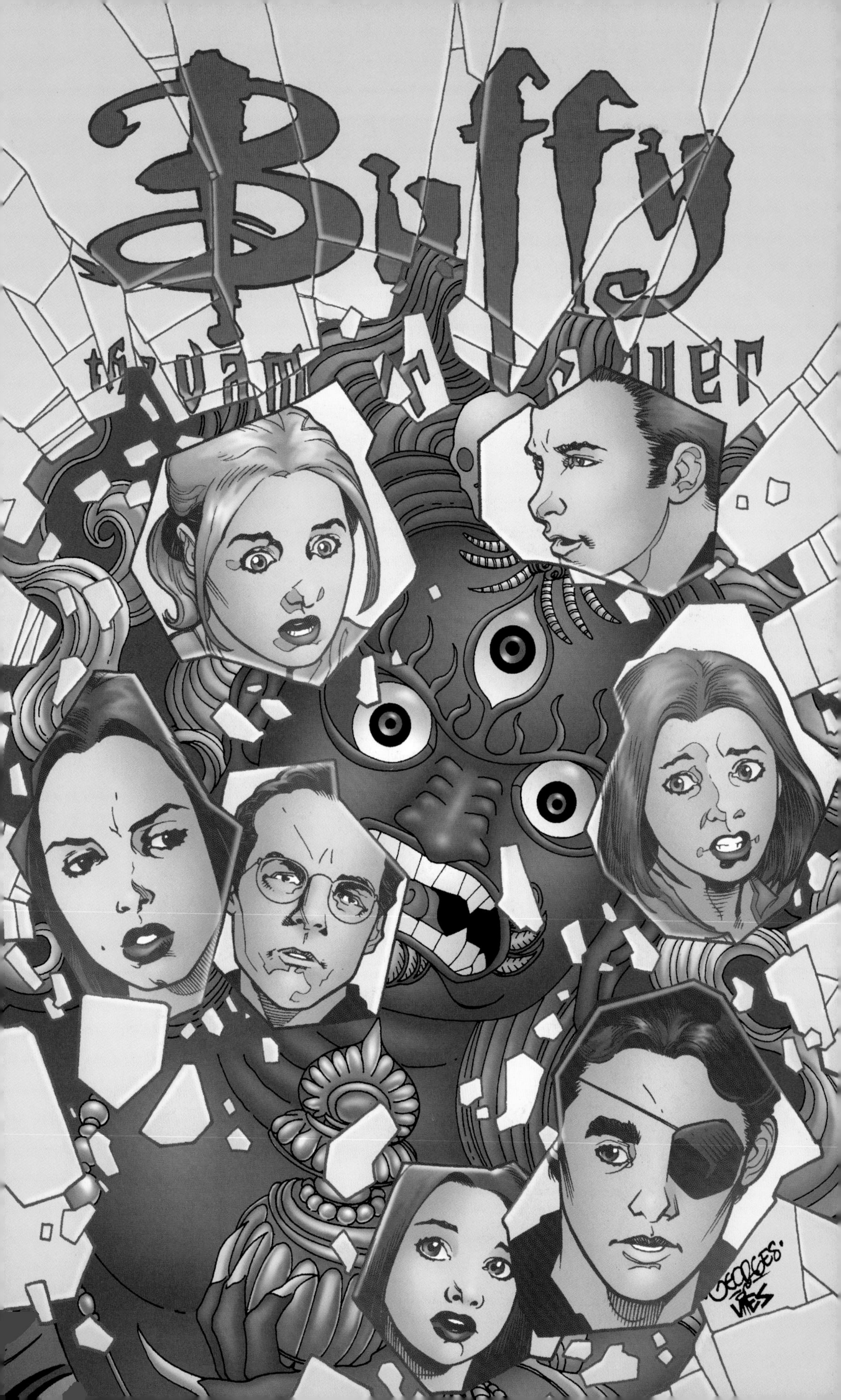
Buffy

SHORT STORIES FROM

MYSPACE DARK HORSE PRESENTS™

"Harmony Comes to the Nation"

Script JANE ESPENSON

Pencils KARL MOLINE

Inks ANDY OWENS

Colors MICHELLE MADSEN

"Always Darkest"

Script JOSS WHEDON

Art JO CHEN

Letters RICHARD STARKINGS &
COMICRAFT'S JIMMY BETANCOURT

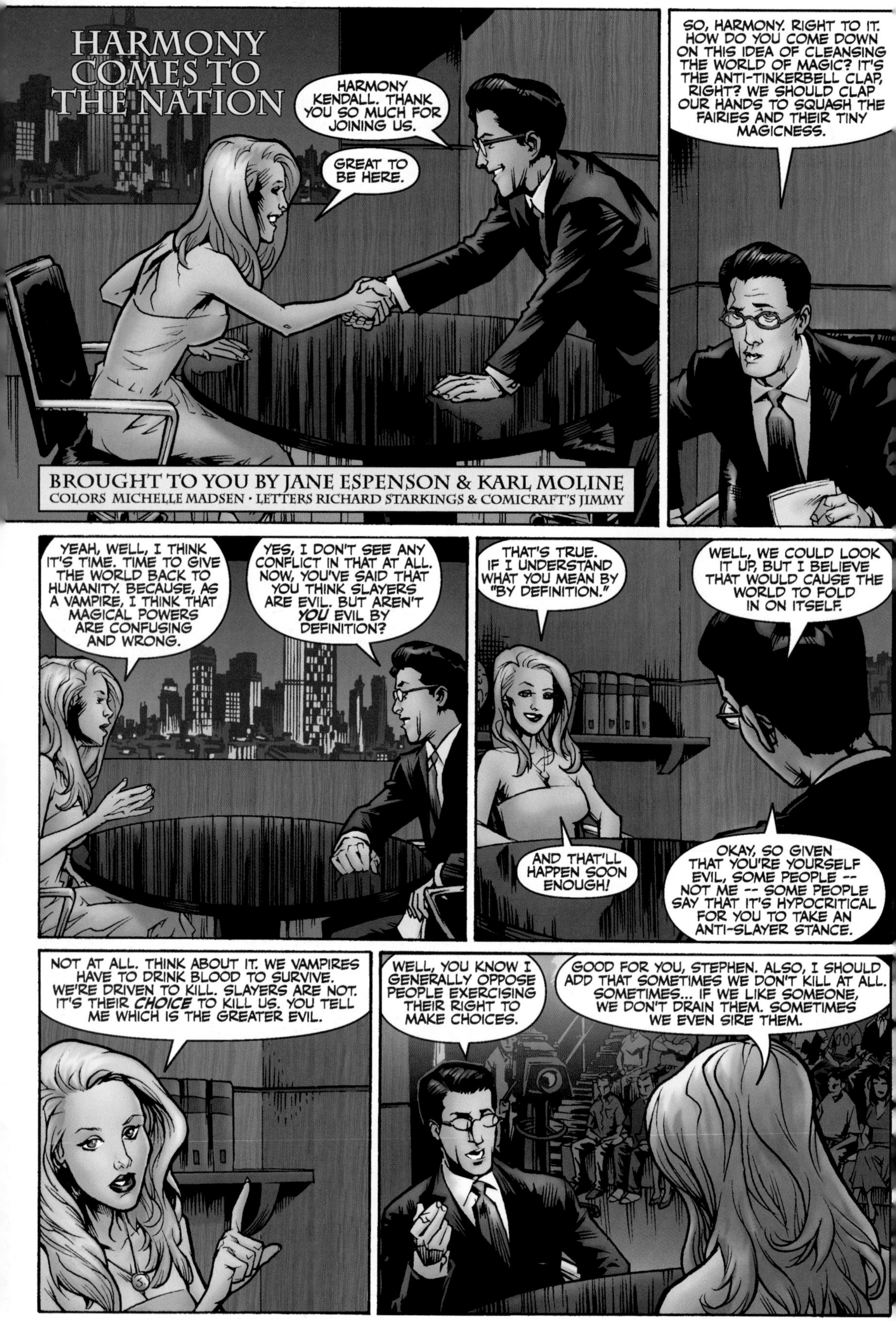

HARMONY COMES TO THE NATION
HARMONY KENDALL. THANK YOU SO MUCH FOR JOINING US.
GREAT TO BE HERE.
BROUGHT TO YOU BY JANE ESPENSON & KARL MOLINE
COLORS MICHELLE MADSEN · LETTERS RICHARD STARKINGS & COMICRAFT'S JIMMY
SO, HARMONY. RIGHT TO IT. HOW DO YOU COME DOWN ON THIS IDEA OF CLEANSING THE WORLD OF MAGIC? IT'S THE ANTI-TINKERBELL CLAP, RIGHT? WE SHOULD CLAP OUR HANDS TO SQUASH THE FAIRIES AND THEIR TINY MAGICNESS.
YEAH, WELL, I THINK IT'S TIME. TIME TO GIVE THE WORLD BACK TO HUMANITY. BECAUSE, AS A VAMPIRE, I THINK THAT MAGICAL POWERS ARE CONFUSING AND WRONG.
YES, I DON'T SEE ANY CONFLICT IN THAT AT ALL. NOW, YOU'VE SAID THAT YOU THINK SLAYERS ARE EVIL. BUT AREN'T *YOU* EVIL BY DEFINITION?
THAT'S TRUE. IF I UNDERSTAND WHAT YOU MEAN BY "BY DEFINITION."
WELL, WE COULD LOOK IT UP, BUT I BELIEVE THAT WOULD CAUSE THE WORLD TO FOLD IN ON ITSELF.
AND THAT'LL HAPPEN SOON ENOUGH!
OKAY, SO GIVEN THAT YOU'RE YOURSELF EVIL, SOME PEOPLE -- NOT ME -- SOME PEOPLE SAY THAT IT'S HYPOCRITICAL FOR YOU TO TAKE AN ANTI-SLAYER STANCE.
NOT AT ALL. THINK ABOUT IT. WE VAMPIRES HAVE TO DRINK BLOOD TO SURVIVE. WE'RE DRIVEN TO KILL. SLAYERS ARE NOT. IT'S THEIR *CHOICE* TO KILL US. YOU TELL ME WHICH IS THE GREATER EVIL.
WELL, YOU KNOW I GENERALLY OPPOSE PEOPLE EXERCISING THEIR RIGHT TO MAKE CHOICES.
GOOD FOR YOU, STEPHEN. ALSO, I SHOULD ADD THAT SOMETIMES WE DON'T KILL AT ALL. SOMETIMES... IF WE LIKE SOMEONE, WE DON'T DRAIN THEM. SOMETIMES WE EVEN SIRE THEM.

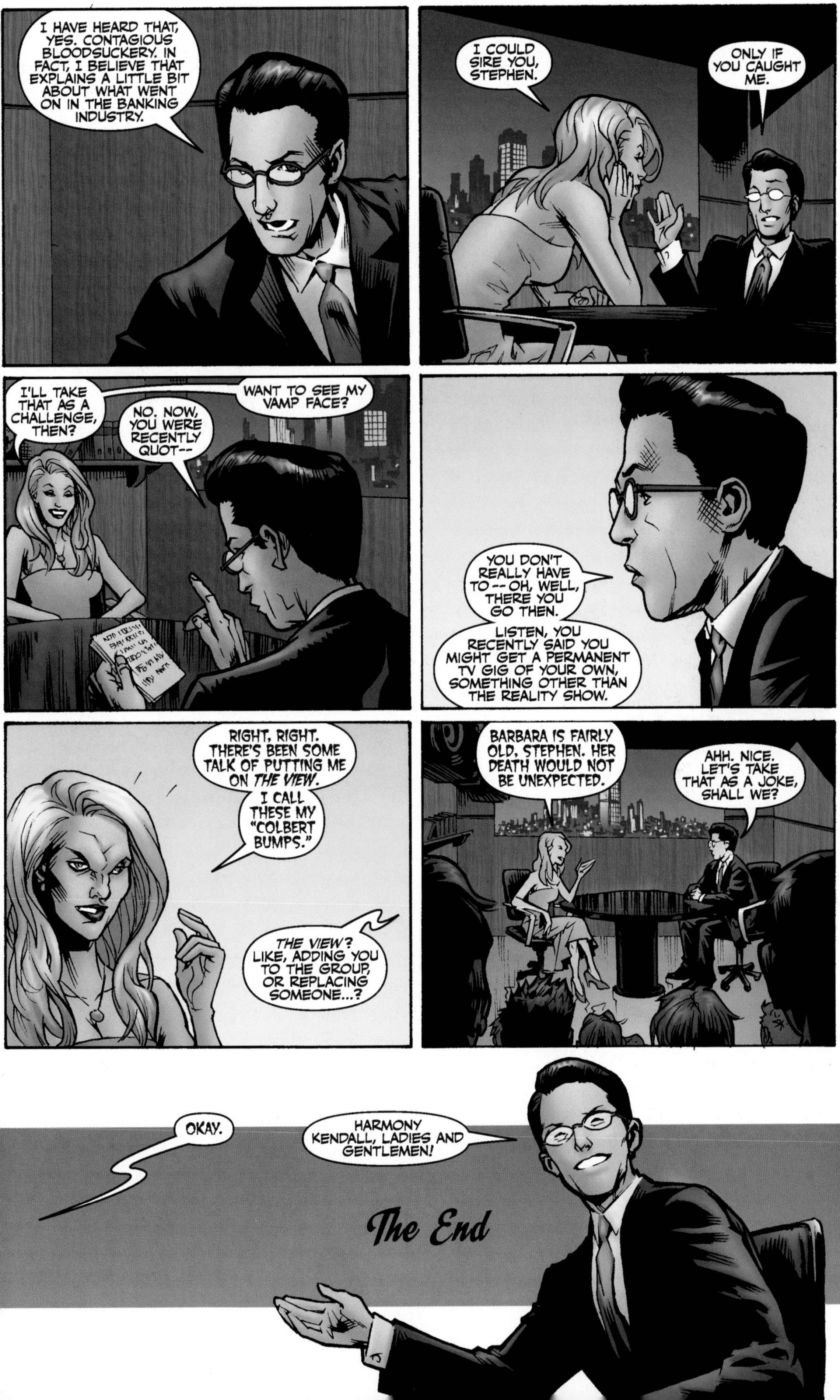
I HAVE HEARD THAT, YES. CONTAGIOUS BLOODSUCKERY. IN FACT, I BELIEVE THAT EXPLAINS A LITTLE BIT ABOUT WHAT WENT ON IN THE BANKING INDUSTRY.
I COULD SIRE YOU, STEPHEN.
ONLY IF YOU CAUGHT ME.
I'LL TAKE THAT AS A CHALLENGE, THEN?
NO. NOW, YOU WERE RECENTLY QUOT--
WANT TO SEE MY VAMP FACE?
YOU DON'T REALLY HAVE TO -- OH, WELL, THERE YOU GO THEN.
LISTEN, YOU RECENTLY SAID YOU MIGHT GET A PERMANENT TV GIG OF YOUR OWN, SOMETHING OTHER THAN THE REALITY SHOW.
RIGHT, RIGHT. THERE'S BEEN SOME TALK OF PUTTING ME ON *THE VIEW*.
I CALL THESE MY "COLBERT BUMPS."
THE VIEW? LIKE, ADDING YOU TO THE GROUP, OR REPLACING SOMEONE...?
BARBARA IS FAIRLY OLD, STEPHEN. HER DEATH WOULD NOT BE UNEXPECTED.
AHH. NICE. LET'S TAKE THAT AS A JOKE, SHALL WE?
OKAY.
HARMONY KENDALL, LADIES AND GENTLEMEN!
The End

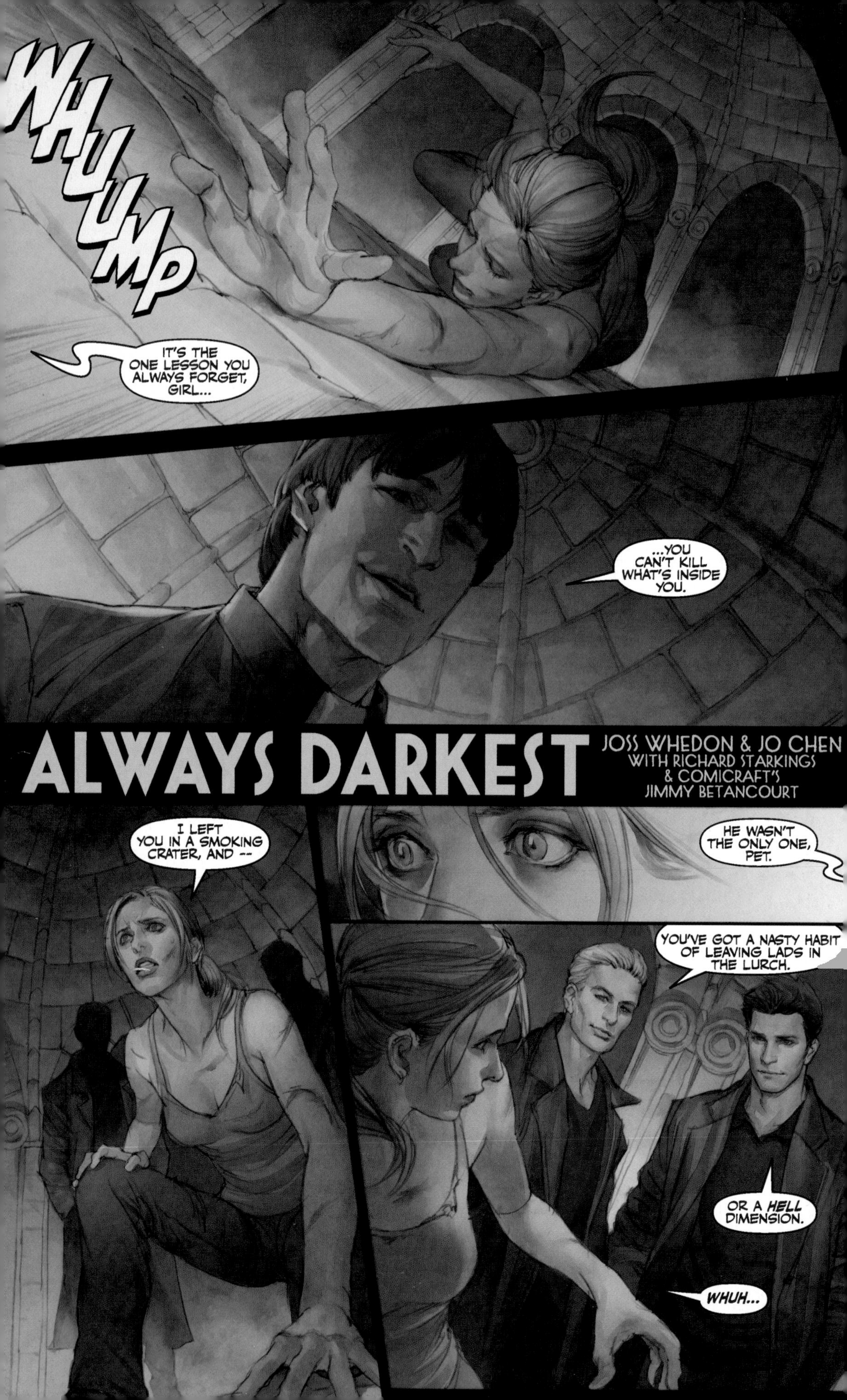
WHUUMP
IT'S THE ONE LESSON YOU ALWAYS FORGET, GIRL...
...YOU CAN'T KILL WHAT'S INSIDE YOU.
ALWAYS DARKEST
JOSS WHEDON & JO CHEN WITH RICHARD STARKINGS & COMICRAFT'S JIMMY BETANCOURT
I LEFT YOU IN A SMOKING CRATER, AND --
HE WASN'T THE ONLY ONE, PET.
YOU'VE GOT A NASTY HABIT OF LEAVING LADS IN THE LURCH.
OR A *HELL* DIMENSION.
WHUH...

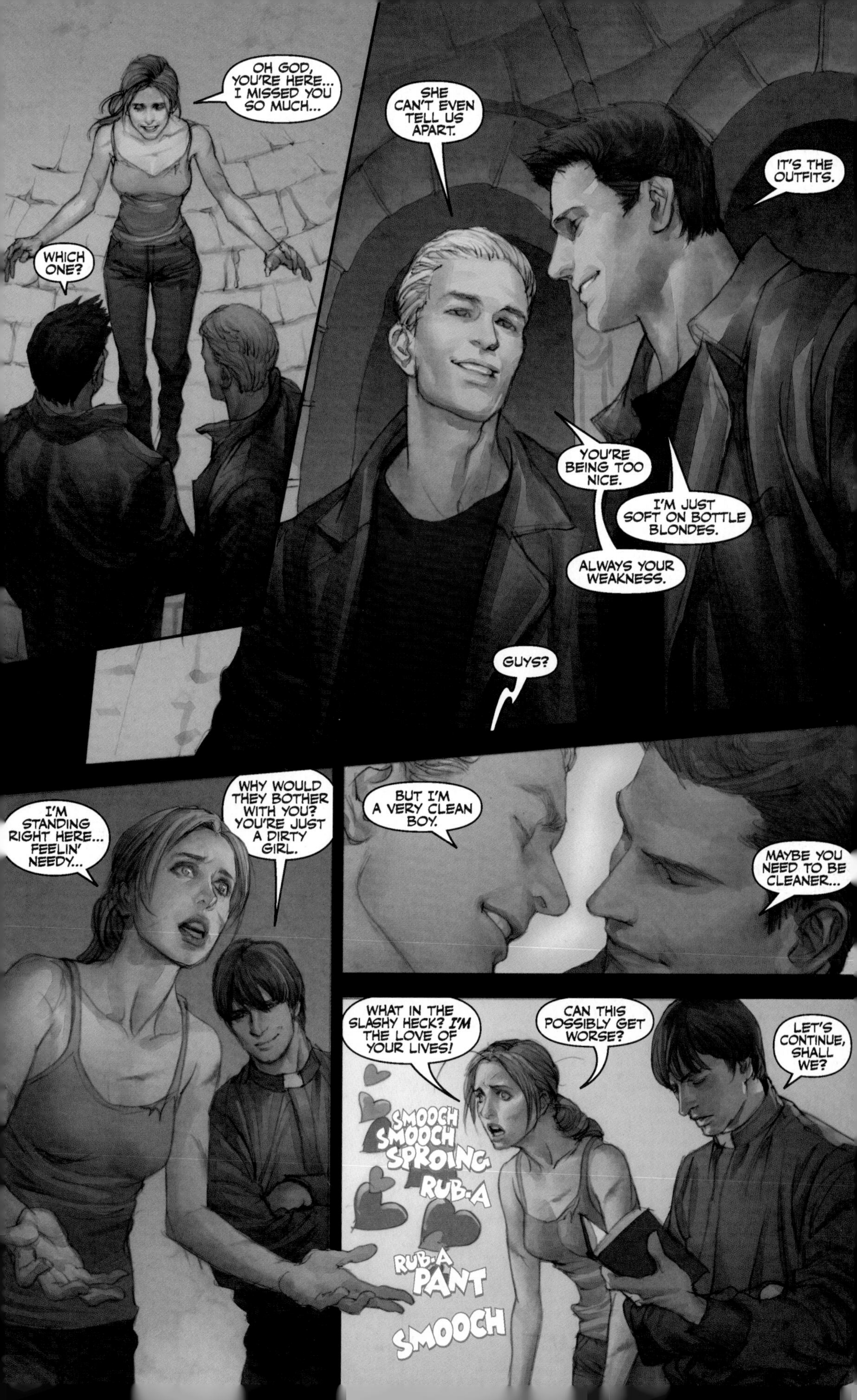
OH GOD, YOU'RE HERE... I MISSED YOU SO MUCH...
WHICH ONE?
SHE CAN'T EVEN TELL US APART.
IT'S THE OUTFITS.
YOU'RE BEING TOO NICE.
I'M JUST SOFT ON BOTTLE BLONDES.
ALWAYS YOUR WEAKNESS.
GUYS?
I'M STANDING RIGHT HERE... FEELIN' NEEDY...
WHY WOULD THEY BOTHER WITH YOU? YOU'RE JUST A DIRTY GIRL.
BUT I'M A VERY CLEAN BOY.
MAYBE YOU NEED TO BE CLEANER...
WHAT IN THE SLASHY HECK? *I'M* THE LOVE OF YOUR LIVES!
CAN THIS POSSIBLY GET WORSE?
LET'S CONTINUE, SHALL WE?
SMOOCH
SMOOCH
SPROING
RUB-A
RUB-A
PANT
SMOOCH

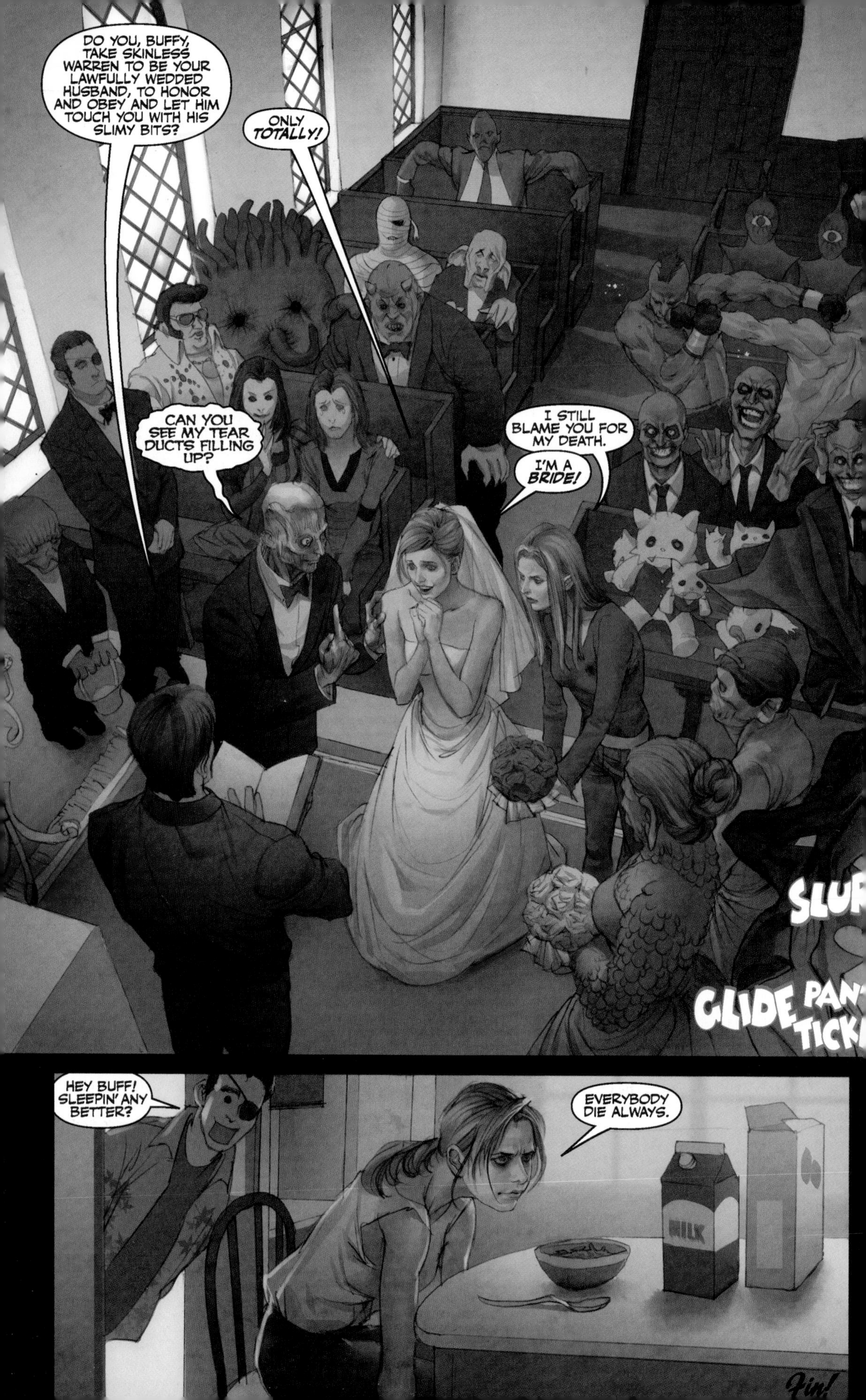

DO YOU, BUFFY, TAKE SKINLESS WARREN TO BE YOUR LAWFULLY WEDDED HUSBAND, TO HONOR AND OBEY AND LET HIM TOUCH YOU WITH HIS SLIMY BITS?
ONLY *TOTALLY!*
CAN YOU SEE MY TEAR DUCTS FILLING UP?
I STILL BLAME YOU FOR MY DEATH.
I'M A *BRIDE!*
GLIDE
HEY BUFF! SLEEPIN' ANY BETTER?
EVERYBODY DIE ALWAYS.
Fin!